RUNNING HOOFBEATS DRUMMED ON THE WIND

Jake heard a shot and a bullet ricocheted inches from his boot. Crouching, he turned and brought up his rifle. Mounted men were springing from hiding and charging in from both sides. The one in the lead he knew from a chance meeting years before. Dos Burton.

Jake aimed, then shifted his sight to the second rider. His shot took the man out of his saddle and he felt something sting his upper arm. Again he fired, awkwardly this time, and a rider's horse went down, rolling, crushing the man beneath it.

Then he was on the ground, not knowing why, and Dos Burton was above him.

"You!" Burton said, pure hatred drawing his lips back from his teeth, his pistol aligning. . . .

RIDE THE
DEVIL'S TRAIL
DAN PARKINSON

ZEBRA BOOKS
KENSINGTON PUBLISHING CORP.

ZEBRA BOOKS

are published by

Kensington Publishing Corp.
475 Park Avenue South
New York, NY 10016

First printing: February, 1990

Printed in the United States of America

To my mother, Cleo Parkinson, with love.

Chapter I

On his twenty-sixth birthday, Jake Creedmore awoke with the resolve that he'd had enough and it was time to move on. It wasn't a sudden resolve. He had been chewing on the notion for months, off and on . . . sometimes avoiding it because no man likes to run away no matter what the situation, other times admitting to himself that there was little reason to stay on. Lately he had come to the conclusion that it just wasn't worth it.

As he had each morning for nearly three years, Jake sat up in his bunk, thumped out his boots and put them on his feet, crammed his old hat over his unruly mop of dark hair, thumbed the sleep from his eyes and stood to stretch himself, avoiding the low rafter poles of the dark little adobe cabin. At six feet two plus boot heels, lanky arms stretched wide to amplify a morning yawn, he fairly filled the tiny place.

Early sunlight poked little dusty shafts through the bullet holes in his slab door to paint bright dots on the battered shutters of the single window on the far wall. Checking the loads in his old Peacemaker, he stuck it into the top of his right boot, then climbed atop the plank table and threw back the roof trap to have a look around. The new sun was a red ball rising out of Texas to the east, flaring the tops of stubby mountains to the west and giving long shadows to the scrub cedar, cactus and spiny locust that dotted the grass prairies beyond his ruined fences.

He took his time deciding there was no one around, then closed the trap, bolted it, and eased his legs to the earthen floor. "Gettin' so it's a surprise when there aren't any surprises," he told himself. With his pistol still riding in his boot, he lifted the bar on the door, opened it and stepped out into cool, bright morning.

Only blackened stumps remained of the sturdy windmill he had built, but he had replaced it with a handpump and his tub and trough were still usable. For a moment he stood, gazing around at the ruined fields between broken fences, the ground still broken up by the milling of driven cattle, then he sighed and began pumping water for a bath.

"Just not worth it any more," he told himself. "Come time to move on, it's time to move on." Stripped to hat, boots and flannel britches, he soaped himself down, rinsed with cold well water and sputtered in the chill. "By rights," he told himself, "what I ought to do first is go find Conrad W. Jackson and kick his tailbone right up between his ears." He toweled off and got out his razor and strop. "Dang shame that wouldn't be polite to do," he shrugged. "Sometimes we're just too civilized for our own good."

It had been a bad few months for Jake Creedmore, beginning about the time that Conrad W. Jackson had changed his mind about selling Jake this land. Jake wasn't quite sure why the banker wanted these dusty acres back—wanted his rough two sections so badly that he had gone to some lengths to drive him off—but it had to do with the water. There were other wells

8

around, here and there, that could supply a house or a cattle tank, but there weren't any like Jake's. He had found it the second hole he drilled, a natural aquifer that flowed artesian most of the year—sweet, cold water in abundance—and even in dry summer had only to be pumped.

Conrad W. Jackson had something in mind for Jake's well. Jake didn't know what it was, but he knew Conrad W. Jackson. The banker was a man who was used to getting what he wanted, and he wasn't partial to paying more for anything than he had sold it for in the first place.

In the past few months it had gotten so that Jake couldn't leave the place without coming back to find damage. He'd had his windmill burned, bullets shot through his shack, fences torn down and cattle driven across his crops. And only once had he actually seen a trespasser.

He had set out one morning, heading for Perdition to buy a bag of flour and a tote of beans, then turned back to pick up some harness that needed mending. He had caught the hardcase on his roof with a bucket of coal oil, and when Jake told him to come down, the man had drawn a gun and opened fire. Jake shot him off the roof, but he had never found out anything about him, not even his name. No one in town recognized him . . . or admitted to it if they did. And Jake had to pay to have him buried.

He had spent two days in town, satisfying Homer Boles and Judge Clinton that he wasn't guilty of anything worse than self defense, and had returned home to find his fences cut in four places. After that, things had just gone from bad to worse.

And now, without a crop to sell and with no profit on his few cattle—thanks to Conrad W. Jackson having jump-shipped a herd to flood the market on him—

Jake decided to cash in and start over somewhere else.

The temptation to leave Conrad W. Jackson with some serious bruises to remember him by was strong, but Jake willed it down. He knew what he intended to do—had decided upon that through a lot of long, lonely evenings—and he would stick to his plan. Conrad W. Jackson would just have to settle for a course of aggravation at the manner of Jake's leaving. He did, though, have some thoughts about the manner of that aggravation. And he had come up with a way for himself to at least break even in the process.

His only remaining livestock was a fourteen-year-old gelding with a swayed back, and now he tossed his old saddle on the beast and started for Perdition one more time, not even looking back at the place he had once thought was his future. "Eighteen miles to Perdition," he told the old horse. "No hurry about it, though, so all you got to do is just don't stop too much. And this evening when I take this saddle off you, you can rest easy because I won't ever be putting it back on. You're fixing to be traded in on something better."

The horse trudged on and Jake slouched in the saddle, keeping his head angled away from the steady wind. The bullet hole through the crown of his old hat had left it breezy inside, and sometimes it got on his nerves.

There wasn't much about this country that he was going to miss. Maybe the chance to see Miss Clara Hayes from time to time when he was in town—no man in his right senses wouldn't enjoy looking at Clara Hayes—he would miss that, though the only time he had ever attempted to be sociable with the young lady, she had clouted him with an axe handle. But, then again, Jake had no hard feelings about that. There were plenty of other young bucks around who had been clouted by Clara. She was a striking woman.

10

There were a few other folks in the vicinity who were decent enough people, but they were a minority, in Jake's opinion. The majority of folks in those parts were a mix of people who worked for Conrad W. Jackson, people who owed money to Conrad W. Jackson and people who tended to socialize with Conrad W. Jackson because he was a man who amounted to something and they hoped it would rub off.

In the close on to three years Jake Creedmore had spent in this part of the territory—dusty country just west of Texas and just north of Texas but otherwise not close to anywhere—he had done his levelest to settle down and be a respectable citizen. It had seemed to him that it was time to shuck the old footloose ways and make something of himself. Every cent he had from his little inheritance, and from what he had saved while kicking around and working for wages for other folks, money that had sat in a bank at Denison during those times, had gone into buying his two sections from Conrad W. Jackson, and then a mortgage on top of that to raise fences and put down his well—a well that he had wished lately could have been an ordinary, dribble-in-summer-freeze-up-in-winter kind of well just like most everybody else's wells.

He was pretty certain that he would never have had the troubles he was having, if his well had just behaved itself and come in stingy and alkaline like most.

He had tried to settle down. He had even taken to attending social occasions, and had got to the point that he could tolerate such events just fine if they didn't last too long.

"Well, all right," he said now to his horse, "sometimes things just don't work out. No sense brooding about it. You just keep on moving and get us to Perdition, then you can rest up and I'll take over from there. Got to make a swap tonight, then tomorrow I

11

got one more social occasion to do."

The sun was rim-down on the mountains to the west when Jake Creedmore led a tired old horse into the stableyard at the edge of Perdition town, shucked off saddle and trappings and wandered across to the stable door to look inside. There was no one there. He ambled around the corner to the bellpost, leaned against it and tugged at the rope. Overhead the old brass bell clanged, clanged again and the door of Sim Hoover's house opened, across the road. Sim peered at him, squinting, then shouted, "Jake, what's the matter with you? You want grain for that bag of bones, you know where it is! I'm busy!"

Jake curled his lip and tugged the rope again. Hoover slammed his door, but when the bell kept ringing he opened it again and hopped out onto his porch, pulling on a boot. With both feet shod he hurried across the road. "Jake, cut that out! You want everybody in town to know I ain't here during business hours? What do you want, anyway?"

Jake pointed at his old horse. "Supposin' I wanted to sell that fine horse there, Sim, what would you give me for him?"

"Not a cent over two dollars," Hoover snapped.

"Why not offer five?" Jake tipped his head, gazing at the stabler.

"Because he ain't worth five, is why. I'd be a fool to go better'n three dollars. That horse is on its last legs."

"Same legs it's always been on, and they've stood up all right. How about four dollars?"

"If it was anybody but you, I wouldn't even think about it. How come you want to sell your horse, Jake?"

"I didn't say I want to sell him. I just asked what you'd give if I did."

"Not a red cent more than four dollars."

"How about the saddle?" Jake asked. "It's still got

some wear left in it."

"Jake, that saddle is so beat up it ain't worth ten bucks. I wouldn't go more than eight on it."

Creedmore nodded. "About what I thought, too. Sim, supposin' I wanted to board out that old horse, how much would you charge to pasture him?"

"For how long?"

"The rest of his life."

"Not a cent less than ten dollars. Extra if you wanted him groomed now and again."

"Would it matter whose horse he was?"

"A horse is a horse. Jake, I ain't got all day. What do you want?"

"Twelve dollars for that horse and saddle, like you offered. And I want him pastured and groomed the rest of his natural life."

Hoover gaped at him. "Do you want to sell him or board him out? I swear, Jake, sometimes you act like you been eatin' yodelberries."

"I want both. You pay me twelve dollars for the horse and saddle, and I'll pay you twelve dollars to tend the horse. I don't care what you do with the saddle."

Hoover shook his head and turned to glance at the house across the road, where a curtain fluttered at the window. "Jake, can we talk some other time? Maybe tomorrow you might make more sense . . ."

"I'm making all the sense I want to, Sim. Is it a deal?"

"Is what a deal?"

"What I said."

"Well, yeah, it's a deal if you say so. But it's a damn fool kind of deal if you ask me."

"Done," Jake said, turning loose of the bell rope. "You going over to the sale barn in the morning, Sim?"

"I reckon. Tuesday is sale day, and I always go."

"I expect Conrad W. Jackson will be there, too, like always."

"Never knowed him to miss a Tuesday sale if he's in town. Why?"

Jake shrugged. "Just bein' neighborly, Sim. You know, shootin' the breeze, like."

"Well, I kind of need to get back to the house, Jake. You want to talk about anything else?"

"Nope. See you around, Sim. Uh . . . who you got waitin' over yonder? Flossie?"

"That ain't any of your business, and it ain't polite to ask, Jake Creedmore!"

Jake pulled off his hat, truly contrite. "You're right as rain about that, Sim. I don't know what made me say such a thing. I s'pose when a body's got a lot on his mind, he gets forgetful."

Hoover nodded, relaxing his face. "I imagine that's right. They been devilin' you again out at your place, Jake? I can't see how you manage to hang on like you do. Most folks out that way has already cashed in, sold out and moved on."

"Well, I'm about to join 'em," Jake told him. "They've plain wore me down, Sim. I'm licked, and I'm fixing to let Conrad W. Jackson have the place back. Thought about dusting him up some first, but I don't see what that would get me."

"Now, Jake, you don't *know* that Mr. Jackson's got anything to do with all that hoorawin' out yonder. Why, Mr. Jackson's a fine man. Most folks bank on him."

Jake eyed the man sadly. "How many horses do you stable for him, Sim?"

"Five. An' he pays right smart for it, too. I even got that prize sorrel of his, right yonder in stall one. He's a man that knows a good stable."

"Still hold the mortgage on your place, does he,

14

Sim?"

"Well, shoot, yes. Just like everybody else around these parts. But that's got nothin' to do with him bein' a fine man. Just proves he is, is all. I wish you'd take better to Mr. Jackson, Jake, and quit this blamin' him for your troubles. Look, if I don't get back over there I'm goin' to have to pay extra. Can we talk some more some other time?"

"Some other time," Jake nodded. "You go ahead on, Sim. I'll put your new horse to the grain trough for you. Tend him right, now, you hear?"

Hoover was already heading for his house. Jake led the old horse into the barn, laid out a bait of grain for it, then walked over to stall one and had a long look at Conrad W. Jackson's prize sorrel. It was a beautiful animal, no question about it—full-bodied and close-coupled with the powerful haunches and trim legs of a racer.

"Understand you can run, hoss," he said, stroking its neck and letting it get the knowing of him. "I hope that's right. Fact is, I'm counting on it."

Nearby on a rail sat Conrad W. Jackson's sleek oiled-leather saddle with its carved trim and matching headstall. Jake ran a finger along its cantle, then left the barn.

A hundred yards along, the road became State Street, a dusty wide place dominated by the Perdition Hotel and the Perdition Bank. Beyond, he turned left on Johnson Street, the town's other main thorough-fare, and walked to Johnson's Emporium. There hadn't been a Johnson in Perdition for two years that he knew of, and the place was owned now by Conrad W. Jackson, but the only person there at the moment was the widow Cole, who ran the store for him.

Jake pulled off his hat. "Evening, Ma'am. I need some store-bought clothes, if you can fit me out in

15

them."

The woman cocked a skeptical brow at him. "You're short on credit these days, Mr. Creedmore."

"Well, Ma'am, I'd pay cash except the bank is closed and I can't get there until morning. But I'll have a ways to go after I come in and settle up my bill tomorrow, so I need to do my picking and choosing now, to save time. I'll pick up my package when I pay my bill."

"Can't see any harm in that, then," she said. "What all do you need?"

He spread his arms, glancing downward at his beat-up attire.

"Everything from hat to boots, I'd say," she said. "That's going to come to a pretty penny, Mr. Creedmore. Fifteen-twenty dollars, at least. Are you sure you're good for it?"

"Soon as I can get to the bank, Ma'am. First thing in the morning."

The package he assembled was complete in all ways but one. The store was short on hats and none of them fit. "Your problem's all in your head, Mr. Creedmore," the widow said. "Most folks' heads are rounder. I had one here that might have fit you, but it was a silver-belly beaver hat and you couldn't have afforded it, anyway. Mr. Jackson took it for his Sunday hat. I stuffed the band so he could wear it."

"Might have been more entertaining if you'd expanded the wart's headbone," Jake suggested.

"I'll thank you to keep your opinions to yourself, Jake Creedmore," she said. "I have enough of my own."

With his shopping done, Jake stopped at Lupe Ramirez' cantina for supper, then walked back to the stable barn. Sim had been by, and put his old horse out on graze. Jake visited the sorrel racer again, fondled its muzzle and scratched its ears.

"See you in the morning, hoss," he told the animal.

"Soon as everybody leaves for the sale barn."

He took his blankets up to the loft and settled in for a night's sleep.

Chapter II

Full morning lay bright on the town of Perdition, and the last outbound traffic had been gone for an hour — buggies and wagons, buckboards and saddle mounts, a southbound caravan headed for Three Forks and the weekly encounter of those who had money to spend and those who had something to sell. It was sale day at the sale barn, and those who were going were gone.

On a quiet State Street, across from the hotel, a splendid sorrel racer wearing tooled-leather gear stood at the hitch-rail in front of the Perdition Bank. Inside, Wilbur Short goggled at the saddle pocket lying on the marble counter, then goggled again at the steady muzzle of the Colt Peacemaker pointed at him through the brass grate. It took him a moment to get his eyes to focus beyond it, on the man who held it. He licked dry lips, tried to speak, then coughed and tried again. "Jake," he said, "you shouldn't be robbing the bank this way."

Outside the teller's cage, Jake Creedmore shrugged, a look of sad resolve on his face. "It's the only way I could think of offhand, Wilbur," he said. "But I wish you'd hurry up and put some money in that poke before Homer Boles or somebody happens along. That would

18

be embarrassing, was the marshal to come in right now."

"I can sure see how it would," Wilbur nodded, fumbling with stacked assets. He had just finished his morning count, and hadn't even closed the safe when Creedmore showed up. Currency and coin lay neatly rowed on the counter before him. Jake's gun twitched suggestively and the clerk picked up the battered saddle-pocket and began putting money into it.

Jake watched him closely. "Give me some of those twenties and fifties there, too," he said. "And don't worry, I don't aim to make a practice of this."

"I hope not, Jake," the clerk shrugged. "Bank robbing can lead to a life of sin, you know." He inserted some twenties and fifties. "Is this on account of not getting top dollar for your cows, Jake? I sure hope that ain't it, because if everybody that didn't get top dollar on their cows was to take and rob banks, that would be a sorry state of affairs."

"You're right as rain about that, Wilbur," Jake agreed. He pointed at the counter. "Are those hundred-dollar bills there, Wilbur? Let me see one of those. I don't remember ever seeing a hundred-dollar bill."

Wilbur handed one across and Jake admired it. "That's mighty pretty. Put a couple of these in there, too, will you? That's right. Thank you."

"Is it because Conrad W. Jackson is fixing to foreclose on you, Jake? Is that why you're doin' this?"

"That's mostly it," Jake agreed. "How much do you reckon I've got there, now?"

"Probably about two thousand dollars. Do you want me to count it?"

"I thought you *were* counting it."

"Well, it's hard to remember to count when you're being robbed. But it's right at two thousand dollars."

"I'll take your word for it," Jake shrugged. "How

about a few of those gold pieces there? Man needs hard cash sometimes, if he goes where folks don't know him."

"Homer Boles will be after you with a posse, Jake. You know that, don't you?"

"I know, but if I can get up around Portales before they catch up, I ought to be all right. Homer wouldn't go any farther than that."

"Most folks would head south. I would, if it was me."

"Yeah, that's why I figure I'll head north instead. Of course, I'd as soon you didn't say anything about that, Wilbur."

Wilbur looked pained. "Now, Jake, you know me. Would I say anything about that?"

"I'd just rather you didn't. How much is in there now?"

"Two thousand, three hundred and fifty-one dollars. How much more do you want, Jake? You're coming near to cleaning us out. This ain't all that big a bank, you know."

Jake thought about it. "Would you say Conrad W. Jackson's sorrel horse is worth five-six hundred dollars, Wilbur?"

"Bound to be," the clerk said. "Or pretty close, anyway. Jake, I really think you ought to reconsider about robbing this bank. Homer Boles might not be the worst that comes after you, you know."

"If you mean those jaybird drifters that Conrad W. Jackson keeps around, Wilbur . . . like that one I had to shoot . . . well, those jaspers have already done about as much to me as they know how to do. That's the reason I'm leaving. But the whole mess of them aren't worth worrying about, as far as I'm concerned."

"I don't know why you keep sayin' Mr. Jackson is behind all that, Jake. Nobody's ever proved he is. But I was thinkin' about some other folks . . ." he glanced around, suddenly nervous.

20

"Yeah," Jake said, "I've heard about Conrad W. Jackson having dealings with that Flanders bunch. But I don't expect anybody's about to sic that bunch on a man over two-three thousand dollars. I expect their services come a sight higher than that." He pondered numbers for a moment, then waggled his gun. "Buckle that tote up, Wilbur. That's enough cash for me."

"At least nobody can say you're a greedy man, Jake."

"Nothing good comes of being greedy." Jake looked around the room, then strode over to the hatrack. A new hat hung there, snow-gray and neatly molded. He took it down, pulled folds of paper out of its lining, and tried it on. It fit as though it was built for him. He tilted it on his head and put his old hat on the rack.

"That there is Conrad W. Jackson's silver-belly beaver hat," Wilbur pointed out. "It's for Sundays."

"That's all right," Jake said. "That horse out front was his, too, 'til today. Would you say all this — cash and everything — would come to about three thousand dollars, Wilbur?"

"I guess it wouldn't miss it very far, countin' the hat. What's this for?" Wilbur stared at the bill of sale Jake had handed him.

"That's for my place that Conrad W. Jackson wants. I've signed it over, paid in full. He just bought it."

"He didn't need to buy it, Jake. If you couldn't pay off your mortgage, he'd get it for a filing fee."

"Well, this way it makes an honest man out of the varmint," Jake allowed. He picked up his saddle pocket and put his gun away.

"He ain't going to be happy about all this, Jake." Wilbur shook his head, not looking any too happy himself. "You know how Mr. Jackson can get when he's crossed."

"Comes of not being crossed enough," Jake decided. "A man's better for his bitter disappointments. They

21

say that in church."

"Amen," Wilbur shrugged. "Comes to that, though, if it was me that wanted to do a mercy for Conrad W. Jackson's everlasting soul, what I'd steal is that picture of him there on his roll-top. Mr. Jackson puts stock in that picture, Jake. I reckon that's because he paid near a hundred dollars to get that Frenchman to paint it for him."

Jake walked across and looked at the picture. A little oil painting of Conrad W. Jackson's face, his expression so stiff and formal that he looked constipated. Jake wasn't impressed. The thing wasn't more than a foot across, frame and all, and certainly not worth any hundred dollars. He knew men who would paint a barn for ten, and provide the paint. But there was no accounting for taste.

"Puts stock in it, does he?"

"More'n a body would think, to look at it."

Jake opened the flap on his saddle pocket and put the picture in with the money. "I'm obliged for the notion, Wilbur. Why, if there was a way I could aggravate Conrad W. Jackson enough that come judgment day the Lord would find him without fault, then I believe I'd have done the varmint a service."

Wilbur sighed. "If aggravatin' him is goin' to save his soul, Jake, I wouldn't be surprised if you'd just assured his place in Heaven."

Jake had started for the door. Now he stopped to look back. "Wilbur, if I didn't know better I'd swear you wouldn't mind aggravating Conrad W. Jackson some yourself."

Short raised his hands in denial. "Not me, Jake. Not on your life. Besides, you're doin' just fine on your own."

Jake shook his head sadly. "Wouldn't have minded doing a little more. Well, nice visiting with you,

Wilbur, but I got to run now."

"Yeah," Wilbur said. "I can see how you got to do that."

Jake stepped out and closed the door behind him, squinting in the bright sun. He tipped Conrad W. Jackson's hat to a pair of bonneted ladies passing by. "Morning, ladies."

"Good morning, Mr. Creedmore," one said. "Doing some banking this morning?"

"Yes'm. Just making a withdrawal. Sure doesn't look like rain again today, does it?"

"No more than generally." She tipped her visor high, looking up at him. "That there looks like Conrad W. Jackson's new Sunday hat."

"Yes'm," he admitted, "it does look just a whole lot like it. But mine fits better than his did."

They went on their way and Jake stepped out into the street. He was tying his saddle pocket onto Conrad W. Jackson's oiled rig when he noticed Wilbur Short at the window, looking out at him. He frowned and waved and Wilbur backed out of sight. The man was just itching to come out and tell somebody that the bank had been robbed. "That Wilbur," he said to the horse, "he knows as well as I do it wouldn't be right to come running out hollering robbery when the robber is still right out front."

He unhitched the sorrel, swung aboard and rode along State Street to turn left on Johnson Street. The sun was just cresting the plank buildings to his right, and shining under the awning of Johnson's Emporium. He dismounted, hitched the sorrel and headed for the door, then stood aside and tipped his hat as Opal Hayes came out, carrying an armload of packages. "Morning, Ma'am," he said.

"Good morning, Jake." She looked past him. "My, but that is a fine horse. It looks like Mr. Jackson's prize

23

sorrel."

"Yes'm, it sure does. My fond hope is that it's as fast as his sorrel, too. Might have a chance to run him, some. Ah . . . is Miss Clara in town with you?"

"Why, no, she isn't, Jake," she said. "I guess you hadn't heard. Clara went off to visit her Aunt Jessy — that's my late husband's sister back home — and might be gone for a while. Jessy is having female trouble."

"Female trouble, Ma'am?"

"That's what she said. Clara decided to go give her a hand. You know how things like that can be."

"Yes, Ma'am, I guess. Well, I'm sorry to miss her, because I'm leaving myself. But I reckon that's how it goes. I hope your sister-in-law's health gets better, real quick."

"There's nothing wrong with Jessy's health," she said. "She just has female trouble."

"Oh." He stood aside for her to pass, then went in to collect his goods and pay his bill.

He knew what was coming. The widow Cole met him at the counter. "I believe that is Mr. Jackson's hat," she declared. "How come you to be wearing it?"

"To keep the sun out of my eyes and the rain off my head," he shrugged. "I been to the bank like I said, Ma'am, so now I need to pay you for that package there."

"Does Mr. Jackson know you are wearing his hat, Mr. Creedmore?"

"I haven't talked to him about it, Ma'am."

"Well, I certainly intend to."

"That's just fine, Ma'am. I hope you'll tell him how much better I look in it than he did." He stepped aside to glance in the dusty little mirror behind the counter. "Just a whole lot better, in fact."

New clothes collected, Jake stepped out into the full sun of morning and paused on the walk to listen to what sounded like a distant commotion, growing a block or so away. Wilbur Short had waited as long as he could, to start spreading the news. Jake tied his packages behind his saddle, swung aboard the sorrel and hard-reined to turn the animal full around in the street, slowly, while he took one last look at Perdition. Slap-up little town, he thought. Not a reason in the world for anybody to stay around here, and sure no reason for any right-minded man ever to come back.

In the distance the ruckus was growing, people shouting and banging doors over on State Street. And somebody had taken to ringing the fire bell.

Solemnly, Jake Creedmore lifted Conrad W. Jackson's hat, a final salute to a place he never intended to see again. Conrad W. Jackson's town, existing for Conrad W. Jackson's pleasure.

"Wasn't for Conrad W. Jackson," he told nobody in particular, "there wouldn't be any reason for this place at all. Puts me in mind of a dung beetle on a cow plop."

He turned the sorrel north then, touched spurs to it and lit out of Perdition like the law was after him — which, by then, it was.

From Perdition, Jake went north, just like he said he would. And Wilbur Short told Homer Boles what Jake had said, just like Jake knew he would. And Homer Boles led his search to the south, just like Jake figured he would. It wasn't much of a posse right at first, just Homer Boles and four others who had joined him at Perdition. But that was only until they came to Three Forks and Homer Boles told Conrad W. Jackson that his bank had been robbed.

They were amazed at how well Mr. Jackson took the news. He just sort of stared at them for a minute or two, then he climbed down into the sale ring with the auctioneer and a hand of polled Herefords and offered an open reward of five hundred dollars for the capture of Jake Creedmore.

They had to postpone what was left of sale day, because after that Homer Boles had seventy-three men in his posse. They combed the country south of there like it hadn't been combed since Chisum's range war. Some of them went all the way to Fort Stockton before they wore out, and eleven of them split off and held up a stagecoach out of Cuervo and never did go back to New Mexico.

So it was several days later before Conrad W. Jackson got back to Perdition and found out that more than some money was missing. His horse was gone, and his silver-belly beaver hat . . . and his picture.

"My picture," he said, over and over, just sitting at his roll-top and looking at the empty place in its corner bin. "He took my picture." Then he would turn to Wilbur Short and ask, "Wilbur, why did that thieving snake take my picture?"

At first Wilbur didn't say anything, but after a while he said, "Maybe he just wanted something to remember you by, Mr. Jackson."

Jackson sat in thoughtful silence for a time, then he got out some paper and a pen. "You don't work here any more, Wilbur," he said.

Wilbur's lip trembled. "You mean I'm fired, Mr. Jackson?"

"Not exactly fired, Wilbur. Consider it a transfer. I'm recommending you for employment with the Great Central and Pacific Investment Company of Big Spring, Texas. You are to leave Perdition immediately, go directly to Big Spring and work there from now on."

"But, Mr. Jackson, that's a long ways off!"

"Yes," Jackson said. "It is."

Then, with Wilbur Short safely on his way to far

places, Conrad W. Jackson called in Homer Boles and what was left of his posse. "Wilbur Short was mistaken in his estimate of what Jake Creedmore stole from the Perdition Bank," he told them solemnly. "I have done a thorough accounting. This bank is short more than twenty thousand dollars. Therefore I am increasing the reward for Jake Creedmore to five thousand dollars, and another five thousand for recovery—intact—of certain personal properties which he also took, specifically one horse, one hat and one small oil painting."

"Never knew a man to be so fond of a silver-belly beaver hat," one of the hunters muttered to another.

"It ain't the hat, you damn fool," the other whispered. "It must be the horse."

"I never heard of a horse worth five thousand dollars," a third told them.

"We better print up some dodgers," Homer Boles decided.

The following day, Conrad W. Jackson declared the Perdition bank insolvent, declared a moratorium on all uninsured accounts, and began foreclosure proceedings on all outstanding mortgages held by the bank.

To stunned debtors attending a town meeting he explained, "Until our losses can be recovered, by means of collection of all debts, the Perdition Bank is temporarily out of business. The outlaw Jake Creedmore cleaned us out. My heart bleeds for all you fine people who must lose your assets all because of what that one man did, but I have no choice in the matter now. It is all Jake Creedmore's fault."

Chapter III

With all that was happening around Perdition and south of there, Jake Creedmore had himself a leisurely trip north to Portales, and stopped off there to visit with his cousin Philo Henderson. He had been meaning for a year or more to go see Philo. They had never been that close through the years, being ten years removed in ages, but each was about the only family the other could lay claim to for sure and they had tried to keep in touch. To Jake Creedmore, Philo Henderson was an island of stability in a sometimes uncertain world.

"Things didn't work out for me down yonder," Jake told the older man. "I cashed in and bailed out and I may have to be scarce for a while."

"Sometimes investments don't pan out," Philo said. "Best thing a man can do then is try to minimize his losses. How come you have to get scarce?"

"Method of my departure probably didn't make just everybody real happy. I had to rob the bank to get my money back."

Philo gazed at him for long moments. "That's pretty drastic, Jake. A man can get himself a bad name doing things like that."

"Desperate situations call for desperate measures

sometimes. I don't expect to make a habit of it, though. The problem now is, what do I do with the money? I hate to just tote it around, and I can't see settling in to reinvest just yet. I wouldn't be surprised if there's two or three hundred dollars' reward on me. I need to let things cool off."

"You might consider cotton futures," Philo suggested. "A lot of criminals get into commodities. Or railroad shares. You remember the Burton boys back home, Jake? Maybe not, they were more my age — outlaws from the day they were weaned, the both of them. It ran in their family."

"I recollect hearing about them," Jake admitted.

"Yeah. Well, they used to steal everything they could get their hands on. Cattle to collar buttons. Made a practice of it. Got to be wanted men and finally had to leave Texas for the territories. But they saved up some money and bought railroad shares and the last I heard they're back in Texas, respectable as you please . . . somebody said they're talkin' about a railroad all their own. Jake, I can't imagine you robbing a bank. How'd you come to such a pass, anyhow?"

"I had something somebody else wanted."

"Problem with investing in land," Philo nodded. "You own land, you own it. Somebody else wants it, they come after it any way it suits them to. Best investment for a man that isn't in position to stand his ground is a floating fund."

They sat on the front porch of Philo's house and watched the moon rise out of Texas, while Phyllis did the supper dishes and put the kids to bed.

"I wish you'd take my money and put it to good use for me," Jake said finally. "I don't seem to be much of a hand at things like that. I buy a piece of Godforsaken desert and first thing you know I've struck water and all hell breaks loose."

29

"Know what you mean," Philo sympathized. "Runs in the family, I reckon. Did that geologist fella from Santa Fe ever show up down there, to find out how come you got all that water?"

"He was around for a while," Jake said. "He scouted around a little, said he thought maybe I'd tapped into a stream aquifer out of the Edwards Plateau or maybe the Ogalala. Said he'd need a survey to figure out where it flowed. I was even thinkin' back then that I might go into the water business. I offered to pay for the survey, but I guess something else came up because I didn't hear any more. Then things started going bad. I probably wasn't meant to get into the water business, anyway."

"Doesn't look like you're going to, now, I guess."

"So will you invest my money for me?"

"Might as well. How much do you have?"

"Two thousand and a bit that I can spare."

"That's a thousand less than you had three years ago."

"Ain't it, though."

"I'll see what I can do. You got any preferences?"

"Just something sound. I kind of favor real property, but you decide. Just whatever's best."

"You want me to call off that surveyor?"

"No," Jake shrugged. "He'd have showed up by now if he was coming. Besides, I never signed any authorization. Not my property anymore, anyway."

"I'll look around," Philo told him. "Two thousand isn't much, but there's opportunities crop up from time to time. Just a matter of gettin' in on them when they hatch." He sat in silence for a few minutes, then started ticking things off on his fingers. "Bunch of Englishmen have been buying up land over around Mesa. Might be some opportunities there. And that Siddons bunch, they've bought about half the Cuero valley. Land knows what they want it for, but they got something in mind, I guess. Then there's that rumor about somebody over in Texas puttin' in a mainline railroad."

"They haven't built railroads in Texas for ten-fifteen years," Jake noted. "How come now?"

"I don't know. Don't even know who's doin' it. It's just a rumor. Big secret, if it's true. Point is, though, there's always *somethin'* goin' on that'll give a man profit on his investment. I'll see what I can find for you."

"I'm obliged," Jake said.

He left Portales the next morning, thinking he might lay over for a time at Melrose. As far as he knew, nobody around Melrose had ever heard of Jake Creedmore. As things turned out, though, he spent the lesser part of ten minutes at Melrose and hid out that night at a burned-out cabin down in the Frio breaks while armed men scouted the countryside trying to find him. It was four days later that he found out why. A dodger on a billboard at Pico carried his name in big letters, with a description right down to the scar on his temple and the color of Conrad W. Jackson's hat. The reward it announced was big enough to make his mouth drop open, and in the little print it told how he had taken twenty thousand dollars from the Perdition bank.

Out of sight of the tiny town he paused, took a deep, sighing breath and told Conrad W. Jackson's horse, "Hoss, there comes times when a man's got to change his notions. I didn't think I wanted to go to Texas, but I was wrong about that."

It hadn't been more than a few years since men on the run had been crossing over from Texas to New Mexico to hide. Lately, though, it had become the other way around. Jake and the sorrel burned some miles for a time, and when they crossed into Texas there were dodgers there, too, so they just kept going.

So much for doing kindnesses, Jake told himself. Try to air out some varmint's immortal soul through the healing powers of restorative aggravation, and what does it get you? A one-way trip to distant places, with saddle sores for company.

Philo Henderson gave serious thought to his young cousin's problems — and to the cousin himself. Somehow, he felt, it wouldn't have surprised him even years back to learn that Jake Creedmore was in trouble with the law. The kid had always troubled him, the way he was. Easy-going, amiable most times . . . shoot, sometimes Jake could charm the ears off a brush Baptist if he took the notion to. But no matter how well a body came to know him, it was always as though he didn't quite know him at all. Jake could shoot the breeze with the best of them, but generally when a body looked back on what he had said, he'd never said one whit more than just what he chose to let on.

It was Philo's observation that some men were talkers and some weren't. Some fellows just rattled on all the time and pretty soon they didn't have a secret left in the world even if they ought to. Others never let on about anything because they never said anything. But with Jake . . . well, Jake didn't hesitate to say whatever came to mind, but when he'd said it there wasn't anything there except just what he had intended you to hear.

In a way it was no surprise that Jake was in trouble. The surprise was *how* he was in trouble. Philo could see Jake's gun getting him into trouble — the kid had always been uncommonly clever with a handgun, though that was another thing most folks never knew about because it wasn't Jake's way to show off or to brag about what mattered. But between a handy gun and a temper that most folks didn't know about either—Jake Creedmore has been known to simmer for years without complaining, then explode like a mortar shell when he'd had enough—Philo wouldn't have been surprised to find Jake running from the law on a murder, mayhem or massive mischief charge.

But to rob a bank? He just couldn't see Jake robbing a bank.

"You know," he told Phyllis, "I just can't see Jake robbing a bank."

"Well, he said he did," Phyllis shrugged.

"And if he said he did, then he did," Philo asserted. "Jake has been known to cloud many an issue in his time, but he doesn't lie."

"Then he robbed the bank," she concluded.

"And then there's *how* he robbed it. If it had been me, and I'd decided to rob a bank, I'd have taken all the money they had. But not Jake. I believe what he took was just exactly as much as . . ."

"Are you thinking about robbing a bank, Philo?" She stared at him, her eyes big and threatening.

"Of course not, pet. Can you see me robbing a bank?"

"I can't see Jake robbing a bank, either. And neither can you. You just said so. Philo Henderson, if you are thinking about robbing a bank . . ."

"I'm *not* thinking about robbing a bank!"

"Then why were you talking about it?" She was bristling now. Philo hated it when Phyllis bristled. Nothing good ever came of it.

"I'm not talking about it!" he sputtered.

"You are so. You said when you rob a bank you'll take all the money."

"I said *if*, not *when!*"

"I don't even know why you're thinking about such things. Why, suppose the children were to find

33

out . . ."

"Phyllis!"

"What?"

"I am not going to rob a bank!"

"Well, I should hope not!"

Philo went for a walk. He needed to think about how best to invest Jake's money for him. Over and over, his thoughts turned to that rumor he had heard—that some investor group over in Texas was putting together a deal to build a new western railroad. Not just some little hob-tailed spur like so many had done, but a real cross-country line. What *was* the name of that outfit? He searched his memory. Great Something and Pacific Investment . . . Great Central and Pacific Investment Company, that was it.

Out of Big Spring, Texas.

Philo turned the notion over and over, toying with it. Rumor had it that those folks were onto something big, and he had a notion they just might have more going their way than even the rumors said.

Two ways for a small investor to profit on a big railroad deal—either have a piece of stock in it and come into a modest share of the wealth, or somehow figure out where the key parts of the deal were and get a trading chip, then deal with the dealers in a seller's market.

Somehow, it reminded him of Jake. Philo made a mental note to go listen very closely to his sources.

Jake hadn't intended to go to Texas. He had seen Texas before. But right now, for a man on the run, Texas was a middling fair place to be. It had achieved that status with all the best intentions. The war between the states was old history—Jake barely remembered it, just something that had been going on

34

somewhere when he was in short drawers — and federal reconstruction had done all the damage it was going to do. Texas had outlasted its carpetbagger government and reinstated one of its own choosing, and everybody decided it was high time for some law and order on a statewide basis. So a few of the high-minded citizens of Texas — and a whole potful of the low-minded ones — went into politics.

What had followed were some eventful years on the glorious road to organized civilization. And their results were obvious. The legislature over in Austin had been passing bills just as fast as it could, meeting for the required hundred and forty days each two years, and the big state now had a body of law that was a wonder to behold. County governments were in total confusion, the court systems were a mess, feuds were springing up all over the state, outlaws were homing on Texas like ducks to water, the Texas Rangers were in political disgrace and what law enforcement existed at all was just whatever each settlement could manage.

There was a strong move afoot to amend the Constitution, to allow the legislature to meet for two days every hundred and forty years, instead of the other way around.

In all, it was a better place for a wanted man to be than any other place Jake could bring to mind. In some ways, it reminded him of Perdition.

Despite the more than two years he had spent around Perdition, he wouldn't miss the place. It had been special to him in only one way. It had been where he first attempted to settle down and become a solid citizen. Things hadn't worked out. But, he told himself, there would be other opportunities after things blew over and the dust settled. He hadn't been at Perdition so all-fired long, at that.

For that matter, nobody had been at Perdition very

35

long. Most everyone there had come from someplace else not too far back, and the little slap-up town just sort of grew. People who lived there were there mainly because everybody is somewhere. Somebody stopped there and built something, then somebody else came along and built something else next door and the first thing anybody knew, there was a town and folks settling in to covet their neighbors' wives and take turns stealing the gold out of one another's teeth. And like any town of the time, there were plenty of folks on the move for it to sift out some population in passing. The big Indian problems were mostly past, the big cattle drives were about done, and there was another economic depression in the east.

Jake had been adrift when he happened on to Perdition . . . one of many. There were drovers laid off from ranches that didn't need spring drives any more, troopers laid off from a field cavalry that had run short on Indians to chase, hunters who came along too late for the buffalo, shooters with no badges to wear, teamsters without teams, muleskinners with no freight to haul — every variety of young buck that the country had called for, molded and then cut loose without purpose.

Jake had been luckier than most. He had some education, a head that worked as well as most and a little money sitting in a bank at Denison waiting for him to decide who Jake Creedmore was going to be some day. He had worked cattle, bucked a plow and clerked in a general store, and he had a notion how it might be to set roots someplace and be a citizen. So he had been looking at opportunities when he wandered into Perdition, and along had come Conrad W. Jackson.

Prince of a man. A real saint. A man who happened to have a few sections of virgin land that he didn't need, and out of the goodness of his heart was willing to let it go for no more than what Jake had in the bank at Denison.

Why, all a man would have to do was drill a little old hole and set a pump and that dry land would blossom to riches in no time. Just see what fine soil that was! Didn't need a thing but a little water on it and a man to tend it from time to time. Sure, parts of it looked a lot like blow-sand, but that was just how this country fooled folks. Why, if it didn't hide its true nature that way, everybody in the country would be out here right now raising figs and racehorses and putting money in the bank.

And improvements? Don't worry about that at all. Conrad W. Jackson happened to own the bank and it would just tickle him half to death to help a young fellow get started off by making a loan to him.

At the top of a rise, Jake hauled rein and turned to look back at the miles of Texas behind him. He shook his head and sighed a rueful sigh. "Varmint," he said, just to hear himself say it.

Twenty thousand dollars the varmint said he took. Twenty thousand dollars out of a two-bit bank that had never had more than five thousand in its safe all at one time in its whole life! Blamed for stealing twenty thousand when all he had come away with was two thousand dollars or so, plus a fair horse and a silver-belly beaver hat . . . and, of course, an oil painting of Conrad W. Jackson. Sometimes of an evening, when coyotes were singing in the hills and Jake chewed rabbit roast beside a lonely fire, he would take out that picture and say a few words to the face of Conrad W. Jackson—words that weren't generally used in public.

He had been tempted to throw the fool thing onto the fire. But then he would recall what Wilbur Short said, about how Conrad W. Jackson put stock in that picture. So he kept it and told himself it was a souvenir.

In those weeks Jake stayed to the back trails, and often went where no trails were, just drifting with noplace in mind to go, no general direction except more or less east, and a feeling that it was better to move on each day or so than to stop anywhere long enough that he might be noticed. Occasionally he saw people — riders skylined in the distance sometimes, or a puncher or two out on the flats working strays for some spread. But he kept to himself as much as he could. Only occasionally did he venture into a settlement — when his supplies ran out and he had to — and each time he moved on as quickly and quietly as he could, then always cut trail and changed direction when there was no one in sight.

Twice he saw dodgers on himself, and each time he was stunned all over again at the size of the bounty Conrad W. Jackson had put up for him. "Set out to aggravate that varmint," he told himself, "I sure never realized what a fine job I was doing of it."

At one place he overheard men talking about a big venture somebody planned — a major new railroad to tie a bunch of little spurs together and then push right on westward, clear out across west Texas and into the territories. A line, they said, that would open up all the central areas to trade. A main line midway between the Atchison Topeka and Santa Fe, and the Southern Pacific. He wasn't paying much attention — just buying his supplies and getting ready to leave — until someone said, "I hear there's gonna be a whole new city yonder, just to serve the line. Someplace called Perdition."

Chapter IV

Riding outlaw trails as he was, it was inevitable that Jake would fall in with outlaws now and then. One bunch he didn't manage to avoid was moseying in his general direction, so he rode with them for a day, shared grub at evening and was making up his mind to go some other direction the next day when they got to talking about rewards.

There were five of them — not an organized gang by any means, just men presently between employments and drifting together. A couple of them, Jake had decided, had a mean streak deep down that made them take to the outlaw trade. The others were just lazy, and none of them were too bright. For a while, lonely and thoroughly tired of his own company, Jake had enjoyed riding with them. But the joy wore thin when Boomer Slade, tall hog at the group's trough, raised his head suddenly and gaped at Jake over the little fire. "Creedmore!" he erupted. "Jake Creedmore! Boys, do you know who we got here? Do you know who this jasper is?"

The rest squinted at Jake. "Who?" a couple of them asked.

"This is the yahoo that cleaned out the Perdition bank. Got better'n twenty thousand dollars, they say."

Foley Size blinked at the number. "Twenty thousand? From Perdition? Boomer, I looked at that bank one time. I bet it didn't have a thousand dollars in it the best day it ever had. Nobody respectable would rob that bank, Boomer. It ain't worth the trouble."

"That's not what the dodgers say, Foley." Slade stared at Jake the way a cougar stares at a lamed deer. "You fellers have all looked at some dodgers. You ever known a dodger to lie?"

Doc Cunningham shrugged. "Maybe not. I got a stack of 'em about me, an' I take pride in the justice they do me."

"You, Foley?"

"Boomer, I got to admit all the ones I know about had their facts pretty straight."

"Rufus?"

"They lied about me. They said I was ugly."

"You are ugly. What I mean is, did you do what the dodgers say you done?"

"They don't know the half of it. But I ain't ugly." He sulked about it for a moment. "Distinctive, maybe, but not ugly."

"George?" Boomer never took his eyes off Jake.

"What?"

"How about your dodgers? Do they say right?"

"How in hell would I know? I can't read."

"Don't matter," Boomer said. "I done made my point."

Jake shook his head. "I never made a study of dodgers, boys, but I never had twenty thousand dollars in my life, much less took that much from that bank."

Boomer scowled. "You did rob it, didn't you?"

"I prefer to consider it a real estate transaction. And all I did was break even. You're looking at the wrong man, Slade."

"Are you sayin' you ain't the Jake Creedmore that

40

robbed that bank?"

"What makes you so sure I am?"

"You answer to Jake Creedmore."

"So does anybody by that name."

"You're a six-footer with brown hair."

"So are half the men in Texas."

"You're about thirty and you have a scar on your cheek."

"Make that maybe a fourth," Jake shrugged.

Boomer grinned. "And you wear a silver-belly bea-ver hat and ride a stud sorrel with the initials C.W.J. on the skirt."

"That does boil it down some," Jake admitted. "You have a real eye for detail, there, Slade."

"I've been praised for it a time or two," Boomer nodded.

"So what's your point?"

"My point is, I reckon you're worth enough in reward money to get me and the rest of these fellers through our present pressing times."

"Not to mention the money he took, if he has it on him," Rufus added.

"Wouldn't mind havin' that there sorrel, myself," Foley decided. "You can keep the hat, though. I never cottoned to white hats."

"Where we gonna turn him in at, Boomer?" George asked.

Slade thought about it. "Might snake on down to Refugio. It ain't too far."

"That's no good. I'm known around Refugio. So's Doc. We'll have to go someplace else."

"We ain't far from Hallettsville, but there's folks there that want to string me up. How about Waco? That's just a few days' ride."

"Waco's out," Rufus snorted. "Them's the ones that said I was ugly."

41

"Boys, I didn't take any twenty . . ." Jake started, but they ignored him, caught up in the planning.

"If we don't decide this, how we gonna collect on him?" Doc asked.

"Might take him back to New Mexico. That's where he's wanted."

"I ain't about to go to New Mexico. That's where I just come from."

"They got any law at Doss?"

Jake said, "How about if I go turn myself in and mail you gents the reward money?"

"Fort Worth?" someone suggested.

"How about Waxahachie?"

"I never been to Beasley. How about there?"

"Them places is a long way off. Gettin' him there won't be easy."

"Shoot him first. That'll make it simple."

"Naw, he'd putrify and how would we prove he's him?"

"You're right as rain about that. We got to take him alive, at least 'til we're close to someplace."

"But that's a problem, Boomer. You know how many ways there are for a man to escape . . ."

"Shut up, Foley. Let's keep an open mind here."

"I have an open mind. You watch your mouth, dumbass."

"Who you callin' dumbass?"

"You, that's who! Shut up!"

"Both of you shut up. Let's hear what Boomer . . ."

"I don't shut up for ugly people!"

They were making such a ruckus that the horses were beginning to spook. Jake said, "You fellows ought to keep it down. You'll spook the horses."

"Shut up, Creedmore! This ain't your business!"

Jake shook his head. "I just think somebody ought to go see about the horses."

"While we're at it, Boomer," Foley snarled, "how much reward have you got on you these days? Funny you ain't said."

"I ain't either ugly," Rufus hissed. "I got a good mind to . . ."

"You ain't got no such thing, Rufus . . ."

"At least Rufus can read, George. Can you?"

"Well, shoot," Jake decided. "I'll go see about the horses."

Two days later he rode out of the hills and down to a little shack-and-shed place named Rosebud, with a railroad spur. He turned the five horses he had "found" over to a depot-master and bought space for himself and the sorrel in a plank-railed stock car on a shunt train bound for Six Bit.

"These little stub lines got more wiggles and cutbacks than a gartersnake at a church social," the woman with the shotgun observed. "And it don't help matters much when the train's got square wheels, either. But it is a way to get from one place to another and I'm not one to complain about such things. Like I used to tell my husband—Pearly, that was the one I used to tell that to—'Pearly,' I'd say, 'Pearly, there ain't any call for a body to fuss about things that a body can't do anything about.' I used to say that to him. Pearly was one to fuss now and again, and I always figured fussing would be the death of him. Told him so, too. 'Pearly,' I'd say many's the time, 'Pearly, fussin' will be the death of you. You just wait and see if it isn't.' Pearly's gone now, bless his soul. Real saint most ways, but he never could help but fuss if things didn't just suit him . . ."

Jake was a little surprised at how many people were riding the stock car. It seemed to be the regular thing to do in this part of the country. The train had a passenger coach up ahead, but he didn't know if anybody was riding it. It seemed to him that everybody was back here with the livestock, and some of them had become quite sociable — especially Annie Coke. A sturdy, gray haired woman with boots and a shotgun, she was one of those people who wouldn't know a stranger if she met one and probably never had. She was one of two women riding stock car this trip. The other was Holly Bee Sutherland, and the two of them were traveling together, along with a pair of saddle mules.

A few of the others had traded names. Some did and some didn't. There was Jud Grover, a rawhide old boy with big hands and a quick grin, and a down-at-heels dandy named Sneed who claimed to be a thespian, and a mouse-faced youngster named Bead who wore a big gun in a tie-down rig and kept throwing suspicious glances at Jake — and others here and there, sharing one end of the plank car with the livestock at the other.

Most of the actual conversation was committed by Annie Coke. She loved to talk, and didn't seem to mind whether anybody else joined in or not . . . though she did involve anybody who'd answer her. She'd started with Jud, tried a turn at Tyrone Sneed and then got around to Jake. "My, but that's a fine hat," she said. "Silver-belly beaver, ain't it?"

"Yes'm, it is." He wasn't paying just a whole lot of attention because he was looking at Holly Bee Sutherland, thinking what a shame it was that she was wearing blue denim pants and a patch pocket coat, and had a floppy hat pulled down to her ears. He would have been happier if she were wearing a dress. She had honey-colored hair and big blue eyes, and had she been wearing a dress he would have had a fair notion of what else she had to go with those features. It

44

was Jake's opinion that a man worth his salt can sort of look right through a dress and have a clear view of the topography beneath. It was an acquired talent. But a man never got the hang of looking through men's clothes because why would he want to?

Holly Bee Sutherland also had a smudge on her face and an attitude like a badger on a bad day, judging by how she kept herself to herself. But it grieved Jake that a woman who might be interesting to look at had decked herself out so there was nothing to see. He felt vaguely that someone had taken away what he considered a natural right and obligation.

"My man Woodrow had one just like that once," Annie Coke was saying, and it took Jake a moment to recall that she was talking about his hat. "Danged fool swapped it for a saddle, though. He wanted to try to ride that hammer-headed roan stud that he traded old man Reems out of. God rest his soul, Woodrow was a saint most ways. But swappin' done him in. I always told him it would. 'Woodrow,' I'd say many's the time, 'Woodrow, swappin's goin' to do you in, sure enough.' And it did, just like I knowed it would."

Jake glanced at her sympathetically. "The hammer-head shucked him, did it?"

"Oh, my, yes. Fourteen times that I know about. But that wasn't what done him. That come from tradin' off his good winter coat to old man Hoot for a hogleg. I told him he shouldn't have did that. 'Woodrow,' I said, 'Woodrow, you shouldn't never have swapped your good coat for a shootin' iron. You know you can't hit the high side of a barn anyhow. You get drunk an' haul that thing out, somebody's plain going to kill you.' That's what I told him, God rest his soul."

Jake looked sympathetic again. "Somebody gunned him down, did they?"

"Would have for sure. Thing was, though, by the

time he taken the notion to go to Longmeadow an' get drunk, we had us a blizzard comin' on. Regular blue norther it was, beatin'est storm anybody seen around those parts for twenty years. And him without a heavy coat, since he'd swapped that off for his gun. Well, I told him, I said, 'Woodrow, you best strap on your gun because it's cold outside.'

Jake tried for a sympathetic look one more time. "I reckon Woodrow froze?"

"No, he drowned. Got likkered up and fell in a cistern, God rest his soul. Most ways, he was a regular saint. All of 'em was, 'cept maybe the first one. God rest their souls."

"Whose souls?"

"My husbands. Let's see. Not countin' the first one . . . I don't count him because he was no account. I told him so, too. 'Slim,' I said—that was his name. Slim. 'Slim,' I said, 'You're just plain no account.' I told him that. But not countin' him there was Pearly, an' Bruce, an' Clyde an' Lester an' Woodrow. Lester's the one that growed up coonass but he mostly got over it. You a married man, Mr. Jones?"

"No, Ma'am," Jake said. "Nor hardly a saint, either."

"Well bless your heart, son, that ain't your fault. Takes a woman's touch to make a saint of any man. Lordy, I done it enough times to know. An' that's somethin' a strappin' young feller like you needs to think about, too. Man ripens on the vine too long, sometimes there ain't much left for a good woman to whip into shape. One of my boys—the third one it was . . . Alfred . . . I could see when he started gettin' overripe so I . . ."

Privately, in his mind, Jake offered his condolences to all of Annie Coke's husbands. He wondered how many of them had been talked to death. He noticed the mouse-faced gun-toter looking at him again and wondered vaguely what was on his mind. Then he went back to looking at Holly Bee Sutherland, wondering if she was as worth looking at as he had a hunch she might be.

". . . taken us a month or two, but we got it done," Annie was saying. "She landed him an' he's well on his way to bein' a saint last I heard. That good woman's got him so whipsawed he can't hardly fart for fear of failure. That puts me in mind of your problem, Mr. Jones. But, Lordy, you won't have no trouble gettin' yourself hooked an' landed. Plenty around ought to be willin' to mend your ways for you, seems to me. You take Holly Bee here, for example. Why, this little gal might could whip a man into fine shape was she to take the notion to. Be a sight better way for her to get shed of her Uncle Roscoe than to keep runnin' away like she's been doin', too. Why don't I sort of get you an' her started out to talkin', an' . . ."

Jake suddenly felt distinctly uncomfortable. "I'm obliged, Ma'am," he said, "but I have some kind of pressing commitments right now. Maybe some other time."

She looked at him with that deep sympathy that a cat reserves for a mouse that just can't get the hang of mousing. "Yep," she said, "I expect you're shy."

The train was slowing, coming to a wood stop. Jake didn't know when he'd been so eager to get out and help load wood into a tender.

Chapter V

All the way to the wood stop, that mouse-faced little fellow had been giving Jake the side-eye, and Jake had wondered about that. Bead, his name was. Neither the name nor the face meant anything to Jake, and yet the fellow acted as though he knew him. A soft-handed, twitchy youngster whose sparse, wiry whiskers sprouting beneath an oversize nose made him seem even younger. Bead wore a tie-down rig that seemed far too big for his scant frame. And he kept looking at Jake. Even Jud Grover had noticed what an interest he had in Jake, and had mentioned it so Jake would notice, too.

Nothing came of it, though, until they were loading wood for the engine's tender. It was common practice on the stub-line roads. They hired cutting crews to haul in stoke-wood and stack it beside the tracks at designated places. Then when a train came it stopped and all the second-class and stock car passengers — and anyone else willing to lend a hand — got off and loaded fuel. Jake was just starting for the tender with his second arm-load when Bead made his move. There was nothing fancy about it — nor too well thought out for that matter. Bead simply drew his gun, stepped up behind Jake, jammed his gunbarrel into Jake's back and said, "Raise your hands, outlaw, for I'm the man who'll collect the reward on you."

It caught Jake off guard, but he did just like the little fellow said. He ducked his head and raised his arms and thirty pounds of stoke-wood cascaded down upon Bead. It knocked his gun out of his hand and dumped him on his backside and there he sat with an armload of spilled wood and his mustache twitching.

Jake kicked his gun aside and squatted beside him. "How come you to poke me with a gun, Bead?" he asked.

Bead dumped the wood he'd caught and peered out from between his hatbrim and his nose. "Because you are a notorious outlaw and I got you dead to rights and I aim to collect the reward on you. Bounty is my business."

"I don't expect you've been in that business very long," Jake allowed.

Annie Coke had hurried over to the commotion, and she leaned over to look under Bead's hatbrim. "Mister, you've made a mistake. This here ain't any outlaw. This is only Mr. Jones, who's about to get sweet on Holly Bee Sutherland yonder, and we don't need you interferin' with a courtship that ain't even hardly begun yet!" Having had her say, she went bustling off somewhere and left Jake to resolve matters.

"How come you to take me for an outlaw, Bead?" Jake asked.

"Because I know you!" Bead snapped, glancing quickly around, this way and that. "Jones is right! You're the notorious train robber Clive Wilson Jones. I got you dead to rights. Where's my gun?"

Jake blinked wide-eyed. "Where did you ever get such a notion as that?"

"Ain't any notion!" Bead was on his hands and knees

49

now, peering around. "You admit your name is Jones, an' the initials on that fancy saddle of yours are C.W.J. Evidence is evidence. Where's my gun got to?"

A fair crowd had gathered and someone said, "The little jaspar's right as rain about that, all right. Seen it my own self. C.W.J., right there big as life."

Jake stood and shook his head. He was going to have to do something about Conrad W. Jackson's saddle. "I'm not Clive Wilson Jones," he said. "I never heard of Clive Wilson Jones, and I never robbed a train in my whole life."

A trainman standing nearby with a shotgun on his arm said, "I don't believe you ever robbed this train, anyway. I'd have remembered that hat."

"I got him dead to rights," Bead insisted. "Has anybody here seen my gun?"

The theptian, Tyrone Sneed, gazed mournfully at Jake. "What tangled webs we weave," he pronounced. "Sometimes it's better to deceive."

"My thought exactly," Jud Grover nodded. "How's come you told us your name was Jones, Jones? Fool thing for a wanted man to just toss out his right name that way. You could have called yourself most anything at all an' we wouldn't have minded, and I bet Mr. Bead never would have figured out who you are. Would you, Mr. Bead?"

Bead was still crawling around, searching here and there. "Not in a million years," he admitted. "I thought sure that thing was over here by the woodpile. How's about some of you folks help me find my gun?"

Jake sighed and shook his head slowly. "If it will set everybody's mind at ease," he announced, "my name isn't Jones. I just said it was."

"That ain't how you do it, Jones," Grover explained. "You ought to have said some other name right off. Changin' now don't do any good."

The conductor came puffing along then from the passenger coach and wanted to know what the trouble was.

"This here is the notorious train robber Clive Wilson Jones," the other trainman said. "That little feller over there found him out."

The conductor looked Jake up and down like he hadn't paid his fare. "Train robber, huh? He ever rob this train?"

"I don't think so. I'd recognize that silver-belly beaver hat if he had." He glanced over at Bead, then raised his voice. "Sir, the Chicago, Shreveport and Pacific Railroad will appreciate it if you'll stop messing up that stack of stoke-wood."

"I can't find my blamed gun," Bead snapped.

"Well, would you mind looking for it somewhere else? That wood is supposed to be stacked neatly . . ."

"How am I going to take that outlaw into custody without my gun?"

"He has one," the trainman indicated Jake. "Use his."

"How am I going to take his away from him if I don't have mine?"

"Do something about this, Chester," the conductor told the trainman. "We have a schedule to keep."

The trainman started to raise his shotgun in Jake's direction, but suddenly Annie Coke was there, her own shotgun pointed at the man's midsection. "You stay out of this, Mister," she suggested. "It ain't your business. Now why don't we all just get back on the train and head for Six Bit like the porter there says."

"Conductor!" the conductor snapped. "Not porter!"

"Well, are we goin' on to Six Bit or ain't we?"

"Not with him, we're not," the conductor said. "I don't allow train robbers on my train."

"It ain't but twenty miles," Annie pointed out. "Be-

51

sides, how many train robbers did you ever know that robbed from the stock car?"

"Makes no difference. He can't ride my train."

"I guess a couple of us could keep him here and you could send some law back for him," the trainman offered.

Annie's eyes flashed. "The very idea! You won't honor a paid passenger's pass to Six Bit, what right have you got to detain him out here where all he done was help you load wood?"

"I got a right," Bead said. "All I got to do is find my gun, and he's my prisoner." He squinted up at Jud. "You got a gun. Will you loan it to me?"

"I make it a habit not to," Jud shook his head.

"This feller's horse is on your train," Annie told the conductor. "What are you fixin' to do, go off with his horse and leave him here? Folks have been hanged for that."

"Then he can go get his horse off the train," the conductor sighed. "But be quick about it. We got a schedule to keep."

Annie glanced at Jake. "You go get your horse, son. I'll stand off these varmints whilst you're about it."

"Did somebody take my gun?" Bead was pleading now. "Come on, folks. I know it was right here somewhere. It's wrong to take a man's sole means of support. Where's my gun?"

The conductor turned away, divesting himself of all responsibility or concern. "Board!" he called. "All aboard for Six Bit and points beyond."

"There ain't any points beyond," the armed trainman admitted quietly. "The Chicago, Shreveport and Pacific don't go anywhere but Six Bit. But he always says it that way, anyhow."

"I can see how it would make him feel better," Jake said, and went to get his horse.

Annie came to a decision. "You, Holly Bee," she said, "go get them mules off the train, too. We'll ride along with Mr. Jones." Turning back to the trainman she snapped, "I don't ride railroads that won't honor a man's pass to Six Bit."

Bead was stomping around, frantic in his search. "What pervert took my gun?" he demanded.

Holly Bee looked toward the stock car, hoisted a contemptuous chin and turned back to Annie. "I don't ride along with outlaws," she said.

But Annie shrugged off the objection. "You do like I tell you, girl. I got me a notion how you and Mr. Jones might just be the savin' grace each other needs."

"But I don't . . ."

"Would you rather go back to your Uncle Roscoe?"

Holly Bee went after the mules.

As the train made steam to pull out, Bead glared through the stock car planks and shook a fist at Jake Creedmore. "Don't you forget, Jones!" he shouted. "I got you dead to rights! You won't get away from me! Bounty is my business!"

Annie Coke settled herself on her saddle mule, shotgun across her lap. "Don't worry about him, Mr. Jones," she told Jake. "He'll be all right. His hogleg is in his saddlebag, right where I put it." Holly Bee Sutherland was already mounted, facing away and making a show of ignoring Jake, except for occasional warning glances in his direction. Annie watched as he swung aboard Conrad W. Jackson's horse, then tilted her head in thought. "You know, that Jud Grover had a point there. Be a whole lot better was you to stop answerin' to the name of Jones."

"My name isn't Jones," Jake said.

"That's the ticket," she smiled. "You just keep that in mind. It's like that duded-up feller — what's his name — said. He said, 'What's in a name?' He said that."

53

"His name is Sneed," Jake said. "Tyrone Sneed. He's a thespian."

"You know, I kind of thought he might be. I can usually spot them kind right off, by how they act."

"My husband Lester, he was an outlaw," Annie Coke chatted as they rode through trackless hills with a lowering sun behind them. "Did I tell you that? About him bein' an outlaw? Most ways he was a saint, rest his soul, but how he made his livin' was by outlawin'. That's what finally done him in, too, just like I knowed it would. He was born coonass and didn't fetch up civilized 'til late in life, so that might be how come he was like he was. But I told him, 'Lester,' I said, 'Lester, outlawin' is goin' to do you in, just as sure as bugs bite.' I told him that, poor soul, but he just couldn't seem to mend his ways."

Long hours and long miles lay behind them now and the wood stop on the Chicago, Shreveport and Pacific was far away, and Jake had been wondering just how long he was to be blessed with the company of the ladies, but so far he hadn't felt it polite to inquire as to why they were still with him, and he wasn't sure he could have gotten a word in edgewise anyway. Annie was on a non-stop chat with no end in sight.

"Point I wanted to make, though," she said, "was that Lester never stayed with a last name hardly any time at all. He changed 'em like most folks change toothpick just ever' whipstitch. 'Bout ten days hand runnin's the longest I ever recollect him answerin' to the same last name. When we was just first married he told me his first last name used to be Tippytoe . . . somethin' like that. Lester Tippytoe. But he was Lester Smith and Lester Coleman and Lester this and Lester that so much it got so's the dodgers on him just said

Lester. Always outlawin', rest his soul, an' many's the time I told him . . ."

"What happened to him?" Jake threw in, just to break the flow.

"Which time?"

"How did he come to die?"

"Oh. Outlawin'. He stole one horse too many."

"Hanged him, did they?"

"Danged horse stepped on his head. You mind if I ask you somethin' personal, son?"

"Ask away."

"Whereabouts are we goin'?"

"Who?"

"Us. Where we goin'?"

"Well," he thought it over, "I thought you and Miss Holly Bee were going to Six Bit, but it appears you've come a mite out of your way. Me, I'm just trying to get to someplace where not so many folks will take the notion they know me."

"I can see how that would ease your mind. Changin' your name wouldn't hurt, either."

"My name is Jake Creedmore," he said.

She thought that over for a moment, then shook her head. "Naw, it's got a right nice ring to it, but it's been used. Some bank robber out in the territories has got hisself in a heap of trouble by that name, an' you sure wouldn't want folks thinkin' you was him. They's some bad folks lookin' for him, the way I hear it. You better think up somethin' else."

Jake decided it was time to take the bit in his teeth. "Ma'am, it's nigh on to sundown and you and Miss Holly Bee are still going the wrong direction. Not that I don't appreciate good company, but don't you suppose you ought to be heading back, if you want to get to Six Bit?"

Her face broke into a serene smile. "Lordy, son, we

55

don't want to go to Six Bit. That was old Roscoe's notion, to send Holly Bee up there to sell these mules. I just come along to keep an eye on her. Roscoe's afraid she'll run off again."

"How come she runs off?"

"Son, if you had to live with Roscoe Sutherland, you'd run off, too. Way he treats that little gal is shameful. I don't believe that old man has did a stick of work since the day he taken her in. Treats her like a hired hand and don't pay her a thing for it. An' her his departed brother's only survivin' kin. Shameful. Why, he don't even allow her to go to barn dances and church socials. 'Fraid she'll hook up with some young buck an' take off, an' he'll have to go back to work."

"Well, if you were supposed to get her to Six Bit . . ."

"I never said I'd do that. I just said I'd keep an eye on her. That's what I'm doin'. You ever thought about callin' yourself Johnson? There's a county or two where folks would shoot you for callin' yourself Johnson, but anyplace else it's a good enough name. Just stay wide of those counties . . ."

Jake had noticed early on that Holly Bee's saddle rig had a sleeve with a rifle in it, but he hadn't thought about that since. But at that moment she hauled the rifle out, sighted and fired, and Conrad W. Jackson's prize sorrel racer came unglued. The horse crow-hopped, hunched and bucked and Jake sailed tail over teakettle into a patch of scrub cedar. He lay head-down for a long minute, trying to get his eyes uncrossed and his lungs to working, then took another minute deciding that no major portions of him were broken, and finally crawled out of the cedars to find Holly Bee sitting her mule saddle twenty feet away, eyeing him curiously.

"What in thunder did you do that for?" he shouted.

She shrugged indifferent shoulders and pointed eastward. "Supper," she said. Two hundred yards away, just at the edge of a stand of brush, a deer lay clean-holed, not even twitching, and Annie Coke came riding back from looking at it.

"Fair shot, Holly Bee," she allowed. "Clean through the neck. Critter never knew what hit it." She turned to Jake. "That's some horse you got there, son. Spooky as a calf at a cuttin'. Man wants to ride a horse like that, he ought to leech on a little tighter."

"I haven't had him very long," Jake rasped. He spotted his hat and started for it, but Annie wasn't through. "You got a sharp knife. Mr. Johnson? Never mind, you can use mine."

"What for?"

"Why, you got to go skin an' gut that deer yonder. You don't expect ladies to do that, do you? That's man's work. Ladies is delicate." She handed him a folding knife and reined around. "Holly Bee, you get on down to that branch yonder an' pick us a camp while I fetch Mr. Johnson's run-off horse. Might get yourself cleaned up a mite, too. You want to look nice for Mr. Johnson, don't you?"

"I don't want to have anything to do with him," Holly Bee declared. "I don't hold with outlaws."

"You just do as I say, girl. Land, I've saw some mighty fine courtin' start off with worse attitudes than that."

Jake went to clean their supper.

Chapter VI

Whatever Holly Bee's drawbacks might have been, she could cook. With water from a clear stream, flour and condiments from Jake's supplies and some spices that Annie carried in a tin, and with the best cuts of the venison that Jake quartered and some greens she found along the streambank, the blond girl put a spread before them that made Jake's eyes bulge and his stomach growl. And he noticed as he wolfed down hot food for the first time in a long time that, with her face washed and her old hat put aside, Holly Bee did look just a whole lot like a girl.

He wondered all over again what she might look like if she was to wear a dress, but he kept his peace. Her attitude toward him didn't seem to have changed any despite the food she served up, and besides he felt it wouldn't be polite to comment to a person about personal appearance — especially to a person who could neck-shoot a deer at two hundred yards from a saddled mule.

Soft sundown lay across green Texas hills when Jake broke out his kit and walked down to the creek. His belly was full of good food and his soul was full of contentment — which, in a young man of his age, amounted to the same thing. Downstream at a clear pool he stripped down, bathed and shaved, washed his old clothes and put on new ones still fresh-wrapped from the store at Perdition. He had come a long way since the day he robbed the bank there, and whether it was the soothing effects of time and distance or just the warm glow in his belly from a good meal, he felt like a new man and it seemed right that he ought to dress like one.

Wearing a new shirt and new britches, carrying his kit and boots in one hand and his wetwash on a stick in the other, he strolled barefoot back to the campsite. Holly Bee was at the fire again, doing something with her skillet, and Annie sat aside on a stump, inventorying the contents of his saddlebags. She looked up as he approached and said, "I swear, son, just look at you! If I didn't know better I'd take you for a ranger. My, but don't you look fine!"

He set down his boots beside his bedroll and hung his wash on a snag to dry, then took a better look at what she was doing. She had emptied both of his saddlebags and had everything laid out in neat order. "You ain't got much money here for a notorious train robber," she said.

"I'm not a notorious train robber. What are you doing with my stuff, Ma'am?"

"Tidyin' up. Object lesson for Holly Bee yonder. Do her good to get a notion of keepin' your stuff tidy. Tidyin' for a man is one of the firstest things in courtin'. She'll get the hang of it once she sees it did."

"Ma'am . . ."

"Who's this jasper in this picture? He looks like he's et a toad."

"That's Conrad W. Jackson. Ma'am. I got to tell you, I don't . . ."

"He kin to you? He don't look like you hardly a'tall."

"I robbed his bank. Ma'am . . ."

59

She gazed at him with renewed respect. "Trains an' banks both? I tell you, son, I don't really hold with outlawin' but I do admire a man as expands on his talents. Did you get a good haul?"

"I didn't take a bit more than what was owed me. I . . ."

Her look of admiration turned to one of benign sympathy. "Is that a fact? Why, maybe you ought to just stick to robbin' trains. I don't think you got the hang of banks yet, Mr. Jones."

"My name isn't Jones."

"That's the spirit."

"I told you, my name is Jake Creedmore."

"No, you listen to me now, Charlie. There's some names a feller just plain shouldn't use, an' Creedmore is one of them. Man gets folks after him like that feller's got, he's gonna wind up dead. You just stick to bein' Charlie Johnson for a while. It's a good enough name."

"Ma'am, I . . ."

"An' besides, the initials fit your saddle. C.W.J. Charlie W. Johnson. Ain't that neat?" She looked at the picture again. "Conrad W. Jackson? C.W.J.? Did you steal this feller's horse, Charlie? I thought you robbed his bank."

"I did. I took his hat, too. This is it."

"My land," she said, and started putting things away in his saddlebags. "Come on over by the fire now, Charlie. Holly Bee is fixin' sugarlumps. That gal's got the finest sugarlumps in Texas, an' I told her I wanted some, but mainly I wanted her to fix 'em so's you'd see what a fine catch she's gonna be."

"Ma'am . . ."

"You'll enjoy 'em, Charlie. Don't argue."

Holly Bee's sugarlumps were as good as any Jake had ever encountered, and he squatted barefoot by the fire putting away six or eight of the little sweet-dough fritters while Holly Bee glared at him and Annie smiled and nodded. Finally she turned to the girl to ask, "How does Charlie Johnson strike you, Holly Bee?"

"Who?"

"Charlie Johnson. We decided on that for Mr. Jones's new name. You wouldn't think less of him for bein' Charlie Johnson, would you?"

"I don't think anything about him at all," Holly Bee said. "I don't hold with outlaws." She finished another batch of sugarlumps and set aside her skillet. "Annie, what are we doin' way off out here with this yahoo? You were supposed to keep an eye on me."

"I'm doin' that, child," Annie said. "Trust me. You been wantin' to get away from your Uncle Roscoe, ain't you?"

"First chance I get."

"Well, this young feller is just the ticket, don't you see? Why, land, if you was his wife, then you . . ."

Jake's head snapped upright so fast he almost broke his neck. "Now hold on there! I don't intend to . . ."

"I don't want to be his wife!" Holly Bee snapped. "I don't even know him!"

"Child, nobody knows anybody 'til they get to know somebody. Everybody knows that. Just take a look at him. He ain't all that bad, is he? I've seen worse. Fact is, I've married worse."

"Ma'am, I think things are about to get out of hand here . . ."

"Hush up, Charlie. We're tryin' to talk. Just look at that face, Holly Bee. Good, strong jaw, eyes set about right . . ."

"Ma'am, me being handsome's got nothing to do with . . ."

"Hush, Charlie. Nobody said you was handsome, so

61

pipe down. What do you think, Holly Bee?"

"I think he's an outlaw and I don't hold with outlaws. Annie, let's you and me just . . ."

"I am not an outlaw!" Jake snapped.

"You are, too. You rob trains."

"I never robbed a train in my whole life. Just a bank."

"See? You admit it."

"But I'm not an outlaw!"

Annie put a soothing hand on his shoulder. "Charlie, will you just hush? I know more about these things than you do. Just let me handle it."

"Handle what? You're supposed to be looking after this girl and here you are trying to snub us up together. What kind of handling is that?"

Annie shook her head. "Charlie, far be it from me to interfere if a full-growed young woman goes mooneyed over some feller an' traipses off with him. That's the Lord's way, don't you see."

"I am not moon-eyed!" Holly Bee flared.

"I don't intend to be traipsed with!" Jake chimed in.

Annie sighed. "I can see this ain't going to be easy. Neither one of you has got the slightest notion how these things are supposed to work."

Jake stood, picked up his boots and turned away, his shoulders sagging with impending defeat. Then he remembered something his cousin Philo had said about women, years before. Women, Philo had explained, will just naturally snooker a man every chance they get. They can't be blamed for that tendency, Philo had added, because it is a natural defense instinct that comes from them being basically aware that men are superior to women in matters of wit, wisdom and will. In his opinion, Philo said, it was incumbent upon a man to recognize that fact and to not be outmaneuvered by the poor dears, but to exercise his natural superiority to the benefit of all involved. A man who lets himself get snookered by ladies, Philo had concluded, has only himself to blame . . . and, worse than that, he does a disservice to the ladies because he undermines their instinctive realization of their natural inferiority and that confuses them no end.

All that had been said a good many years before, prior to Philo being landed by Phyllis, but Jake didn't see how that should change a basic truth. And here he was, backing down in the face of blatant snookering. He owed it to these ladies, he decided, to put his foot down.

So he turned around and did—square in Holly Bee's hot skillet.

There was no question that they were impressed. He went hopping around on one foot, hollering through clenched teeth, and he had their full attention.

But when finally he could speak, he made his point. "This has gone as far as it is fixing to," he said. "Much obliged to both of you, and no hard feelings, but come first light I'll be heading out on my own, all by myself, without any further use for company. It's my best suggestion that you ladies just head on back to Six Bit or wherever, and forget that you ever laid eyes on the likes of me."

Two days later they crossed Little Clay Creek, climbed a long hill and looked down on what was left of the town of San Galena. It wasn't much of a town, just a few beat-down buildings, a dusty street, some dry hedgerows and a dozen acres of holding pens at a rail siding surrounded by beanfields. Just another little down-at-heels spur line town, the kind that had sprung up along the quiet side of Comancheria back before

Texas was tame. Most such places existed for a few years, then just dried out and dusted over and sprang up again someplace else. But having a railroad changed things. Towns of that sort that found themselves on rail would dry out and dust over, just like other places, but they didn't quite disappear. The railroad saw to that.

"Not much of a town, as towns go," Annie Coke allowed.

"I don't like that place," Holly Bee said. "Let's go someplace else, Annie."

Jake didn't say anything, just started down the hill toward town. He was thinking it might be time to try riding a stock car again, partly just to rest and partly to break trail in case there *were* hardcases looking for him like Annie thought.

He didn't want to ride a main road. Folks tended to look at folks riding the mains, and to get curious about them. But hardly anyone ever paid any mind to folks riding the stublines. Texas was full of them—little spur railroads that had sprung up mostly in the seventies, a lot of them financed by carpetbaggers trying to reinvest their thievings before Reconstruction ran out. If there was one such line in Texas, Jake supposed, there were a hundred. Little two-bit railroads that went from just most anywhere to a mainline siding somewhere, and every last one of them named like it had been the grandest rail venture in the history of locomotion. San Galena's was called the Victoria, Waxahachie and Great Western Railroad, though as far as he knew it didn't go anywhere except to Fort Worth.

And to his mind, San Galena filled the bill as a good place to catch a train. He reined in just outside of town and looked the place over. Peaceful as a graveyard it seemed. The only living souls in sight were a pair of bewhiskered codgers who had taken root on a bench in front of the general store. Beyond was a dusty depot and a hedgerow, and past that were fields and hills.

"Right nice little town," he said to nobody in particular. "Ought to be a monument here: 'On this spot, in the year of you name it, nothing at all happened.'" The idea pleased him and he turned to grin at Holly Bee Sutherland. "That would be a sight, now, wouldn't it?"

She glared at him. "How many times do I have to tell you I don't talk to outlaws?"

He glared back. "How many times do I have to tell you I'm not an outlaw?"

Annie Coke shook her head and tished her mule. "If th' two of you ain't th' beatin'est!"

Holly Bee glanced around, nervously. "I don't like this place, Annie."

"It's just a town, Holly Bee," Annie said. "You ever been here before, Charlie?"

Jake squinted, trying to remember. In those years of kicking around he had seen a sight of little towns. "Maybe so. Seems familiar. Just like every other little scrub-grass cowtown around, though."

"I don't like it," Holly Bee insisted. But when they went ahead she trailed along, peering suspiciously here and there, her nose quivering like a cottontail rabbit's. She pointed. "What's that yonder?"

"Where?" Jake squinted.

"Line of bushes yonder."

"Hedgerow," Annie said. "Farmers plant 'em. Protects the fields from wind-scour."

"In cattle country?"

Jake saw something else, then. Out by the loading pens were barbed-wire fences — tall, tight fences everywhere he looked. The dusty wind had obscured them from a distance.

Annie saw them, too. "Lordy, don't times change,"

she said. Then she chuckled. "One of my husbands— Clyde, it was—he always used to say that. 'Times change,' he'd say. Got him into trouble now and again because there's plenty of folks that don't hold with that kind of talk. It aggravates 'em. But he went right on sayin' it, bless his soul. Real saint he was, most ways. But he'd say, 'times change,' an' as often as not pretty quick there'd be some yahoo a'thumpin' his head for him . . ."

"Why are there people in the hedgerow?" Holly Bee asked.

". . . but it never changed his ways none. I recollect Mrs. Biddle sayin' to me, 'Annie,' she said, 'Annie, that man of yours has got the soul of a philosopher sure enough . . ."

Jake squinted, trying to see through the haze of dust. "What people?"

Holly Bee nudged her mule forward. "Annie, I see folks in those bushes. Do you . . . ?"

" '. . . might have the soul of a philosopher, bless his heart, but he ain't got the brains God gave a goose, settin' folks off like that . . .'"

"Holly Bee, you're right as rain," Jake said. "There *are* folks in that hedgerow. I wonder what they're up to?"

"I wasn't talking to you."

". . . finally told him so, too. 'Clyde,' I says, 'Clyde, somebody's sure enough goin' to beat your head in if you keep on sayin' times change. Notions like that upsets some folks just somethin' fierce. Like politics an' religion an' the weather . . ."

They were into the town then and Jake noticed that the brace of codgers wasn't on the store bench any more. Then he heard sounds, and turned. Mounted men were boiling over the hilltop behind them, coming full tilt with guns in their hands, spreading as they came.

It got Annie's attention. She turned, gaped and clapped her straw hat down tight on her head. "Oh, my!" she said. Before Jake could react she had spurred her mule and was heading for the center of town at a full run, with Holly Bee just behind her.

Jake cancelled all thoughts of a monument to serenity and dug his heels into Conrad W. Jackson's prize sorrel. Within fifty yards he was neck-and-neck with the two women, and just noticing that the hedgerow had spilled its people. The men were spilling across the tracks, coming up the street at a run, yelling war cries. There were a lot of them.

He never figured out who opened fire first — whether it was those behind or those ahead — but suddenly the little street was full of thunder and the whine of angry lead. His Peacemaker was in his hand then and he was selecting a target, a red fog of sheer aggravation before his eyes. It wasn't polite to shoot at women. But before he could fire, a couple of the combatants had already learned that. Annie Coke had swiveled around and taken a rider out of his saddle with a load of birdshot, and Holly Bee's rifle spread-eagled one of those ahead with a shot that took the heel off his boot.

Jake slammed his gun away, stuffed his mouth full of reins, grabbed a mule halter in each hand, knee-turned the sorrel and all three of them thundered full tilt into the mouth of a little alley hardly wider than a buckboard — which was what was at its other end, coming their way.

Chapter VII

The little alley was no more than a space between long, low buildings, and it took them more than half its length to get stopped. By then the sorrel and the buckboard's dapple were shoulder to shoulder, threatening to climb all over each other, and the dapple had its head under Jake's arm, slamming him in the ribs with its headstall. The woman driving the wagon was standing, fighting her reins and shouting, "Get out of the way! You can't come in here!" Annie was shouting, "Let go of my mule, Charlie! I got hooraws to shoot!"

Behind them, out in the open street, it sounded like a war was going on. Jake spat out his reins, turned loose of Holly Bee's mule and tipped Conrad W. Jackson's hat to the lady in the buckboard. "Sorry, Ma'am," he said. "We just got here ourselves. Can you tell us when the next train is due?"

"Thursday," she snapped, trying to see past the intruders, to see the street beyond. "I knew it would come to this. I told that bonehead . . ."

"I don't hold with folks shootin' my direction," Annie fussed. "Charlie, let loose! I still got another load."

"I got six," Holly Bee offered. "Which ones you want shot, Annie?"

But it was too late to retreat. Facing doors on both

68

sides of the alley banged open behind them, blocking the passageway, and beyond them were the sounds of men piling from doors, running toward the street. "Go get 'em, boys!" a man's voice shouted. "This has gone far enough! Now you can earn your wages!"

The lady in the buckboard stretched on tiptoe to see over Jake's head and shouted, "Don't say I never told you, Chub Whatley! This whole mess is your fault!" With a sigh of irritation she worked her reins, backing the buckboard off a few steps . . . a thing Jake greatly appreciated. The dapple had taken to chewing on his shellbelt.

"I told him," the lady explained, turning her attention finally to those with her in the alley. "I said, 'Chub Whatley,' I said, 'you let grangers fence up the holding pens, you're just asking for a war. Those drovers will be down here like ticks on a woods cow.' I told him that. Land, anybody knows cowmen don't hold with their pens being fenced, and you think grangers are going to stand and watch them cut wire? You'd think Chub would have better sense, wouldn't you?"

"Men," Annie sympathized. "Bless their hearts, they're all just alike, ain't they?"

"Not a one of them's got the sense God gave a goose," the lady agreed. "My name is Harriett Fletcher. I didn't get yours."

"Annie Coke," Annie nodded. "Yonder is Holly Bee Sutherland. We're both from out around Rosebud. This here gent is goin' by the name of Johnson right now because it's better he don't answer to his right name."

Jake tipped Conrad W. Jackson's hat again. "Howdy, Ma'am," he said. Past the obscuring doors, in the street beyond, the shouting and shooting were beginning to sound organized. "That Chub Whatley you mentioned just then, I take it he's the law around here?"

69

"If you want to call him that," Harriett sneered. "He's town marshal." She glanced at his saddle. "What does the C.W. stand for, Mr. Johnson?"

"Well, actually, Ma'am, those aren't my initials. The saddle came with the horse. The initials stand for Conrad W. Jackson."

"Your horse is named Conrad W. Jackson?"

Beyond the door-barred alleyway there was a renewed burst of gunfire, then a loud voice barking orders in sudden silence.

"Sounds like the marshal's got things in hand out yonder," Annie said.

"Either that or they're all dead," Holly Bee allowed.

"Not likely," Harriett Fletcher shook her head. "Last two times they had it out on that street out there, the only casualty was Maude Clark's milk cow. There isn't a one of those men out there that knows how to hit the side of a hill. Chub will round them up and lock them in the depot barn . . ." she sighed, ". . . then when the train gets here Thursday Judge Moody will turn the drovers loose and Judge Hanover will turn the grangers loose and pretty soon they'll be at it again."

Annie clicked a solacing tongue. "That kind of thing can give a town a bad reputation."

"Doesn't really matter any more," Harriett said. "Hardly anybody left here who cares one way or another . . . at least not enough to file charges with the sheriff. Only reason San Galena keeps its town charter is to give those lunatics a place to fight, and to keep Chub Whatley supported on the fines they pay for the privilege. Local law! They wouldn't get off easy if they pulled stunts like that in the sheriff's jurisdiction."

"Tough sheriff hereabouts?" Jake asked.

"Tough as a boot. Why don't you use your right name, Mr. . . . ah . . . Johnson?"

"Never know it to look at him," Annie jumped in,

70

"but this here is a wanted man. He was goin' by the name of Jones, but some dribblebritches bountyman tried to take him in for bein' the notorious train robber Clive Wilson Jones. So we decided he's Charlie Johnson. I been tellin' him, names can label a body if he ain't careful."

"*Are* you Clive Wilson Jones?" Harriett asked Jake.

"No, Ma'am, I'm not . . ."

"You're gettin' the hang of it," Annie said.

". . . and I never robbed a train in my whole life."

"Then what are you wanted for?"

"He robbed a bank," Holly Bee said. "I heard him say so."

"I see." Harriett gazed at him with eyes that seemed to see right through him.

"It was a business transaction," Jake explained. "Nothing else to it." He wanted to change the subject. "If you'll haul on those reins, Ma'am, maybe we can get you backed out of here."

"Wouldn't want none of this to go any farther, of course," Annie said. "I mean about this young feller's circumstances an' all. 'Specially not in a county with a tough sheriff. Who is sheriff here, anyway?"

Harriett Fletcher hauled her reins and began backing away. "I am," she said.

Jake had seen a few lawmen in his time. Mostly— more often than not—they were men of the cut of Homer Boles, men who settled into a thankless job and did it as well as they could and learned soon on that it was easier to keep the peace than to reestablish it afterward . . . men who often were fifty and florid and, like Homer Boles, got to carrying a portly gut around in front of them because of the hours of sitting their work required. And mainly, every lawman Jake had ever known, seen or heard about was a man.

This Fletcher woman was trim and thirty or forty

and didn't carry any gut in front of her. All she carried in front was what women generally do. And where most lawmen carried a gun or two on visible display, this lady didn't have a weapon in sight unless it was a pair of cold-steel eyes that looked like they could cut a man down if they needed to. Sheriff? She surely didn't look to Jake like a sheriff. On the other hand, when a fellow has a grip on a lady's halter and is fine-steering her rear-end in a narrow alley, that is no time to argue.

"Did you steal Conrad W. Jackson, Mr. Johnson?" she wondered as her rear wheels cleared.

"No, Ma'am, I sure don't believe so."

"Then where did you get him?"

"Who?"

"Your horse. Conrad W. Jackson."

"This horse isn't Conrad W. Jackson, Ma'am."

"Oh. I must have misunderstood. Who *is* Conrad W. Jackson, then?"

"That's the varmint Charlie stole the horse from when he robbed his bank," Annie chipped in, helpfully. "Prob'ly deserved it, too. Jasper looks like he's swallowed a toad."

"I see," Harriett said.

"Charlie's got a picture of him, to remember him by."

"My."

She sawed reins and the dapple cleared the wagon out of the alley and backed a few steps further, leaving room for the rest of them.

Duty-bound for the sake of the ladies, Jake lifted his flap and pulled out the banker's painting, holding it up for the lady sheriff to see. "This is him. He runs a bank and swindles folks on the side."

"My," she said. "What a fine likeness. Does it look like him?"

"Near enough, considering it was done by a Frenchman. Conrad W. Jackson puts stock in this thing, is why I keep it around."

"Along with his horse."

"Yes'm, and his silver-belly beaver hat. Maybe I got just a mite carried away."

"All he taken was only what the varmint owed him," Annie added. "Can't see much harm in that, I guess, only it does make Charlie here a wanted man. But we'll get his ways mended quick enough with Holly Bee here gettin' sweet on him . . ."

"I am not!" Holly Bee chirped. "Annie, you know I don't . . ."

"Hush, child. These things take time."

From the street beyond the alley came the lock-step scuffling of many men being led away for incarceration.

"I suppose I'll have to arrest you, Mr. Johnson," the lady sheriff said. "But I'd prefer not to do it here. This is Chub Whatley's jurisdiction, technically, though it's in my county. Besides, he'll have that depot barn packed with prisoners."

"No jail?" Annie wondered. "What kind of town ain't got a regular jail?"

"There used to be one, but the Oakley brothers tore it down."

"How come?"

"They wanted out, I suppose." Harriett pursed her lips in thought. "Would you ladies prefer to be arrested for aiding and abetting, or deputized to help escort a prisoner?"

"I'll help," Holly Bee volunteered.

"I don't think you ought to arrest Charlie," Annie said. "He's no hardcase nor anything like that. No rough edges that a good woman can't smooth out."

"There would have to be mitigating circumstances, Mrs. Coke. Otherwise it really is my duty to arrest and detain wanted people. But let's discuss it later. Right now I have to give all those lunatics the opportunity to file complaints with the county court. It's a waste of time—none of them will—but they have to have the opportunity." She looked Jake up and down, speculatively. "Have you ever killed anyone, Mr. Johnson?"

"Yes, Ma'am. Once."

"What was the reason."

"I just couldn't tolerate him, Ma'am."

"Why not?"

"Because he was shooting at me."

"That seems straightforward enough. That was the only time?"

"Yes, Ma'am."

"Then you may keep your gun for the time being, but I would like for you to come with me."

"Am I under arrest?"

"Potentially." With her three acquisitions following behind, Harriett Fletcher flipped her reins and headed for the depot, circling around the buildings that faced on the main street.

"Where do you aim to take Charlie if you arrest him?" Annie asked.

"The county seat is at Limestone," Harriett said. "We'll go there."

"Gonna wait 'til Thursday and catch the train?"

"Of course not. It's only twenty-three miles to Limestone."

"These mules are pretty tuckered."

"Are they your mules?"

"No, they're Roscoe Sutherland's mules. He thinks they're at Six Bit."

"Then leave them here. I imagine there are just any number of horses that have wandered out of Chub Whatley's jurisdiction since the shooting started. I will confiscate what we need as abandoned stock, and the county will trade them to you for Mr. Sutherland's mules."

"My," Annie said, impressed at how simple things could be if a body was a sheriff.

Harriett glanced back at Jake. "I suppose you will attempt to escape from custody at the first opportunity. Everyone does. But I really wish you would wait until we are out of San Galena, for your own safety. Will you do that?"

"Am I in custody?"

"Potentially. Will you wait?"

"Yes, Ma'am. I'll wait."

Chub Whatley was a big, hard-looking man with a sour face and galluses. He and a motley dozen deputies had just finished packing prisoners into the depot barn—drovers on the hay side and grangers on the hardware side. Harriett pulled up to the wide doors and stepped down to peer inside. "I told you this would happen, Chub. It always does. Any casualties this time?"

He turned, scowling. "Nothin' serious. Two bullet burns, a few bruises and scrapes and one feller was dusted pretty good with birdshot. How come you're here, Harriett? Haven't you got anything better to do?"

"I could do a whole lot better right here than you're doing," she said. "Do any of these man have the sense to file charges and get this business into county jurisdiction where it belongs?"

He sneered at her. "You know better'n that, Harriett. None of these boys is gonna have anything to do with you or the damn county."

Nevertheless, she strode into the barn and asked her question of all and sundry inside, then came back out looking disgusted. "Not a working brain among them," she muttered.

"What did you expect, Harriett?" Whatley growled. "This county's the laughin' stock of the state, with a woman for sheriff. But I reckon what happens in San

75

Galena just ain't goin' to be any of your business, is it? There ain't been a shot fired nor even a hard word spoke anywhere outside of my own civil jurisdiction, so you just run along home an' have a tea party. Anything hereabouts is men's business."

The lady turned a nice shade of pink at that, and glared up at the marshal. "Armed conflict? Mayhem? Attempted murder? By rights that's the law's business, Chub."

Whatley ignored her, looking over the three with her. His eyes lingered a moment on Holly Bee, then turned to Jake and began to widen. "Hot damn," he muttered. "Who is this here?"

"These people are with me," the sheriff said. "They're none of your concern."

"Damned if they're not!" he stepped closer to Jake and squinted up at him, his eyes taking in features, hat and horse, then dropping to the initials on his saddle. Recognition hit his eyes like a light striking, and a slow grin began to form. "Well, by golly. I got a dodger on a feller that matches this'n to a T. Robbed a bank, and there's a damn fine reward on him. An' here he sits, right square in my jurisdiction." He reached for his gun and Harriett stepped between them, but a brawny hand hurled her aside. "Mister, you're mine."

Whatley got his gun out of his holster, but that was as far as it went. He froze in place, staring into the business end of Jake's Peacemaker a foot from his nose.

"It ain't polite to lay hands on a lady," Jake snapped. "Now you drop that gun or I'll blow your fool head out from between your ears."

Whatley dropped his gun.

"Tell your boys to do the same."

The deputies didn't wait to be told. They had seen Jake's gun snake out, like nothing any of them had seen before, and they disarmed themselves in a hurry.

76

"My land, Charlie," Annie rasped. "How'd you do that. I never seen a handgun drawed so fast!"

Jake glanced down at Harriett. "Ma'am, this jaybird owes you an apology. What kind would you like?"

"It's all right, Mr. Johnson," she said, her eyes wide.

"No, Ma'am, it isn't. It isn't a bit all right. Would it be all right with you if this here marshal squared his account?"

Whatley went white-faced. "Mister, I'll apologize. Whatever you want. Just . . . just don't shoot."

"What I think you ought to do," Jake suggested, "is write out an affidavit about the recent ruckus in San Galena and give it to the sheriff so's the county can do whatever counties are supposed to do. Will you do that?"

Whatley went from white to red, Jake's finger on his trigger went from brown to white and Whatley went white again. "I'll do it," he said. "Yes, sir. I'll do that right now."

Five minutes later Harriett Fletcher had her jurisdiction restored and the back of her buckboard full of guns, Annie and Holly Bee had their saddles on fresh horses and Chub Whatley was hearing how many felony charges he personally would face if he let any of his prisoners loose before the county court had had its day with them.

On their way out of San Galena, headed north toward Limestone, Jake asked the sheriff, "Did I mitigate your circumstances enough back there that you might reconsider about arresting me, Ma'am?"

"I'm still thinking about it," Harriett Fletcher said. "Just don't try to escape before I make up my mind."

Chapter VIII

When they had gone, Chub Whatley paced back and forth in front of the depot barn for a time, tossing cusswords and threats around in random order, then he headed for his little office behind the general store. It took him a while to find the dodger, because he couldn't remember what name had been on it and he went through the stack twice searching for a Johnson. But then he found it, and as he read it a mean grin spread across his heavy features. Jake Creedmore. There wasn't any doubt about it, that yahoo with the she-male law had been Jake Creedmore. And the reward that banker had put on him! Five thousand dollars for the man, five thousand for return of stolen property. It was enough to make his eyeballs wobble.

Dodger in hand, he walked back to the depot and rousted out the Western Union telegrapher. Referring to the dodger, he sent a wire to Homer Boles at Perdition, requesting more information about the fugitive Jake Creedmore and a more precise description of the stolen property for which the reward was offered. What, exactly, was it that the sponsor of the reward wanted returned to him? And what were the instructions for the care and delivery of the stolen property if recovered?

"Say it's urgent," he told the telegrapher, "and tell him to send the answer to me at Limestone, as soon as possible."

Back at the barn he went around to the corral and put a loop on Sid Hagen's big bay racer, tied it at the gate, then went for his saddle and gear. As he had expected, Hagen was waiting for him when he returned.

Of all the crowd of toughs Chub Whatley had hired on as deputies, Sid Hagen was the biggest and meanest, and Chub had kept an eye on him. He had a good thing going here in San Galena—had until today, at any rate—and sooner or later he expected Sid to call him out, to try to take it over. It hadn't happened yet, because Sid was afraid of Chub Whatley, but sometime it would. Still, things were different now.

"Is that your rope on my bay, Chub?" Sid frowned at him.

"It's my rope," Chub said. "And this is my saddle."

"What do you think you're doin', Chub?"

"Well, Sid, I was thinkin' you and me might make a trade. You been talkin' around a little about how you think you could run things in San Galena, right?"

"What if I have?"

"The only thing between you and the chance to try your hand is me, Sid."

"So?"

"So I just got to thinkin', I'm gettin' a little tired of this marshal business, Sid. Maybe I might just move on. But I need a good horse, so I just figured, why, I'll just swap with ol' Sid. My badge and this town for that racin' bay of his. He ain't ever gonna see a better deal than that."

Hagen gawked at him. "Trade? My horse for your operation?"

"Sounds like a real winner from your side, don't it?"

79

Sid's brow lowered again, speculatively. "I can think of a better deal yet," he said. "If you're movin' on, then I'll just appoint myself marshal like you did, and keep my horse into the bargain."

Chub shook his head. "I don't work that way, Sid. I've made you the best offer you're fixin' to get."

"And what if I don't take it?"

Chub swung his saddle onto the rail and turned, his hand brushing the gun at his belt. "You been thinkin' you'd try me on for size, Sid. Either we swap now like I said, or you get the chance to try me on now. Either way, I'm takin' the bay. It's up to you whether you're alive to see me leave."

He didn't expect Sid to draw. Generally folks backed down before Chub Whatley. But Sid had seen Chub outdrawn once today—some hooraw with a white hat, riding with the woman sheriff, had made the marshal look downright silly. Sid sidestepped, shucked out his gun, and realized his mistake an instant too late.

"I thought maybe you had better sense," Chub muttered, looking down at the fallen man. When others came around the barn, drawn by gunfire, he said, "You boys take a good look at this. Sid sold me his horse, then tried to take it back. He drew on me and I had to kill him. You all see it that way?"

They did.

"Then one of you had better get a message off to that woman sheriff. Tell her what happened, and that there wouldn't have been trouble if she hadn't undermined my authority. Oh, and tell her there ain't any law in San Galena as of now, because the marshal quit."

A rider carried the message from the Three Forks telegraph office to Perdition to deliver it to Homer Boles, and he put on his hat and went to find Conrad

W. Jackson. He didn't like walking around town these days. It seemed like every time he looked around there were more vacant buildings, more boarded-over doors and shuttered windows. And hardly anybody on the streets. Since the day Jackson had closed the bank after Jake Creedmore robbed it, things had been going from bad to worse. Jackson had been calling in his loans and foreclosing on mortgages as fast as he could — to recoup so he could reopen the bank, he said — and a lot of people had just pulled up stakes and moved on. Boles suspected that Jackson probably owned half the town by now, and had harbored some suspicions about that. But, on the other hand, he couldn't see how Jackson stood to profit. He owned a lot of property thanks to his foreclosures, but with the town dying out none of it was worth anything.

Homer found the banker over at Johnson's Emporium, doing inventory. The store was one of the few businesses still doing business in Perdition, and a lot of what it was selling was the supplies that folks needed to leave.

At the main counter the widow Cole was wrapping a package for Opal Hayes and Homer tipped his hat. "Mornin', ladies. Is Mr. Jackson hereabouts?"

"In the stockroom," the widow Cole said.

"Thankee, Ma'am. Heard anything from Miss Clara lately, Miz Hayes?"

"Only that she's staying on a little longer with her Aunt Jessy, and might bring her along when she comes home. Aunt Jessy has female trouble."

"Yes'm." Homer lowered his eyes, feeling just a little embarrassed. He went on past and found Jackson in the stockroom. "Got an inquiry about my dodger on Jake Creedmore," he said. "It just come in from Three Forks, but it's from someplace yonder in Texas. Town marshal over there wants more details about Jake, and he wants to know exactly what property it is you've put your price on and how it should be handled."

Jackson set down his counting pad. "Have they caught him?"

"Well, no, sir, this marshal didn't say he'd caught him. Just asked about him. I'll tell him what I can, but what do you want me to say about the stolen property?"

"Tell him I want it returned intact and unharmed."

"Yes, sir. You mean your horse and your hat both?"

"I mean my picture! I put stock in that painting, Homer. I want it back, just like it left my desk, without a scratch on it. I'll pay five thousand dollars for that, but not a cent if it has been tampered with. You tell him that."

"Yes, sir." Homer made notes on the back of his message. "Uh, should I say Jake has to be brought back here to get the reward on him?"

"I don't care what they do with Creedmore. I just want that picture back."

"I guess they can try him wherever they find him, if you'll go there to be a witness, Mr. Jackson. Otherwise I don't know how they're gonna make a case . . ."

"Tell them to shoot him on sight."

"Uh . . . I can't say that, sir. It ain't just exactly legal to put a blood bounty on a body, not unless he's been convicted and is a threat to life and limb runnin' loose, you see . . ."

"Then tell them whatever you need to tell them, Homer. I just want him caught and my picture returned."

"Yes, sir. And about the money . . . ?"

"What money?" Jackson looked blank for a moment.

"Uh . . . the twenty thousand dollars he took from your bank, Mr. Jackson. We ought to take steps to get that money returned when they catch him."

"Oh, that. You do whatever is best, Homer. You're

the law. Just make sure they know to get that picture back to me, untampered."

"Yes, sir." Homer tipped his hat and turned to leave.

"Homer, where was that message from, exactly?"

Homer turned back. "Place called San Galena. I never heard of it, but there's a Western Union there."

"San Galena," Jackson nodded, thoughtfully.

"Yes, sir. But I'm supposed to send the response to another place, called Limestone. I reckon that's where that marshal is fixin' to be."

"Do you know where Limestone is?"

"Only that it's in Texas. Maybe I could find it on the map."

"Never mind, Homer. I have a map of my own."

When Homer had gone, Jackson sat for a time in brooding silence. Then he stood, put on his hat and left by the rear door. Someone in Texas had a lead on the whereabouts of Jake Creedmore. It was time to take action to make sure that his property was returned, intact and uninvestigated, and the matter was far too important to leave to chance or the bumbling efforts of some two-bit marshal somewhere in Texas. There was too much at stake to count on less than the best.

It was time to get in touch with Royal Flanders' outfit.

While Homer Boles was wording his message to Chub Whatley, to be sent off to Three Forks for telegraphing to Limestone, Texas, a thing kept nagging at him. What it came right down to, it seemed, was that Mr. Jackson didn't care too much about the loss of his silver-belly beaver hat, and didn't even particularly care about the fine sorrel racer he had lost. All he really seemed to care about was that little painting of himself that Jake Creedmore had taken while he was robbing the bank. He was willing to pay five thousand dollars to get it back.

There was just no accounting for taste. Homer had seen the painting, any number of times, and had never thought much about it one way or another. He had seen far better paintings. He shook his head, lost in the mystery of it all.

But what kept nagging at him was that Mr. Jackson had forgotten about the money. Just for a second there, Homer had had the feeling that Jackson wasn't even aware that Jake Creedmore was running loose with twenty thousand dollars that he shouldn't have. How could anybody forget losing that much money?

And that brought back the two different stories he had heard: Wilbur Short had seemed pretty definite about Jake stealing two thousand dollars and a horse, hat and picture, and Homer had never known Wilbur to be wrong about amounts of money.

But then Mr. Jackson had said Wilbur was mistaken, that Jake had taken twenty thousand, not two thousand and some. And when Homer went to ask Wilbur about that it turned out that Wilbur was gone somewhere— Mr. Jackson nor anybody else could tell him where— and wasn't expected back.

It was a puzzle, sure enough. But Homer could make no sense of it so he stopped worrying about it and went back to work.

Far to the east, at the town of Big Spring, Wilbur Short was trying to get the hang of his new job. It was a bit difficult because no one had exactly told him what he was supposed to do. The fact that the letter he had brought from Conrad W. Jackson had put him on the payroll of the Great Central and Pacific Investment Company told him that Mr. Jackson was associated with the company in some fashion, but no one had told him just how. The fact that the Great Central and

Pacific Investment Company was collecting money from a great many people in many places and issuing shares in a railroad venture told him that the company was in the railroad business. And the fact that there were clerks issuing vouchers for payment of surveyors, road crews and tie-cutters told him that the project was in full swing. But the only thing he was sure of that was expected of him was deliveries. Each day, sometimes several times a day, someone would hand him a pouch or a box or a stack of papers and tell him to deliver it to someone else.

One time it had been Uno Burton himself who sent him on a delivery.

"These securities are to be delivered to the Big Spring Bank, Warren," Mr. Burton had said. "Take them there promptly and give them to Mr. Hamilton at the second window. If Mr. Hamilton isn't there, wait for him to come in and give them to him. Don't give them to anyone else. Do you understand?"

"Yes, sir," Wilbur said. "Uh . . . it's Wilbur, sir."

Burton glanced up from his desk. "What?"

"Uh . . . I said, it's Wilbur, sir."

"What is?"

"My name, sir. It's Wilbur."

"Congratulations. Now get on with that delivery."

"Yes, sir."

Wilbur felt it was a feather in his cap, professionally, to have been addressed in person by the president of Great Central and Pacific. It was an honor, and he felt his career with the investment company was definitely on its way. He hadn't met the other Burton brother, Dos, and he understood that Dos was rarely in the office, spending most of his time in the field as he did, but he looked forward to making his acquaintance when the opportunity came.

And it was Uno Burton's instructions that had led

Wilbur to learn something else of interest. Alex Hamilton had not been available at the Big Spring Bank when Wilbur arrived, and didn't show up for more than an hour. To pass the time, Wilbur had thumbed through the securities listings which he was delivering. Among them, buried in the stack, was a different document — a transfer of title to various properties in and around the town of Perdition. He read it, and read it again, surprised. He had never realized how much of Perdition Conrad W. Jackson owned, but Conrad W. Jackson didn't own it any more. It had been transferred to the Great Central and Pacific Company in lieu of cash payment for accepted shares in the company's railroad venture. Mr. Jackson hadn't fared very well on the price. Wilbur estimated no more than a dime on the dollar, but it was enough to make up the difference between an eighteen thousand dollar investment and a twenty thousand dollar investment.

When Alex Hamilton arrived at the bank, Wilbur dutifully delivered the documents to him, then asked, "What does a bank like this do with real property put up for cash shares?"

Hamilton shrugged. "Just like anybody else. We put it on the market and sell it for what we can get, and hope it covers what we've granted on it."

It was a marvel to Wilbur, and a lesson in how things are valued. All the time he had lived in Perdition, he had thought of the little town as just about his whole world. But now he was out in a bigger world and chance had given him a look at hard values. Somebody, somewhere, was fixing to have the opportunity to buy virtually the entire town for not much more than what Jake Creedmore had taken from the bank there.

Chapter IX

Harriett Fletcher was fascinated at the idea of the straightforward, polite young man she had found being an outlaw and a bank robber, but she didn't question him about it. She had a notion that if she asked him flat out whether he had robbed a bank, he might just tell her about it. And that would pose a moral dilemma. The two women riding with him — one tough and motherly and full of talk, the other a striking young blonde who rarely said anything — had both told her that Charlie Johnson was a confessed robber with a price on his head. But they seemed to be going solely on what he had said to them, and there was no law against a man saying anything he had a mind to . . . as long as he didn't say it to a sheriff.

She didn't want to arrest the young man, and she wasn't quite sure she would be able to if it should prove necessary. That business with Chub Whatley, when the young man had faced the marshal down in his own town . . . well, Harriett had seen some sights in her life, but she had never seen anything quite like that. Charlie Johnson — she knew that wasn't his right name, but she wasn't sure she wanted to know what it was, either — seemed for all the world a thoughtful, plodding, laconic soul, the type who would think out every situation, plan every move and do nothing either rash or abrupt. If there was a word that suited him — at least as he seemed to be — the word was slow. Not slow-witted . . . no, he wasn't that . . . but slow to act, slow to react, slow-talking and slow-to-methodical in his actions.

Yet when Chub Whatley had offended him — by being rough with her — the transformation had been remarkable. She had never seen a handgun drawn with such lightning reflex, had never seen such cold intent in the dressing-down of one man by another.

She had never heard of Chub Whatley being out-drawn by anybody, and she had never heard of him ever backing down. He was considered a dangerous man, and most men she knew were afraid of him. But not Charlie Johnson. If Charlie Johnson had been inclined to kill, Chub Whatley would be dead.

She wasn't quite sure what to do about him. In the sheriff's office at Limestone she had folders full of wanted men, dodgers with names and sometimes pictures, descriptions of their crimes and the charges against them, and often with a reward for their capture and return to where they were wanted. In that folder, she suspected, was a description of Charlie Johnson complete with details of his crimes, and a true name. It would be her duty, once she could link him with specific charges somewhere, to detain him. And that, she felt, would be unfortunate.

Heading north toward Limestone, they stopped at a ford on Rock Creek to rest their horses. The creek wound down from higher country just west, a series of stone tanks and rippling runnels carrying clear water from springs above off toward a river somewhere. Jake took it upon himself to set the horses to water, two at a time, while the women refreshed themselves upstream. He unhitched the lady sheriff's buckboard horse and led it and Annie's to a gravel bank where they could drink. Then he put neck-loops on them and set them out in a little meadow with good graze and went back for his horse and Holly Bee's, taking his sweet time and sort of drifting farther down the creek as he worked.

When the two horses were watered he led them up to another patch of graze, neck-looped Holly Bee's mount, took a good long look around and swung into his saddle. "Been mighty nice getting to know y'all," he breathed, "but there comes a time a man's got places to go and things to do. So y'all take care now, you hear?" A quick grin touched his cheeks. "Come on, hoss," he said. "Let's just ease on downstream a ways, then see about making ourselves some miles."

Within fifty yards he was out of sight of where he had been last, and he allowed himself a sigh of sheer relief. Things had been going from bad to worse, saddled with a bunch of women, and it had seemed to him that things were mighty near out of hand. But now there wasn't a thing keeping him, and all of Texas lay ahead. Just the low sun at his back, the long shadows of cottonwood and scrub cedar on the hills, birds flitting here and there, squat limestone juts on the slopes . . . and a blond girl on top of the nearest one with a rifle pointed in his direction.

He hauled sharp on the reins and his mouth dropped open.

"Get on back yonder," Holly Bee told him. "Nobody said you could leave."

Some distance upstream, Harriett Fletcher glanced at the lowering sun and said, "I expect he is escaping about now."

"Prob'ly so," Annie Coke agreed. "Bless his heart, he's bound to try it. Wouldn't be natural if he didn't."

"Will Holly Bee have any trouble with him?"

"Don't see how," Annie shook her head. "Short of doin' her violence, I don't suppose any man could get past Holly Bee once her mind is set, an' I know folks well enough to know that young feller just ain't got it in him to do harm to a female."

"I've had the same impression," Harriett agreed. "Doesn't it just seem . . . well, unfair, though, the advantage any woman has over any decent man?"

"I've thought on that some," Annie shrugged. "But it ain't exactly unfair. It's just the Lord's way, I reckon. Them that has a duty gets the powers to get it done."

"Duty?"

"My land, yes. No man born ever civilized hisself. It's up to us to do that. So since we got it to do, I reckon the Almighty seen fit that we should be equipped to do it."

"I never thought of things in exactly that way," Harriett admitted. "But it does make sense. Pity it only works on decent men, though. There's plenty around that I wouldn't have wanted to set a sweet thing like Holly Bee to corral."

"Men are just like any other critters," Annie warmed to her subject. "Them as matters has got to be housebroke and saddle broke to be worth their salt, and it's up to women folks to see that's done. But some of 'em are just plain no account . . . my first husband was like that . . . and they're a different matter."

"So what do you recommend regarding that other kind?" Harriett was curious.

Annie shrugged. "Shoot 'em, I reckon."

Harriett chuckled. "The law frowns on simple solutions," she said.

"Law says what's legal and what ain't," Annie pointed out. "It don't necessarily say what's right and what ain't. How'd you ever come to be a sheriff, anyway? I never heard of a woman sheriff before.

Leastways not in Texas."

"It's just temporary," Harriett said. "Last elected sheriff in this county got shot, and nobody would run for the job. I was practicing law, and Judge Burris appointed me as interim sheriff. I guess he thought it was a good object lesson for some of the men . . . let them know that when there's an elected office open somebody had better file for it or see here what might happen. There has already been a petition for a new election, so I don't expect to be sheriff very long."

"That how that Whatley hooraw got a'holt of San Galena, was while nobody was sheriffin'?"

"You might say so. Chub Whatley is the man who shot the last sheriff."

"I don't much care for that feller," Annie allowed. "Got a streak of mean in him, I believe." She peered downstream, squinting. "Yonder comes Holly Bee, bringin' Charlie back. You s'pose he's got it out of his system?"

"For the time being, I guess."

"You might just let him go," Annie suggested. "I don't believe he's apt to hurt anybody. That young feller just don't have the makin's of an outlaw, even if he did rob some popinjay's bank to get his money back."

"I've been thinking about that," Harriett said. "What bothers me is, with everybody under the sun chasing after him, sooner or later he might *have* to be an outlaw." She paused, watching thoughtfully as Holly Bee herded Jake back toward the ford. "You know, Annie, there's retribution and there's restitution. Your friend there—according to hearsay—put himself outside the law and when he did that he set himself up to ride the devil's trail. I just don't like to see a thing go unresolved. But maybe there *is* more than one way to balance the scales."

91

"I do love to hear fine talk," Annie grinned. "What does all that mean?"

"It means that I am considering giving that young man a chance to get off the devil's trail by doing a community service."

Lottie Camber gathered her skirts and marched up the steps of the Rossville schoolhouse, pausing on the porch to look back the way she had come. The bell overhead continued to clang enthusiastically, but there was no one else visible outside the school except herself. Only a few animals—a pair of tired horses in the farrier's corral, a dog asleep in the shelter of a pole barn—and a dust devil chasing old worn-down tumbleweeds along the dirt street. Everyone who was coming was already here, she decided. They were waiting for her inside.

She opened the door and went in, accompanied by a gust of dusty wind. The door slammed behind her and she paused, letting her eyes accommodate to the sudden gloom. The room was full of people—some sitting on benches, some standing in groups here and there. She didn't need to count heads, she knew there were about thirty present. Women of various ages, children of various sizes . . . the only man in the place was old man Tuttle, backed defensively into a corner with his wife and daughter shielding him there.

Lottie took a deep breath, nodded to a woman or two, then stepped around the bell-cove. "You, Billy Mills," she said, "You stop ringin' that bell now, for there's nobody else comin'."

The boy shrugged and tied off the bell cord. Lottie strode to the front of the room and turned, waiting for silence. When she had their full attention she said, "You all know I wrote a letter to that lady sheriff over

92

at Limestone, about the trouble we got here—"

"Knew you was going to," Jessy Wheeler interrupted, "but I told you at the time it wouldn't do any good. She isn't even in our county."

Lottie glared at the older woman, then started over. "I wrote a letter to that lady sheriff over at Limestone, like I said I would. I know she isn't in our county, but she's the only woman law I ever heard of and it didn't hurt none to ask her if she could lend us a hand. I told her how things has got here at Rossville with most of the menfolks gone all this time and us not even knowing where they went to—"

"And how's she gonna know where they went if we can't find out?" Jessy Wheeler interrupted again.

Lottie glared at her again, then turned her attention to Clara Hayes. "Miss Clara, do me the kindness to tell your aunt Jessy that the best way for a body to hear what's fixin' to be said is to hush herself up long enough to listen."

Clara turned to Jessy. "Aunt Jessy, she said if you'd—"

"I heard what she said," Jessy said, "And far be it from me to interrupt a body if they'll just say what's on their mind."

"Thank you," Lottie said. "Like I said, I wrote a letter to—"

"You already said that," Jessy interrupted. "Get on with it. How come you to bell us all down here on a day like this, Lottie?"

"Because I have something to tell you all!"

"Well, what is it?"

"Did you hear back from her, Lottie?" another woman asked.

"Does she know where all our menfolk went to?" someone else put in.

"I guess I'll mosey over to the saloon and get myself

a drink," old man Tuttle declared, then paused, rubbing his white whiskers. "Naw, can't do that. Danged thing's been shut down nigh six months. Like most everything else around here. Where's everybody got off to?"

Lottie Camber waited them out, then continued. "I told her—"

"Who?"

"The lady sheriff at Limestone! I told her how a lot of our menfolk used to be railroad builders, and how they'd figured out that the railroad was goin' to come through here so's they all chipped in all their money and bought this land for a townsite—"

"Bunch of boneheads—"

"And then the railroad went to Big Spring instead—"

"Land, Lottie, that was all six-seven year ago. Did you happen to think to tell her what happened lately?"

"Won't do any good. She's in a different county."

"Well, Lottie could be right about her knowin' how to find folks, though. She *is* law, and law's got its ways—"

"Order!"

"What?"

Lottie glared at the lot of them. "Are you all gonna let me tell this, or not?"

"You got the floor."

"Thank you. Yes, I told her what happened lately. How there's this bunch at Big Spring that are fixin' to build rail on west, and how thirty-one men from Rossville went down there and hired on as a crew—"

"Thirty-two."

"What?"

"There was thirty-two of them scamps," Jessy pointed out.

"Thirty-one. We made a list, remember?"

94

"I remember. I remember you didn't want to count my Harold when we made it, too. But countin' him there was thirty-two."

"Harold Wheeler doesn't count," Lottie said.

"He most certainly does! It was him that got wind of that project in the first place, wasn't it?"

"Well, I don't count him because he isn't a road-builder like the rest of 'em are . . . or used to be."

"He went with 'em! I say he counts!"

"Oh, all right! Thirty-two. And I told her how they said it was all gonna be a big secret about where the line was going because there was delicate negotiations involved—"

"That's a shifty bunch down yonder. Them Burtons wasn't ever any better than outlaws 'til they got rich and turned respectable."

". . . delicate negotiations involved about the route, so they had agreed to work incom . . . inco . . . secret and have their pay sent back here from Big Spring."

"Well, I haven't seen a red cent since the day Clyde left."

"Nobody has, Mabel."

"No, but Clyde's not shiftless like the rest of 'em. He wouldn't—"

"Are you sayin' my Walter is shiftless?"

"You better not be sayin' that about Roger, Mabel. I'll take a strap to you—"

"Order!"

"You don't have to holler, Lottie. This ain't that big a room."

Old man Tuttle gritted what teeth he had. "Danged if I don't wish that saloon was still open."

"Hush up, Mose. You don't know the first thing about female troubles."

"Did you hear back from the woman sheriff, Lottie?"

"Yes, I heard back! That's what I'm tryin' my level

best to tell y'all! I told her we don't know where them men have got off to, but with them gone the whole town has fell into rack and ruin and all the businesses are shut down and we can't even get by decent 'cept for the bean crop and could she please give us a hand."

"I'd like to give that scamp Clyde a hand, for disappearin' like that and me with children to feed. I'd like to give him a hand full of hickory bat. Knock some sense into that—"

"Told you he was shiftless."

"He ain't shiftless! You mind your mouth, Nora Bennett!"

"Order! Does anybody want to hear what the sheriff lady said, or not?"

"I hope you're fixin' to tell us, Lottie, 'cause I ain't got all day."

"I'm tryin' to tell you!"

"Well, get to it, then!"

"Well, I will! She wrote me back a nice letter . . . real print-shop paper and everything, with her name right up there at the top just like a regular sheriff might. 'Harriett Fletcher,' it said. 'Sheriff of—"

"Get to the point! What did she say?"

"She said she'll see what she can do."

Chapter X

Uno Burton didn't trust Conrad W. Jackson. He hadn't trusted him two years back when Jackson first visited Big Spring with that crazy story about a big artesian spring in the New Mexico territory eighteen miles out of someplace called Perdition, and he didn't trust him now. The man was a weasel, and Uno Burton was one to know a weasel on sight. Still, when he had sent his baby brother Dos out there to look, Dos came back with confirmation. Sure enough, there was a good, flowing well out on a little slap-up stead eighteen miles from town. Artesian, Dos said, and water enough to supply a good town and irrigate several miles around it. Water enough, properly handled, to pay out all the advance financing on a mainline railroad and leave the line itself clear profit for its owners.

There seemed to be somebody living on the place, Dos said, but there was nobody around when Jackson showed it to him and Jackson was ready to sell it at a price. Negotiations had followed, and Jackson's price became a piece of the action. He would accept shares in the railroad venture, provided he kept the franchise on developing the town that would be there. Then Uno himself had gone out to look.

"You already got a town," he told Jackson, gazing in contempt at the little assemblage of structures that was Perdition. "How come you want another one?"

"That's where the water is," Jackson retorted coolly. "Out here, water is money. Towns come and go . . . but a town with water, and a mainline railroad . . ."

He was talking Uno's language, and the two of them reached an agreement. Jackson signed over the water place on the spot, with his provisions in the contract, and Uno issued him half the shares he wanted. The other half were to be forthcoming upon payment of twenty thousand dollars cash. Barter was well and good, Uno philosophized, but he felt better about things when some money changed hands.

It was a test of Jackson's good faith, demand for twenty thousand dollars. And Jackson had, indeed, come through. It had taken time, but abruptly, not long after Jackson had sent the clerk from Perdition with a letter requesting that Uno employ him and keep him in Big Spring, the remaining money had arrived.

Conrad W. Jackson had passed Uno Burton's test. He had made good his part of the contract. Which made Uno wonder even more what the man was up to.

And then there was the matter of the clerk he had sent. Wilbur something. Uno had been suspicious when the man showed up, carrying a sealed letter from Jackson that requested Great Central and Pacific hire him and keep an eye on him. If the man was a spy of some kind, why would Jackson ask them to keep an eye on him?

Uno had made a point to speak to Wilbur personally, had sent him on an errand of some sort to test him. If Wilbur *was* a spy or a plant, he certainly didn't seem like one. He seemed to be just what he seemed to

98

be — a two-bit bank clerk displaced from a two-bit bank and ready to go to work somewhere else. Burton had been intrigued by his response to the question, "And how is Mr. Jackson these days?"

"He's fine," Wilbur had said. "I expect he's aggravated because Jake Creedmore robbed his bank, but mostly I think it's because Jake took his picture while he was at it. I told Jake he sure enough was gonna aggravate Mr. Jackson if he done that, but I reckon that's what he had in mind all along."

"The bank was robbed?" Burton was surprised. He had seen that bank. It wasn't one that he would have considered robbing, even in the old days. "How much was taken?"

"Two thousand, three hundred and fifty one dollars," Wilbur told him.

"Two thou . . ." Uno gaped at him. "How much was in the bank at the time?"

"Oh, there was twice that much, at least. But Jake's too proud a man to take more'n his share. Even robbin' the bank, he was fair about it."

"I swear," Burton swore.

Still, he had learned nothing that seemed pertinent to his dealings with Jackson, and concluded for the time being that Wilbur Short was nothing more than he seemed to be. Which might, on the surface, indicate that Conrad W. Jackson in turn was just what he seemed to be. Which made Uno Burton distrust him all the more, since such seeming straightforwardness could be evidence of intelligence.

It was Uno Burton's fundamental rule of business, and he had told his baby brother Dos many a time, "Don't ever expect folks to do what you expect them to do, nor to be what you expect them to be, because if you do the smart ones will skin you every time and the dumb ones are just going to rob you first chance they get, anyway."

It went along with Uno's ethic: skin everybody you can as soon as you can and make enough money that they can't skin you back.

As far as Uno could tell, baby brother Dos had no slightest interest in such complexities. Dos was in his element when he was in the field, backed up by three or four capable gunsels, which he almost always was.

But trust Jackson or not, the man had cut himself a piece of Burton's pie and the Burtons were stuck with him for a time—as long as it took to get their right-of-way all the way from Big Spring to the water stop in the New Mexico territory. And that was when Uno Burton expected that he and Jackson would part company. Jackson would pull some weasely stunt like try to establish control of the artesian well property he had already sold to the railroad, then hold them up with it for more money.

And when that happened—or something like it—then Uno would take the necessary step. He would send Dos out to deal with the problem. Dos did enjoy dealing with that kind of problems.

In the meantime, all he had to do to deal with Jackson was to encourage him in development of his new town west of Perdition, and keep him guessing about everything else.

Now Uno Burton glanced at his calendar and decided it was time to throw Mr. Jackson another bait. He rang the little bell on his desk. Within seconds his confidential secretary, Wesley, was at attention before him. "Wesley," Uno said, "I want you to send another letter to Conrad W. Jackson. Tell him that the Great Central and Pacific Investment Company will accept his request for timbers to build a watering tower, but that our people advise us that a thousand board feet of milled planks is adequate for the tank . . . not four thousand as he requested. Tell him that if he wants to build private facilities alongside he can damn well use his private funds to do it. Then tell him that our acquisition of rights-of-way is progressing nicely, and you may hint that he might want to look at some nice properties northeast of his site, for his own purposes, of course. Oh, and give him my best regards."

Wesley finished his notes. "Yes, sir. Ah . . . sir?"

"Yes, Wesley?"

"Ah . . . the new reports show that the line will approach from somewhat south of east. If Mr. Jackson is purchasing property north of east from the site, he will miss the advantages of having inside knowledge."

Uno grinned at the secretary. "Precisely, Wesley. Please get that off promptly. We wouldn't want Mr. Jackson to think we had forgotten him, would we?"

As they approached Limestone in the cool of the evening, Harriett Fletcher hauled up at a crossroads within sight of the town. She turned to gaze for a moment at Jake Creedmore, then made up her mind. "Come here, Mr. Johnson," she said.

Jake reined the sorrel alongside her buckboard. "Ma'am?"

"I wonder if you would do me a favor," she said. "I just plain forgot that I was supposed to pick up a title document from Bert Froome, and it's getting late. I wonder if you would mind going after it for me."

Jake arched a surprised brow. "You want me to take off and run an errand for you?"

"If you would be so kind. It won't take very long. Mr. Froome lives just down the road, the second house out. It isn't more than two miles. Will you be so kind?"

He peered at her in the dusk. "You want me to go pick up something for you, two miles away, by myself?"

101

"It won't be any problem," she assured him. "You can handle it."

"Yeah, but what if I take a notion to just keep going? Aren't you sort of planning to arrest me as soon as you find out what it is I might have done?"

"Well, of course if you're running an errand for me, I would certainly hope you wouldn't escape until you have completed it. You wouldn't, would you?"

"I reckon not," he admitted. "But what if I did?"

"Then I would be very sorry that I sent you."

"Yeah, I guess you would." He nodded. "Okay. What do I do?"

"Just go find Bert Froome, tell him you are from me and pick up the title document he has for me. Then come on into town and meet me at the sheriff's office. It's right next to the courthouse. You can't miss it."

"I wouldn't mind," he muttered.

"What?"

"Missing the sheriff's office. I wouldn't mind. Uh, this thing I'm supposed to pick up . . . it isn't anything anybody would start shooting about, or anything like that, is it?"

"Bert Froome is the county clerk. I told him I'd stop by on my way back and pick it up."

"Yes, Ma'am." With a sigh he turned the sorrel and headed west in twilight.

Annie watched him go, then reined close to the sheriff. "Ma'am, it ain't my call to say so, but that's got to be the dumbest stunt I ever heard of a sheriff pullin', lettin' a armed felon loose so's he can run errands. You maybe just lost yourself a prisoner."

"I thought you didn't want him arrested," Harriett said.

"Well, I never thought he deserved arrestin', but I never said to let him go, neither. He's liable to just fiddlefoot off, an' . . ."

102

"I hope not, but there was really only one way to find out."

"But if he does, who am I gonna match up Holly Bee with?"

"You're not going to match him up with me!" Holly Bee hissed. "I told you, I don't hold with outlaws."

"He ain't a outlaw, Holly Bee. He's just knuckle-headed an' misguided in his ways. Lordy, he'll tame down just fine given half a chance. But he ain't ready to let loose yet, neither. How come you to do that, Ma'am?"

"To see if he'll come back. If he does, he might be just what I need to help a lady with serious female trouble. I told the lady I'd see what I can do."

"You did?"

"I'll tell you about it later. Come along, now, I'll find you ladies a place to stay the night . . . now where did Holly Bee get off to?"

Annie looked around, startled. There was no sign of Holly Bee Sutherland. Abruptly and without a sound, she had disappeared.

Sid Hagen's racing bay was a fine rough-country horse, and Chub Whatley pushed it unmercifully. His first thought was to swing around through the hills and get to Limestone ahead of the woman sheriff and those with her. It wasn't likely that any answer had come yet from his wire to Perdition. The place didn't even have a Western Union. But he wanted to be in position to see what the woman sheriff did with Jake Creedmore. He intended to collect on Creedmore, one way or another. But at the creek ford he caught sight of them, a mile ahead just topping a rise, and changed his plans. Instead of outrunning them and waiting at Limestone, it would be better just to follow them. That

103

way, even if Creedmore made a break for it and got away from the petticoat law, Chub would have no trouble finding him. The more he thought about it, the more convinced he was that a wanted man wasn't going to just ride tamely into the county seat with a woman sheriff. Creedmore would get away at the first opportunity, and that would solve all the problems about how Chub was to take him away from a sheriff.

So he followed, watching the shadows lengthen, watching the sun finally dip behind the western hills, wondering when the outlaw was going to break and run. But still they went on, together, and he stayed back and followed.

Limestone was in sight ahead and dusk was falling when Chub angled through a gully, topped a rise and hauled up. Just ahead was the south fork crossroad, and the buckboard was stopped there, the petticoat sheriff still aboard and the other two women on horseback alongside. At first he didn't see the man he knew was Jake Creedmore, then he glanced around and found him and gawked. The outlaw was riding tamely off down the west road, not running, not even seeming to be in a hurry. And the sheriff and the other women were just sitting there, watching him go. Chub had no idea what that was all about, but it suited him just fine. He had expected a chase—maybe a long one. But there Creedmore was, all five or ten thousand dollars worth of him, and he was just ambling along in no particular hurry.

Just let him get out of sight of Harriett Fletcher—off on his lonesome—and the man was fair game. Chub wheeled the bay and headed west, staying low and out of sight of the west road. He was familiar with these parts. The road ran out by Olmstadt's place, then on past Bert Froome's little farm, then wandered across the old Bonehandle Ranch range and into the next county, which pleased Chub Whatley. Creedmore was heading for the next county, and that was just fine. He would pick him up along the way and take him there personally, then find a jail to put him in and wait to collect the reward. Past Olmstadt's, he would ambush him, get that damn quick gun away from him and maybe lay some bruises on him to get even for the treatment he'd had at San Galena.

He might even break his legs, he decided, and the more he thought about that, the more it seemed the thing to do. A man with broken legs wasn't likely to try to run off on the trip ahead.

He circled wide around Olmstadt's, then followed a draw for a half-mile and cut across a field toward the road where it passed Bert Froome's place. There were some trees there, and a tall windrow, and it would be as good a place as any to take himself a prize. He might even get Froome to go in to Limestone and send a telegraph message ahead for him, so the law in the next county would know he was coming with a fair-caught wanted man.

He edged into the clear of the road and peered eastward, and there was Creedmore, still ambling along, coming right to him. Chub backed off, got down and led the bay into the shadows of the windrow. Then he edged into cover beside the road and drew his gun.

Jake wasn't looking at the trees as he approached. He was looking past, where lamplight had appeared in the windows of the house he was supposed to go to. And so he didn't see the man waiting in the shadows until he was right beside him. Then he saw him, saw the gun in his hand and heard the gunshot, all simultaneously. By pure reflex his gun came to hand and centered on the assailant, but something was wrong. The man had been standing and pointing a gun at

105

him, but now he was falling, and Jake realized it wasn't his gun that had fired. The man hit the ground, rolled and whimpered, and Jake urged the sorrel forward to stand directly over him.

"Put that gun down," he told him. "Drop it, right now."

The gun fell from a limp hand and Jake said, "Now get away from it." The man rolled away, and Jake saw his face. "Well, my land," he said. "You just don't ever learn good manners, do you?" The man on the ground tried to glare up at him, but his face contorted with pain and he rolled over again, trying to sit up. "What's the matter with you, anyway?" Jake asked. "You fell like you'd been shot."

"I have been shot," Whatley said in a high, tight voice. "Oh, shit, it's my legs. Oh, sweet Jesus . . ."

"How can it be both of your legs?" the voice behind him brought Jake around in his saddle so fast he near whipsawed himself. Holly Bee Sutherland was there, just beyond on the road, putting away her rifle. "I only shot one of your legs, mister. Don't go blamin' me for both of them."

Jake gawked at her. "Holly Bee? What are you doing . . ."

"Shut up," she told him. "I ain't talking to you." To Chub Whatley she said, "I saw you side-trailin' this jasper, mister. Figured you'd try to help him get away from the sheriff." She dismounted, picked up Chub's gun and put it in her belt, then stepped closer for a look at him. Jake edged the sorrel aside, keeping a clear line between himself and the San Galena marshal. "Well, for mercy's sake," Holly Bee declared. "I *did* get both legs, didn't I? I guess that's what comes of standin' with your legs together." There were voices beyond the hedge, and lamplight coming closer. Holly Bee stepped back and glanced up at Jake. "Your friend

106

here won't help you get away now, so you just get what you're supposed to get and get on back where that lady told you to. She might trust you, but I ain't about to."

Chapter XI

Far to the southwest, where a tall trestle was taking shape above the rocky bed of a meandering river, Dos Burton massaged his gloved fist and looked at the battered man at his feet. The man was on hands and knees, shaking his head slowly from side to side while blood dripped from a broken lip and smashed nose. Dos clicked his tongue in sympathy. "I really hate to have to get surly with you boys," he said, and kicked the man in the ribs, flopping him over onto his back. "It's just that I can't have you tryin' to run off like that, you see." He kicked him again, then gestured at a pair of gunnies standing to one side. "Pick him up," he said.

Large and ungentle hands lifted the bleeding man to his feet and held him upright when his legs went limp.

Dos stepped close to peer into the man's blinking eyes. "Just where did you think you were goin' to, anyhow?"

"I . . ." the man shuddered, wheezed and started again. "I . . . I just thought I'd get a message off to my woman back home. Just to let her know I'm all right. That's all. Honest, I wasn't going to say anything to anybody."

"Oh, I don't suppose you were," Dos nodded. "But don't you see, it's like we told you boys when y'all signed on, we just can't take any chances on that. Just not any at all." He looked around, making sure his voice carried to the group of workmen gathered at the foot of the trestle. "That's why the boys here had to go get you and bring you back, don't you see. And that's why I had to mess you up like this, is because lots of times folks get forgetful, just like you did today, and it's just better that none of you take the notion to head off somewhere again because after this, we'd just have to kill anybody that did.

"You boys just don't have any idea of what a delicate thing it is to be tryin' to build a railroad in this day an' time. You work and you plan and you figure, and you raise money and hire plans drawn up, and you go out and try to pay a fair price for rights-of-way without anybody knowin' what you're buyin' it for because if they knew they'd try to cheat you . . . and linin' up rights-of-way takes a long time even in the best of situations, but you can't just sit back and wait to get it done. No, there's your investors to consider, and investors won't hold still for just quiet purchasin' of rights-of-way. They've got to see that grades are bein' laid and trestles built and track and timbers on order, or they get the notion that *they're* bein' cheated.

"Delicate work," he warmed to his subject. "Mighty delicate. Why, even out here where it's six miles from one rabbit track to the next, there's just no way of keepin' it a secret when you set out to build a railroad. You start shapin' a grade and in just no time at all everybody and his dog knows that somebody is fixin' to build a railroad and everybody just gets to itchin' to find out who's buildin' it and where it's goin' and all. Just let one wrong word slip out . . . just *one* . . . and we'd have so many land sharks on us that we might as well just shut down and not build any railroad at all."

"I wouldn't say anything," the battered man still

hung, limp as sacking, in the hard hands of Dos Burton's toughs. "I just . . ."

Dos shook his head sadly. "All you boys just *have* to get this clear. We don't take any chances. Not any at all." With a sudden turn he planted his fist in the man's belly, then turned back to his audience. "That's the way it is, fellers. Just like my brother Uno said. Incommunicado for the duration of the project. Now let's not have any more of this foolishness. I hate to bury men that work for me."

He walked away, followed by the four burly toughs who were his constant companions, and workmen came to pick the injured man up and carry him to a tent. They got him down and resting, and one of them said, "That was a dumb stunt, Clyde, tryin' to get off to town thataway. Wonder they didn't kill you for it."

"All I wanted to do was let Mabel know . . ."

"Well, you heard what they told us, just like the rest of us did. And we all agreed to it. Incom . . . inco . . . you know, *secret*. Besides, your woman is all right. They're sendin' all your wages straight back to her, just like with the rest of us."

"I was wonderin' about that," another man said. "How do we know for a fact that the company is payin' our wages to our women back yonder? We haven't heard from any of them any more'n they've heard from us."

"That's how come I tried to get a wire off," Clyde said.

"And dang near got yerself killed for it."

"I been havin' some second thoughts, myself, Walter," another chimed in. "I mean, bein' out of work is one thing, but bein' kept like in a chain gang is another."

"The whole mess is Harold Wheeler's fault," the second said. "If he hadn't come back from Big Spring

110

all et up with this great opportunity . . ."

"It ain't my fault any more'n anybody else's!" Wheeler snapped, thrusting his head into the tent. "All I did was hear about a good thing and tell the rest of you. Nobody made you take this here job!"

"He's right as rain about that," Walter decided. "But then, work's scarce when there hasn't been anybody built a mainline in west Texas for near on to fifteen years."

"Lord," Tom Bennett breathed. "I don't like to think about what Nora might do if it was to turn out that she *wasn't* gettin' my wages like I told her she would."

"Get riled, is what she'd do, Tom. Same as with the rest of our womenfolk."

"You ever seen that many women riled all at once?"

"No, nor ever hope to, either. Lord only knows what they might get it in their heads to do. Women can be downright strong-headed time to time."

"Can't they ever!"

"Well, it's a peace to know they're all gettin' good wages for our time while we're out here buildin' this secret railroad that everybody in Texas knows about. My advice to Clyde—and the rest of you—is just to keep in mind that everything's fine at Rossville and there ain't any womenfolks gettin' riled, and let's get this here job done as soon as we can so we can all go home."

With understandings reestablished at his work camp, Dos Burton headed for his own tent, then stopped when the lookout up on the trestle called, "Hey, Dos!"

He turned and shaded his eyes. The man on the trestle pointed. "Riders yonder! West! Comin' this way!"

"How many?" he called.

"Can't tell! Maybe half a dozen or so!"

Dos turned to his followers. "Get our horses," he said. "We don't need company."

A mile west of the trestle camp they saw the riders coming toward them, and a half-mile further on they counted them. Seven men, armed and mounted, men who rode with the steady, mile-eating pace of far travelers or hunters. Dos and his men spread out in a wide line and stopped to wait for their approach.

At fifty yards the intruders reined up, and one—a lean, hard-eyed man with at least four guns visible on himself and his saddle—stepped his mount forward. "Looks like you boys are puttin' up a trestle yonder," he shouted. "Buildin' a railroad, are you?"

Dos responded, "What we're doing is our own private business, and if you mean to pass you'll have to swing wide around. This is private property."

The man eyed him for a moment, and a wolfish grin twitched his cheeks. "Well, my, my. Sonny, if we wanted to make your business ours, not you and thirty more just like you would slow us down at all. But we got other things to do right now. We're lookin' for a wanted man, and we aim to have him."

"We don't have any wanted men here."

"Young feller," the man continued. "Tall, dark hair, prob'ly ridin' a stud sorrel and wearin' a silver-belly beaver hat. Calls himself Jake Creedmore. You seen anybody like that?"

"We haven't seen anybody at all," Dos shook his head. "We're busy here, so go about your business."

"I reckon you're tellin' it straight," the man said. "Expect he's on over east of here someplace. Whose railroad is this gonna be?"

"I told you that's none of your business," Dos snapped. His fingers hovered at the butt of his gun,

112

and he knew his men were ready to draw, too. He had chosen them carefully. They were all sudden men with their guns, almost as quick as he himself. "Now go away. We don't want you here."

The man facing him barely seemed to move, but abruptly there was a gun in his hand, thundering. Dos heard bullets clip air past both his ears, seeming to pass at the same time, and he froze. All of the men facing him now held guns, and they all had grins on their faces.

"Best thing you might learn, Sonny," the talker said, "is to find out who you're talkin' to before you get frisky. You'd be dead now if anybody was payin' my price for you, and it wouldn't be all that high a price, either. Now you get on back yonder and think about how lucky you are that I don't give a hang about you or your railroad . . . because if I did you'd learn another lesson right now an' it would be your last one. There ain't many men that ever threatened to draw on Royal Flanders and lived to reflect on it."

Casually, then, the large long-riders reined their mounts and angled away to go around the construction site. Dos Burton and his four toughs sat where they were, guns still in their holsters, and watched the dusty riders pass. Dos felt as though his ears were singed, but gape-mouthed shock held him motionless. Flanders! He had heard of Royal Flanders. Nobody within a thousand miles of New Mexico badlands hadn't heard of Royal Flanders, though few could say they had ever seen him.

Dos didn't know who Jake Creedmore was, and was sure he had never seen the man. But just for an instant he felt sorry for him. His days were distinctly numbered.

A little way north, one other had heard the gunfire and reined in to try to see where it was coming from. Alex Hamilton couldn't tell whether he had heard one shot, or two closely spaced, but it was his practice in the event of gunfire to determine its location and try to avoid those who had caused it. In the distance, south of the trail he followed, was a rising structure of new timbers that he took to be a bridge of some sort, but the shot or shots hadn't come from there. They had been farther away, and more to the southwest.

Squinting, he peered in that direction, partly blinded by the afterglow of a new-down sun. At first he saw nothing, then, tiny in the distance, a group of riders moving sedately eastward, far beyond where his path led.

With the assurance that no one of a mind to use guns was headed his way, Alex Hamilton settled into his saddle and proceeded westward, wishing he were back in Big Spring. But, it was part of the job of junior officers of the bank to make periodic sales trips. The bank kept a list of investors and speculators who now and then bought off the accumulated property holdings that the bank itself had no use for. Generally these were closer to Big Spring, and a trip might take two or three days with towns spaced closely enough that a man could sleep in a bed almost every night. Recently, though, the bank had acquired a batch of real properties from the Great Central and Pacific Investment Company, properties entirely beyond the accepted border of Texas . . . properties out in the badlands somewhere. And nobody in the vicinity of Big Spring was buying New Mexico badlands.

So it became Alex Hamilton's unpleasant duty to take the title documents closer to their source and try to peddle them to someone who might not know any better. He was now in the third day of his journey, and hadn't seen a settlement since yesterday. He might have gone most of the way by rail, but it would have been as harrowing a trip because there was no mainline rail westward from Big Spring. Gossip had it that the Burton brothers were in process of building one, but no one knew much about when it would be operational or even exactly where it would go. The Burtons didn't discuss such things with the bank—or with anyone else, so far as Alex knew. "Those two have the souls of outlaws," he told himself now, thinking about them. "It's probably how they stay in business."

It was Alex Hamilton's fear that he might have to go all the way to Portales to unload the "Perdition properties," though he hoped he might find a buyer somewhere closer at hand. But it was his instruction to go all the way to Portales if he had to. That was about as far as the bank's investors list went, and the pickings were slim that far away. Only one possible buyer was listed at Portales itself—an occasional speculator named Philo Henderson who had once parlayed eleven thousand dollars' worth of graze in Welton County into twelve thousand dollars' worth of preferred stock in a hot-air balloon venture and cashed in just before the balloon went down. Henderson considered himself a shrewd and successful investor. The bank considered him a nut, but it was possible that if no one else would buy something called "Perdition properties," Philo Henderson might.

Alex Hamilton was instructed to try for twelve thousand dollars on the properties, but he was authorized to go as low as twenty-four hundred. It was a puzzle to Alex why the bank had ever picked up such properties to begin with, but a lot of things had puzzled him since the bank president became involved with Great Central and Pacific Investment Company.

"Souls of outlaws," he told himself again. "It's almost

115

as though the Burtons had put a gun to his head."

Then, thinking about that, Alex decided that notion wasn't as implausible as it seemed.

Beyond the trestle area and upstream a few miles, he crossed a rocky creek and began looking for a place to camp for the night. Maybe tomorrow, or the next day, he would find a buyer for the "Perdition properties." Maybe he wouldn't have to go all the way to Portales and unload them on Philo Henderson.

Jake Creedmore came to Limestone in the dark of evening, leading Chub Whatley's bay racer with Whatley tied across its saddle, and with Holly Bee Sutherland following along behind to keep an eye on him.

By lamplight he followed the little town's main street until he found what seemed to be a courthouse, and beside it a sheriff's office. And Harriett Fletcher was waiting for him there. As he tied reins at the hitchrail the door opened and she stepped out. "Well," she nodded, "I'm just delighted that you came back, Mr. Johnson. Have you seen . . . oh, there she is. We wondered where she had gone. I . . . who do you have there?"

"Chub Whatley," he told her, tipping his hat. "Holly Bee shot him through both legs."

"That jasper was aiming to help this jasper run off," Holly Bee said. "Good thing I went along to watch, or you'd have lost him."

"No such thing," Jake said. "Beg pardon, Miss, but that wasn't how it was. You see, Ma'am, this fellow was laying for me out by Bert Froome's place and came at me with a gun. Hadn't been for Holly Bee I'd have had to shoot him myself, so don't put any blame on her. She did the right thing, even if it was for the wrong reason. Mr. Froome's wife bound up his legs to

116

stop him leaking, but he needs a doctor. Is there one around here?"

"Take him inside," Harriett said. "The doctor can tend him in his cell, then he's going to have a long visit with the judge. He killed a man in San Galena and took his horse."

Jake carried the groaning Whatley into the office and through to the jail, and dumped him on a cell cot. Holly Bee tagged after him, carrying her rifle, but the sheriff stopped her at the cell door.

"I've arranged a nice room for you and Annie, Holly Bee," she said. "You'll get a good night's rest at the boarding house. Annie's already over there. I'll show you the way." To Jake she said, "You can sleep in one of the empty cells. Just take your pick."

He frowned, glancing around at her. "Am I under arrest, Ma'am?"

"Not at the moment, Mr. Johnson," she assured him. "I haven't had a minute's time to review my warrant files since I got back, and I don't think I'll get to it until tomorrow . . . after you and I have had a nice chat about community service and restitution."

"What restitution?"

"Why, we shall talk about that first thing tomorrow," she smiled. "Come along, Holly Bee. Have a nice sleep, Mr. Johnson."

Chapter XII

"I'm not going to do any such thing!" Jake's roar overrode the clatter of the knife and fork he dropped onto his plate. Eyes wide with indignation, he glanced around for support and found none. Annie Coke was staring at the lady sheriff with undisguised admiration and Holly Bee was looking out the window, ignoring the whole thing. "I'm not!" Jake emphasized. "I got better things to do."

Across the table, Harriett Fletcher simply raised a decorous brow. "Just what is it you object to, Mr. Johnson? It doesn't seem such an outrageous request, considering."

"I'm not going to go and take care of a bunch of women with female troubles," Jake said flatly. "I don't even know what female troubles are, but you've got the wrong man for the job."

"Sounds all right to me," Annie offered. "We'll go along an' help. I know all about female troubles. My husband Woodrow . . . bless his heart, he was a saint most ways . . . he used to say to me, 'Annie,' he'd say, 'Annie, are you havin' female troubles?' And I'd say to him, I'd say . . ."

"What are those men doing over there?" Holly Bee turned her chair for a better view of the street beyond the dining room window.

". . . I'd say, why, bless your heart, Woodrow, of course I am, but don't you worry your head about it none. It comes with the territory."

"I don't believe you exactly understand," Harriett told Jake. "I'm only suggesting an escort service . . ."

"What kind of man do you think I am, Ma'am?"

"Woodrow just never could get the hang of female troubles, neither. Many's the time I'd tell him, 'Woodrow,' I'd say, 'Woodrow, there's things God just never equipped menfolks to . . .'"

"There's no dust this morning," Holly Bee pointed out. "Why do they have bandanas on their faces?"

"I think you are basically a right-thinking young man who just found himself on the devil's trail," Harriett was telling Jake. "It seems to me you might . . . what?" She turned to the window. "Where?"

"Over yonder, across the street. Those four men with the bandanas on their faces." Holly Bee pointed.

"Oh, heavens!" Harriett stood, shoving her chair back. "That's the bank. And I left my gun . . . where did I leave it? Oh, I was driving nails with it, to fix the drainboard. I must have . . ."

Across the wide street, four riders had dismounted in front of the bank. Their faces were covered, but Jake recognized them. They were four of the five he had trailed with, out in the hills. "Those folks in Waco were right," he muttered. "That Thurgood *is* ugly, even when he hides his face." He wiped his mouth, set his napkin aside and picked up his hat. "Don't worry, Ma'am," he told the sheriff. "I'll help."

Annie's voice trailed after him as he left the room, "I don't believe they need any help, Charlie. They seem to know how to . . ."

Three of the outlaws had entered the bank, leaving one outside, and Jake was glad it was George Floom they had left. In his estimation, Floom was the dimmest of the bunch. He wondered what had become of Boomer Slade, but saw no sign of him.

He tipped his hat at a rakish angle, then strolled across the street, grinning as he approached the waiting outlaw. "Morning, George," he said. "You boys making a deposit here, are you? Like to see a man invest his . . ." with one final stride he swung from the knee and cold-cocked the outlaw. Floom had just started to draw his gun, and Jake plucked it from his fingers as he fell. He turned, waved it toward the boarding house window, then tossed it out into the street and went through the door, into the bank.

There were two clerks at the counter, their hands held high, and the three robbers were spread in front of them. They started to turn and Jake cocked his Peacemaker. "Don't move another inch, boys. Just drop those . . ."

Thurgood and Foley Size froze where they were, but Doc Cunningham dropped to a crouch and swivelled, bringing his gun around. Jake's Peacemaker thundered in the little closed room and Doc was flung back against the counter.

". . . guns," Jake finished.

Doc's gun had already fallen. Two others followed it and Foley Size looked around, raising his hands. "I be damned," he said. "It's him again."

"I don't suppose these fellers came in to make a deposit," Jake glanced at the nearest clerk.

"No, sir, I don't believe they did. Who are you?"

"Just happened along," Jake said. "The sheriff will be here directly." He turned to Foley Size. "What did you boys do with Boomer Slade? I don't see him around."

"Sold him," Size growled. "What's the matter with you, mister? Can't you go find your own bank to rob?

It ain't polite to butt in like this, you know."

The door opened and Harriett Fletcher entered, holding George Floom's gun in both hands. "What is going on here? Are you men robbing this bank?"

Size and Thurgood pulled off their hats. "We thought we might, Ma'am," Foley nodded. "Then this jasper had to come and butt in."

"We didn't actually get right down to robbin'," Thurgood added. "So if you'd just let down that cannon there, Ma'am, we ought to be on our way before the sheriff shows up."

Foley glared at Jake. "From now on if you'll just let us know which banks you want, we'll try to stay away from them. Can we go now?"

On the floor, Doc Cunningham was moaning and cradling a bloody arm. Harriett gazed at him, assessing the damage, then turned cold, level eyes on the other two. "I *am* the sheriff," she said. "You men are under arrest. Thank you for your assistance, Mr. Johnson."

"He ain't Johnson," Foley Size snapped. "He's Jones."

Thurgood glanced around at him. "Then how come Boomer to say he was Jake Creedmore?"

With the two of them supporting their companion, Harriett and Jake herded them outside where Holly Bee stood over a stunned and frightened George Floom, her rifle's muzzle an inch from his nose. Harriett added Floom to her catch and they herded all four down the street to the jail. With five prisoners, the place was fairly filled. As Harriett was locking them in, Jake asked, "How'd you boys manage to sell Boomer Slade? I'd have figured it might be the other way around."

"Got the drop on him," Foley shrugged. "After you taken off like you did—which wasn't just real polite if you don't mind me sayin' so — ol' Boomer got down-right mean about things so we had to do somethin'. So we sold him."

"Where did you sell him? Last I heard, you boys couldn't agree on anyplace to go."

"Didn't have to go anyplace. Bountyman came along and we sold him Boomer. Not for much, but not too bad a deal, considerin'."

"You always stand a loss goin' through a middle-man," Jake sympathized. "Sometimes the convenience is worth it, though. Man on the run ought to invest through third parties. I know I do."

They exchanged a look. "You do?"

"Sure. You ever hear of Philo Henderson, out at Portales?"

None of them had.

"Right shrewd investor," Jake told them. "And a man you can trust. He's looking after my portfolio right now. Thing is, he might pool some of my funds with some of his own and maybe somebody else's, and all together there's enough to get in on the ground floor of some pretty good deals. Lots of folks have got rich that way, you know."

"They have?"

"That's how I hear it. The thing is, you have to make sure your middleman knows what kind of in-vestments you like, otherwise he might be brokering your funds into short range capital gains when what you really had in mind was institutional security and long range cash flow."

"You're right as rain about that," Foley nodded. "My brother Finley, he come into some money one time up in the territories, and since he wasn't of a mind to stay around and get recognized he had a feller invest it for him. Trouble was, the feller put it all into commodity futures and it turned out Finley didn't have all that much future. They hanged him two weeks later at Grayson."

"Mr. Johnson . . ." Harriett was waiting at the cellblock door, tapping her foot.

"Yeah," Jake told the prisoners, "Philo Henderson is like that, too. He goes for preferred stock issues and commodity futures and buying on the margin, so I had to tell him to keep my capital channeled. I like real property, myself. It's slow on the gain, but God sure isn't making any more of it."

"Mr. Johnson, couldn't you continue this at another time?" Harriett sounded almost snappish. "I swear, men get started talking they just don't stop."

"Yes, Ma'am." Jake touched his hatbrim. "You boys take care of yourselves now, and remember what I told you. Man can waste his money if he doesn't put it to good use."

He followed Harriett out into the office and she locked the door behind him. Annie and Holly Bee were waiting for them there.

"Now back to what we were talking about, Mr. Johnson," Harriett said. "It isn't all that far over to Rossville. Two days at the outside, and I'll send a letter of introduction with you so Lottie Camber will know you come from me—"

"Ma'am," he shook his head firmly, "I just can't see me going off to do emergency service for a bunch of women—"

"Not emergency service," she interrupted. "Community service. It's a whole different thing."

"It doesn't matter what it is, that isn't what I had in mind to do. I don't even know those women."

"You will," she said. "They need help and I told them I would see what I can do. You have two choices, Mr. Johnson. Either give me your word that you will go over to Rossville and attend to those women, or you just sit down here and wait while I go through my warrants file and see what I can find out about you."

"He'll go to Rossville," Annie decided. "You don't have to worry none, Harriett. Holly Bee and me will go along and see he behaves himself. Won't we, Holly Bee?"

"Annie, I . . ."

"Sure we will."

"I would like Mr. Johnson's word," Harriett said.

"Then you have Mr. Johnson's word," Jake sighed.

"That isn't good enough," she amended. "I want *your* word, whatever your name is."

"Ma'am, no good is going to come of this. I'm in no position to be doing for a bunch of strange women right now. I can hardly do for myself these days, much less . . ."

"Your word," she insisted.

"One thing I want to know. What makes you so blamed sure you can trust me just because I give my word? I've know fellers I wouldn't trust if they gave me the mortgages on their mothers."

"So have I," she assured him.

"He just can't get the point," Annie said.

"No, he can't seem to, can he? But it doesn't matter. Do I have your word, sir?"

Jake surrendered. "You have my word. But only until I get the troubles at Rossville tended to. By the way, what is the trouble?"

"They've lost their men."

"All of them?"

"Quite a few. As I understand it, they're railroad hands who signed on as a crew to build a railroad, and the ladies have lost them."

"I don't suppose it occurred to them to just sort of look where the railroad is being built?"

"Of course it has. But they don't know where that is. I trust you will resolve their problems for them."

"Well, I'll give it a shot. But why me?"

"There are some things it takes a man to handle, Mr. Johnson."

There was a marshal's office at Big Spring, with a telegraph office right next door and four large safes within half a mile. There was a safe at the Big Spring bank, a safe at the Wells Fargo barn, a safe at the Western Union office and a safe in Uno Burton's office not far away. These circumstances had made Big Spring a handy center for the transaction of bounty business in these years when law in Texas was just about whatever each community chose to make of it.

Bounty transactions were standard business for Marshal Toliver Gibbs, about as standard as any part of his job. Rarely did a week pass that some bounty hunter didn't show up with either the person or the remains of some felon upon whom someone had put a price. It was a nice side business for the marshal, and the town itself appreciated it because they didn't have to pay him a regular salary. The bountyman would show up with his prize, Gibbs would stow the felon either in his jail or at the undertakers, then Gibbs would verify, for a reasonable fee, that the felon was in fact the felon in question, and would wire off for the bounty due upon him, certifying that he had him in custody. Pretty soon the money would come back, Gibbs would take his cut and hand the rest to the bountyman, and that gentleman would go forth to find other felons. Gibbs had seen the operation a hundred times, and there wasn't much that could surprise him.

What did surprise him one bright morning was the pair that walked into his office. The big one was twice the size of the little one and had his hands bound behind him and a large pistol tied in place at his throat, pointing upward at his gullet. The little one held the pistol's grip and used it as a come-along. Marshal Gibbs gawked at the pair. The big one he knew from old times — Boomer Slade, sure as the world, except for a pronounced nervous twitch that seemed to overtake him each time the little one tugged on his pistol. The little one looked like a mouse with a large hat. Little was visible of his face except a plentiful nose and outthrust whiskers that twitched this way and that.

"My name is Bead," the little one said. "I'm here to collect the reward on this man."

"I do believe that is Boomer Slade you got there, Mr. Bead," Gibbs said.

"I know who he is," Bead said. "Bounty is my business."

Because of a dispute between widely-separated jurisdictions as to which had first call on dealing with Boomer Slade, it took most of a day to collect bounty on him and part of a second day to transmit invoices and affidavits before the vouchers were in hand to pay it off. During that time Bead sniffed around Big Spring, looking for leads on other wanted men. Texas was full of them these days, but still it took work and single-mindedness to trace them. Like flocks of geese, firing generally into the flock seldom put meat on the table. Bead preferred the more orderly, professional approach to the bounty business: pick out one, get a line on him and track him down, then go on to another.

Bead's choice for his next quest was a well-known bandit with a high price on his head, and he had reason to think he was in the right locale. The man would be here or had been here recently. He was sure of it. Even the four who had sold their leader to him had helped to verify it. They knew him by description: tall, young, dark-haired, with a silver-belly beaver hat and a stud sorrel racer with the initials C. W. J. on its saddle. Bead described him in detail, and they knew him and pointed the way. But here in Big Spring it was as though he had hit a wall. He talked to person after person, repeating the description a dozen times, then a dozen more. But no one had seen the man. No one even knew of anyone who had.

The only thing anybody at Big Spring recognized about him was his name—Clive Wilson Jones, the notorious train robber.

When Bead went back to the marshal's office to collect his money on Boomer Slade, Toliver Gibbs had heard who he was looking for. People of the town had repeated Bead's questions to him. But Biggs was no help, either.

"I don't believe you'll find him here," Biggs said. "If anybody of that description had come through, somebody would remember. One thing you got going for you is, you know what he looks like. I never heard anybody say what Clive Wilson Jones looked like, before. How come you know all that?"

"I've seen him," Bead admitted. "Had him dead to rights once, but he got away. But never mind, I'll get him again. Bounty is my business."

"Well, when you get him," Biggs smiled, "you just haul him on back here. I'll be glad to handle the reward arrangements for you."

Chapter XIII

Jake Creedmore was sullen most of the trip from Limestone to Rossville, torn between ominous hunches that things were going from bad to worse in his life and bleak assurance that he was on his way to hell in a handbasket. What was it the woman had told him? About his having chosen to ride the devil's trail? He had grave doubts about that. It just didn't seem to him that aggravating Conrad W. Jackson was all that sinful a thing to do, and aside from taking back what was fairly owed to him that was all he had done. But he had surely taken a wrong turn somewhere.

"The idea was," he told Conrad W. Jackson's racing sorrel, "We were going up to Portales and visit with Philo, then just sort of get lost and let everything blow over. You remember me telling you that? That was how it was going to be. There never was anything in the plan about stringin' off cross-country with a couple of stray women, and sure enough not anything about going over to Rossville to help a bunch of women who can't keep track of their men-folks."

When the horse didn't respond, he reached around and hauled out the little painting of Conrad W.

Jackson from his saddlebag. "And as for you," he told the painting, holding it out at arm's length, "as for you, my constipated American friend, you know as well as I do I didn't take any twenty thousand dollars. If there was twenty thousand dollars there to take, and if it's gone, then you and I both know who took it, don't we?" He grasped the corner of the frame, ready to sail the thing off into distance and limbo, then changed his mind again. He had carried the fool picture this far on a pure whim, he might as well carry it a little farther. "If Wilbur hadn't told me how you put stock in this painting . . ." With a shrug he slid it back into his saddlepocket and noticed that Annie Coke was riding alongside, just a pace away, looking at him with motherly sympathy.

"Crenshaw Haynes used to go to talkin' to hisself just like that there," she said. "He leaned toward moods, and sometimes he just set off talkin' to hisself. I used to tell him, 'Crenshaw,' I'd say, 'Crenshaw, that talkin' out loud to yourself is gonna do you in, you mind what I say.' But, bless his heart, he just went right on doin' it like I knew he would."

"One of your husbands?" Jake asked, absently, lost in bleak reverie over his misfortunes.

"No, not one of mine. He was my sister Liza's husband. Second or third one she had, as I recollect. A saint most ways, he was, but broody like I said. Used to talk to hisself. Trouble was, on top of bein' broody he had a right smart temper an' was one to take offense at slights, an' sometimes he'd say things to hisself that he just couldn't tolerate havin' said, then he'd get off into these quarrels so fierce that, land, Liza was afraid he was goin' to kill one another before he saw his way clear to quit."

Jake glanced around, half-listening. "Kill . . . one another? Who?"

"Crenshaw Haynes. An' hisself. Never in my life saw such a hot-tempered pair when he an' him got goin'. I recollect times he got so mad at hisself he wouldn't talk to hisself for two-three days. When that happened an' he didn't have anybody to talk to he'd go out an' talk to his pole barn."

"His pole barn."

"Sure enough. But that didn't always work out just right, neither. Sometimes he'd say somethin' to his pole barn that he just plain couldn't agree with, an' so he'd have to butt in an' set hisself straight on the matter an' there he'd go again, fussin'. I told him that was goin' to do him in, but he never paid any mind."

"So what happened to him? Did he kill himself?"

"Oh, lordy, no. Not Crenshaw Haynes. No, Old Man Alf Worthy shot him, bless his heart. Old Man Worthy was Crenshaw's best friend an' they'd get together an' drink whiskey an' play pinochle most Saturdays, out in the pole barn. Always filled their pockets with corn when they done that, so if they got drunk and went to sleep out there the pigs'd wake 'em up Sunday mornin' in time to go to church."

"Remarkable," Jake shook his head. "So why did his friend shoot him?"

"Oh, Crenshaw got to talkin' to hisself about politics. He should have stayed off that subject because Crenshaw never could agree about politics. But this one time he got into an argument about it an' Old Man Worthy tolerated it just as long as he could then he shot him down, 'cause he didn't hold with anybody sayin' that kind of things to a friend of his."

Jake had the feelings his ears would eventually accommodate to Annie. Like locust hums and steady wind, with a little luck he might get so that he wouldn't hear her at all. "That doesn't make much sense," he noted.

"You'd have to have knowed Crenshaw," she explained. "Them as knowed him got confused sometimes as to which one of him was which. To his dyin' day, Old Man Worthy never was sure he'd shot the right one."

The trail they were following was little more than a cowpath meandering through rolling hills, but Harriett Fletcher had suggested it. "Likely you'll want to stay off roads," she said. "Have you thought about reshaping your image? That might help. And change your name? I mean, there's nothing wrong with Charlie Johnson, but some people change their names when they're trying to change their ways. It's just a suggestion."

"It's getting so I don't know for sure what my name is any more," he told her with some truth.

He carried a letter from her, addressed to Mrs. Lottie Camber at Rossville. His instructions were to deliver the letter to Mrs. Camber, which would qualify him as arrived help, then to listen to Mrs. Camber when she told him what the problem was that was deviling the ladies at Rossville. From there on, the instructions were unclear. "Just do what seems right," Harriett had ordered him. "Use your judgment and do what's best and I'm sure God will bless you for it."

I could use a little bless about now, Jake told himself. From somewhere ahead came the sound of a distant bell.

"There's men on that road yonder," Holly Bee observed, and Jake squinted at the distant, rising plain beyond the hill they were climbing. He hadn't noticed until then that there was a road off there, but now he saw it, and there were riders there.

They topped out on the hill, watching the riders in the far distance, then lowered their gaze. Just below, in a barren little valley between two rising plains, was what might have passed for a town if a body wasn't particular about definitions. Two short, intersecting dirt streets with a cluster of buildings, and thirty or forty houses of various descriptions scattered around.

"Must be Rossville," Annie decided. "This is about where Harriett said it was."

"I don't see any shortage of men," Jake observed. The little town seemed to be full of men. From where they sat, Jake could count close to forty of them in the dusty streets — some on horseback, some afoot, some driving wagons, men who looked as though they had just stepped out of church with slicked hair, trimmed whiskers, starched collars and fresh-blacked boots. What was not visible, anywhere he looked, was women. There was not a female to be seen.

He shaded his eyes. The road north wasn't the only one that had traffic on it. There were other men coming from three other directions.

The tolling bell's sound seemed to be coming from what appeared to be a little schoolhouse, right in the middle of town.

"I don't like this place," Holly Bee said. "Why are those men totin' flowers like that?"

Jake squinted. She was right. At least a half-dozen of the men on the streets below were carrying what seemed to be bouquets of prairie flowers. In addition, several had guitars or banjos slung on their backs, and one was lugging around a huge, curled brass horn.

"Seems like this ought to be Rossville," Annie frowned. "I don't see how we could have missed it. I reckon we best ride down an' have a look. You lead off, Clifton. We're right behind you."

Jake flinched at the name. He wasn't sure he would ever get used to being called Clifton. Annie had insisted, though, and he had finally agreed. For the duration, pending further aliases, his name was Clifton W. Jenkins. At least it matched the initials on his saddle.

As they started down the hill, though, Annie reminded him again, "You just remember, son, come time to call names, you answer to Clifton Jenkins. Holly Bee an' me, we won't let on otherwise, so there's no reason anybody in these parts shouldn't think that's who you always been."

At the edge of town, where the cowpath trail entered the west road, a recently-polished carriage rolled by them. Two sun-darkened men sat stiffly on its seat, both scrubbed, shaved, brushed and polished and both looking thoroughly uncomfortable. As one, their faces swivelled toward Holly Bee, and they almost went off the road gawking. They passed them, and one's voice floated back, "You see that'n, Pete? Hoo-ee, I b'lieve we done come to the right place!"

Both of them carried bouquets of flowers in work-hardened hands.

Jake and his escorts stared after them, wondering what it was all about.

Men were everywhere in the little town—wandering around, gathering here and there, talking, loafing, but most eyes were on the little schoolhouse at the intersection. Its doors and shutters were closed tight and its bell was ringing. They rode toward it and Jake glanced back to see that they had picked up a crowd. Twenty or thirty men were following along behind them, with more joining in. More specifically, the men were following Holly Bee—although when the crowd became unwieldy some of the older ones veered aside to tag behind Annie Coke.

Jake paused where a knot of men stood in the shade in front of a boarded-up tavern. He looked at them and they looked at him, then he nodded. "After-

133

noon, gents. I'm looking for some women."

"Aren't we all," one of them leered at him. "You'll have to wait your turn, though. Most of us been here since yesterday."

Jake cocked his head. "What I mean is, I'm supposed to find a woman here with female troubles."

"With what?"

"I got a letter of introduction."

"Now that's a notion I hadn't thought of," another man said. "All I brought was flowers." He gazed at the schoolhouse. "For all the good it's done me," he added. "That is one standoffish bunch yonder."

"Is that where they are?" Jake looked across at the schoolhouse. Behind him Holly Bee shrieked and he turned just in time to see Annie lay the barrels of her shotgun across the skull of a man holding flowers.

"Y'all just back off and mind your manners!" Annie shouted. "Lordy, didn't anybody never tell y'all it ain't polite to . . . here, now!" Her shotgun arced again and another man went to his knees. "Charlie! We could use a hand, here!"

"I thought I was Clifton," Jake muttered. He drew his Peacemaker and fired two shots over the heads of the crowd. "Back off!" he roared. "All of you! What in blazes do you boys think you're doing?"

"Courtin'," several said, looking at him in wide-eyed surprise.

"They with you, mister?" someone asked.

"They're with me," he assured all present.

"Then what are you doin' here, anyway?"

"I'm looking for women."

"Lord, some folks don't never have enough."

Still holding his Peacemaker, Jake waded the sorrel into the crowd, cut out Holly Bee and Annie and herded them toward the schoolhouse.

"Crazy as loons," Annie said. "What kind of town is

this, anyway?"

"B'lieve it's called Rufflesville, Ma'am," a man nearby said. "It's full of loose women, but they won't come out of that schoolhouse yonder."

The ringing of the schoolhouse bell was beginning to give Jake a headache. He hitched the sorrel out front, walked up the steps and banged on the door. For a moment there was no response, then a bullet ripped through the panel, barely missing his hat. He dived backward, missed his step at the top of the stairs and rolled all the way to the bottom. From across the street, someone called, "We'd thought about tryin' that, mister, but we thought we'd wait 'til somebody else tried it first. We're all obliged to you."

Holly Bee gazed down at him, shook her head in disgust, then circled her horse out in the street, raised her rifle and fired at the bell tower. Instantly the bell stopped ringing and in the silence was the sound of a rope falling to plank floor somewhere inside.

Annie Coke stepped down from her saddle, clucked sympathetically as Jake got to shaky feet, then marched up the schoolhouse stairs. Standing back from the frame, she rapped on the door and called, "Y'all can stop shootin' now, ladies. Sheriff Fletcher sent us to look out for you."

After a moment there was the creak of a bar being lifted, and the door opened an inch. Annie grinned at the inch. "Your worries is over, ladies. Harriett Fletcher sent Clifton Jenkins to solve your problems for you. Can't hardly ask for better than that."

The door opened further and Annie beckoned. "Get on in here, Charlie . . . I mean, Clifton. Don't pay to keep ladies waitin'."

Across the street, several dozen potential suitors began a migration toward the schoolhouse, hats and flowers in their hands. Holly Bee reined her horse

135

around, her rifle leveled toward them. "Git!" she ordered.

They got.

With the street again cleared, Holly Bee backed her horse to the schoolhouse hitchrail, stepped down without taking her eyes from the mass of male humanity staring across at her, tied her reins then scampered up the schoolhouse steps and through the door. She closed it and someone dropped the bar into its racks.

Her eyes were still adjusting to the dim interior when she heard Annie's voice: "Neighborly of y'all to let us in like that. My name's Annie Coke. Yonder is Holly Bee Sutherland and this here is Mr. Jenkins. We're lookin' for Miz Lottie Camber."

A muscular woman with hard eyes stepped forward. "I'm Lottie Camber. What was that you said about the sheriff?"

"Sheriff Fletcher," Annie said. "Sheriff *Harriett* Fletcher — ain't that the beatin'est? — she sent us over here to see you. Said you had problems."

"We certainly do." She turned to glare at Jake. "How come you shot our bell-rope?"

"I didn't do that, Ma'am." Jake shuffled his feet, realizing for the first time that he was the only man present so far as he could tell. He felt like a rabbit at a foxtrot. "Maybe I best wait outside."

"Hush up, Clifton," Annie told him. "Miz Camber, that was Holly Bee that shot your bell rope, not Mr. Jenkins."

"Well, how come her to do that?"

"Y'all were makin' a terrible racket," Holly Bee said flatly.

"We were tryin' to call in some help," Lottie Camber said. "All those men out there . . . well, it's downright shameful."

"It was your own doin', Lottie," a gray-haired woman with a shawl spoke up. "I told you it'd be just as well if not just everybody was to find out that we're alone here. But no, you had to . . ."

"Now, Jessy, all I did was tell the mail rider to see if anybody had any notion where our men got off to. I never told him he could spread gossip."

"Varmint's been tellin' everybody in a hundred miles that Rossville's full of loose women," Jessy explained for Annie's benefit. "Now see what's come of it? All them damn men . . ."

"A bad situation is no call for bad language, Jessy," Lottie Camber scolded. She turned then to Jake, eyeing him from top to toe the way a meat buyer eyes a hog in a sale lot. "How do I know you're from Sheriff Fletcher, Mr. . . . ah . . ."

"Jenkins," Annie said. "His name is Clifton Jenkins. Tell her about the letter, Charlie."

"Clifton," he reminded her. "I have a letter, Ma'am. Miz Fletcher sent it for you." He dug around in his coat, found the letter and handed it over. While she read it, he stared around, trying to count noses. There were forty or fifty people here, all women and children . . . he amended that at sight of a bearded oldster asleep on a bench in the corner . . . mostly women and children. He couldn't be sure how many there were, because some were moving in and out of another room at the back.

"Well, I reckon you're all right," Lottie Camber decided. "What are you going to do to help us?"

"I haven't the vaguest idea," Jake admitted.

"Well, while you're deciding, I'd better introduce you around," she said. "Ladies! Ladies, can I have your attention?" Two or three glanced around at her, but most paid no attention. Some of the women were at windows, peering out through cracks in the shutters. Other were carrying things in and out of the back room. Some were tending children and there were several conversations or arguments—Jake couldn't tell which—going on simultaneously. Lottie Camber stamped her foot. "Ladies, please!"

Annie glanced around the room. "Hard to get folks' attention sometimes," she muttered. Matter-of-factly she raised her shotgun and emptied both barrels into the rafters. Silence and pattering birdshot descended.

Lottie gaped at her for a moment, then snapped her mouth shut and raised a hand. "Ladies, your attention please. Sheriff Fletcher from Limestone has sent a man to help us. This here is Mr. Clifton Jenkins, and he's—"

"No, it isn't!" a voice from beyond one of the rearward groups cut in. A skirted figure pushed through and Jake's eyes went wide.

"He isn't any such thing," Clara Hayes corrected. "That there is just Jake Creedmore, except he's got Conrad W. Jackson's hat."

138

Chapter XIV

Since trouble had been a regular and invited occurrence in the neighborhood of San Galena, in the south part of the county, the people of Limestone in the north had grown accustomed to seeing hard men come and go. It was one reason some of them had gone along with the bizarre step of appointing a woman as interim sheriff. The logic had been that, with a woman in office, there wouldn't be anyone to stir things up in the south and maybe all the hardcases would just stay down there and not fool with Limestone.

The fact that somehow things *had* been upset at San Galena—the former town marshal from there was in the county jail at Limestone now, with bullet holes through the meat of both legs—and that subsequently someone had tried to rob the bank at Limestone just heightened the feeling that the best law is no law at all and the nearest thing to no law is a woman as sheriff.

Only an enlightened few were aware that the lady sheriff had in fact had something to do with the collapse of San Galena's little private jurisdiction, and those didn't say much about it because they couldn't understand how such a thing had happened.

But, the bank robbery had failed—thanks to some stranger with a quick gun stepping in on the sheriff's behalf—and so far no great harm had come of it all. Still, it was no surprise to anyone when a trail-dusty band of dark-coated men with enough guns sprouting among them to arm a battalion showed up in Limestone. Then when T-bone Shaw, in a fit of sobriety, recognized the men and spread the word, everyone's direst predictions arose like ghosts to haunt the sunlit street.

"Royal Flanders," Shaw told a breathless audience at the Come On Inn. "That there is Royal Flanders an' his bunch just bigger'n hell won't have it."

Royal Flanders. The name evoked images of blazing guns bringing a sort of law to the badlands of New Mexico, and later images of blazing guns putting that law six feet under when it got in the way.

Within minutes of first sighting, the word had spread up and down the streets of Limestone. By the time Flanders and his men were dismounting in front of the sheriff's office, there were people peering through cracked doors all up and down that block, hoping somebody would politely point them toward San Galena and that maybe they would never come back.

Harriett Fletcher had the impression of several massive dark shadows ghosting through her office door, and suddenly the room was very small. The man in the lead, a sun-dark dusty man with several visible guns, glanced at her, looked around and shrugged large shoulders under a dark and dusty coat. "Set," he told the others with him. "We'll wait."

They took seats, pulling chairs around so that every part of the little room was under surveillance, and Harriett, working at her desk, scowled. The men hadn't said a word to her—just entered and occupied the office. She looked from face to face and recognized none of the four. She had the impression there were at least two more outside, guarding the front. She coughed and all those inside glanced around. At sight of her frown the leader blinked, then pulled off his hat and hissed something at the others. They shucked their hats, too, then resumed their vigil. Harriett noticed that the man who seemed to be in charge had iron-gray hair and a face that looked like the dry bed of an intelligent creek. All that seemed to live there—except for a pair of eyes that wouldn't miss seeing anything worth seeing—was potential. He looked like a smile that had been waiting for years to happen and hadn't yet found a reason.

She coughed again and asked, "Is there something I can do for you gentlemen?"

"No, Ma'am," the leader's cheeks rose just a hint as he shook his head. "You just go ahead with what you're doin'. Don't mind us." He waited patiently for another minute or two then said, "Crone, go get somebody to ask."

One of the men stood, put on his hat and went out. He was back in a matter of minutes with Bert Froome sort of high-stepping ahead of him, half-dangling from a huge hand on his lapel. "Found this'n right next door," Crone said.

"He'll do," the leader nodded. Without any visible malice he said to Froome, "Sorry to bother you, mister, but we're here to see the sheriff. Do you know where he might be?"

Froome blinked huge eyes. "The . . . the sheriff?"

"That's right. The sheriff."

Froome glanced confusedly at Harriett, then back at the big man sitting before him. "Ah . . . what sheriff are you lookin' for?"

141

"The sheriff of this county," the man explained, patiently. "Do you know the sheriff of this county?"

"Ah . . . yes, sir, I'm proud to say I do."

"And do you know where he is right now?"

"Ah . . . yes, sir, I surely do."

"Where?"

"Right there." Froome pointed. "Sheriff Harriett Fletcher. She's him."

A wide, hard mouth that might never have shown surprise in all its years dropped open in astonishment, and the others followed suit. Having effectively disappeared in their confusion, Bert Froome scurried out the door and closed it behind him.

The seated ones all stood, their full attention on Harriett now. She had the impression that a forest of dark oaks had abruptly grown around her.

"You?" the leader rasped, then cleared his throat. "Ah . . . is that right, Ma'am? You're the . . . the sheriff here? Like he said?"

Harriett sighed. She nodded. "Always seems to come as a surprise," she said. "Yes, I am the sheriff. Who are you?"

Recovering a little, the big man glanced around at his chair, started to sit and remained standing. Harriett wondered how many guns he carried under his coat. With every motion he made, she saw a few more. "Please," she said. "Sit down." They sat, pulling their chairs around to face her in an attentive row, their hats in their hands. In that instant they looked like so many oversized schoolchildren. "Now," she said. "Is there something I can do for you gentlemen?"

"Ah, yes, Ma'am," the leader leaned forward, started to offer a huge hand, then withdrew it uncertainly. "Ah . . . my name is Flanders, Miss . . . ah, Ma'am. The boys and me, we've come a long way,

142

trackin' a man that's wanted real bad back in our territory. Heard there was a feller here that might give us a lead on him, if we could just talk to him a little. Feller named . . . ah, C. Whatley. He's a lawman of some kind, supposed to be here in your fair city."

"He's here, all right. What do you want to talk to him about?"

"Well, Ma'am, that's kind of . . . are you sure you're a sheriff? Honest to pete?"

"Honest to pete," Harriett assured him. She took her badge from her purse and held it so they could all see it.

"I declare," Flanders said. "I do declare."

Harriett put her badge away. "Who is it you are looking for, Mr. Flanders?"

"Like I said, a feller named Whatley. Just want to talk to him a little, that's all."

"You said that. But who is it you are after?"

"Well, Ma'am, it's a jasper that robbed a bank out our way. The banker's all upset because of a picture he stole. Seems like it has something to do with a railroad project, though he doesn't say much that's very clear about that."

"What is the banker's name?"

"Uh . . . his name's Conrad W. Jackson, Ma'am. But he ain't the one we're trackin'. He's the one puttin' up the reward, you see."

"I understand," Harriett nodded. "I believe I'm beginning to understand better all the time. Can you describe the person you are out to . . . what *are* you out to do, exactly? Kill him or apprehend him?"

"Apprehend, Ma'am. What a lot of folks that hire us don't understand is that we ain't hired guns — even if appearances are deceivin', which sometimes keeps a body healthy out in the badlands. But we do

143

go after folks for rewards, if that's what needs doin'."

"Describe him, please. The one you are tracking."

"Well, he's young . . . not a button, but he ain't hit thirty yet . . . and tall, dark brown hair . . . no prior record that I could find although that banker says he's a real bad'un. And chances are he's wearin' a silver-belly beaver hat and ridin' a blood sorrel with a trimmed saddle that has the initials C.W.J. on it. Name's Creedmore, if that means anything. Jake Creedmore."

Harriett thought it over while they waited in silence. "I don't know anyone by that name," she said, finally. "And descriptions can be so vague. But you know how it is, Mr. Flanders. There's just no telling what a person might not remember."

"Yes, Ma'am." Flanders nodded his understanding. "Well, I guess we better talk to this Whatley. Is he around?"

"You know, Mr. Flanders," Harriett said, "This has been a long, hot morning. I was considering a glass of lemonade. They serve excellent lemonade at the boarding house diner. Do you suppose you . . . ?"

A smile that was like granite pulverizing spread across his face. "Why, Ma'am, I would be delighted. Just flat out delighted."

"Good." She stood and they all jumped to their feet, parting ranks so she could lead the way. "And while we're having our lemonade, perhaps you can tell me more about Conrad W. Jackson and the railroad venture. I find that very interesting."

"Somebody has given you boys a serious misapprehension," Jake said, speaking from the top of the schoolhouse steps. "And not that it's your fault, considering how you've been misled, but you all have like to scared the bejeezes out of all those ladies in there. You just haven't got any idea what they been thinking since you all showed up."

"We heard they was loose women," a man in the crowd below squinted up at him. "You tellin' us that ain't so?"

"Not only not loose," he assured them, "but also not even unattached. They have a complete set of menfolk someplace, they just don't know quite where at the moment. It's a real sad set of circumstances."

"How can they not know where their menfolks are?" a man asked. "I mean, one or two, maybe . . . but *all* of 'em?"

"I haven't quite got that all sorted out yet. Seems like they went off somewhere to build a railroad, and the ladies haven't heard from them since."

"Well, the poor things!" someone said. "That's just awful."

"Been some talk down at Big Spring about somebody buildin' a mainline west," another offered. "Don't know as I've heard any more about it, though. It all just sort of hushed up a while back. You suppose that's where these ladies' men went? To Big Spring?"

"I been to Big Spring," someone said. "It ain't all that hard a place to leave."

"Wonder if whoever it is, is still hirin' crew?" a burly man with wilted flowers scratched at his whiskers. "Me, I could use the work."

"Couldn't we all!" another added, emphatically.

"I heard a rumor, clear out at Portales," Jake recalled, "about some folks at Big Spring gettin' involved in something big. Any of you ever hear of the Burton brothers?"

"Used to know kin of theirs," a man nodded. "Is

that where they are? Big Spring?"

"That's what Philo Henderson heard, and he's usually right. He's a cousin of mine and I got him handling my investments because he usually knows what's going around."

"That's a high-rollin' pair," the man said. "If they're down at Big Spring I got a notion to go nose around there a little. Might be opportunities there."

"Now, hold on," a freckled redhead with a rifle and cactus roses snapped. "I thought we was here to chase women, not to find work!"

"Times change, Ruby," a dour mustanger told him. "First things first, an' I ain't had steady work in near on to a year. Besides, this gent says those women in yonder are all took."

"He didn't say they was *all* took. Maybe some ain't, yet."

"That Henderson you was sayin' about," a top-hatted man with cut clovers raised his hand. "Does he do mutual funds?"

"I expect he does," Jake nodded. "Though I wouldn't think he'd go heavy on single-issue debentures. Too much market fluctuation there, and you lose your liquidity."

"Best money used to be in metals," a man with glasses pointed out. "But I kind of think transportation and communication stocks is the way to go nowadays. I wouldn't mind havin' a piece of a railroad."

"Not me," someone else said. "Too many stub-lines has gone bust since Reconstruction, an' how you gonna know who's got mainline projects with capital structure? Nobody lets anybody know what they're doin' for fear of right-of-way holdup, so you wind up sinkin' blind money into preferred stocks and lose your dividends when some yahoo takes a notion to recapitalize."

"You're right as rain about that, Ray," a long-jawed individual agreed. "I think kindly of common stocks, myself. But I wouldn't go into railroad finance without I had inside knowledge of who's doin' the tradin'. Hard for just anybody to find that out these days."

"Speculators has got the whole mess screwed up," a surly man said.

Ruby the redhead was staring around in disbelief. "Here we all come all this way to chase women an' y'all take to talkin' high finance instead? What's the matter with you boys?"

"No women to chase, Ruby," the mustanger shrugged. "These around here is all done chased."

"One of th' Lord's blessin's on earth is a chaste woman," the mustanger intoned. "Not that them kind bring a whole lot of relief to a man that's been on the prowl too long."

"I got close to fifty dollars in a posthole safe back home," the long-jawed man said. "You suppose a man like Philo Henderson could put that to use for me?"

"Depends on what kind of investment you prefer," Jake told him. "But generally even split options take a little more than that."

The man with the drooping posies was gazing in speculation at the long-jawed one. "Are you thinkin' what I'm thinkin', Hank? There's enough of us here to prob'ly come up with a pooled mutual, an' if that Henderson feller knows how to ride a market, we could maybe get a line on who's backin' that railroad project while we're down around Big Spring."

"You goin' to Big Spring?" the top-hatted man glanced around. "What for?"

"Ain't we all?"

147

"That's the first I'd heard of it."

"Why would we all go to Big Spring?" a man somewhere in the crowd asked.

"Because that's the best place to start lookin' for them women's menfolks," Drooping Posies pointed out. "We all come to offer them our services, didn't we? What are we gonna do, turn tail in their hour of need?"

"That wasn't the kind of services most of us had in mind, Bill," someone said.

"Well, it's about the main kind they require, as things turn out. So what about it? Who wants to go to Big Spring?"

"Are there loose women there?"

"They's an opportunity for financial recompense."

"Might be jobs, too."

"And we can get a line on what railroad stock we want points in."

Jake wisely kept his mouth shut and let them run with it. He couldn't, he decided, have worked it out better himself. The ladies of Rossville were well on the way to having their female troubles ironed out—their men found and returned to them—and their potential suitors were just liable to make a profit on the deal. He doubted whether any corporate secret had ever faced a more massive concerted effort to uncover it at its source. If anybody could find a secret railroad and the men working on it, this bunch could.

Feeling as though a load had been lifted from him, he grinned, tipped back Conrad W. Jackson's silver-belly beaver hat and thought about where he would go now that his responsibilities here were at an end.

He had it narrowed down to either New Orleans or Bugtussle when the schoolhouse door opened and several women stepped out onto the porch. Instantly the hubbub of conversation in the street went silent and hats were pulled from heads.

"If you gentlemen have nothing better to do," Lottie Camber addressed the crowd, "Most of us could use some help loading wagons. Mr. Jenkins has volunteered to lead us westward on a search for our menfolks."

Jake's mouth dropped open. "I never volunteered to do any such . . ."

"Hush up, Clifton," Annie nudged him with her shotgun. "I volunteered you."

Chapter XV

By the time Royal Flanders learned that Chub Whatley was in the county jail and not going anywhere for a while, Harriett Fletcher had learned a great deal about Conrad W. Jackson, the badlands of New Mexico, the erratic history of law and order in the territories and the emergence of unexplained railroad trestles in the three rivers country of west Texas. Royal Flanders had learned to like Limestone lemonade and the bright eyes of lady sheriffs. He had also learned a lesson in intuition.

"I don't doubt that the Perdition bank was robbed, Mr. Flanders," she told him. "And I don't doubt that this Jake Creedmore, who may or may not have been in Limestone recently, robbed it first. But I doubt very much that he robbed it the most."

"It is just a mite odd that Homer Boles got two different stories about how much was missing," he agreed. "That's why I had my men do a little checking before we set out, but there wasn't a lead on where that bank clerk got off to, and he was the only prime witness to the robbery. On the other hand, any number of folks back there saw Jake Creedmore wearing Conrad W. Jackson's silver-belly beaver hat and riding his sorrel horse."

"That kind of limits the enforceable charges to hat-and-horse theft, doesn't it?"

"Well, Conrad W. Jackson seems pretty certain he can make his charges stick . . ."

"Which would indicate to me that Mr. Jackson knows where the clerk is."

"Possibly. But the oddest thing of all—he doesn't seem nearly as concerned about getting his twenty thousand dollars back . . ."

"Which makes one wonder if he ever lost it."

". . . as he does about getting his painting back."

"He probably put stock in it," Harriett mused, recalling something the man known as Charlie Johnson—now Clifton Jenkins—had said.

"He acts like he thinks Creedmore is toting around his twenty thousand dollars in that picture."

Maybe he is, Harriett thought, but that thought she kept to herself. Instead, she asked, "That trestle you and your men saw—out in the middle of nowhere, you said—was there a work crew there?"

"We didn't look close, but it was under construction so I reckon there was. Why?"

"Oh, there are some ladies over in the next county who have misplaced some odds and ends, and there could be a connection. Do you know who was building it?"

"No, and they sure didn't want us to find out, either." He chuckled. "Of course, that's just the way things are these days. Man'd be a fool to let on that he's buying right-of-way. Prices would go right out of sight. Not like it was back when the carpetbaggers and the government were doing that. Eminent domain has its drawbacks, but it sure cuts down on rampant speculation." He pushed back his chair. "Are you through?"

She glanced at her empty glass. "Why, yes, I

suppose so."

"I didn't mean that," he said. "I meant are you through interrogating me? Lady, I haven't been so scrupulously grilled since the first time I took a territorial marshal assignment — back before I turned honest."

Her smile rewarded him. "Yes, I believe I have a nice, clear picture now of . . . well, of some things that had puzzled me."

"Then I don't suppose you can tell me where Jake Creedmore is?"

"I can tell you he left Limestone three days ago. I can't tell you where he is." She raised a brow. "Do you know the name Philo Henderson, Mr. Flanders?"

He nodded. "Creedmore's cousin. Lives out at Portales. You certainly are full of interesting bits of information, Ma'am."

"Oh, that's just a name a young man mentioned the other day. A young man with a sorrel horse and a silver-belly beaver hat. He was discussing investment with some men who tried to rob the bank here."

"Did they get it robbed?"

"No, they didn't. He stopped them. You know, Mr. Flanders, not everyone who rides the devil's trail is necessarily all bad."

He stood, offering his arm. "I know that, Ma'am. Might be I put in a few miles on that trail myself . . . back before I turned honest."

On a bright morning six big, dark men mounted on rangy horses topped out on the rise overlooking little Rossville, and paused there, shading their eyes. "That town is deserted," one said. "Is that Rossville?"

"It's where Rossville is supposed to be," another

nodded.

"Well, there isn't anybody there. It's a damn ghost town."

"No, there's somebody. Horse at a rail just past that barn yonder. I see its shadow."

From old habit they spread wide, coming down on the town in a quarter-circle that left nothing hidden to them as they approached. From the edge of town Royal Flanders could see the tired horse hitched outside a vacant, leaning barn, and the man who sat in shade just inside, smoking a pipe. He was within easy gun-range before the man saw him, again from old habit. But no stealth was necessary. The pouches on the horse said the man was a mail-rider.

Royal approached and leaned down, crossing his arms on an upslung knee. "Howdy," he said. "No customers today?"

The man shook his head. "Damned if I know where everybody's got off to. There just ain't anybody here anymore. I looked all over town."

"Mail to deliver?"

"Not much. Letter for Miz Camber from the sheriff over at Limestone an' a dun for Miz Jessy Wheeler. I reckon it's a dun, 'cause it's from a investment office down at Big Spring, but of course I don't run around readin' people's mail."

"Of course not. You looked all over town?"

"All over it. There ain't that much of it to look over. Looks to me like everybody's done pulled out. They're all gone."

"Folks do that, sometimes," Royal said. "Hard times."

"Yeah, but a bunch of women? Wasn't hardly anybody left here anyway but a bunch of loose women."

"Loose women?"

"Well, women that didn't know where their men had got off to. I got some rounds stood for me here an' there when I mentioned there was a town full of loose women over here. But there ain't anybody here now." The mail rider put away his pipe and stepped out into the sunlight, squinting. "Who are you?"

"I'm the one who'll take delivery on those letters you mentioned," Flanders said, quietly.

"Now look here," the mail rider stared at him. "You don't want to interfere with the U.S. Mail. I got to deliver these letters to the addresses or else take 'em back."

Flanders shrugged and casually drew a large pistol. "I'll take them off your hands," he said evenly.

When the mail rider had gone, and while his men combed the little town for sign of occupancy, Royal Flanders opened the two letters. He grinned at the first one, a hastily scrawled note that must have been written and sent while he was having his little talk with the lady sheriff's prisoners at Limestone. It was from Harriett Fletcher to one Lottie Camber, and it warned the addressee that there might be men showing up looking for "Mr. Jenkins." It urged her to keep him hidden, and implied that there were some false charges against him that would be cleared up shortly.

"That woman bears watchin'," he told himself. "She is a slick one."

The second letter was a somewhat threatening note to a Mrs. Jessy Wheeler of Rossville, stating flatly that the man she inquired about . . . no name given . . . was gainfully employed and in good health, and that it would not be advisable for her to pursue further inquiries. It suggested without actually saying it that either his employment or the state of his health might be in jeopardy if the sender had any further indication of meddling on her part. It was

154

unsigned, but the careful handwriting indicated it might have been done by a clerk or secretary . . . and it was on printed letterhead. The Great Central and Pacific Investment Company of Big Spring, Texas.

Royal Flanders looked from one to the other of the letters, deep in thought, then folded them and put them away in a coat pocket. There was certainly more going on here than met the eye, and he recalled the careful questions Harriett Fletcher had asked him over lemonade at Limestone. Questions about railroad trestles and about Conrad W. Jackson. Questions about the charges against Jake Creedmore. Comments in passing about the odd reaction of a banker who had lost — he said — twenty thousand dollars, but was more concerned about losing a painting of himself.

And a sudden intuition hit Royal Flanders. Even supposing he was to bring back Jake Creedmore — and, of course, he would unless he decided not to — what guarantee was there that Conrad W. Jackson even *had* the cash money to pay the reward he had offered? What was the possibility that the reward itself depended upon delivery of Jake Creedmore — or of the painting?

"That lady sheriff just could have a point," he told himself. "Wouldn't be the first time all the chickens was stole while everybody's out chasin' the wrong fox."

Only in Texas, he thought. Out in the territories, things were simpler. A man does this, this or this he's committed a crime and stands to be punished for it. It was that way in Texas once, and would be again one day. But not now. Since the end of Reconstruction, Texas had bred politicians like a swamp breeds mosquitos, and all those politicians were over in

155

Austin making laws on top of laws, laws contrary to laws, laws to mitigate laws, laws to eliminate laws . . . the effect in fact was that Texas lacked consistent laws and would remain so until the courts got around to cleaning up the legislature's playhouse.

An interesting problem, he told himself. A man committed a crime in the territories, he could be tracked into Texas and brought back for a reward . . . unless the reward itself was bogus. But what if a man in the territories was committing crimes in Texas? Who would pay for his recovery? Rewards are paid by those who have the wherewithal to pay. He looked at the letter on the fancy paper. Somehow, the Great Central and Pacific Investment Company sounded a whole lot more substantial than Conrad W. Jackson.

Royal Flanders looked around at the tiny, deserted town. It never had been much of a place—a few buildings thrown into place by people who never got around to doing it any better—and now it was empty. And what is an empty town? He thought about it. Without people, a town was just an ugly little junkheap taking up good graze . . . it was less than nothing. Pretty much the way Perdition, out in the territory, had looked when he passed through to start tracking Jake Creedmore. He had thought at the time how strange it was that one man could put an end to a town. Conrad W. Jackson said Jake Creedmore was to blame out there. Jake had robbed the bank. Therefore the bank had gone out of business and called in its notes. Therefore a lot of people who couldn't pay off their mortgages lost their securities, all of which went back to Conrad W. Jackson, who would sell them off—probably already had sold them off—to someone remote and indifferent who would use the deeds to raise funds for something that

156

would have nothing at all to do with the little town whose carcass had fed the process.

He thought about it again now. One man can kill a town. But *which* one man had done it? Perdition was dying — probably dead by now, just like this little place that somebody had called Rossville — and Conrad W. Jackson was offering a lot of money for recovery of a painting of himself.

"He must put stock in that painting," Flanders told himself.

His men were coming back, finished with scouting the area. "Nobody here now," Hank said, "but they haven't been gone very long. Better'n a hundred folks around here within the past day or two . . . a lot more than could have lived here." Michael came in then to add, "Most of the tracks go south and southwest, but not the way we came. There's a wander-trail southwest, off the roads, with wagon tracks. Several wagons, buggies, maybe a surrey or two, and some riders, and folks walking. Women's shoes, some of them. The ones south are on the road, toward Big Spring."

Sam had found some tracks on the west road, four riders. "Might be the same ones we passed yesterday," he suggested. "A redhead, a mustanger and a couple of others. You recollect, they went wide to let us by."

"Found some pantries," Cal said, "all empty . . . cleaned out. And racks where water barrels sat, but the kegs are gone."

"Little change of plans, boys," Royal told them. "We need to swing down to Big Spring and nose around a little. I got a notion we been goin' after little fish when there's bigger ones to catch."

"Then what about Creedmore?" Hank asked.

"He'll keep," Royal assured them. "We know where he is, and we can get him when we need him. Let's

157

go see what else there is to turn an honest profit on in these parts."

In the county jail at Limestone, Foley Size pounded on the bars of his cell with a bedrail while a pale and subdued Chub Whatley watched bleakly from the next cell. Ever since the visit from Royal Flanders, Chub had been withdrawn and jumpy, a condition that went far beyond the scabbed-over bullet scars in his legs. He was like a man who has seen ghosts . . . or like a fox that has encountered a wolf and will never again be bold in his foxhood.

Foley banged rhythmically on the bars until the connecting door opened and Old Hack the jailer poked his head through to find out what the commotion was about.

"Need to talk to the sheriff," Foley said.

"She's busy," Hack said.

Foley began banging on the bars again.

Finally, Harriett Fletcher came in, and the prisoners removed their hats.

"Ma'am, we got a request," Foley said timidly.

"Yes, Mr. Size?"

"Ma'am, we was wonderin' if you could let one of us off on furlough for just a little bit, to go to the bank."

"You've already been to the bank," she reminded them. "That's why you're in here."

"Yes, Ma'am, but this is different. This time we need to make a deposit."

"A deposit?"

"Yes, Ma'am. If one of us could go to the bank . . . you could put a guard on us, if you want to . . . then just stop off at the telegraph office, then come on back here, we wouldn't make any more commo-

158

tion about it."

"You want to go to the bank, then the telegraph office, then back here?"

"Yes'm."

"Why?"

"Well, we got to figurin', what little money we got amongst us ain't doing us any good whatsoever in our pokes, but if we was to put it all in the bank, then get a voucher an' send it off to be invested for us, why then the time we spend here would be time put to good use because we might show a profit out of it."

"I see. Request denied." She turned away.

With a shrug, Foley began banging on the bars again.

"I can't let any of you out to go to the bank," Harriett turned back, "so forget it."

"Yes, Ma'am. But in that case, we was wonderin' if you could maybe go and take care of that for us." He held up a grimy fist. "Here's all our money. We'd trust you . . . especially if you was to bring us a receipt."

Harriett sighed. "Where do you want the voucher sent?"

"Feller out at Portales. His name's Philo Henderson, an' from what we hear he knows how the cow ate the cabbage where investments is concerned. Only one thing, though, we don't want to get into any commodity futures or rollover debentures or like that. You tell him we want our money in somethin' sure, like real estate or capital-intense fixed improvements."

159

Chapter XVI

At the first noontime stop, Jake Creedmore realized with a sinking heart that the situation had gotten totally out of hand. The women had decided — how they could "decide" anything with their constant bickering and wrangling was beyond him, but they had, somehow — that they didn't want to go to Big Spring because Big Spring would be out of the way if their missing husbands/rail builders had gone west from there. So, though there were plenty of men willing to escort them to Big Spring, Jake found himself virtually alone with a disorganized wagon train — train didn't describe it, he decided; mob was a better word — bound back more or less the direction that he, Annie and Holly Bee had come from Limestone.

"Single file!" he had shouted after five hundred yards of travel with Rossville barely put behind them. A quarter-mile later he was riding more or less in the midst of a shifting oval of wheeled vehicles and conveyances which veered, swerved, closed and reorganized with no regard to the lay of the land but was dictated mostly by the desire of each female in the group to be so situated as to hear whatever others might be saying about her behind her back.

"Close up the ranks!" he had barked, three miles out. Less than a mile beyond that he found himself plodding along as escort to three heavy wagons while the dust of lighter, faster vehicles settled on the wind far ahead. It was nearly noon before they got back together. Those in the lead had decided to wait for those behind, because most of the food and virtually all of the water was aboard the slower heavy wagons.

"Circle up yonder and we'll take a noon rest!" he called the order as they came down into a little valley with a rocky stream meandering through it. "Let's have a cookfire over there by those willows!" A half-hour later he sat on a rock gnawing a hank of jerked venison and trying to ignore the fact that there were more than a dozen separate picnics going on all up and down the valley, each driver, group or family having independently decided on its own version of a suitable place to have lunch. There were even some separate camps up on the hills on both sides.

Annie came up from the creek, with Holly Bee tagging after her and scowling at Jake as they approached. But Annie was beaming. Hands on her hips, shotgun dangling from one arm, she turned full circle, taking in the be-wagonned landscape. "Ain't this a sight," she grinned. "Does a body's heart good to see folks takin' the initiative like this here, don't it. An' it's all your doin', Clifton. Why, if you hadn't come along an' volunteered to help these ladies out of their miseries, they might still be just a-settin' back there at that dried-up little town, just waitin' for their men to come back. This here is what I call positive action!"

"It's what I call disaster," Jake muttered. "Do you

161

realize that we're going the wrong direction?"

"Why, we ain't either," she blinked at him. "Those men are bound to be out yonder west of Big Spring someplace."

"I mean for me," he shrugged. "This is the wrong direction for me. I had in mind to go east."

"You can go east some other time," Annie waved it away. "How many chances does a body get to help the needy in this life?" She paused, thoughtfully. "I been meanin' to ask you, Clifton . . . how come that sweet thing with the axe handle called you Jake Creedmore?"

"Because that's who I am."

"Misunderstandin's like that can sure enough cause trouble. We almost had us a difference of opinion in that schoolhouse meetin' back yonder . . . while you was outside settin' them men straight. Some of th' ladies noticed that the letter from the sheriff was about Clifton Jenkins, then that gal called you Jake Creedmore. Why, some of 'em was about to step outside an' shoot you if you didn't tell 'em what you done with Clifton Jenkins."

Jake shook his head and chewed off another chunk of jerky.

"What do you mean, that's who you are?" Annie rounded on him. "I thought we all decided you was going to be Clifton Jenkins."

"I'm Jake Creedmore," he said. "I don't know how many times I have to tell you that."

She thought that over. "Well, if you *was* Jake Creedmore, how come some little ol' sweet thing in Rossville to know about that?"

"Clara is from Perdition," he said.

"Well, bless her heart, she can't help that none. Everybody's from someplace. But how's come her to call you by name?"

"Because she knows me. Perdition is where I'm from . . . lately. I robbed the bank there. I don't think she knows that, though."

"Oh." Annie let it soak in, then she leaned close to ask in a low voice, "She ain't anything . . . ah, particular to you, is she? I mean, I sure wouldn't want to think you just been a-toyin' with poor little Holly Bee all this time."

"He hasn't been doin' *anything* with me," Holly Bee erupted. "He's an outlaw! I don't associate with outlaws!"

Jake almost strangled himself, trying to swallow unchewed jerky. Finally he caught his wind, stood, put on his hat and strode away to get his horse. It was time to move, if this bunch was going to be anywhere particular by nightfall. Swinging near to Lottie Camber's wagon he waved his hat and shouted, "Get 'em formed up, Ma'am. Time to move on. Let's get a good tight group to start, right up on that hill."

An hour later, or a bit more, they were all packed and ready to go on but still spread out across the valley and for a half-mile each way. And Jake had invented some new swear words that he didn't suppose anybody had ever heard before. He rode up to the westward slope and waved his hat, a signal for them to come ahead. Most of them did, though one wagon bogged in the only soft place on the little creek within miles, two others decided to turn north and find a gentler place to cross, some of those already across turned south for some reason he couldn't fathom, and a buggy crammed with two women and about eight children did a few figure-eights out on the bald prairie and then started back

163

toward Rossville, nobody but its team in charge.

Finally Jake raised his eyes to heaven, had a little man-to-man chat with his maker, then spurred the racer toward the nearest wagon, which was just topping the hill. "Hold up right there," he shouted. "I mean right there! That's right! Stop those horses right where they are! Now stay there! Don't y'all dare so much as move an inch!"

From there he reined hard around, caught up with a surrey just heading off by itself, spurred the sorrel to crowd in close and turn it, then herded it back to where the stopped wagon waited. "Now stop!" he shouted. "Stay right here and don't move! Not a step!" With two of them anchored in place by hard words and surprise, he went after another.

The sun was entering its final quarter when he scanned the horizons from a high knoll and decided he had them all accounted for. He rode down to the little knot of wagons and stepped down, glaring at them one and all. "We'll make camp for the night here!" he barked. "One fire! Everybody all in one place! First one that decides to scatter, by God, I'll shoot your horses!"

From the cluster a phalanx of angry women marched out, their eyes glittering. "What do you mean, camp here?" one of them demanded. "Why, we had our nooning right down yonder. We ain't come a half a mile. How come you want to stop?"

"Because we're going to get something settled before we move a step farther. Number one, either I'm in charge of this outfit or I'm not!"

"Then you're not," a couple of them said in harmony.

"If that's all you got on your mind, we'll put somebody else in charge," another said. "Now let's get movin'. We got ground to cover. You just lead."

"I'll be in charge," Lottie Camber decided. "Now let's everybody . . ."

"Who says you'll be in charge?" a woman nearby snapped. "Why, Lottie Camber, I recollect the time you was going to be in charge of the barn-raisin' for—"

"Let's have a meeting!" someone else interrupted. "We'll vote on it!"

"We can't stop to vote. We got ground to cover. What's this jasper stoppin' us here for?"

"Shut up!" Jake roared.

In the sudden silence, Annie's voice rose querulously, "Charlie, I don't think that's very polite, to—"

"I said shut up!"

"You want me to shoot him in the leg, Annie?"

"Shut up!"

About the time he figured he had their attention, there was an eruption of screeching, giggling children from the clustered vehicles and a tendril of smoke arose from the open bed of a haywagon. Old Mose Tuttle cursed in a high, whining voice and drew a bucket of water from one of the barrels lashed to a high-side, then hobbled across to slosh it into the burning wagon's bed. "You little varmints behave yourselves!" he shouted.

Some of the women broke ranks to corral their children, and Jake found himself facing a diminished crowd. "If you ladies want to go anyplace, the first thing that has to happen is, we have to get this caravan organized," he explained. "Now, do you want me to help, or not?"

"You said you would," Lottie Camber reminded him, sternly.

"Actually it was Miz Coke that said he would,"

165

Jessy Wheeler pointed out. "You ought to try to keep things like that straight, Lottie."

A pair of aging sisters with matching mother-of-pearl shawl clasps—Jake recognized them as the occupants of one of the morning's runaway surreys—marched purposefully out from the wagons to accost one of the women in the leadership delegation. "You ought to keep an eye on them children, Flossie," one of them said. "It was Elmer and Emory that tried to set fire to Janey's wagon yonder."

"What do you mean, organized?" Lottie Camber asked Jake.

"I mean organized so everybody has some notion of what everybody else is doing," he said slowly. "I mean organized so when we travel we all travel together and not scatter off in all directions like a bunch of goats that's got into a yodelberry patch. I mean organized so whoever's in charge is in charge and everybody else knows it. That's what I mean by organized."

"I got to admit, that's a good idea," Nora Bennett agreed.

"Sounds all right to me," Henrietta Price nodded. "Who *is* in charge?"

Lavinia Tuttle looked thoughtfully around. "I thought maybe Jessy Wheeler was, but if Lottie wants to . . ."

A pair of freckled youngsters crept past the fringes of the gathering, sighted in on Jake and, in unison, let fly a pair of dirt clods that smacked the sorrel glancing blows on its rump. The horse squealed, reared and danced, and Jake clung to his saddle.

"Now Elmer . . . Emory . . . that wasn't a nice thing to do," Flossie Todd scolded.

Jake had stood all he could stand. Bringing the

racer under control, he put heels to its flanks and spurred directly toward the mischief-makers. They stared in awe at the juggernaut coming at them, then turned as one and ran.

The tide of voices behind him rose—"Land a'mercy! . . . For pity's sakes . . . What in the world is he . . . Don't shoot him just yet, Holly Bee! . . ." but Jake ignored them all. Bent low over his saddlehorn, he reined the sorrel alongside the fleeing pair and leaned down to snag one and then the other, angry fingers hoisting them by their bib-straps to fling them across the horse's withers. He reined in, then, anchored them firmly in place and paddled their squirming bottoms with a callused hand. When he was satisfied that they wouldn't sit for a while he slid them to the ground—not gently—and pointed back toward the wagons. "Git!" he roared. They got.

It was a quieter crowd that he returned to face, and he wheeled to before them. "Well?" he demanded.

"I got an idea," Lottie Camber said in a small voice. "Why don't you be in charge, Mr. Jenkins?"

"Johnson," Annie Coke corrected. "I mean, Creedmore. How about it, Charlie? You want to be in charge?"

"I don't want to be here at all," Jake snorted. "But since I am, I'm in charge, and I want every last one of you to damn well . . . pardon, darn well remember it. Now, we camp right here for the night, and spend the time getting organized. One fire. One camp. No stragglers. And no changing your minds!"

He turned the horse and headed off for a private chat with himself. Behind him someone asked, "Who is that man, anyway?"

It took Jake a while to simmer down, and it didn't

167

help at all to review the series of circumstances that had led him here . . . a wanted man, with a price on his head, going the wrong direction in the wrong place, and somehow suddenly having responsibility for twenty-one women, sixteen children, four dray wagons, a horsecart, a haywagon, two surreys, a two-up carriage with a wobbly wheel, a buckboard and various livestock, not to mention a gimpy old man named Mose Tuttle. It helped a little to have the chance from time to time to look at Clara Hayes, whom he had never expected to see again and who had taken to toting an axe handle almost from the minute he showed up. And it helped just a bit that Coryanne O'Keefe, who shared a carriage with Amber Quinn and Ophelia Lashlee and the Lashlee girls, was well worth being looked at herself, and that Mabel Hornby had a way with biscuits.

If he hadn't made a promise to Harriett Fletcher, though, he decided he would just drift away right now and never look back . . . provided he could get a few miles behind him before Annie Coke got the notion to send Holly Bee out with her rifle to keep close herd on him. Come to that, he hadn't the slightest doubt that Conrad W. Jackson's sorrel could outrun Holly Bee's paint horse with ease. But that wasn't a pleasant idea. Jake felt he could live with the knowledge that he was an outlaw because of having robbed a bank, but it would be far more difficult to live with the notion of having escaped from a bunch of women by outrunning a honey-haired slip of a girl in a cross-country chase. Somehow, that just didn't fit Jake's picture of himself at all. On impulse, he hauled out Conrad W. Jackson's picture and gazed at the face that had started all his troubles.

"You'd do it, wouldn't you?" he said to the face. "You wouldn't give it a second thought, to break a promise to a lady sheriff, or to get loose from a responsibility by outrunning a girl, or probably ever even care what might happen to a bunch of rattle-brained females out on their lonesomes without a man to look out after them. You wouldn't give it a thought, would you, Conrad W. Jackson?"

The face in the picture stared back at him with the sour smugness of one who has just swallowed a toad.

"It's no wonder your hat never fit you right," Jake said caustically. "There isn't enough gumption in you to fill out a whole head. Had to pad the lining to wear it, didn't you? Just like this here picture is padded. Big, thick frame to mount a little picture of a little man."

Disgusted with his own pettiness, Jake thrust the painting away in his saddlebag. But the thought buzzed around him for a moment—why was that picture so thick? Felt like the whole back of it was padded with paper, just the way the inner lining on the man's silver-belly beaver hat had been when Jake first took it as partial payment on his lost money.

Movement in the distance westward drove away such notions. A mile away, or a little more, a rider was on the trail, coming toward him. And for an instant he had an impression there were two riders out there, one in plain sight in the distance, a second farther away and furtive. But when he shaded his eyes for a better look, there was only the one. The quartering sun must be playing tricks with his eyes, he decided.

The rider came on, dim against a lowering sun and banked clouds on the horizon that caught and

169

rebounded the sun's light. At a quarter mile distance, Jake thought it looked like someone familiar, but still couldn't make him out. Then the rider hesitated, stood tall in his stirrups, swept the tall hat off his head and executed a sweeping bow—or as near to it as a man on horseback might come.

And Jake recognized him. This world is getting smaller every day, he told himself, because yonder comes Tyrone Sneed, the thespian.

Chapter XVII

As shabby as ever, and with several days' growth of stubble murking the outlines of his mustache and goatee, Tyrone Sneed straddled an old horse with a steamer trunk strapped atop its rump, and seemed overjoyed to have discovered a familiar face . . . or any face, for that matter. But particularly Jake's.

"Ah, the redoubtable Mr. Jones!" he intoned. "Robin Hood of the ranging reaches, nemesis of the potentates of portation, benefactor of the ill-befallen . . ." his gaze went to the cluster of vehicles at the crest of the hill beyond Jake. ". . . ah, would those perchance be your merry men?"

"About the merriest you ever saw, if they're men." Jake studied him askance, recalling what Annie had said about thespians, wondering if maybe she had been righter than he thought. "What do you want, Sneed? What are you doing way out here? I thought you were on your way to Six Bit."

"The vagaries of vagabond rumor have played me afoul," Sneed gestured broadly, and Jake had fleeting impressions of people spreading falsehoods. " 'Twas my understanding that the fair city of Six Bit sported an opera house, and my intention was to

171

offer my services there for modest remuneration. Unfortunately, truth be known, the little hell-hole *operates* a *sporting house* and I became separated from my meager sustenance virtually within hours of my arrival."

"You lost your money?"

"In a manner of speaking, yes."

"Sorry about that. But how'd you get way off over here?"

"Fickle fate tempered by providence, as the Bard might have said. While quaffing a measure of recuperative ale to drown my sorrows, I seem to have drowned my faculties as well, at least temporarily, and I found myself the next morning bound for the metropolis of Buffalo Bone aboard a conveyance operated by the Transcontinent and Nacogdoches Railroad Company. Having no wherewithal to reimburse that railroad for my fare, I was given the opportunity to make repayment in kind."

"You went to work for them?"

"I cleaned stock cars all the way to San Galena. That is where I acquired this fine mount. Strangest country down there, there are saddle horses—with saddles—simply wandering around loose and waiting to be adopted. Then I came looking for you."

"For me?"

"Absolutely. While at San Galena I was privy to a conversation among gentlemen occupying a stable— several deputy marshals and quite a number of detained guests awaiting justice—in which you were described quite accurately and referred to by several different names. It became clear to me then that your path and mine were destined to cross again, so that I could offer you a splendid opportunity."

Jake just looked at the man, waiting.

172

"Mr. Jones," Sneed said, "I admire a man who saves and invests his money, no matter what his means of coming by it . . . which is to say, I hold not the slightest ill will for a professional train robber. Had I the talent for it, I might rob a few myself."

"Sneed, how did you happen to find out where I was?"

"Why, I stopped off at Limestone and a dear lady there was kind enough to buy me a glass of lemonade in return for an hour's pleasant conversation. Then she told me I might find you at Rossville, and set me on this path. But here you are! I believe that proves that we are destined for each other."

Jake backed his sorrel off a step, his eyes suspicious in the brim-shadow of Conrad W. Jackson's silver-belly beaver hat.

"Mr. Jones," Sneed explained, "I come to offer you the opportunity to invest in a road company production of King Lear."

As the sun sank beneath banked clouds in the west, while Tyrone Sneed strutted among the ladies, expounding bits of grandiloquent prose and helping himself to Mabel Hornby's biscuits, Jake counted things. Using the papered back of Conrad W. Jackson's picture as a pad and a sharpened bullet for a pencil, he counted wagons and buggies, horses and cows, supplies and gear. He made an inventory of the wagon party, listing everything from the names of all present to the condition of wheels and harness. Then he sat by the fire and reviewed his catalogue, trying for a reasonable estimate of how far this group was capable of traveling without coming to grief. The results were not reassuring. We'll be lucky, he told himself, if we make ten miles. Still, beneath the bickering and backstabbing that seemed to be the favorite group entertainment of his charges, he sensed an iron determination that they seemed to all share. Annie had voiced it, earlier. "Don't let these ladies' chatterin' fool you, Charlie," she said. "This ain't any lark with them. Their minds is made up, an' they intend to have their menfolks back if it hare-lips half of Texas."

He had suspected as much, but still it gnawed at him. "Why me, though?" he asked. "Why don't they just go ahead on their own . . . or get somebody to lead them who's *willing* to?"

"Because they trust you, Charlie," she said, simply.

The notion had set him back a smart step. "Me?" he gaped at her. "Why?"

"I'll be switched if I know," she admitted. "But they do. Just like that lady sheriff trusts you, an' I don't know why she does, either. Come to that, I ain't real sure why Holly Bee an' me trust you. But I reckon we do."

"I don't," Holly Bee pointed out. "Not for one minute." Her blue eyes glittering in the evening light, she glared at him. "And don't you get any notions about kissin' me, neither," she said. "I'll brain you quicker'n you can say scat."

"Don't get any . . ." he ran out of words, simply stared at her for a moment. "What makes you think I'd . . . ?"

"Word gets around," she said, archly. "Way I hear it is, you kissed that Miss Clara Hayes once and she clouted you with an axe handle."

Jake stared at her, dumbfounded, and Annie smiled a secret smile and rubbed her hands together.

174

"I hear tell that when you get gussed up an' go into town for a social, you get right frisky," Holly Bee expanded. "So I'm tellin' you, happen you get notional about me, I'll give you cause to regret it." She turned away, then turned back, anger blazing from her. "An' that goes for Clara Hayes, too . . . an' Coryanne O'Keefe, too. You just leave us alone, Clinton."

"Clifton," Annie corrected. "But his name's Jake, ain't it, Charlie?"

Jake didn't answer. He was watching the angry backside of Holly Bee Sutherland stalking off across the wagon camp. He was wondering how she would look in a dress.

"Oh, my, this is goin' along just fine," Annie said smugly. "I believe that's the first time that gal has said two words straight at you since the day we all met." She straightened, then, and cast him a knowing glance. "You mind what she says, though, Charlie. Don't you go to kissin' on that gal right yet, 'cause you got other things to do right now an' no time for lollygaggin'."

So Jake busied himself with the counting of folks and things and set his mind to how to organize a wagon train from the raw materials listed on the back of Conrad W. Jackson's painting. It wasn't going to be easy.

He made the rounds once more, pausing to have a word with Mose Tuttle, then completed his count of water barrels and leaned against the rear wheel of the Wilkinson, Stuckey and Todd wagon to review his notes. He appended a note about a leaky keg at the bottom of his repairs-to-be-made list, then scanned upward, taking things item by item: list of tarps and wagon-covers which could provide shelter;

175

list of food supplies (they were going to have to do some foraging, he could see); list of two milk cows and who must milk them; list of draft and riding stock (at least, all the animals seemed to be in fair condition); list of conveyances—two medium wagons with double-hitch, one tandem carriage, one buckboard with slats, one light wagon, one haywagon, one horse-drawn cart, two surreys, one slab-side wagon, single hitch, two dark, questioning eyes the color of oak bark in the evening . . . he blinked.

Clara Hayes stood before him, gazing at the painting in his hands. "That is Conrad W. Jackson," she said. "Why do you have Conrad W. Jackson's picture?"

He pulled off his hat. Conrad W. Jackson's hat. "It's a sort of souvenir, Miss Clara," he said lamely. "I keep it in fond remembrance of the gentleman, and because I might need something to wipe my boots on one of these days. It surely is a pleasure to see you again, Miss Clara. I really didn't have a chance to tell you back there . . ."

"I just can't imagine you robbing Conrad W. Jackson's bank," she said. "Couldn't believe my ears when I heard about that."

"How *did* you happen to hear about that, Miss Clara?"

"Word gets around. And now you are a notorious outlaw, with people chasing around trying to collect rewards on you. I just can't for the life of me understand . . ."

"It just sort of happened," he said. "One thing led to another, and . . ."

"I don't mean that. I mean, I can't understand why a man on the run would hire on to guide a wagon party."

176

"I don't seem to have ever had a chance to not do that," he shook his head. "I'm not just real sure how that came about, but at least there's one nice surprise that came of it. Seeing you again is . . ."

"I hope you'll take note that I am carrying an axe handle," she pointed out.

"Yes, Ma'am, that's hard not to notice. A thing like that can bring back memories . . ."

"Beg pardon!" Ima Lou Stuckey and Flossie Todd strode between them, heading for the back of the wagon. Ima Lou was leading her impish Paddy, who dragged his feet and stopped long enough to stick out his tongue at Jake. Flossie had Elmer and Emory, by the ears, one in each hand, guiding them along. At the rear of the wagon Ima Lou lowered the tailgate and hoisted Paddy into the bed. "Now you get your shoes off, you hear? And you roll up in that soogan yonder by the linen trunk, and get to sleep. And no nonsense!"

At Flossie's command Elmer and Emory climbed into the wagon bed and were given similar instructions. "Now you boys get to sleep," she told them. "And leave space for us an' Miz Wilkinson. Lord knows, we are all gonna have to sleep narrow for a spell."

They clapped the tailgate shut, said, "Evenin'," to Clara, glared suspiciously at Jake and went off toward the cookfire.

"I never thought you'd rob a bank, Jake Creedmore," Clara said. "All I ever thought you were good for was drillin' water wells."

"Well, I did that up brown, if I do say so myself," he admitted. "That was really where all my troubles started, you see . . ."

A shrill howl erupted from the canvas-covered

177

wagon at his back, followed by another, and the wagon began to rock from side to side, its spring-straps creaking. "Did too!" a child's voice raged. "Did not!" another chimed in. "Did too!" "Did not!" "Hit him a good lick!" "Ow!" "Get off, I want to sit on his head!" "You varmint!" "Ow!"

The wagon rocked and shuddered, and suddenly there was a grinding, splintering shriek and the wheel at Jake's back pitched outward, throwing him against Clara Hayes. He grabbed her, lifted her, jumped . . . and tripped. The heavy wagon groaned and collapsed behind them.

Jake whistled through his teeth, started to raise himself and ducked as an axe-handle whizzed past his head. Clara hissed, "Get off me, Jake Creedmore! How dare you . . ." She drew back to strike again and he pinned her arms. "Miss Clara, I'm not . . . that wagon . . ."

She twisted, trying to get her axe-handle into action, and they rolled completely over. There were voices all around: "Ah, the grand passions of youth . . ." that from Tyrone Sneed; "Charlie, you let that gal alone! Behave yourself, now . . ." Mose Tuttle's creaky voice, "Hee, hee! I recollect when . . ." "Mose, you shut your mouth!" "What is that man doing to Clara?" "Who *is* that man, any-way . . . ?"

Something hard collided with the back of Jake's skull and he went limp, his face falling into the thick, dark hair of Clara Hayes, his lips just at her ear. But he was in no condition just then to appreciate such comforts.

Clara Hayes dragged herself from beneath the inert man and scrambled up, smoothing her skirts around her. Mose Tuttle leaned down to peer at

Jake. "He ain't dead, is he?"

"He ain't dead," Holly Bee said. "All I did was thunk him a little bit."

"Well, I hope you didn't thunk him too hard," Annie Coke said. "There's a wagon that's got to be fixed before mornin', an' fixin' wagons is man's work. Ladies is too delicate for that."

In the dim hush before dawn, Coryanne O'Keefe awakened from dreams that excited and disturbed her—dreams of a tall, handsome young man in a white hat, a man whose dark eyes held roaring passions hidden and barely in check . . . a man who could ride down and paddle errant youngsters, then in a voice of angry thunder take charge of everyone around . . . a man who, while wagons and things collapsed around him, threw himself into the abandonment of passion with the nearest available female . . . a female who, in her dreams, sometimes was herself. She awoke trembling and flushed, and couldn't go back to sleep.

Quietly, not to disturb the others sleeping around her—her sister Amber, snoring slightly, her round belly a mound beneath her blanket, and Ophelia Lashlee and her little girls, Sue and Sally—she folded her bedding and dressed herself, then stepped out into the cool hush of gray dawn. Coryanne strolled around for a bit, enjoying the cool and the quiet, then gravitated to a vantage point from which she could see across the little jumbled circle of wagons. Just there, small metallic sounds emanated from where lanterns lit a circle of ground, and her breath caught in her throat. He was there, the stranger. Stripped to the waist in lantern light, he

179

was fitting a wheel into place on Maude Wilkinson's old wagon. There were others there, too—the tall-hatted actor, Tyrone Sneed, sitting with his back propped against a front wheel, and old man Tuttle—Callie Smith's father—curled up on the hard ground. Both of them were asleep. But the young man worked rhythmically in the lantern light, fitting a reinforced wheel onto a rebuilt hub, pushing this way and that to get it into place on an axle held up by a wagonjack.

Still feeling the disturbing, delicious effects of her dreams, Coryanne crouched in shadows and watched for a time, then climbed up on the high side of Ophelia's carriage for a better look.

Until Clara Hayes came from the territories to visit with her aunt Jessy Wheeler, Coryanne had been the only single woman in Rossville—of an age for suitors, but unlikely to attract any in a place where all the men were gone. Now, with Clara Hayes and the newcomer, Holly Bee—Coryanne wished she had hair like Holly Bee's—there were three of them in the group, and they had shared some interesting conversation. All of which, along with the abrupt events of the past evening, had contributed to disturbing her dreams.

From the top of the carriage, she could see better. He had the wheel in place, and was setting pins or bolts to keep it there. Lantern-light gleamed on the sweat-slick contours of his back, shadowing the lean, rolling muscles of his shoulders and arms. Coryanne watched in fascination, then looked away, her eyes adjusting to the dim, growing light of dawn on the prairie.

She looked around, leisurely, then frowned and squinted. There was a horse out there. Just past a

180

little rise, a saddled horse, its silhouette clear against the pale grass slope beyond it.

Why was it out there? She glanced toward the rope corral on the other side. All the rest of the stock seemed to be contained. How had that horse got loose? And why was it wearing its saddle?

With a shrug, she climbed down and went to get it.

Sore-headed and grumpy, Jake had worked half the night to fix the wheel on the Wilkinson, Stuckey and Todd wagon. Tyrone Sneed and Mose Tuttle had both come out to offer to help, then had both gone to sleep, so he had worked alone, accompanied only by occasional complaints from inside when he jarred the wagon or made too much noise.

The wagon's hub had splintered, and he had no choice but to make a new one. It had taken hours. But now, with the first touch of dawn, it was finished and he worked the wheel into place, pinned the fresh hub and let down the wagon jack — slowly, so as to arouse no further complaint from the ladies sleeping inside.

With the wagon once again standing on its four wheels, he drew the jack from beneath it, lifted it and looked around, trying to remember which wagon he had borrowed it from. His mind was made up. He had a fierce headache, he was tired and sore, and he was going to get some sleep and it didn't matter a whit what these women wanted him to do. Whatever it was, it could wait.

He started toward the Tuttle wagon, where the jack belonged, and suddenly there were scuffling steps behind him and the unmistakable cold muzzle of a gun was thrust against his back.

"Raise your hands, Clive Wilson Jones," a familiar voice said. "I've got you dead to rights."

Chapter XVIII

It didn't take long for word to spread around Big Spring that there was a search on for a bunch of missing railroad constructors. Men who had recently descended on Rossville to look into the rumors of loose women there now descended upon Big Spring to spread word of the sad plight of a band of brave ladies whose cherished husbands, fathers, brothers and neighbors were unaccountably missing. From eating house to boarding house, from saloon to blacksmith's to farrier's shop, the questions were passed. Who was building a mainline railroad? Where were they building it? How was it being financed?

And what would be the best way to get in on the profits?

Chivalry was important in Texas, and many a man doffed his hat and went watery-eyed at the tale of those poor, courageous ladies set out cross-country in search of their men. But first things first, and men who hadn't given serious thought to much of anything since the bad times set in now found their minds turning to questions of their own: What was the chance a man could buy a piece of wasteland out yonder somewhere in time to charge the railroad ten times its worth for a right-of-way across it? Who would get the contract on cutting ties? On hauling rail? On terrorizing landowners who tried to highjack right-of-way prices? What were a man's chances of getting in as an investor in the profit-sharing trust? Or getting pre-development prices on preferred stock? Of getting work on the line itself? Of getting a mail contract?

And with the influx of strangers in town, nobody much noticed the six large, quiet men who wandered about here and there, never seeming to listen to the questions but always happening to be within earshot of the answers.

"I ain't heard about any railroad," a bartender shrugged. "Y'all might ask somebody over at the Great Central and Pacific Investment Company. They been gettin' a lot of mail lately, maybe they heard about it."

"Recollect several wagonloads of folks rollin' out of here one night, few months back," a lounger in front of the smithy said. "Never heard where they was goin', but they had picks an' spades an' like that." He paused, remembering. "Recollect it, 'cause Dos Burton was ridin' along with 'em, him an' them toughs he keeps around. Don't see ol' Dos around here much these days."

"Rossville?" a barber scratched his head. "Sure, my wife's sister's husband has a cousin that used to live up there, but seems to me like he found work someplace an' hauled out. He used to be a trestle-builder back when the carpetbaggers was puttin' in stub lines all over hell's half acre. Don't know what he's doin' now, though. Seems like Fannie said he went west."

184

"Don't seem right to me that a local bank would be loanin' money on town lots way out in the territories," a merchant sniffed. "I know for a fact they did that, an' I ain't too happy about it, 'cause they sure wouldn't loan *me* any."

Royal Flanders sat in a dark corner of a dim saloon, drinking lemonade—he had become fond of lemonade—and listened to the reports as they came back. He had heard of the Burton brothers years back. Couple of hell-raisers who had turned respectable if not honest, and now the rumor was they were on their way to getting rich through an investment company. The Great Central and Pacific Investment Company of Big Spring. The happy light of coincidence danced in his dark eyes, redoubling when he heard about the complaint of a townswoman talking to a clerk at the morning market. Her husband, it seemed, had been sent off westward to try to market titles to a bunch of town properties that the bank had taken as collateral on a loan to Uno Burton. She didn't know when he would be back, or what she would do if it rained before he returned, because he hadn't finished fixing the roof. Seemed to her, she said, that if Uno Burton wanted to sell the town of Perdition, he ought to just do it himself and not go slipping around using the bank as cover for his transactions and causing Alex to be away when he ought to be home patching roofs.

"We may have a line on something real good, here, boys," Flanders told his men. "Let's listen around some more and see if the name Conrad W. Jackson pops up."

"Sure," one of them said. "But what about that

Creedmore jasper that we came to get?"

"We can pick him up anytime," Flanders said. "He won't be hard to find."

"It's another one," Philo Henderson turned mystified eyes on his wife. "Nearly nine hundred dollars this time, from a bunch of cowboys over in Texas somewhere. With a message. Says Mr. Jenkins recommended me."

"Who is Mr. Jenkins?" Phyllis asked, just as mystified.

"I haven't the vaguest idea, any more than who 'Mr. Johnson' is that recommended me to that last group. Phyllis, this makes nearly two thousand dollars that's come just in the past few days. What should I do?"

She shrugged. "Invest it for them, I suppose. That's what they want."

"Does it seem a little strange to you that all of a sudden people I never heard of are asking me to be their investment broker? When I've never been an investment broker?"

"Not necessarily, Philo. You know how word gets around. You've done all right with your investments. I guess people hear about that and want you to do the same for them."

"All I did was make a little money on that hot air balloon business. I don't see how any of these people could know about that."

"Maybe that bank over at Big Spring told them about you . . . the one that keeps sending you fliers on stock options."

"Maybe so," Philo shrugged. "What should I do

186

with all this?"

Phyllis thought it over. "What are you going to do with Jake's money?"

"I don't know. I just figure something good will turn up. I've been asking around."

"Well," she said, "it seems to me whatever is good enough for Jake ought to be good enough for these people. When you find something to buy for him, just buy some more of it for them."

The wagonjack weighed a little over forty pounds, and when Jake raised his hands the jack did the inevitable thing. It arced over his head and fell directly behind him. He heard a thump, a whoosh of expelled breath, a thud and a groan. He turned, kicked away a pistol that had fallen to the ground, then squatted on his heels before the mouse-faced bounty hunter who sat spread-legged, cradling the wagonjack in both arms. "I wish you'd quit poking me with your gun," he said. "Don't you have anything better to do?"

"You can't get away from me, Jones," Bead sputtered. "I got you dead to rights. Bounty is my business."

"I don't know how many times I have to tell you, my name isn't Jones. Now how'd you get here?"

"I followed that actor. I figured you two was in cahoots, and I was right. What is this thing, anyway?"

"It's a wagonjack. I was fixing to put it back where it belongs. But then you went to sticking your gun in my back again. When are you going to stop that?"

There were questioning voices here and there, among the wagons, then Annie Coke came hurrying up to them, resplendent in red flannel nightgown, hat and boots and shotgun. She gaped at the man on the ground. "Why, land sakes! Is that you again, Mr. Bead?"

Bead tried to tip his hat but gave it up when the wagonjack dug painfully into his abdomen. "Ma'am," he said. He set the jack aside and clambered to his feet, peering around in the uncertain dawn-light. "You might as well just give up, Jones," he said. "I've got you this time. Where's my gun?"

Beside the wagon wheel Tyrone Sneed snorted, came awake, rubbed his eyes and gawked around him at the various women out and running around in their night clothes. He stood, removed his hat, licked down his mustaches, and put on his best smile for one and all, then noticed Bead and hunkered low for a good look at the visible portions of his face. Bead's nose, prominent and seeming to support the brim of his hat, had gone red. His whiskers twitched this way and that. "Did you take my gun?" he demanded of Jake. "Give it back!"

"I don't have your gun," Jake said. "You dropped it."

"I know I dropped it, but it isn't here now. Where is it?"

Coryanne O'Keefe entered the camp, leading a saddled horse. Annie Coke went over to look at it and Maude Wilkinson climbed out of her wagon followed by Ima Lou Stuckey, Flossie Todd and three young boys. Maude examined the repaired wheel on her wagon and straightened. "My, but you done a fine job on this. Who's that?"

188

"His name is Bead," Jake said. "He's a bounty hunter."

"Lookin' for somebody small, is he?"

"No, Ma'am, he's looking for his gun. He dropped it and now he can't find it."

Helpfully, several of them started looking for Bead's gun while Tyrone Sneed followed various of them around, looking at them.

"This isn't one of our horses," Annie called from across the way. "Ask Mr. Bead if this is his horse."

Bead looked up. "That's my horse, all right. What's it doing here?"

"Didn't you bring it with you?" someone asked.

Jake sighed. "Bead, I sure wish you'd quit this nonsense. You're after the wrong man."

"I know who I'm after," Bead snorted, stooping to look under a wagon. "And I've got you dead to rights, too. Where in blazes did my gun get off to?"

"I got one I can let you use, if you need it," Mose Tuttle offered. "Even sell it to you, for a fair price."

"He'd just lose it," Jake said, but Mose had already gone to get his gun. Bead expanded his search, looking under neighboring wagons.

Jake followed along. "Bead, have you ever seen this Clive Wilson Jones you're so hot to catch?"

"You know damn well I have," Bead looked around. "We were on the same train from Rosebud halfway to Six Bit."

"That was me you saw," Jake explained.

"I know it was you! I got eyes." He stood, glaring around at the crowd. "Somebody took my gun. I want it back. Who's got it?"

No one answered, but Mose Tuttle came back

just then, peering down the muzzle of an ancient Colt Dragoon. "There's some mud in here," he said. "Hold on a minute." He pointed it into the air and touched it off. Its roar was deafening. "There, now." He looked into it again. "That reamed 'er out."

Just beyond him Bead's horse reared, whinnied, thundered off between wagons and set a course south. "That was my horse!" Bead shouted.

"We ain't doubtin' that, Mister," Jessy Wheeler assured him. "Man says a horse is his horse, most of us will take his word on it."

Mose Tuttle extended his gun. "You want this or not?"

Jake stepped to him and took it, handing it over to Lavinia Tuttle. "Take this and put it away, Ma'am. We won't be needing it."

Bead was already running for the gap between wagons where his horse had gone. "I'll be back for you, Jones!" he shouted over his shoulder. "I'll be back, you just wait and see. Bounty is my business!"

Janey McCoy and Henrietta Price had just come from their bunks in Janey's haywagon. "Who was that?" Janey asked.

"That was a professional bounty hunter," Annie Coke said. "His name's Bead."

"Who is he looking for?" Henrietta wondered.

"Right now he's looking for his horse, and it's on its way to Big Spring."

Mose Tuttle was squatting beside the abandoned wagonjack, examining it. "This looks a whole lot like mine," he said to nobody in particular.

The sun was high when everyone finished breakfast, and Jake changed his mind about taking a nap. A cold wash in the creek, followed by a morning shave during which he had caught glimpses of several pairs of pretty eyes watching him—he didn't know which were more interesting, the smoke-dark eyes of Clara Hayes, the gold-flecked brown eyes of Coryanne O'Keefe or the suspicious blue eyes of Holly Bee Sutherland—had helped. Then getting his belly full of Mabel Hornby's biscuits and Sedonia Mills' crisp fried bacon, topped off with a mug of Fredonia Whisenhunt's blackstrap coffee, had made a new man of him.

"Time to move out," he told them, starting toward the rope corral but veering aside to haul Tyrone Sneed out of cozy conversation with some of the younger women. "You'd best behave yourself," he told the man. "Those women have husbands, you know."

"Not right now, they don't," Sneed put on an injured look. "Abandoned! They stand abandoned as prairie flowers deserted by the sun! A measure of solace, a word of reassurance, a modicum of charm to fill the awful void of the bereft . . . it's the very least I can do, I think."

"One modicum too many and you'll have some jealous husbands to contend with," Jake warned him. "When we find them." He glanced around at the women and children packing their wagons for travel. "I believe the real least you can do is get busy and help some of these ladies hitch their teams."

At the rope corral he saw Holly Bee, her paint horse already saddled and packed, swinging aboard. Long-legged and lithe, and without the bother of skirts to hinder her, she forked the animal as natu-

191

rally as any man, and thrust her rifle into its saddle-sleeve. At sight of him, she reined away, looking back at him, alert and suspicious. He shrugged and went to his packs, dug through them, then stood and looked around the camp. His painting of Conrad W. Jackson was not there, and for a moment he couldn't think when he had last seen it. Then he recalled having it in his hand when the Wilkinson, Stuckey and Todd wagon collapsed. He walked back across and looked around. The painting was nowhere in sight.

Clara Hayes came around the tailgate of the next wagon, her arms full of bedding. Jake pulled off his hat. "Miss Clara, I wonder if . . ."

She looked up, saw him and stopped, then stepped back warily. "You let me alone, Jake Creedmore! You just stay away from me now."

"Yes, Ma'am. I was just wondering if you'd seen . . ."

"You should learn to control yourself."

"Yes, Ma'am. I'll try. I was just looking for Conrad W. Jackson's picture. I lost it somewhere."

"Well, I don't have it." She started around him, then stopped as a thought crossed her mind. "That Holly Bee Sutherland . . . what is she to you?"

"N . . . nothing. Not that I know of. She just showed up with Annie Coke."

"Well, she thunked you like she knew you."

"That was all a misunderstanding, Miss Clara. You see, this wagon wheel popped off its spindle and . . . well, things got a little confused. That's all."

"How come she wears pants?"

"I don't know. You might ask her."

"I'm asking you. The way Annie Coke acts, you

192

and Miss Sutherland are . . ."

"Well, we aren't."

"Nobody likes a womanizer, Mr. Creedmore. Especially women."

"Miss Clara, I am not a . . ."

"You couldn't prove it by me. Mercy!" She scorched him with a final look, then headed wide around him and went on her way. Jake stared at her departing form, then started to put on his hat and jumped when another voice, right beside him, startled him.

"Told you off pretty good, didn't she?"

It was Clara's aunt, Jessy Wheeler. Jake pulled off his hat again.

"Sweet thing's always had a way with words," she told him, looking him up and down the way a buyer judges a beef. "Been wonderin' what Jake Creedmore looked like. You're the one that brought in the water out in that hell-hole, right?"

"I got a good well," Jake admitted. "But I had to give it up. Conrad W. Jackson wanted it."

"Conrad W. Jackson's a varmint," she said. "Met him when I was out yonder last time. Man looks like he'd eat toads. Understand you robbed his bank, too. What for?"

"Two thousand, three hundred and fifty one dollars. That, throw in a hat and a horse, kind of broke us even on the place he wanted back."

"Well, you got gumption," she decided. "Not a whole lot of sense, maybe, but gumption. What did you do with the money?"

Jake felt he was being grilled, and wondered why. "I left it with Philo Henderson to reinvest."

"Stocks and bonds?"

"I favor real estate, generally."

"Good thinkin'. Acreage or town lots?"

"Well, acreage is really what I had in mind, but whatever Philo comes up with will do."

"Don't overlook town lots," she advised. "Man ought to get a lot while he's young."

"Yes, Ma'am."

"Far as I can see, you're all right," she decided, still studying him. "No great shakes, but all right."

Jake didn't know what this was all about, but he'd had about enough of it. He wondered where Conrad W. Jackson's picture was. It had his travel roster written on the back. "I always thought I'd do, Ma'am," he told the older woman. "I'm not rich, but I'm handsome."

She put a thoughtful hand to her chin, looking at him more closely. "No," she said, finally, "that's not the word that comes to mind. Matter of fact, I don't quite see what Clara sees in you. But you're all right, I guess."

Still wondering what that was all about, Jake went back to saddle his horse and found it already saddled. Coryanne O'Keefe stood holding its reins, smiling shyly at him. "I thought I'd saddle your horse for you, Mr. Creedmore," she said. "You got a lot on your mind, so it's the least a body can do."

Flustered, he swept off his hat again. "Well, thank you, Miss. That's neighborly."

"Oh, it was fun," she said. "I never saddled a horse before."

Before he could respond, a shadow fell across him and he turned to find Holly Bee looking down at him from her paint, her expression ominous. "You behave yourself, you hear?" she said.

"Holly Bee, do you know where my painting is? I can't find it."

"Not your painting. It's that bilious man's painting. But Annie's got it. She picked it up last night when you left it lyin' around."

"Well, then, where's Annie?"

"Big Spring. She said go on along an' she'll be back directly."

"Why did she go to Big Spring?"

"Didn't say. But she said for me to stay and keep an eye on you, so that's what I'll do. You just behave yourself."

With a warning glance that took in both Jake and Coryanne, she heeled her paint and rode off, sitting straight and imperious atop her horse.

"Thank you for saddling my horse, anyway," Jake told Coryanne, blinking at the light from her big brown eyes. He put on his hat, stepped to his stirrup and swung . . . down, around and under. Abruptly he was on the ground, among the sorrel's feet with fifty pounds of saddle and gear atop him. Only then did he recall that Coryanne had never saddled a horse before.

Chapter XIX

Annie Coke wasn't sure what the papers were that had been hidden inside the back wrapping of Jake Creedmore's picture of Conrad W. Jackson, but there were a lot of them, all neatly stacked and bound, and printed in fancy letters with green and red scroll borders. She tried to read one or two of them, but even the words that had letters she could decipher were mostly words that she couldn't pronounce.

Two things she was sure of, though: they were important and they looked like trouble.

In her time, Annie had seen other papers printed so fancy that a body couldn't make out what they said, and they had always been trouble. Eviction notices sometimes looked like that, and services of foreclosure. Past-due tax notices, federal marshals' arrest warrants, impoundment orders and death certificates, Annie had seen them all at one time or another, and a cold sense of impending doom swept over her when she found these in the back of the painting. She had become fond of the young man who insisted that he was Jake Creedmore. More than fond, she had a lot of time and effort invested in him and the notion of his being swept away to

196

oblivion on a tide of evil papers didn't set well with her at all.

She hardly slept all night, for worrying. She thought about getting some of the ladies to look at the papers and figure out just what they portended, but she decided that might be the worst thing she could do, because whatever evils were lurking ahead of Jake Creedmore, everybody in the group would know about them. By the same token she didn't want to ask Jake about them, because she was certain he didn't know he had them and Annie was of the conviction that what a man didn't know wouldn't hurt him.

So she lay awake through a long night, worrying, then decided the best thing to do was to find a disinterested party to tell her what the ominous papers were. At first light, she saddled her horse, strapped the painting into one saddlebag and the fancy papers into the other, and headed south toward the nearest town where Jake Creedmore might not be known. And that was Big Spring. Annie had never been to Big Spring, but she knew where it was, and from having listened to the men who came to Rossville looking for loose ladies, she had the impression that Big Spring was just full of people who knew what important papers meant.

It was past noon when she came to the town, and she was a little disappointed. From what she had heard, she expected Big Spring to be big. It wasn't big, maybe two or three times the size of Limestone, and it wasn't especially impressive. It was just a town.

Still, there were plenty of people in the town, and

she was sure somebody could help her. She rode slowly along the main street, identifying buildings and offices. At the end of the street was what might be a courthouse, but she didn't want to go there. Annie had seen some courthouses. Nothing good ever came from courthouses. The same applied to marshal's offices, of which there was one two doors down from the bank and across the street from something called G.C.&P. Investments. Annie decided to try the post office, next to the bank. She hitched her horse, slung her saddlebags over her shoulder and went inside, then stopped with a frown. The place was full of people, all waiting in line to get to the counter, and there wasn't anyone visible at the counter.

"Ain't this a sight?" a man commented casually. "Gets like this every Tuesday, when the mail's in." He glanced at her shotgun. " 'Course, if you're here to rob the bank, Ma'am, you come in the wrong place. Bank's next door." He grinned, as one who suddenly feels the need to make sure someone knows he's joking.

"I just come in to get some information," she told him. "Don't anybody work here?"

"Clerk's back in the back, someplace. But if all you want's information, you'll have a long wait here."

Annie had decided the same thing. She left the post office, stood on the walk for a minute, looking at the other buildings, then went into the bank. It was busy there, too, but at least there were people at the tellers' windows, waiting on the people in line. She found a bench and sat down to wait. After a while the door opened and the same man she had talked to in the post office entered.

He went to the railed enclosure where bank officers worked and asked someone something, then turned away, frowning. Glancing across the lobby he saw Annie and his eyes widened slightly. He walked across and tipped his hat. "I hope I didn't give you any notions about robbing the bank," he said.

"I'm just waitin' 'til there's somebody I can talk to," she said.

"Me, too," he told her, and sat beside her. "Generally I make my deliveries to Mr. Hamilton, but come to find out he's out of town. I'll have to wait for somebody else."

"What do you deliver?"

"Securities, mostly. Sometimes title deeds and like that. I work for G.C.&P. We do a lot of business with this bank." As he spoke, he folded out a sheaf of papers, illustrating what he delivered. Annie stared at them. Mostly they were fine-printed papers with scroll borders of various kinds. And the gentleman seemed to be familiar with what they were.

She pulled out her own parcel. "I come in to find out about these here," she told him. "Maybe you can tell me, Mr. . . . ah . . ."

"Short," he nodded. "Wilbur Short."

"Annie Coke," she said. "Howdy." She unwrapped the sheaf of printed papers on her lap. A man sitting on the next bench — a big, stone-faced man with gun bulges under his dark coat — raised a brow as he glanced at them. Wilbur Short looked them over and his eyes went wide. "Hoo-ee," he said.

"Ma'am, I sure do know what those are. Those are primary securities of a capital stock issue." He looked closer. "Well, my land! That's G.C.&P. special issue. Preferred stock. I didn't think there were any more of those around. Only ones I ever saw are some that Mr. Burton has, he's the principal partner in G.C.&P., you know . . . an' some that Mr. Jackson got one time out at Perdition. Where in the world did you get all these, Ma'am? I bet ever Mr. Burton don't know there's this much special project stock out loose."

"They aren't mine," Annie admitted. "They belong to Jake Creedmore."

The big, dark man's eyebrows rose slightly and Wilbur Short looked as though he were about to drop his teeth. "Jake Creedmore? *The* Jake Creedmore?"

"Only one I know," Annie said. "He says that's what his name is." Disturbed at the unexpected reaction, she gathered up the papers and slipped them back into her saddlebag, then put her foot on it.

"Well, my land," Wilbur Short said. "Jake Creedmore. I ain't seen him since the day he left Perdition. He robbed the bank, you know. Didn't take any more than what was due him, but he did rob it, sure enough. I know because I was the one that got robbed. Jake Creedmore. Land sakes, I figured he'd be out of the country by now, or in jail. Fine young feller most ways, but I never felt right about him robbin' Mr. Jackson's bank. Took his horse an' his hat, too. An' a paintin' that Mr. Jackson put stock in. My land! Ol' Jake must be doin' just fine,

200

if he's accumulated all this just from that two thousand, three hundred an' fifty-one dollars he got from the bank. Lordy, I guess he's a major stockholder in the special project now."

"He's doing all right," Annie nodded. "He believes in investin' his money. Heard him say so, many's the time."

"Well, I hope he's got those stocks certified," Wilbur said. "Has he done that? Sometimes folks don't know to do that."

"How does a body do that?"

"Well, you see, all those certificates say is what they are and what number each of them is in the security issue. Trouble is, if they aren't certified an' a person loses them, then they just wind up belongin' to whoever finds them. Let me see one of those again."

Annie pulled out a single sheet. Wilbur turned it over and frowned. "That's what I was afraid of. Jake must have never got around to that. But any bank can certify a body's stock, as long as it don't belong to the bank itself."

"Can anybody do that for him? I don't know when he's goin' to have a chance to do any bank business."

Wilbur grinned. "I hope he never does any more like he done before. Told him at the time he hadn't ought to rob that bank. Things like that can lead to a life of crime." He rubbed his head thoughtfully. "Seems to me like, with both of us to vouch for ol' Jake, an' both of us know him personal, this bank right here ought to certify his stocks for him. Far as that goes, they can be put in safe deposit, so they don't even have to be carried around." His gaze fell on the un-stood-on side of Annie's saddlebags, where a corner of the painting showed. He grinned and pointed. "I bet I know what that is!"

"It's a painting of Conrad W. Jackson," Annie said. She hauled it out so he could see it.

"As ever was," Wilbur beamed. "My, but don't that look just like Mr. Jackson. Looks like he just et a toad. I'm proud Jake hung onto this and didn't throw it away. Mr. Jackson paid a Frenchman a hundred dollars to paint this for him. Can you imagine that?"

"No," Annie studied the picture. "For the life of me, I can't."

"Mighty fine likeness," the big, dark-coated man muttered.

Annie glanced up. "I reckon. You know Mr. Jackson, too?"

"It must look like the varmint," the man said, "because it sure doesn't look like anybody else that I ever saw."

"Jake took it to aggravate him," Wilbur said. "Figured that might help him get to heaven easier."

"Sounds to me like Conrad W. Jackson's a man can use all the help he can get in that department," Annie allowed.

"Might even deserve a boost," the big, dark man said, but this time he said it only to himself.

With Wilbur Short's help, Annie got Jake's "special project" stock certified and registered to Jake's name, and had it locked away in a vault. She asked

202

once or twice what "special project" meant, but no one seemed to know . . . except that the G.C.&P. company had issued the securities to raise money for a big project of some kind.

"Prob'ly tryin' to build a railroad somewhere," Wilbur suggested. "Nobody tells me anything, but that'd be my guess since it's a secret. What else would anybody try to keep secret?"

And that gave Annie some new things to think about, too. But she learned nothing more that day in Big Spring. If there was a railroad being built, nobody was talking about it.

When she mounted to leave, Wilbur Short came from the G.C.&P. place across the street to see her off. "You give ol' Jake my best when you see him, Ma'am," he said. "An' you tell him I surely got no hard feelin's about him robbin' the bank that time. He was right gentlemanly about it, in my view."

As she headed out, turning from the main street onto the side street that led to the trail northwest, a man stepped out of shadows in front of her and tipped his hat. At first she thought it was the same big, hard-faced man she had seen in the bank, but then she decided he wasn't . . . not the same one, just another one like him.

"Mr. Flanders asked me to head you off, Ma'am," he said politely, though she had the feeling—as with the other—that if he stopped being polite somebody had better light a shuck in a hurry. "He said you might want to know about the railroad trestle we saw the other day." He pulled a scrap of paper from a deep pocket and handed it up to her. "Fact is, he thought you just might want a map to show you

203

how to get there."

She took it and glanced at it. It was rough, but it looked like a useable map. "Who is Mr. Flanders?"

"Oh," the man grinned—a grin that on his face was even more ominous than the somber look it replaced, "he's just a man that likes to see things sort of come out even in the long run. And just lately he's taken to drinkin' lemonade."

The man thumbed his hat again, politely, and eased back out of her way. Annie rode on down the narrow little street, then glanced back when she heard a horse coming fast behind her. It was the little bounty hunter, Bead. Annie had been wondering whether he'd made it to Big Spring and whether he had found his gun in his saddlebag, where she'd put it. Apparently he had, because it was in his holster, and now there was a length of stout leather thong flapping beside him, one end attached to the gun, the other to his belt.

The street narrowed even more where a gristmill's loading chute stuck out across the walkway, its brace-poles thrusting out at an angle. Annie eased her mount over to let the other rider pass, and waved at him. He glanced at her, raised a hand to his hat, and his belt-thong looped around one of the chute braces. In an instant his gun drew itself, wedged itself into the angle between brace and chute, fired a charge upward through the mill's awning and took up the slack on Bead's thong. The little man seemed to hang suspended in midair for a moment, his legs still bowed around the belly of a horse that was no longer under him, his hand at his hatbrim in salute and his whiskers twitching beside

204

his nose. Gravity took over then, and he fell, swinging in a long arc beneath the sturdy bracing, a doubled-over pendulum suspended by a leather thong.

Annie, swivelled around in her saddle, stared back at the swinging, dangling man and shook her head. "I never," she muttered. "I declare."

Following the map that Annie had brought back from Big Spring, Jake swung the caravan south of west and had the feeling he was retracing his own steps. The route would cross midway between Limestone and San Galena, heading him right back the way he had come. "I don't have any intention of going back to the Territory," he said flatly. "I said I'd help these ladies find their menfolk and I will, up to a point. But that point is going to come soon. I'm a wanted man out there, remember? And by the way, what did you do to Conrad W. Jackson's picture? It's skinny all of a sudden."

"Back tore open," Annie said blandly. "But I fixed it, it just ain't padded as much."

She hadn't mentioned any of the transactions at Big Spring. She had thought about that, and decided it would keep. Since neither Jake nor Holly Bee had the slightest notion yet that they were going to get married, she didn't want to complicate things by having Jake start thinking that Holly Bee might be marrying him for his money.

"Far as goin' back to the Territory," she told him, "I don't believe that trestle that man said about is anywhere near the Territory. I don't expect it's much

205

past Rosebud."

At least, for Jake's peace of mind, there had been no further disasters with the wagons. No wheels had broken, no teams became tangled and the ladies of Rossville were conducting themselves with a certain degree of organization. The latter was a credit to Jake's planning. He had enlisted Tyrone Sneed—since the thespian seemed to have no intention of leaving just yet—to keep track of who was feuding with whom among the ladies, and give him reports at each stop. So far, it was working. At present he had Aunt Jessy Wheeler and Lottie Camber together in mid-train because they weren't speaking to each other today, while Janey McCoy and Nora Bennett, who were at the hair-pulling stage, were at opposite ends of the formation. This left him with only minor spats to cope with until the wagons stopped again to rest their stock.

At night camp the ladies without vehicles—Annie and Holly Bee, as well as Fredonia Whisenhunt who rode her husband's black horse—shared a tent, and an elaborate system of standing guard had worked itself out. Jake spread his soogans so as to keep an eye on the stock, and an eye on Tyrone Sneed to keep him away from the ladies. Jake didn't for a minute believe the actor's story about walking in his sleep. In turn, Holly Bee tended to stand guard over Jake on the theory that he must not be allowed to either run away or wander too near the night quarters of either Clara Hayes or Coryanne O'Keefe, Annie Coke kept an eye on Holly Bee because it was her duty, and the rest of the ladies took reluctant and highly-argued turns standing guard on the camp, the children, and their imagined personal territories.

All in all, it was working, and on the third day out they came in sight of a railroad.

"Maybe that's the one," Lottie Camber pointed. "But I don't see any trestle."

"No, Ma'am," Jake explained. "That yonder isn't a new railroad. It's an old one. It runs from San Galena to Limestone and its name is the Victoria, Waxahachie and Great Western. We have to cross two or three of these little stub lines before we get out where that trestle might be and see if your menfolks are there."

Approaching the railroad, they saw smoke to the south. It was Thursday, and a train was coming. A second train, pointed southward, sat immobile just ahead.

Chapter XX

With the repossession and subsequent transfer through the Big Spring bank of the properties he had financed in and around Perdition, Conrad W. Jackson recovered most of the money he had invested in prime issue shares of the Great Central and Pacific Railroad project — money that he had taken from his own bank after Jake Creedmore's robbery, blaming the entire loss on Creedmore.

And with funds at hand once more, he began buying land — various parcels along a line from the Texas border — abutting land there which his sources had confirmed was now owned by the Burton brothers — to Jake Creedmore's old place with its good well. Conrad W. Jackson intended to take no chances in dealing with the Burtons. When it came time for them to reveal their rail and their route, and thrust westward into the Territory, he intended for the land they needed to belong to him. And as a prime stockholder in the investment pool, he intended to dictate exactly where the line must run to reach the water-stop at the old Creedmore place. Generally, he felt, things were going well. He was in position now to dictate the route west from Texas, he would soon be in position to sell the land that route would follow, and he had already had the franchise for a townsite at the wellhead. The Burtons would howl and squirm when they realized they had been out-foxed in their own game of fox, but there wouldn't be much they could do to recoup. He congratulated himself on the best-laid scheme of his career, and counted his cards.

There was only one missing at the moment. He still hadn't heard anything from Royal Flanders about recovery of his painting . . . and the stock certificates it contained. That was worrisome, and would be until he had them back. None of the shares were certified to him, for the simple reason that if he had certified his ownership, the Burtons would have learned how much he owned.

But he had faith in Flanders and his outfit. They frightened him a bit—they frightened everyone, for that matter—but it was Royal Flanders' reputation and stock in trade that he had never in his career failed to recover that which he set out to recover. The man was a legend in the badlands. It was also Royal Flanders' claim, they said, that he had never done a dishonest job nor been involved in one. In a way, to Conrad W. Jackson, that part of it was comical. Men like that—they dealt with robbers and horse thieves and clear-cut, barbarian motives— what could they possibly know of the fineries and subtleties of stock manipulation and corporate piracy? When they brought in Jake Creedmore—or at least word of his death and the return of Jackson's stock shares—they would never doubt that, once again, they had operated on the side of the angels.

Simpletons, he told himself. Like almost everyone

he knew, in one degree or another, they were simpletons. The world was full of simpletons, and it would be a real waste of talent if there weren't a few Conrad W. Jacksons to profit from all that simplemindedness.

He regretted not yet having his stock in hand, but he had faith that he would have it when he needed it. And that wouldn't be far in the future. The Burtons over in Texas, he had decided, were also simpletons in their own way. Becoming respectable had destroyed their old devil-take-the-hindmost dash. Now they were a couple of penny-pinchers who might drag out a railroad project for years if they thought they could save a dollar here and there on right-of-way. But Conrad W. Jackson had his own ideas about that. He sat now in the sunlit interior of what had once been the Perdition bank, and gazed around him with satisfaction. Along one wall were large, fresh-painted signs ready to be posted, one on the front of his office, declaring *Clearwater Townsite Development Company, Conrad W. Jackson Prop., Choice Townsites Available, Commercial and Residential* . . . and below, in garish letters, *Clearwater, Central City on the Great Central and Pacific Railroad.*

And on the desk before him were final drafts of the advertisements he would soon be sending out to newspapers at San Antonio, Austin, Galveston, Forth Worth, Santa Fe and Big Spring. The advertisements said much the same thing as the signs, but in more detail. Conrad W. Jackson was preparing to go into the townsite business in a big way, and the Burtons would learn of it just like everyone else — when they read about it in the newspaper.

210

He glanced up as one of his crewmen rapped on the door and came in, pulling a folded paper from his coat pocket.

"Surveyor's out at the townsite, Boss," the man said. "But he says he can't start his survey until you give him the authorization for the easements. He wants you to sign this."

Jackson glanced at the document, then signed his name to it and handed it back, irritated. The damned surveyor would certainly charge him for the time he had sat there at the townsite, while a crewman rode all the way to Perdition and back to get a permit signed for him. He shoved the thought aside, though, still basking in the glow of how thoroughly he was outsmarting all the simpletons around him.

It wasn't until late that evening that he realized the surveyor had arrived a week ahead of schedule, and he didn't think much about it. The man had probably been in the area—maybe somewhere not too far away like Three Forks or Portales—and had been wired by his company.

At the townsite, meanwhile, the crewman had handed over the signed easement authorization to the surveyor, who looked at it, frowned and then looked again. "What is this name?" the man asked.

"Conrad W. Jackson. That's his own signature. I saw him sign it."

"I thought this land was owned by Jake Creedmore," the surveyor said.

"Naw, Creedmore used to have it, but Mr. Jackson owns it now. All this is his."

"Well, who's going to pay me?" the surveyor

wanted to know.

The crewman shrugged. "Conrad W. Jackson, who else? This is his land and that's his signature. What more do you need?"

"Nothing, I suppose," the surveyor said. "Nobody ever tells me anything." With his authorization stowed away, he set up his tools and went to work.

The little wood-stoker that ran from San Galena up to Limestone each Thursday was called the 4:20 in honor of the time of its arrival at Limestone on some long-ago day when somebody took a notion to call it something. It was one of two engines that ran this road, both on Thursdays. The Sunrise Special, the first one most Thursdays, was a market train that ran a circle each week, northbound from Abilene to Hobbs Corner, then west to Proxy where it switched onto the Victoria, Waxahachie and Great Western's stub track to run south through Limestone and San Galena down to Meridian, then to another short line circling back to Abilene. Generally it was off the Victoria, Waxahachie and Great Western tracks before the 4:20, coming from the west and its own weekly route, switched on northbound. Usually it worked that way.

In honor of those times when it didn't, there was a two-mile sidetrack midway between Limestone and San Galena to allow the two trains to pass. This was one of those Thursdays.

As Jake Creedmore's wagon convoy came down out of the hills to where they had a long view of the tracks, they saw a train sitting idle directly ahead of them—a southbound stopped to wait—while a mile or so south was the smoke plume of a train coming north.

Jake would have found it interesting to watch the trains pass, except that he had other things on his mind at the moment. Just in the past few minutes his carefully planned order of march had disintegrated. His wagon train had gone back to its old ways and was no longer a train, but just a mess of wagons and buggies veering here and there, all going more or less the same direction but with no semblance of order at all. And what had demolished its orderly progress was a simple thing. Amber Quinn, without so much as a by-your-leave, had gone into labor.

Now wagons, surreys, riders and carts zigzagged this way and that, often precariously, as women aboard various vehicles shouted suggestions, questions and related comments back and forth, their teams mostly ignored and selecting their own paths.

Jake's immediate reaction was to stop right where they were, see to the young pregnant woman's comfort, then get himself as far away as possible while the women tended to whatever needed to be done for a woman having a baby. But the women saw it differently. By what amounted to a rolling committee decision, they decided that Amber would last another mile or two and the place to stop was "them trees off yonder, where there's shade."

The shade was some distance ahead, well beyond the tracks of the Victoria, Waxahachie & Great Western Railroad. Outvoted and outranked in what Jake considered a moment of dire emergency—

though most of the women didn't seem too concerned about the fact that birth was fixing to happen right out here in front of God and everybody—he set his mind to getting them to that shade as rapidly and efficiently as possible. He had noticed from the outset of this trip that one of the women was obviously great with child, but the notion of the inevitable next step had never crossed his mind. Now that it did, he was near to panic. Jake didn't consider himself a finicky man, nor one to back down in the face of crisis. It was just that he suddenly realized he would rather wrestle a bear than be faced with the notion of a woman having a baby. Some mysteries were better just left alone.

With every rider in the party pressed into service to guide teams, he reorganized them after a fashion and headed for the railroad and the hills beyond. Gathering speed on easy ground, the convoy arrowed toward the waiting Sunrise Special, where curious faces lined the windows, and Jake guided them toward the front of the train, to go around. The train coming from the south was visible, but still distant, and he decided not to wait for it.

He was almost at the tracks when he saw that the only graded crossing was blocked by the engine sitting idle on the sidetrack. Elsewhere, as far as he could see north and south, the rails sat high atop bare ties. For wagons, the tracks were wheel-busters.

Jake, riding alongside the lead wagon, slewed its team to a halt and raised his arms, signalling those behind to stop. He peered southward, where the northbound train was still just a distant plume of dark smoke, then spurred the sorrel across the first tracks to the engine beyond. The engineer and fireman looked out at him from their cab.

"Howdy," Jake thumbed his hat. "Need to get you to move this train, if you don't mind. You got the grade blocked."

"We're waitin' for another train to pass," the engineer scowled at him. "We'll move when it's by."

"No," Jake said, "I want it moved now."

"Why would I move this train for you?"

"Because there's a woman in one of those wagons over there—that high-side carriage yonder is the one—that's just about to have a baby."

"Well, what difference does it make which side of the tracks she has it on?"

"It matters to all those ladies," Jake told him. "They don't want that baby to be born over here. They want it to be born over there. Besides that," he drew his Peacemaker and pointed it at the man's face, "if you don't move right now I'm probably going to shoot you."

"Well, why didn't you say so in the first place?" The engineer blinked at him. "Lord knows I'm a reasonable man."

"Then you just put on some steam and reason this train forward far enough for us to get those wagons across this grade."

"If you miss the varmint from there," Annie called from the assembled wagons, "Holly Bee can pick him off from here."

At sight of the drawn guns, most of the passengers lining the windows had raised their hands. Some of them began pulling out wallets and pocket watches.

The engine had been idling, just holding its pressure while it waited, and now clouds of steam hissed from gaskets as the engineer put it into motion. Jake rode alongside, keeping his gun pointed at the reasonable man, while Annie rode forward across the main tracks to cover the rest of the train with her shotgun. The train eased forward, lurched and eased again, and Jake looked back. At the grade crossing, Annie was still facing train cars. "Go on," he yelled at the engineer. "You've still got us blocked."

"I should have backed up," the man shouted back. "We're running out of sidetrack." Still, he kept it moving.

Jake looked back again and Annie waved, but he wasn't sure what she meant, so he urged them on again. By the time he was satisfied, the engine's wheels were poised over the switchpoints and its cowcatcher was jutting out across the mainline tracks. "I guess that's far enough," he told the engineer. "Now you just wait here while we get those wagons across."

"I can't just sit here like this," the man said. "You see yonder? That's the 4:20 coming. I'm blockin' his track!"

"Then tell him to stop," Jake suggested. "Because if you move before those ladies get their wagons across the grade, I'll come back up here and shoot you."

He headed back toward the crossing, ignoring the passengers at the windows who goggled at him as he passed. Behind the train, Tyrone Sneed and

Fredonia Whisenhunt were leading wagons across. Clara Hayes and Aunt Jessy Wheeler crossed with their buckboard, then Lottie Camber in her surrey and Sedonia Mills in her old phaeton, holding baby Hope on her lap while her other three gawked at the train.

At the rail switch, the Sunrise Special's whistle was howling mournfully, and in the distance the 4:20 responded, short blasts that sounded like engine talk for "get the hell out of my way."

The Tuttle wagon with its two-up hitch crossed sedately, old man Tuttle shouting his ire at the errant train while Callie Tuttle Smith drove. Then Mabel Hornby's light wagon with Bubba, Willie and Aristotle hanging out over the tailgate. Nora Bennett's cart was next, with Ferdinand and Matilda bouncing up and down as the rails jolted its hard axles, and Janey McCoy's haywagon followed, children's faces peering through its slats. The sisters Pleasant and Serenity Higgins, both staring straight ahead with the prim expressions of deaconesses on their way to church, wheeled their surrey over, and Maude Wilkinson came behind, hauling reins while Ima Lou Stuckey and Flossie Todd gave her overlapping instructions. In the bed behind them, Elmer and Emory Todd and Paddy Stuckey chunked dirt clods at the rear of the train.

"Come on!" Jake shouted. "Get that last one across! She isn't having it yet, is she?"

Beside the final carriage, Annie looked around at him with worry on her face. "We might have misjudged, Charlie," she said.

"Well, come one! Get moving! You all said you

217

wanted to cross, so cross!"

Ophelia Lashlee climbed from the interior out onto the seat and took up the reins. She flicked them and the carriage creaked into motion. Holly Bee rode her paint forward to confront Jake, her rifle cradled suggestively on her arm. "Don't you go yellin' at ladies when they're in a family way," she warned him.

With Annie leading and Ophelia Lashlee at the reins, the carriage climbed the grade and started across . . . then sagged to a grinding halt as the off rear wheel parted company from its hub and rolled away.

"Oh, good Lord," Jake breathed. There were ominous sounds coming from the enclosed bed of the carriage, rising in tenor to match the ominous bellowings of two trains and the screeching of distant wheels on iron rail. A grinding crash resounded behind him and the train beside him lurched and shuddered. He looked back. The engineer of the approaching 4:20, it seemed, had waited an instant too long before setting his brakes. The noses of the two engines now were delicately intertwined, cow-catcher to cow-catcher, and the 4:20's guide wheels sat on ties beside their rails. Neither train was was going anywhere for a while.

Jake spurred to the broken carriage, arriving alongside just as Annie did. "That horse can't drag this thing off here," she said. "Maybe we can hitch up another horse . . ."

"Get ropes on it," Jake said. "We can pull. No, you all are going to have to move Miz Quinn to another wagon. This one won't make it as far as those trees."

Annie's eyes widened. "What do you want us to go to those trees for?"

"Well, that's where you all said we had to go, so the lady can have her baby! That's what you told me!"

Ophelia Lashlee cast him a sympathetic look and turned to Annie. "Poor thing, he don't know a stitch about all this, does he?"

"We just thought them trees would be a nice place to wait while Amber done her labor," Annie explained to Jake. "We just miscalculated. It's her first one, an' a body never knows for sure."

Jake was almost in a frenzy. "Well then, dammit, what are we supposed to do? Where do you all want her to have that baby?"

"It ain't our choice, Charlie," she smiled thinly. "That's all been decided. She'll have it right here."

Chapter XXI

The birth of Amber Quinn's son Harold Sean, on a West Texas railroad track midway between Limestone and San Galena, was a festive occasion attended by the child's Aunt Coryanne and nineteen other women and sixteen children recently of the town of Rossville, as well as two judges, fourteen shackled feud participants on their way to Limestone to stand trial, four part-time deputy marshals, a dentist from Abilene, nine trainmen, two whiskey drummers, a man who traveled in ladies' ready-to-wear, six out-of-work cowboys, a Mexican family enroute from Matamoros to Stinnett, a thespian, a codger and a wanted man in a silver-belly beaver hat who celebrated the occasion by erecting a wagonjack beneath little Harold Sean's place of birth and remounting a pin-sheared wheel.

"If I live to tell of this," he muttered as he worked, "I swear I'll never get within a mile of a woman the whole rest of my natural life."

"Will you stop crankin' that jack!" Jessy Wheeler's voice came from inside the carriage. "We're tryin' to have a baby in here!"

"If I get through this," Jake promised himself, "I'm going to paint the word 'Texas' on a shingle

220

and nail it to a pole and head off yonder and not stop 'til I find a place where nobody knows what that word means."

"When you find the time," a railroader called from the respectful distance most of the men were keeping between themselves and the natal carriage, "I need to talk to you about these trains. I don't know who's supposed to pay for the damages."

"If I ever once get shed of this crowd," Jake swore, "I'm going to go to New York City and live on plum pudding and venture capital and never look at a damn water well, windmill, wagon or woman again."

Holly Bee Sutherland, who had been crouched on the carriage's boot, watching the proceedings inside, leaned over the top and prodded him with her rifle. "You mind your mouth," she ordered. "There's ladies in yonder."

"I know damn well what's in yonder," he rasped. "Female troubles. That's what I got, is female troubles. I expect I got half the female troubles in Texas right now, not to mention bounty hunters and babies . . ."

"You know what causes that, don't you?"

"Yeah, it's because I'm an outlaw, just like you said."

"I don't mean bounty hunters. I mean babies. You know what causes that?"

He glanced up. High sunlight haloed golden hair and shadowed a pair of intense blue eyes. He felt himself turning red, and looked down quickly, trying to concentrate on his work. "I know what causes it," he muttered. "Absent-mindedness."

From somewhere nearby he heard Annie Coke's chuckle. "Believe we're doin' just fine," she said, though he had no idea who she was talking to.

He got the errant wheel in place, set a new pin, crimped it and released the wagonjack. Inside the carriage, Amber's rhythmic puffs and gasps were interrupted by a groan, and Lottie Camber's head appeared at the curtained window. "That's enough of that," she told him. "You jerk this wagon one more time I'll take a flatiron to you." Inside, the gasps and pants settled once again to a steady rhythm. The Mexican man had come over to watch Jake work on the wheel, and when Jake squatted to haul out the jack the Mexican squatted down beside him. "This is your first borning of a child, Señor?"

"First and last as far as I'm concerned," Jake gritted. "I don't ever want to go through this again."

"It becomes easier," the man shrugged. "Maria and me, we have six. Maybe we will have six more, who knows?" His dark eyes twinkled. "When I saw you draw the *pistola* to make the train move, at first I thought maybe you would rob us. Then I learn there is to be a baby and I understand. My first baby, I went to the cantina and shot holes in the walls. My second baby I went to Hermosillo and shot holes in Juan Flores. After that, each time a baby is born to Maria, I take a little money and buy corn futures. Babies are a good sign to buy corn futures."

Jake was pulling out the jack. He paused and looked at the men. "I never thought about that," he admitted. He dragged out the jack, hoisted it to his shoulder and looked around, trying to spot the

Tuttle wagon. One of the cowboys, squatting on his heels nearby, puffing on a hand-rolled cigarette, said sourly, "My uncle went bust in corn futures. Don't trust 'em, myself."

"Corn futures are not for everyone," the Mexican admitted.

"Flour mills are a good property," the cowboy said. "Money to be made in flour mills up in the high plains. Winter wheat's the big thing nowadays, but you can lose your socks in wheat. That's why mills is the way to go."

"Irrigation projects ain't bad," one of the shackled prisoners from San Galena allowed. "They're marketin' debentures at Fort Worth for big irrigation projects up north, with a roll-over option on cash crops as an enticement. I got six hundred dollars in that game, myself."

"That wouldn't be for me," a judge tossed in. "Institutionalized investments don't let a man see what his money's doing."

"No different from mutual funds and pooled capital," Jake said. He spotted Tyrone Sneed hanging around the carriage and beckoned him. "Tyrone, get away from there before those ladies get mean! Come get this jack and take it back to the Tuttle wagon for me." He handed the jack to the thespian and lifted his hat to wipe sweat from his face. "I been moving around a good bit just lately," he told the judge, "so I just put my money with Philo Henderson over at Portales and let him handle it. Saves a lot of worry to have a middle man."

"What kind of investments does he handle?" one of the trainmen asked.

"Oh, most anything. He shops around and finds what looks good, and plays the markets."

The dentist pulled at his lip thoughtfully. "I've always been afraid I'd get over-collateralized if I didn't tend my own investments. You had that problem?"

"Not with Philo. Dang near lost my liquidity on a real estate deal of my own, though. I had to cash in and pull out on that one. But I broke even."

"Public works," the man who traveled in ladies' ready-to-wear interjected. "Safest investment a man can make is public works, the way I see it."

"No question about the security angle," a deputy marshal offered, "but you'll never get rich on public works unless you're in a position to contract materials or select easements. An' them things usually ain't market-driven. Politics gets involved too much. Me, I buy life insurance."

"That's good, but it's hell to collect on it," a cowboy allowed.

"Would you write down that fellow's name and address for me?" the dentist wondered. "The one out at Portales."

Jake wandered across to the rear stage of the stalled train and borrowed paper and pencil from a porter. He wrote out Philo's name and address and gave it to the dentist. Most of the other men sifted around them, glad to have something interesting to talk about since they obviously weren't going any-place for a while. The fireman from the Sunrise Special had been sent north to bring help from Limestone, but it would be evening, at least, before anybody came.

"How about letting me have that name, too," the porter requested. "I got a few dollars I might want to put to work."

"I been' thinkin' about buyin' some Fort Worth municipal bonds," a drover with long mustaches drawled. "They got a new stockyards issue."

"What kind of payback are you lookin' at?" one of the whiskey drummers squinted at him. "Fixed or scaled?"

"Sliding scale," the drover explained. "Ninety-day option on second issues, too, if a man wants to exercise it."

"Bonds are all right for low profile long term," one of the prisoners pointed out. "For the little investor, though, he's just as well off putting his money in an interest-bearing account. It ain't any way to get rich. To my way of thinkin', oil is where the money's at."

"Oil?" the drover sneered at him. "You're about as like to find oil options as you are to find feathers growin' on a pig. Folks back east got that all tied up. Has been for years."

"There's oil in Texas, too!"

"There is? Where?"

"I don't know. I just heard there was."

"That Henderson, does he know anything about oil?"

"He keeps a bucket of it in the barn to dress his tackle," Jake shrugged. "I don't know, maybe I'm old fashioned, but I just favor real property mostly."

Annie hurried by, carrying water from the Sunrise Special's boiler tap. She paused at the comment, remembering. "Feller in Big Spring told me

225

to say howdy to you, Charlie. Said he knowed you from way back."

"Who was it?"

"I don't remember. Stand aside, I got to hurry."

She hurried on, and Jake stared after her, remembering that he had never found out why she went to Big Spring. Some of the other men followed his glance. The carriage standing on the railroad track was a beehive of activity, women hustling about, carrying things, doing things, peering into its windows. Holly Bee and Coryanne were on top of it now, trying to see everything at once, and Clara was up on the seat on her knees, leaning to look past the tonneau curtain.

"What are they doing over there?" a man asked, vaguely.

"Who knows?" another said. "You know how women can get. Anybody here ever had experience with import and export commodities?"

Thin wails arose from the carriage and some of the men glanced around again, then returned to the business at hand. Tyrone Sneed had returned from the Tuttle wagon and stood listening for a time, then tilted his hat and grinned. "One of the real sleepers is entertainment," he told the group. "I know people who have made fortunes in road company shares."

"My baby brother Zeb bought shares in a circus one time," a shackled granger from San Galena frowned. "It went belly-up six months later and he wound up with a dog act. You ever try to hunt hogs with a dog act? Zeb said he tried it, but the only hog he brought home was one that died

226

laughin'."

"Give me a nice little limited debenture any time," the dentist decided. "With a certified line of credit on the profit sharing trust."

"Escrow," a cowboy said. "Earmarked escrows keeps the varmints honest."

"What are y'all doin' out here, anyway?" one of the trainmen was looking at the wagons and buggies scattered here and there over a quarter-section of countryside.

"These ladies are from Rossville," Jake explained. "We're looking for a railroad."

" 'Pears to me you done found one."

"Naw, we're looking for a new one . . ."

"Some folks are hard to satisfy."

". . . that it seems like somebody is trying to build on the sly. Those ladies' menfolks are rail hands. They went off to work on a project and haven't been heard from since."

"I own a quarter interest in a warehouse and dray outfit at Abilene," the dentist said. "They've been stockpiling track for somebody, but it's all blind orders. Don't know who it's going to. The orders come from Big Spring, though."

"Likely the same outfit," a drummer suggested. "There hasn't been a railroad built in Texas in ten-fifteen years at least. Don't seem likely there'd be two of them now."

"How would anybody keep a railroad secret?" a drover marveled.

"Probably couldn't for very long. Soon as they start layin' line, everybody's goin' to know about it."

"We heard somebody is building a trestle west of

here," Jake said. "That's where we intend to look."

"I wonder if there's shares to be had," a prisoner cocked his head, looking west. "I wouldn't mind having stock in a railroad. You suppose that Henderson has leads on railroads?"

"He keeps his ear to the ground," Jake shrugged. "I don't think he misses much."

"Why don't you let me have his address, too."

"You can't go off making investments," one of the judges reminded the shackled man sternly. "You're under indictment for . . . what are you indicted for?"

"Disturbing the peace," the man said.

"Maybe we can work out a mutual fund through the court," the judge rubbed his whiskers thoughtfully. "Be a shame for any man to miss out on an investment opportunity just because of due process."

"Amen to that," another prisoner said.

Annie approached again, from the engine, bearing hot water. She looked happy and excited.

"I take it you've done all right, dealing through this Philo Henderson?" the dentist asked Jake.

"He suits me."

"You have quite a few stocks, do you?"

"Lord," Annie declared in passing, "this young feller's got stocks he don't even know about."

Jake swiveled around, wide-eyed, his mouth open to say something, but she was already gone, heading for the carriage where the activity levels seemed to have grown feverish. Women were crowding around, smiling and cooing.

"Any special thing to know about him, if a body wanted him to be his broker?" a drummer asked.

Jake turned back, thoroughly puzzled. "What?"

"Henderson. Anything to know about him?"

"Oh. Well, just be sure he knows what kind of thing you want to get into, I guess. He can't read minds."

"That's understandable."

The Mexican was staring at the carriage, beginning to get the drift of what was happening over there. A wide smile lit his face. "Ah," he breathed. *"Un muchacho. Un poquito bravo. Bueno."*

Some of the others turned to look. "Well, my land," someone said. Jake turned. A spearhead procession of cooing, chattering women had come from the carriage, led by Ophelia Lashlee who cradled a small wrapped bundle in her arms. She stopped in front of Jake, smiled and handed him the bundle, and suddenly he found himself holding something he didn't recall holding ever before. He swallowed, tried to speak and swallowed again.

"I told them you should see him because you're the one responsible," Coryanne O'Keefe glowed.

"His name is Harold Sean," Flossie Todd said. "He's a boy."

"She doesn't mean *responsible,* like responsible," Clara Hayes hurried to explain. "What she suggested was that since you are responsible . . ."

"Behave yourself," Holly Bee warned him. "If you drop that baby I'll shoot you dead."

"Sure is somethin', ain't he?" Annie Coke glowed, drawing back a fold in the fabric to uncover a tiny, squinched face. "Kind of reminds me of my husband Lester. He was an outlaw, but a saint most ways. But he'd get to lookin' just like that when

229

things didn't go to suit him . . ."

Most of the men had hauled their hats from their heads, and one or two murmured congratulations to Jake. The Mexican man stepped close to suggest, "If I were you, Señor, I would put a little money in corn futures now."

Jake finally got his tongue untangled. "Now hold on, y'all, this isn't *mine*, for pete's sake!"

"Ah, Señor," the Mexican soothed him. "How can one ever know such things for sure? When I look back now, sometimes I regret that I went to Hermosillo and shot holes in Juan Flores."

Chapter XXII

With the trestle completed, Dos Burton saw no further reason for secrecy concerning the westward portion of the route. It was time to lay rail, and he had a starting point — huge stockpiles of rails and ties that lay waiting, hidden at a remote, burned-out ranch spread not twenty miles from the border of New Mexico territory. It was what had gotten the Burton brothers into the railroad business in the first place, that stockpile. They hadn't assembled it or put it there in the first place. That was someone else's doing, entirely. But in their outlaw days the brothers had stumbled upon it — guarded trains of stacked flatcars rolling in secret to a marshalling yard outside Fort Worth, then with switched crews being shunted off into the maze of little stub-line railroads that wandered off to the west and south.

"Nowhere Lines," some called them. Little railroads that went to places like Mobeetie and Four Square and Hitchcock, then met other little "nowhere lines" that went off who knew where. There had been a time at the end of Reconstruction when a lot of people in Texas found themselves with a lot of money that they had to either spend or account for, and it seemed like every second one of them had decided to build a railroad.

And somebody was using some of those roads, the Burtons discovered. Somebody with enough panic capital from back east to cover the costs, and enough hands in enough pockets in Austin to keep it secret, was importing and stockpiling more rails. The secret trains rolled out from Fort Worth and seemed to fall off the end of the world out yonder, then eventually they came back empty to be loaded again.

Pure happenstance, that the Burtons had stumbled across that. But once discovered, they had grown curious, and eventually had found the stockpile . . . and come up with their idea. It took them the better part of three years to come into possession of all that material hidden out there in the lonesomes. People had died in the process, and a few politicians had either simply disappeared or left Texas and never came back. But, eventually, Uno and Dos Burton found themselves in sole possession of an unassembled railroad, and within months the Great Central and Pacific Investment Company was born. They headquartered at Big Spring, began stockpiling more supplies at Abilene and began the painstaking job of accumulating capital and acquiring rights-of-way.

In order to attract the kind of investors they required—men controlling large sums that they could invest secretly, with the Burtons' hard-won rail stockpile and the assurance of right-of-way as security, they had to have a route to talk about. The eastern terminus could be Big Spring, with an adjoining line to Abilene to complete the main, or maybe—and Dos was certain he could handle this—just maybe that little line from Abilene might become theirs with the right persuasion. So that left a westward destination, and then along came Conrad W. Jackson with the answer. They got out their maps and made their decision. With the watering spot that Jackson promised, they could push right out into the territory to that big well, let Jackson provide a town for them there, and send branch lines north to Santa Fe to meet the Atchison Topeka and Santa Fe, and southwest to El Paso to meet the Southern Pacific.

Neither Burton trusted Conrad W. Jackson at all, but so far he had come through as far as they could tell. He had bought his stock, paid for his stock despite someone robbing his bank during the transaction, and he had the water. They had both seen it.

Now, with completion of the main trestle that would join the east route coming out from Big Spring with the west route into the territory, Dos was ready to begin his end. For four days his crew had been moving westward, nearly a hundred men strong now with twice that many draft animals, scraping here and filling there to put down a rough subgrade. The main grade work would be done on the way back, eight miles at a time as the rails went down, from the hidden stockpile right back to the trestle.

By the time Uno Burton finished his paperwork and started laying rail west from Big Spring, Dos would have a useable track from Trestle Point westward right to the final plunge into New Mexico.

The brothers seldom were together these days, but when they were they just couldn't help a few chuckles of pure glee. Nobody they knew of had ever pulled off a venture like this. It stood to reason, then, that there just wasn't anybody else around who was as smart as them. Even that pea-brained Jackson had fallen right into step.

Jackson would have to go, of course. Once they had their line to the waterstop, he might be a nuisance. But he was useful for the moment.

Flanked by his four toughs, Dos rode to a high point to survey the progress being made. Below, out on the flats, men sweated their teams and tools glistened as another mile of subgrade was completed. Dos shaded his eyes and looked west. Just out there — another day or two away — was the stockpiled material to begin building a railroad. Handcarts and team-drawn rail wagons waited there to begin building back toward the trestle, and the manpower was here to do the job. Among the men sweating out there on the flats were maybe thirty experienced railroad builders, hired as a crew for the duration of the project. The rest were Mexicans and a few drifters they had picked up — men whose presence wouldn't be missed anywhere while they worked here. Idly, Dos wondered whether Uno had in fact been sending wages to those railroaders' families back in that little town they came from. It didn't seem likely that he would. They had better uses for the money, and what was going to come of it anyway? What could a bunch of women do about anything? And who else was going to care?

Dos frowned as furnace winds eddied up from the

flats, kicking up little whorls of dancing sand. The cloudbank to the west, that had been just a haze out there for the past two days, was becoming a cloudscape—growing and defining itself. Sunlight glistened on high, shredding tops, and the distances below were shadow-dark. The wind kicking up said those thunderheads would grow and move.

It did not please him. Men could drag up sub-grade in desert heat, if they had to. But rain would slow the work.

"This never was much of a town anyway," Homer Boles said, looking sadly around at the boarded-up buildings that were now most of the town of Perdition. "Couldn't ever get itself a railroad, nor even a decent stage line."

"Only town I know of nowadays that never even managed to get a telegraph," Sim Hoover agreed. "But it *was* a town, though. I don't know what it is now."

"Empty," Homer decided. "It's just empty. I bet there ain't a hundred folks within twenty miles of where we're standin' right now, Sim. Used to be close to four hundred right here in town . . . least-ways whenever we had a social."

"Pretty soon there won't be anybody here at all." Sim leaned back against the stable wall, spreading his long legs out in front of him. His expression went sour as he gazed across at what had been his house before Conrad W. Jackson called in all the mortgages. Now the building was vacant and boarded-over, and it had a little linoleum sign on its door that said it was the property of a bank at Big Spring, Texas. Sim now lived in the loft over his stables. "Only thing that keeps me here is, I still get business from that outfit that Conrad W. Jackson was workin' out at Jake Creedmore's old place. He's fixin' to build up a brand new town out there, is what they say."

"Might make a go of it," Homer shrugged, sprawled in the shade beside the stablekeep. "That's one hell of a good well ol' Jake brought in out there. If we'd ever had water like that here, Perdition might have been quite a town. Seems like it would take somethin' more than good water to make a town get started, though."

"They say Conrad W. Jackson's got somethin' more in mind. Somethin' pretty special, he says. He's layin' out enough town lots out there for a thousand people or better, the way I hear it."

Homer shook his head. "I don't know. Just havin' good water—even a high artesian like Jake's big well—don't seem like that would attract people all by itself. Have to be somethin' else. I was wonderin' if maybe he figures on buildin' a sale barn an' takin' the trade away from Three Forks. But even if he could do that, I don't see how . . ."

"I hate those damn signs," Sim muttered, still staring at the linoleum rectangle across the street. Most of the vacant buildings in Perdition sported similar signs, all from the same bank over in Texas.

"Well, what was he gonna do with all this fore-closed property, Sim? Sit on it? He had to sell it off to get his money back after Jake robbed the bank."

"I reckon. Twenty thousand dollars is a lot of

236

money to lose. I just wish they hadn't come out an' put up those signs. Makes everything here seem kind of useless."

They sat in silence for a while, Sim glaring at the sign on his old house, Homer deep in thought. Finally Homer tilted his hat and scratched his head. "I just ain't real sure that's how it happened," he said.

"What?"

"About Jake takin' twenty thousand dollars out of that bank."

"What about it?"

"Lot of things. Like the only witness there was, was Wilbur Short, and Wilbur told me clear as day that what Jake took was two thousand, three hundred and fifty-one dollars."

"He took Conrad W. Jackson's horse, too," Sim pointed out. "I know that for a fact, because he took it right out of this very stable."

"Did you see him take it?"

"Naw . . . I was kind of busy at the time . . ."

"That was about the time Flossie was in town, as I recollect," Homer grinned.

"That ain't anybody's business! Mind your mouth. But I know he took that horse because plenty of folks seen him ridin' it out of town. He was wearin' Conrad W. Jackson's silver-belly beaver hat, too."

"But nobody saw him take anything, except Wilbur Short said he saw him rob the bank, an' what Wilbur said he took was a whole lot less than what Mr. Jackson said he took. Besides, Wilbur left right after that an' nobody knows where he is."

"Lot of that goin' around," Sim shook his head.

"Opal Hayes got word from Miss Clara little bit back . . . Miss Clara's off seein' about her Aunt Jessy back in Texas, y'know . . . female troubles . . . well, Opal says th' female troubles turns out to be Aunt Jessy's son Harold is missin' . . ."

"Mighty sorry to hear that."

". . . him an' about thirty others all from the same town."

Homer's eyes widened and he looked around. "What?"

"I said . . ."

"I heard what you said. What happened? County seat war or somethin'?"

"No, seems like they all taken off to work on a new railroad an' just haven't showed up since."

"Who'd build a railroad these days?" Homer goggled at him. "Nobody builds railroads these days, an' even if somebody did, an' a body wanted to find people workin' on it, it's no great shakes to find a railroad."

"Well, I guess it is to find this one. It's a secret."

"What is it, underground?"

"It's just nobody knows anything about it."

"That's the silliest thing I ever heard."

"Well, that's what Clara said was goin' on. She said there's a sheriff over yonder someplace that might help 'em find out about it, though. Only thing is, that there sheriff is a woman."

"Sounds to me like it's time for Opal to be gettin' that girl of hers home. Secret railroads an' woman sheriffs! Land, I don't think Texas is good for her."

"I hate those damn signs," Sim growled, again looking across the street. "Somebody ought to shoot

Jake Creedmore for what he done to this town."

"What makes you so sure it was him that done it?"

"Well . . . Conrad W. Jackson said so."

"Uh-huh."

Sim turned to scowl at the former marshal. "Are you sayin' he didn't rob the bank?"

"I don't say he did and I don't say he didn't," Homer drawled. "I just ain't all that sure about what really happened."

"Well, if Jake didn't take the money, then who did?" His question was interrupted by movement up the street, and they both turned to watch a man setting up a tripod-mounted transit. "How come you suppose that feller is surveying way off over here? He started out surveyin' Jake's old place for Conrad W. Jackson, but ever since yesterday he's been here in town, sightin' lines northwest."

"I know," Homer said. "This mornin' he was over by the hotel, drivin' stakes right out in the street."

"Did you ask him what for?"

"No. Should I?"

"If I was marshal here, I guess I would."

"I ain't marshal any more. Am I? Nothin' left here to marshal."

"Well, if you aren't, who is?"

Homer stood and stretched his arms, yawning. "If you're so danged curious, I'll go ask him what he's doin'. But only because you're curious."

Sim watched him stroll away, then turned his attention again to the linoleum sign across the street. That had been his house once. But it wasn't any more. And he just couldn't figure out why some bank way off over in Texas had been willing to buy up so much of Perdition from Conrad W. Jackson.

Clearwater, that was what they said Conrad W. Jackson planned to call his new town out at Jake's old place. Clearwater. Well, it had that, all right. Compared to the water that flowed from that big well Jake had brought in, every dinky little well in Perdition gave dark alkali.

Sim leaned forward to peer beyond the awning at the clouding sky. A wind had picked up and little whorls of sand danced here and there in the street. "By golly," he muttered, "I believe it might rain. Hope it does enough to charge the cistern."

Thoughts of Perdition's water had clouded his mood, just like those thunderheads building up overhead had clouded the sky. He thought about having cistern water to drink instead of brackish well water, and couldn't decide which he preferred. The one tasted of gypsum, the other of bird droppings and dead rats.

Homer Boles came back eventually, looking puzzled. "I thought you said that surveyor was working for Conrad W. Jackson," he said.

"That's what I heard. He's been out at Jake's old place. Who else would he work for?"

"He says he works for a geologist up at Santa Fe. He says he's charting a aquifer for Jake Creedmore."

240

Chapter XXIII

Of all the erstwhile suitors who had descended upon Rossville then gone on to Big Spring with the best of intentions regarding finding "those poor women's missin' menfolks," only two — Ruby and the mustanger Willis Holt — actually learned anything of value. Most of the rest, by the time they reached Big Spring, found their chivalrous spirits somewhat abated by trail dust and decided to do their research in whatever saloons had space enough to hold them. Some found other interests as well — females more in need of immediate attention than of noble quests — and quite a few had forgotten the Rossville dilemma entirely in favor of thinking out investments plans.

But the redhead and the mustanger happened to be within earshot when the big, dark-coated man — one of several they had noticed hanging around Big Spring — stopped Annie Coke in the street and told her about a railroad trestle being built out in the middle of nowhere. They exchanged glances, watched with amazed interest when the woman with the shotgun rode on and the little mouse-faced man with the thonged handgun attached himself to the millchute, then set their hats firmly on their heads

241

and went in search of the big man they had seen. He wasn't hard to find, and they accosted him in a deserted alley.

"We don't want any trouble," Ruby assured him, "but we need to know all you can tell us about that railroad trestle out yonder."

The man studied them with dark, hooded eyes and a slight smile played across his face. "I'll take into consideration the first part of what you said," he told them. "Now stand aside."

"What first part?" Ruby's pugnacious jaw thrust out.

"About you not wanting any trouble. You boys just be on your way right now, and I don't expect you'll get any." The man brushed them aside and started for the next street, in no particular hurry.

"I be damned," Ruby growled. "Mister, I don't think you understand. We want to talk to you."

The man didn't even look back. Ruby bristled and glanced at the taciturn Holt. "I guess he needs persuading," he said.

They spread, flanked the big man and rushed him, fists swinging. A moment later they were both flat on their backs on the ground. The man looked down at them coolly. "I guess you weren't serious about not wanting trouble," he said. "Want any more?"

Swearing and panting, they came off the ground and charged him again. And again they both found themselves sprawled. Blood trickled from Ruby's split lip, and the mustanger was shaking his head slowly from side to side, trying to clear the ringing from his ears. Ruby raised himself on his elbows.

242

"Who the hell are you, anyway?"

"Nobody you ever heard of," the man said. "You might have heard of my boss, though. Name of Royal Flanders."

Holt's head jerked up and Ruby's eyes went wide. "Flanders? The badlands . . ."

"That's him," the man said. "You boys all right? Wouldn't want to be impolite about it, but I got things to do."

"We need to know about that railroad trestle," Ruby growled. "If you don't tell us, who's goin' to?"

"I surely don't know," the man said. "Maybe Mr. Flanders would, but probably not. And I don't think you want to go after him like you went after me. Royal Flanders gets tough sometimes." He gazed at them almost tenderly. "How come you boys want to know about other people's business?"

Holt shook his head a final time, still dizzy. "Women," he said. "There's a bunch of women tryin' to find out where their men went, an' Ruby figures maybe if we help them out, well . . ."

"*I* figure?" Ruby glared at his partner. "I don't see you fightin' shy of women, Holt."

"Anyhow," Holt continued, "we wouldn't mind them bein' beholden to us, if you catch my drift."

"Some of them must be worth lookin' at," the man said.

"Some of them sure as hell are."

"Well, I'm not going to tell you anything. But if I was you boys, I believe I'd go hang around that G.C.&P. investment office yonder and see what I could see. Might be some folks that would just as soon not have a bunch of females out scoutin' the

243

wild country."

Without another word, he glanced down at them one more time, then turned and walked away. Holt got to his hands and knees and frowned at Ruby. "You want to go try him one more time?"

"Do you think I'm crazy?" Ruby stood on rubbery legs, wondering if he had ever been hit so suddenly and so hard. "I just want a place to sit down for a while."

"Suits me," the mustanger got his feet under him and stood swaying.

"Let's go sit by that G.C.&P. place," Ruby suggested. "You sit in front and I'll sit in back."

"Couple of cowboys pretty set on mixing in," one of Royal Flanders' men told him. "Reckon they set out to chase women and wound up chasin' for 'em. I said they might want to listen around that investment outfit, maybe pick up a notion or two there."

"Won't hurt," Flanders said. "You get Creedmore and those women directed?"

"They'll be on their way out to that trestle, I guess."

"That's fine," Flanders allowed. He turned to another of them. "You said you got word back about that Jackson?"

"A little," the man said. "Partly from the bank here, partly from the wire to Three Forks. Seems like Conrad W. Jackson came out just fine on his bank bein' robbed. Paid off on some shares he'd bought, then called in mortgages and transferred title to that G.C.&P. for working capital. The bank

244

here picked up the paper, and they've got somebody out peddlin' the stuff. Right now Jackson is out yonder planning a new town, puttin' everything he has into it."

"Kind of sounds like he's got the inside track on something big, doesn't it?" the first man suggested.

"Big as railroads," the other nodded. "Far as cash on hand, though, Royal, I can't see where he's got two nickels to rub together."

Flanders' brow lowered briefly. "Man that's offering a reward on somebody ought to keep the money on hand to pay it," he muttered.

"Royal, I hope we're goin' to make some money on this deal," one of them said. "We've invested a lot of time and travel here."

"Oh, we'll come out one way or another," Flanders nodded. "Had a little talk with the bank here in town. They pay twenty-five cents on the dollar for disclosure and recovery of collateral fraud."

"This bank loaned money to Jackson?"

"No, to the Burtons. But most of the collateral is Perdition property, and the rest is first-issue stock held by Conrad W. Jackson. He co-signed for the note."

The second man grinned. "I don't think Conrad W. Jackson has any first-issue stock."

"Surely doesn't look that way, does it?" Flanders returned the grin. On his face, the expression was like clouds rolling back to let the lightning through. "Boys, I believe we've been here long enough. Let's head back out to the Territory. Things might get interesting out that way pretty quick."

"We gonna shadow along after those women?"

Flanders turned to the first man. "How do you feel about those two cowboys, Henry?"

"They got gumption. Not much sense, but gumption."

"Kind of like Jake Creedmore," the other noted.

"They ought to be able to handle things there, then. So I guess we can just head straight on back. We'll need an extra saddle horse, though. Wilbur Short doesn't know it yet, but he'll be going with us."

If anybody noticed Ruby sitting on the sill of the back door of Great Central and Pacific Investment Company's building—Uno Burton's private door—they didn't think much about it. It was obvious the redhead had either taken a fall or been stomped by somebody, and a man with such aches just naturally finds himself a handy place to sit and suffer. There would have been no question that Ruby was suffering. He sat in silence, leaning sideways against the closed door, one cheek pressed to the panel, eyes nearly closed and blood drying on his chin.

And just beyond the door, at that moment, Uno Burton was announcing a decision.

"I'm not ready to have everybody and his dog find out what Dos is doing out there," he told his private squad of guntoughs. "Those damned women should have just stayed home and kept quiet, but no, they're out there someplace looking for their men, and in the meantime half the people in Big Spring are asking questions about railroads. So you boys know what to do. I want those women stopped. I don't care what it takes, you just get out there and find them and stop them."

Outside the door, Ruby's eyelids hooded eyes that smoldered with indignation. A man of his time, Ruby felt strongly about women and about a man's duty toward them—namely, to protect them against everyone except himself.

He got to his feet, choking back a groan, and went to find Willis Holt.

The mustanger had a knot on his head and a big, purple bruise under his left eye. He sat on the front porch of Great Central and Pacific Investment Company, cradling his head in his hands.

"We got to get our horses and pack for a trip," Ruby told him. "There's some varmint inside yonder that's sendin' hardcases out to stop those poor, defenseless women."

"What are you gettin' us into this time, Ruby?" Holt looked up at him, then slowly got to his feet.

"Nothin' we can't handle," the redhead assured him. "Shoot, have you ever seen a situation you and me couldn't handle?"

"As I recollect, yes," the mustanger reminded him. "Not more than an hour ago, I believe it was."

Far to the west, Alex Hamilton had come to Portales. Trail weary and tired, he sat with Philo Henderson at Phyllis's kitchen table and displayed his wares. He had managed, at various stops on the way out, to unload everything except the Perdition properties but he was about convinced that this last stop was a waste of time. He had tried a dozen

247

times to sell the Perdition titles, and to people much more likely to take a flier in such things than any Philo Henderson was. No one had been the slightest bit interested in them. Some had even laughed at him.

"The bank's prepared to take a loss on these," he admitted to Philo, "for the sake of liquidity. Might even think about half the face value, if a man wanted to take the whole chunk."

"Pretty chancy stuff," Philo frowned. "Bunch of town property, someplace nobody ever heard of."

Phyllis leaned over his shoulder. "But, Philo, that's . . ."

He raised a hand, scowling. ". . . not the kind of thing I normally buy, anyway," he covered. "I don't know, Mr. Hamilton. I surely don't feel real inclined toward this."

"A third," Hamilton said. "Maybe a third of its face value. I think we could manage that, for a cash transaction."

"These little old towns," Philo said, shaking his head. "Man just never knows what'll come of them. Most of them just dust over and blow away. I mean, look, considering what you're offering, this must be the whole town!"

"Oh, no. Just bits and pieces."

"I don't know, Mr. Hamilton. If your bank has picked up this much property in one little town, there sure must be something wrong with the town."

Phyllis was dancing on her toes, behind Hamilton, trying to get her husband's attention. "But, Philo," she said, "what about . . ."

He frowned and shut her up with a wave. "About

248

my other investments. I know. Pretty hard to justify putting this much money into something that looks this chancy."

Hamilton sagged in his chair. "Maybe if you'd just write down a figure . . . something you'd be willing to talk from . . . then maybe we could discuss it." Philo was already writing.

He looked up and thumbed to another deed. "What's this property here? It says hotel."

"It's a hotel. Closed down, but it is a hotel."

"Would this include the street in front of the hotel?"

"Well, not by itself, it wouldn't. But there's another one in here, a lot across from the hotel. Those two together would give you the street. Why do you ask about the street?"

"I just sort of like streets," Philo shrugged.

"Street in front of the hotel," Phyllis breathed. "Why, Philo, isn't that where . . . ?"

"Where the hitchrack is, yes," he said quickly.

"I'll tell you what," Alex said, "I was really hoping to place all this as one package, but I'd even consider splitting it up, if there's some parts of it you might be . . ."

"Oh, I'll buy it all," Philo said. "For this price right here. Cash on the barrelhead, take it or leave it."

"I'll take it," Alex blinked.

They shook hands and the deal was completed. Hamilton signed over the papers on behalf of the bank in Big Spring, and Philo gave him a draft on the bank in Portales.

When Hamilton was gone, Philo sagged in his

chair and stared at Phyllis. "Next time I decide to buy somethin', Hon, it might be a gag to put over your mouth when I'm talkin' deals."

"But Philo, isn't this all what . . ."

"Go get that letter," he said.

She went and got it and brought it back, and they read it again together. It was a letter from a geologist at Santa Fe, addressed to Philo for delivery to Jake Creedmore. The surveys had been completed . . . somebody named Jackson had authorized the access and easements . . . and the geologist was prepared to identify and locate Jake's aquifer. It was a fault-flow, too deep in most places for a normal well to tap it. It probably, the geologist theorized, originated up in the Sangre de Cristos and it likely terminated as a bluff spring somewhere along the Rio Grande. But in between, his studies indicated two places where it could be tapped to provide a big well. One, as Jake had discovered, was where he had hit it. The other, by the geologist's best calculations, would be in the town of Perdition. He gave measurements and quadrants, then described it in layman's terms. The most likely place to bring in a good well from this aquifer would be in the street in front of the old hotel in Perdition town.

"I wonder how Jake's going to feel about you investing his money in Perdition town property," Phyllis murmured.

"He left it up to me," Philo said. "Besides, it isn't all his money. I put in some of that other money that people keep sending us, too. Like you said, what's good enough for Jake ought to be good enough for folks we don't even know."

"Have you invested everything that's come in, then?" They both were somewhat boggled at the phenomenon of various sums of money arriving from here and there, vouchers sent by wire, with instructions from people they had never heard of that Philo was to invest it for them.

"Oh, no," he shook his head. "I've pooled it all in a trust, with accounting of what is whose, and there's still a lot to go. But I think now we know what the plan should be. First, I'm going to send someone to Perdition to drill a deep well, to get to that water vein or whatever is in . . . aquifer. Then I need to buy some outside land beyond the town — east, I think, those people south toward Three Forks are too land-proud to deal reasonably, and there isn't much of value west, and that Jackson has the north all blocked — then declare a capital trust and issue shares for all those people who have money in it . . . mercy! Real property, pooled trusts, capital improvements and venture shares, all in one deal. It's wonderful!"

Chapter XXIV

As the days passed, each as unpredictable and chaotic as the one before, Jake had begun to grow numb to his predicament. The scrap of map that Annie had mysteriously brought back from Big Spring—all she knew was that a man gave it to her and said there was a railroad trestle where the X was—proved to be misleading in its relation of distance. Few enough landmarks were noted on it, but somehow Jake had expected them to be closer together. The fact was, what he had judged to be ten-mile intervals on the map had proven to be more on the order of thirty-mile intervals, as though the map had been drawn by someone with the habit of covering great distances by fast horse, and who had no patience with the plodding pace of wagons, buckboards and carts.

But then again, when he thought about it, he himself had covered those same vast distances without paying them much mind. But that was back in the days—somehow it seemed a long time ago—before he had started acquiring women. When it had been just him and Conrad W. Jackson's racer, with nothing ahead but miles and miles of miles and nothing behind that much mattered . . . He shook his head irritably and glanced back at the straggling line of rolling stock coming along behind him. He had the sisters Higgins—Serenity and Pleasant—in the lead today, with Lottie Camber bringing up the rear. Surreys ahead and behind and everyone else in between. It was a good, strategic placement, sort of averaging out the relative speed of the vehicles. But that wasn't the main reason he had them spread so. The real reason was that the sisters and Lottie had got into it the evening before on the issue of appropriate dress for cotillions as opposed to afternoon wear for tea occasions, and all three had been pale and stiff-lipped since. He had to keep them separated until it blew over, otherwise they would have every woman in the crowd choosing up sides.

It was the first time he had seen Aunt Jessy Wheeler take sides with Lottie Camber about anything, and of course that had been disastrous, too. Lottie had politely told Jessy to mind her own business and stop interfering, and that had set Clara Hayes off on a roaring tizzie, and when the baby started crying Amber Quinn had made a cutting remark to Clara about the way she wore her bonnet, and Nora Bennett—who wore hers the same way—had taken extreme umbrage and made a comment that the reason the baby was crying was because it was Sterling Quinn's offspring and therefore probably not too bright . . . and about that time Jake's head had started aching from trying to keep track of who was mad at whom and about what.

He glanced back again and cursed under his

253

breath. Mabel Hornby apparently had decided to have a little chat to pass the time. She had broken ranks to pull up alongside the Mills wagon, threatening the ribs and wheels of both. Jake reined around, rode back down the line and took a deep breath before pulling off his hat. "Ah, Ma'am," he said, "I surely would take it as a favor if you'd get back to your place in line. Do you suppose you'd do that?"

"Certainly," she smiled at him, then turned toward Sedonia. "Thing is, most folks use too much saleratas, seems to me. Biscuits' insides ought to be like little, soft shingles, not like rows of lumps. What I do is weigh out the flour, then for each ounce of flour I . . ."

"Get back in line!" Jake roared.

Children's heads popped out of both wagons to gawk at him, and the two women favored him with disapproving scowls. "Nothing was ever accomplished by a loud and imperious manner," Sedonia Mills said. Mabel looked like she was going to give it some thought and have her say later. But she did get back into line.

"If I keep my sanity through this," Jake promised himself, "I'm goin' to donate ten dollars to a Franciscan monastery." He turned toward the front just in time to see a sack of meal arc outward from the Wilkinson, Stuckey and Todd wagon, to land with a thump on the ground. Jake spurred the sorrel forward, leaned from his saddle to lift the fifty-pound sack, then headed on to catch the wagon that had dropped it. The wagon hadn't even slowed. At the tailgate he peered inside, nodded to Maude Wilkin-

254

son and said, "Ma'am, you dropped this."

"I didn't drop it," she said. "I threw it out."

"How come you to throw it out, Ma'am? This is good meal."

"Well, it isn't ours."

"Whose is it, then?"

"As far as I know, it belongs to Henrietta Price. If she wants it, she can carry it."

Jake chewed on his tongue, needing the pain to keep him courteous. "Ma'am, Miz Price doesn't have a wagon to carry this in. That's why we put her stuff in other wagons."

"Well, I was willing to do her that favor, but not if she's goin' to talk about my husband behind his back."

Jake sighed. "What did she say about Mr. Wilkinson behind his back?"

"She said he isn't here!"

Jake looked around. "Well, Ma'am, that seems to be factual enough. He *isn't* here."

"Well, it isn't what she said so much, it's how she said it."

"Ma'am, I'm fixin' to chunk this meal back into your wagon, so you ought to get out of the way . . . because if you don't I just might knock you right on your delicacy with it."

One trick Jake had discovered early on, women tended to work together better and get along better if they all had somebody to be mutually mad at. Generally, that was him.

Maybe he would donate more than ten dollars to a Franciscan monastery. Maybe twenty-five or fifty.

He glanced back again, then cut through the line

255

to accost Tyrone Sneed and Annie Coke, riding alongside the train. Jake pointed beyond them. "Why have those two stopped?" In the distance, Ophelia Lashlee's carriage and Sedonia Mills' wagon had left the line and halted, side by side in the scant shade of a honey locust tree.

"They're trading babies," Sneed said, shrugging.

"They ain't either," Annie corrected him. "They're *changin'* babies." She glanced back, looking thoughtful. "That reminds me, Charlie, we need to find us a crick and lay over. They's a lot of wash to be done."

Jake peered into the hazy distance, trying to recall what he had seen of this country before. The hills went on and on, arid, sandscrabble rises with the vegetation of land just on the verge of being desert. Yet here and there, wandering through it down little rocky draws and widening valleys, were streams that carried good water. In the distance a hazy line of pale green marked what might be a stream. Beyond the hills stepped away and away, and rising above them were clouds—faraway thunderheads that had been there each of the past five or six days. They seemed a little nearer now.

"If we can persuade these folks to keep moving along," he said, "we might be at water by tonight. Where did Holly Bee get off to?"

"We're low on vittles," Annie said. "She went to get us all some supper."

"I wish you'd keep an eye on her, like you promised her uncle you would," Jake rasped, shaking his head.

"Matters to you, does it, Charlie?"

Sneed had ambled back to see what was keeping the stopped wagons. A half-mile north, another rider plodded along, a silhouette on the skyline except for the flash of color where sunlight caught his white whiskers.

"Hot dang," Jake muttered. "Now I've got to go fetch Mr. Tuttle back again. I wish his wife and daughter would keep him with their wagon. If he gets out of sight he'll get lost."

With an exasperated sigh, Jake wheeled the sorrel and headed out to retrieve the old man.

Annie looked after him, her eyes narrowed by a trace of smile. "He ain't about to admit anybody is important to him," she said to herself. "Not Holly Bee, not Clara Hayes, not old man Tuttle—not the whole dang lot of us. Don't matter even a whit to him, do we? Not so's he'd admit to it, we don't." The smile built. "Just like my husband Woodrow. Like him as peas in a pod, some ways."

To the west, the wagon string was still rolling, moving on. But even now, without the determined presence of Jake Creedmore insisting on a semblance of order, they were beginning to scatter, and Annie felt a moment of real pity for the young man she had latched onto. "I bet he'd rather be drivin' cows than tryin' to tend a bunch of women," she told herself. "At least cows got a herd instinct." She heeled her horse and headed out after the receding bunch. She probably, she felt, ought to have a talk with some of the ladies.

In midafternoon, Holly Bee showed up, coming in from the north. Strung to her saddle she had a brace of long-legged rabbits, a prairie hen and a turkey. She showed them to Annie, apologetically. "All I could find," she said. "Game is scarce along here." She raised high in her saddle to look around. "Where's what's-his-name?"

"Who, Charlie?"

"Whatever."

"He went on ahead to look at a crick. I told him we needed a place to do the wash."

"You shouldn't let him go off by himself," Holly Bee frowned. "What makes you think he'll come back?"

"Because he's an honorable soul, Holly Bee. Sets on him like a horsehair shirt would, an' it itches him somethin' fierce, but he is, anyway."

"He's an outlaw."

Annie studied on that for a moment before responding. "No, he isn't," she said finally. "He robbed a bank—leastways he says he did, but he's no outlaw. I know about outlaws. Married one once."

"Well, you shouldn't trust him. What if he just keeps on goin'? He don't like bein' with us any more than I like havin' him around."

A slight twinkle came into Annie's eyes. "Matters to you, does it, Holly Bee? I mean, whether or not he comes back?"

"I need to hang these critters on one of the wagons, to keep for supper," Holly Bee said. "How come those two wagons are so far behind everybody else?"

"They stopped so Sedonia and Amber could change their babies. That thespian is yonder, leadin' them in."

"They better keep their heads up an' their skirts

258

down," Holly Bee allowed. "That varmint ain't to be trusted, any more than what's-his-name is."

"Sight less, some ways," Annie agreed. "I been thinkin' either that man ain't a thespian or I've had the wrong notion about them. I believe he likes women just fine."

"Well, it's just as well that what's-his-name isn't all that keen on 'em. Annie, somebody ought to talk to that Coryanne O'Keefe. I seen her moon-eyein' that outlaw a couple of times now, an' somebody ought to put a stop to that. It . . . well, she's too young to know better, but it's not in her best interest."

"I declare," Annie muttered, covering it with a cough. "But it don't matter to you whether he runs off or not?"

"Not the least bit." Holly Bee had untied the game from her saddle and was flagging down Janey McCoy's haywagon. "None of my business what he does."

The sun was low, sinking toward rising clouds, when Jake returned. Stopping on a rise, he removed his hat and shook his head slowly in disbelief. The wagons were scattered over a good hundred acres of rolling prairie. The only saving grace that he could see was that they were all there—somewhere—and they all were still moving in more or less the same direction. "My God," he breathed. "Lord. If I ever get out of this I think I'll go join the Spanish navy."

By the time he had them assembled again, rolling in line as he was determined that they should, the sun was behind the clouds and evening's clear light lay across the land. Once again, the lead vehicle

259

was the Higgins sisters' surrey, so he pointed them at where he wanted them to go. "Right off yonder," he showed them, "where you see those green tops, there's a good stream there. It's only about a mile and a half, and there's a rock tank where whoever wants to can wash clothes. If you ladies can just sort of guide a straight line in that direction, I'll do my best to get everyone else to follow you."

As the wagons rolled past him he waved his hat, signalling to Annie, Holly Bee, Henrietta Price, Fredonia Whisenhunt and Tyrone Sneed. When he had them around him he said, "From now until we get to that creek yonder, I want these wagons in single-file order. That's because there are gullies and breaks above the creek, and I'm tired of fixing wagons. So if you ladies would ride along close, two on each side of the line, and *please* try to keep them in line, I'll go ahead and lead. Tyrone, you bring up the rear and don't let anybody straggle."

They nodded and started for their assigned stations, but Holly Bee paused and turned back. "I don't take orders from you," she pointed out.

Jake held his temper in close check. "I'm just asking as a favor," he said.

"Well, I'll do it because I feel like it," she said. "I just want it clear that I don't take orders from you."

"All right," he sighed. "You don't take orders from me. Now will you please just . . ."

She was already heading away. "I'll bet it was the brightest day in your uncle Roscoe's life," Jake muttered, "the day you ran off from him and didn't come back."

They made it to the slope of the creek's little

valley without trouble, and Jake rode ahead of the Higgins wagon, choosing a smooth route down toward the stream. Because of the thunderheads in the west, and because of the unsettling tendency of pretty little streams to become raging torrents in the event of flash floods, he had located a likely ford and now he led them across and up the far bank to a wide, cottonwood-studded shelf beyond. It was a sheltered, pleasant spot, and he chose it carefully — deadfall for fires, graze for the stock, space for children to run and play, easy access down to the creek for the women who had things to wash . . . and a shady place off to one side where he could throw his bedroll and maybe just sleep for the duration.

The crossing was roundabout — an angling path down to the creek, then upstream along its low bank to where he had found the easy ford, then across and back downstream to where there was an easy climb to the campsite. He led the Higgins wagon in among the cottonwoods, then counted them as they followed — the buckboard, the Tuttles' two-up wagon with Fredonia Whisenhunt riding alongside on her black horse, the Mills wagon, Janey McCoy's haywagon led by Holly Bee on her paint, Nora Bennett's drawn cart, the carriage with Ophelia Lashlee driving while Amber Quinn sat beside her nursing her infant and Coryanne O'Keefe smiled at him from the boot, then the Wilkinson wagon with Henrietta Price leading aboard her gray . . . one by one they crested and he counted them, satisfied for once with their performance.

He sighed with relief as Lottie Camber's surrey

crested the rise, followed by Tyrone Sneed, brushing dust from his tall hat.

"The Rubicon is crossed and we the victors here assemble," Sneed orated, looking smug.

"Help me get them circled . . ." Jake started, then stopped as a shout and a crack like splintering wood echoed just behind him. He looked around.

At the last instant, Lottie Camber had noticed the Higgins sisters climbing from their surrey and changed her mind about where she wanted to park. Veering to go around them, she had edged too close to the high bank. Now her surrey hung canted over the ledge, one forward wheel turning merrily in thin air above a six-foot drop. From the way the surrey seemed to crouch there, Jake knew what the noise had been. Its front axle was broken.

Chapter XXV

"What I ought to do," Jake stormed, tying off a winch line to the trunk of a cottonwood tree, "is just get on my horse and go find a town with a jail and turn myself in. Just walk in and say, 'Howdy, I'm Jake Creedmore and I robbed a bank, lock me up.' That's what I ought to do." He made no attempt to keep his voice down. He didn't care who heard him. "Restitution! Blame that woman sheriff anyway for talking around in circles. Restitution, she said! Restitution instead of retribution! Little old Community Service, she said. Redemption! Chance to get off the devil's trail, just do a little old favor for a few ladies with female troubles! Female troubles, my left foot! Dang biddies don't have female troubles, *I* have female troubles!"

Hauling his drag rope around a second tree he stamped to the rear of the unhitched surrey hanging on the ledge and tied the other end of the rope to its rear axle. "I could have been clear to New Orleans by now!" he griped. "Or Springfield, Missouri! Or Springfield, Illinois, or Springfield, Massachusetts! But no, not me. Here I am wet-nursin' a bunch of squabblin' women across half of Texas, goin' right back the way I meant to be coming from and takin' time out to fix busted wagons every whip-stitch! If I had the brains God gave a biscuit I'd just go find a sheriff and turn myself in!"

Around him, children gawked and scrambled to stay out of his way. Some of the women pretended to ignore him, others were haughty and stiff-lipped, offended at his rude behavior, and still others gathered up great baskets of fabric and garments and headed for the creek, wanting to be nowhere near a man in such a mood.

Finding tools, Jake drew the bolt pin from the surrey's rigging and removed one of its harness shafts, swinging it like a long club as he ranted. People disappeared behind trees and wagons, and Tyrone Sneed scurried beneath the buckboard.

"If I'd ever had a lick of sense in my life I wouldn't have listened to that woman sheriff!" he blustered. "And if I hadn't stopped off at San Galena I'd never have run into her in the first place! And if I'd had gumption enough to just head off and leave by myself out yonder where the horse threw me, I'd never have gone to San Galena! And if I hadn't let a couple of females throw in with me at that woodstop I'd never have been thrown by that horse!"

Warming to his subject, he wedged the surrey rail into the ropes at the snug-tree, hauling them together to make a loop. He tugged at his makeshift windlass, turning it a half-turn, and the surrey behind him groaned and scraped against the ledge. "If I hadn't got on that train at Rosebud I'd never have been at that woodstop to start with," he growled, setting his back to the task. "If I hadn't tied in with outlaws I'd never have gone to Rosebud in the first place! Come to that, if I had just shot Conrad W. Jackson instead of robbing his bank, I'd probably have been a town hero instead of a wanted man! And if I hadn't dug that damned well out yonder . . ."

Something stung his back and his hand slipped off the windlass rail. It sprang back and whacked him in the shin. He spun around and Serenity Higgins stood there, threatening him with a willow switch. "You mind your tongue," she said. "Us ladies don't have to tolerate profanity."

"You ladies . . ." he grabbed the switch, jerked it out of her hand and threw it on the ground. "I'll tell you what's hard to tolerate. You ladies are hard to tolerate. Damn near impossible! Bunch of self-centered, gossipin' busybodies that can't even stay in line when a body tries to help you! I don't think it's any wonder your husbands disappeared."

Serenity's face went white and her eyes went liquid. Abruptly she turned on her heel and walked away, ramrod-stiff. Jessy Wheeler hurried from the buckboard to intercept the older woman and comfort her. Jake saw Clara Hayes staring at him, her eyes blazing with anger. "Don't you butt in, either, Miss Clara," he warned. "I'm in no mood to be reasonable right now, and I know you understand that because I doubt you've ever been reasonable in your whole life. Hitting men with axe-handles! I swear!"

Lottie Camber peered from behind a tree. "Mr. Creedmore, I believe you ought to just calm down and . . ."

"Not another word!" he pointed an angry finger at her. "Just don't you talk to me! Look at that surrey! I'll probably be up all night splinting that axle because you couldn't be bothered to see if there was solid ground under your wheels! Oh, no, just drove right off a gully cliff! Lord!" He glared around at all and sundry. "If there was an entire brain in this whole outfit, somebody would take it out and play with it! Half of you squabblin' like biddy hens all the time and the rest not payin' enough attention to even keep going the same direction! Mis Hornby can't drive a wagon for thinking about how to mix dough! Miz Wilkinson can't tolerate Miz Price and slings sacks of meal out on the prairie! And you, Tyrone Sneed! I see you under that buckboard! You tag along and strut and brag but I haven't seen you lift a finger to help me keep these wagons fixed! Ow!" he lost his grip on the windlass again and it whacked him on the other shin.

Annie sighed, hurried across and took the windlass from him. "Let me hold that 'til you run down," she said.

"Don't you get righteous, either!" he shouted at her. "You got me into this in the first place!"

Over near the carriage, Holly Bee called, "Do you want me to shoot him, Annie?"

Jake ignored her. "What kind of women take off half-cocked to go looking for men who probably don't want to be found? What kind of women stop on railroad tracks to have babies? What kind of women ain't got sense enough to stay home where they belong and let folks that know how tend to

266

their problems?" Shaking a furious finger, he stepped away from the windlass, and Holly Bee raised her rifle. Jake stared at her, then put his fists on his hips.

"You, Holly Bee Sutherland!" he barked. "Just look at you! Slouch hat, boots and damned old britches, and that fool rifle you're so proud of. What are you goin' to do, shoot me? Just look at you! These damned fool women may not have the sense God gave a raisin, but at least they *look* like women! Why in hell can't you put on a dress and behave yourself?"

From the strange light that glowed in her blue eyes, Jake thought for an instant that she *would* shoot him. But then her chin quivered and he saw that the strange light in her eyes was evening's glow shining on tears. She stared at him for a moment, then turned away.

"Charlie, turn around," Annie said.

Still furious, he swung around. Annie squinted at him and turned loose of the windlass rail. It flipped up, caught him square under the chin and Jake saw stars come out. The next thing he knew he was flat on his back and Annie was kneeling beside him.

"I might have misjudged about you," she said, sadly. "I thought better of you than to go turnin' mean like you just did."

He rubbed his chin, trying to sit up but still too dizzy. "I said what needed saying," he grumbled. "This whole outfit is . . ."

"You just hush. I heard what you said. What you said to Miz Higgins yonder, that was uncalled for, Charlie. Don't you know the Higgins ladies ain't out

267

to find their husbands? They don't have husbands. They're both widows. They came along because they'd have been lonely with everybody else gone."

"Oh." Jake rubbed his sore chin and looked at the ground. "Well, I didn't realize that. But . . ."

"An' you think the rest of 'em *wants* to be out here like this? They had to go lookin', Charlie. They was about out of anything to eat there in that town. What's on those wagons is all they had left."

"Well, damn it, I didn't know . . ."

"No, you didn't. So you had to get it out of your system. You think you got problems, Charlie, an' maybe you do. But if you think you're the only one with problems . . . you shouldn't have said what you did to Holly Bee, either. I'm ashamed of that."

"Well, dang it, she's always deviling me, Annie—"

"Holly Bee doesn't wear a dress because she doesn't have one."

Jake didn't say another word to anyone all evening. He dragged the Camber surrey off the shelf, cut cottonwood splints to bind its front axle and reassembled its rails. He went down to the creek and washed himself, staying clear of the rock tank where some of the women had an assembly-line wash operation going on, with ropes strung in the trees for clotheslines, then went back up to the shelf, searched his pack for a bit of jerky or biscuit, found none and decided to do without. He kept to himself and everyone else avoided him.

He was tending the stock, securing the rope corral and watching the clouds in the west when he noticed Coryanne O'Keefe coming across from the fire. She had a tin plate and a mug, and for a moment he thought she was going to bring them to him. But she simply put them down beside his gear and turned away without a glance.

By the time it was dark, lightnings danced in the high clouds to the west, and the thunder when it came was distant and deep. There was a flurry of activity as women collected their children, brought in their wash and stowed things in shelter, but Jake stayed to himself. Gusts of wind chattered in the treetops, but the air had no scent of rain. Still, it was raining somewhere to the west, and the clouds in the distance flared with stuttering light.

It was a silent and brooding camp that night, among the cottonwoods. For once, nobody had much to say to anybody. It was as though Jake's mood had stunned them . . . or as though his anger had stung them. Even Tyrone Sneed slunk around, quiet and morose, then rolled up under a rock shelf and went to sleep.

They slept that night to the sound of distant thunders, and when they awoke to a fresh dawn Jake Creedmore was gone. It was as though he had never been there, and even Holly Bee couldn't find enough tracks to tell which way he had gone.

"I don't generally misjudge menfolks," Annie Coke admitted to them all, "but this time I reckon I must have."

"So what do we do now?" several asked, of her and of one another.

"I don't know what else we can do, except go on," Lottie Camber said. "We can't go back. And even if

269

we could, why would we?"

In the silence as they thought about that, they heard Amber Quinn's voice, coming from the carriage, crooning quietly. "Hush little baby, don't you cry. We'll find your daddy by and by."

"I can't stand that," Annie said. "I still got the map, an' I reckon we'd best go on and try to find that baby's daddy. And all the rest, too."

"But we don't even know where we are," Mabel Hornby said, sounding as though she was about ready to cry.

"Oh, I know where we are," Annie assured her. "So does Holly Bee."

"I do?" Holly Bee looked up. "Where?"

"Don't you remember, child?" Annie pointed northwest. "We crossed this crick before, though we was upstream a ways. That was where Chester stepped in your fryin' pan."

Clara Hayes looked up from folding clothes. "Who?"

"Chester . . . Charlie. Jake. Whatever his name is."

Holly Bee stared at her, incredulous. "We come all this way, just to end up at Six Bit?"

"No, Six Bit is way off yonder. We're goin' where the map says, just about straight west. We're goin' to take a look at that trestle out there."

Ophelia Lashlee gazed out at the shadowed glade where the children already were running and shouting in the cool morning air. High clouds stood, as they had, to the west. Sue and Sally Lashlee had taken offense at Elmer Todd and had him down, pummeling him with little fists while his brother

Emory stood aside shouting taunts at all three of them. Ophelia took a deep breath, then let it go. They weren't hurting one another. "What happens if we don't find them?" she asked.

"The men? Of course we'll find them." Nora Bennett put an arm around her shoulders and nodded assurance. "We have to find them."

"But what if they aren't there? What if they aren't anywhere we can find?"

"Then we just keep on looking."

"I felt better about it when we had a man helping us," Henrietta Price said. "Even if he did turn out to be no account, I always sort of figured he'd come up with some way to lead me to wherever Pasco is."

"I guess it was the same with me," Mabel Hornby admitted. "I never realized he was so upset about me gettin' out of line back there."

"You weren't the one that broke an axle," Lottie said. "It was my fault."

Coryanne O'Keefe stirred the coals of the breakfast fire, then looked up at one and then another of them. "He left because of me," she said. "I told him how grand I thought it was about Amber having a baby, and I . . . well, I said I couldn't hardly wait to have one, too."

"Knew I should'a shot that varmint," Holly Bee glittered.

"Oh, he didn't do anything. Fact is, after that he wouldn't even hardly talk to me. I guess I made him mad."

"Doesn't matter who set him off like that," Ophelia said. "I just felt better when we had a man to sort of look after us."

271

"Well, you still have one!"

As one, they turned. Tyrone Sneed stood there, managing to look hurt, angry and capable, all at once.

"I'm sorry," Ophelia blurted, "I didn't mean . . ."

"It doesn't matter," he said, clearing his throat. "And you're probably right. I may not know a trail from a trilogy, and I've never repaired a wagon wheel in my life. But if it makes you ladies feel better to have a masculine voice hollering at you whenever you get out of line, then I'd be right proud to do that."

Annie gazed at him with sudden approval. She had misjudged another one, she decided. Tyrone Sneed was no more a thespian than she was. "We'll rest here today," she decided. "Give our stock a chance to graze, and maybe Holly Bee can find us some meat. Tomorrow we'll pick up and move on. There's another crick yonder, somewhere. We might be able to make it there by tomorrow night."

The contraption was Sterling Quinn's idea, and not many thought much of it. But it was the only idea they had, so they helped. It was nothing more than the groundcloth from a tent, ripped out and formed around a framework of elevation poles and spadehandles, then coated with tar. But it was the best they could do, and as night fell — a sodden night of pounding rain that came down in blind sheets while lightnings danced overhead and the little creek below the embankment became a rushing river — they crept from shelter and lowered it on

272

ropes. It would have two passengers—Sterling Quinn because it was his idea and Harold Wheeler because he drew the short straw. Clyde Hornby wanted to go, too, but they didn't let him. He was still stove up from being beaten by Dos Burton, and was in no condition to run a flash flood in the dark of night.

"You boys watch yourselves," Frank Camber told the two in the canvas boat. "If any of them guards see you, they'll probably shoot you."

"They won't see a thing," Harold grinned in the stormlight. "They're all under wraps, waitin' out the rain."

"All you got to do is just get to a town," Frank said. "Anyplace with a telegraph. Just let the women know where we are, and tell 'em . . . well tell 'em . . ."

"We'll take care of it," Sterling Quinn said, clasping his hand. "You all just cover for us here as long as you can, then make out you didn't know we was gone and the rest of you had nothin' to do with it."

The two eased down into the little craft and cast off its ropes. For a moment it turned and eddied at the bank, then its long end caught the flow of water. It spun out, crashed against a timber, broke loose and was gone in the darkness.

273

Chapter XXVI

As dawn's banners climbed the hills ahead his second day out, Jake put the miles behind him, a grim rider on a fast horse. With light enough to see the land, he let the sorrel have its head to run as God and its breeders had intended, and didn't slow until the horse was foam-flecked and panting. He could have run it more, but didn't.

"It wasn't your fault, hoss," he muttered. "It's my fault. Nobody else's, just mine. Philo was right about me. I wait too long to get mad, then when I do bust loose I do more damage than good. Sometimes I don't think I'm fit to have around."

When the sun was warm on his shoulders he walked the animal a mile, then gave it water from his canteen. From a rise he studied the land, seeing the landmarks and knowing where he was. Ahead was an old, abandoned stead, a relic of the Comanche and Jicarilla days in these dry hills. Leading the sorrel, letting it cool and get its wind, he walked the mile to the old place to rest for a bit in the shade of a locust tree. As the sorrel crunched at seep-grass he flanneled it down and rubbed its sleek neck. "You're not Conrad W. Jackson's horse," he said slowly, gazing off into the distance. "You're my

274

horse. I gave plenty for you."

On impulse he pulled the hat from his head, held it at arm's length and gazed at it. Except for being dusty and a little stained around the band, it was the same hat he had taken at the bank in Perdition. With a grimace, he turned it front-on, gripped the felt brim on each side and rolled it, pressing it tight. When he released it it sprang back, but only part way. Where there had been a flat brim, now it swept up jauntily. He put one hand inside the crown and creased it with the other, pressing the crease this way and that until it suited him. "You're not Conrad W. Jackson's silver-belly beaver hat," he said. "You're my hat . . . by God." He put it on his head again and tugged it to a comfortable angle.

He opened a saddle pocket and pulled out the painting inside, looking at it with distaste. The painted face stared back at him, haughty and presumptuous. "As for you," he said, "you're not my picture. You're Conrad W. Jackson's picture and you ought to be properly displayed." He got out his knife, poked a hole through the top of it and hung it high on a wind-scored post that might once have been a corral gate. It gleamed in the morning sun.

Before he put away his knife, he walked around the sorrel, pausing on each side to throw back the leathers and shave the initials from the hand-tooled skirts. "You're not Conrad W. Jackson's saddle," he said. "You're my saddle."

The ritual was a venting of spleen, he knew, but somehow it was more than that, as well. Somehow he felt just a little cleaner than he had before. "That lady sheriff was right," he told himself. "I've been riding the devil's trail, and I'm not the man I thought I was, because of it." Nobody made me rob that bank, he thought. I did that all by myself. I'm guilty as sin of doing that, and the guilt slops over onto everything. "Hell," he said aloud, his voice thin on the winds, "I don't even know how to be polite any more."

He rested a half-hour in the sparse shade, feeling moody and small, then took up his reins and led the sorrel out into sunlight. He swung aboard, leaned to pat the horse fondly and said, "Let's go, hoss. Nothing holdin' us back now."

Behind him, Conrad W. Jackson's painting stared biliously at the morning, but Jake didn't look back where it hung.

When the sun was high he crossed a rock-bottom gully that normally would have held no more than a trickle of water. But now it was wide and flowing, belly-deep to the horse and rising. He splashed across and looked back. "Real storm out yonder last night," he muttered. He was glad he had reached the stream when he did. By nightfall, it would be bank-deep and uncrossable, and it might be tomorrow before it receded.

In midafternoon he saw distant smoke and rode to high ground to squint at it, shading his eyes against the quartering sun that made the far reaches haze and dance. The smoke was a tiny plume, moving. He nodded. "Chicago, Shreveport and Pacific," he said, wrinkling his nose. He turned a little south and went on.

He came to Rosebud in the evening. It wasn't much of a town—just a little shack-and-shed place with a railroad depot, just like it had been when he saw it before. He rode in, hitched the sorrel in front of a ratty general store and went inside. The aproned man behind the counter gave him a sour look and Jake gave it right back. Then he walked around, getting an idea of what merchandise was available, and returned to the counter. "Just so you'll sleep better," he told the man, "come morning, after I've looked up Roscoe Sutherland and had a little sleep, I aim to be a cash customer of yours. Right now, though, I need a place to tend a tired horse and a tired man. And we both need to be fed."

With completion of his new office at the Clearwater site, Conrad W. Jackson brought wagons and hauling crews down to Perdition and loaded the last of his equipment and personal effects. His desk, cabinets, chairs, benches, lamps and signs—these draped with muslin because they were nobody's business just yet—were carried out of the old bank building and loaded into wagons. From the back room came his bed, nightstand, lavatory, mirrored dresser, closet and an array of trunks and crates, things he had not unpacked since moving out of his house and into the bank.

He sent men to Sim Hoover's livery to fetch his buggy and gather his riding horses for driving to Clearwater, where he would headquarter from now on, and wagons to close out the last of the inventory at the emporium, which would be reopened at Clearwater when its building was complete.

With his livery stables empty, Sim Hoover walked up the road to watch the loading and departure. Homer Boles was already there, just standing in the shade of a weathered awning and looking moody.

"My God," Sim said, gazing around at the desolate remains of the little town, "it's like watchin' the sod fall on an old friend's casket, ain't it?"

Across the street, Conrad W. Jackson directed the tying down of things in a dray wagon, while his horse and buggy waited at a nearby hitch to follow the procession out of town when everything was loaded.

"This is the most activity I've seen in Perdition for months," Sim intoned, his voice as hollow as a preacher's at a gravesite. "But it's the last hurrah, I reckon. Those fellas that came to get the horses, they said they won't be needin' stablin' any more. Conrad W. Jackson's goin' to have his own stables up at the new town . . . Jake's old place." He glanced up and down the once-busy street, seeing the linoleum signs everywhere. "I hate those signs," he muttered. "Don't make any difference now, though. I reckon I'm out of business as of today."

Homer Boles squinted at him, thoughtfully. "That's all the business you had? Just Jackson's stock?"

"Oh, there's your horse and mine, and Opal Hayes' pair, an' maybe a few days' board on some horses that was rode in yesterday from Portales, but not enough to keep goin' on. I'll have to shut down an' move on, I reckon."

Across the street, wind whipped a corner of the muslin covering on one of the big, plank signboards

278

in Jackson's dray and a crewman hastened to tie it down. Boles scratched his chin, looking thoughtful.

"You got any idea where you'll go, Homer?" Sim asked. "Not much future in bein' town marshal in a ghost town."

Homer didn't answer. He just stood and watched.

Down the street, a handful of men emerged from the shuttered hotel. Sim nodded in that direction. "Those are the ones that came down from Portales. I wonder what they're so interested in them survey stakes for?"

"Maybe they'll buy the place," Homer said, thoughtfully.

"Buy what? Perdition?" Sim shook his head. "I'd sure make them a good price on a livery stable, but if they wait around a few days they can have it for free." He waved a forlorn arm, indicating the length of the street. "What's here for anybody to buy, Homer? Bunch of empty buildin's waitin' to fall down? Damn. I kind of liked this place, back when it was still a place . . . back before them damn linoleum signs."

The sun rose higher and wagons appeared at the intersection, loaded wagons coming from the emporium. As they approached, the crewmen across at the old bank finished their strapping and climbed aboard their wagons, and Conrad W. Jackson — looking smug and pleased — stepped up into his buggy and took the reins. He swung out into the street and headed sedately for the north road, all the wagons following.

"Not so much as a fare-thee-well," Sim grunted. "Used to think I liked that fart, too." He shrugged.

"Well, I guess the party's over."

"I guess it is," Homer said. "Did you see those signs that Conrad W. Jackson loaded on that wagon?"

"Couldn't see what they said," Sim shrugged. "He had 'em covered up."

"Well, I saw one of 'em. It said, 'Clearwater Townsite, Central City on the Great Central and Pacific Railroad.' "

Sim stared at him. "A railroad?"

"That's what he's been up to," Homer nodded. "I reckon that's why he wanted Jake's old place so bad, with all that water. Somebody's buildin' a railroad."

Sim's mouth hung open until he remembered to close it. "Well, I'm jiggered," he declared.

Odd sounds came from up the street, and they turned to look. The Portales men had spread out, and now were coming along both sides of the street, removing linoleum signs as they came.

"By damn," Sim breathed. "Maybe you're right, Homer. Maybe they *are* buyin' the place."

A tall, hook-nosed man with a round hat strolled down mid-street, making notes on a pad. When he noticed Homer and Sim he came over to them and held out a hand. "Good morning," he said. "My name is Henderson. Philo Henderson. I represent the Creedmore Investment Trust."

"Creedmore?" Sim gawked at him, then shook his head. "Sim Hoover. This here's Homer Boles. He's town marshal . . . or was. Did you say Creedmore?"

"Pleased to meet you," Henderson said. "That's right. Creedmore Investment Trust. We have purchased these properties here."

"You bought Perdition?"

"Well, not all of it," Henderson said. "But I guess it comes to most of it. Lot to be done here, isn't there?"

"You *did* say Creedmore?"

"That's right. Creedmore."

"Ah . . . what Creedmore is that?"

"Oh, that's Jake Creedmore. He's our initial investor in the trust." He looked around. "We're going to need timbers, I suppose, since they'll use a rotary rig . . ."

"A what?" Homer blinked.

"Rotary rig. We'll be drilling a water well over there. Jake hit a feeder strata at his place, but the big water is here, about a hundred and twenty feet down we think."

"Jake Creedmore robbed the bank here!" Sim blurted. "At least, we think he did. Or I thought he did, anyway."

"Well," Philo grinned, "I doubt he'll do that again. He owns it now."

Two thoroughly wet and shaken men pulled themselves from the roiling waters of a draw that was now a river. They dragged themselves up limestone banks and flopped there, exhausted, to watch the remains of their pole-and-canvas boat wash on downstream.

"You all right, Harold?" Sterling Quinn asked, trying to catch his breath.

Harold raised himself, then sagged back, resting

on his elbows. "I guess so, though if there's a place on me that don't hurt, I haven't found it yet."

"I'm about the same," Quinn admitted. "Land, I was beginnin' to think we'd go all the way to the Gulf of Mexico."

Through the night and into the morning they had tried to stop the spinning, bucking contraption, grabbing at roots and rock banks as they veered past, but the velocity of the flood had carried them on and on like a leaf dancing on a torrent. Only when the canvas boat had smashed against a stone shoulder at a bend, throwing both of them into shallow water, had they escaped.

Out of the water finally, they sprawled on arid ground under a blazing sun and let their dizziness subside. Below them the floodwaters thundered and foamed. Above, a wandering turkey buzzard circled, waiting to see if they were dead.

After a while, Quinn got his feet under him and staggered to the high bank of the floodway, climbed it and stood, looking around. He had little idea where they were, except somewhere east of where they had started. Nowhere was there any sign of buildings, roads, no sign of people anywhere. But they had to find a town. He had to get a message to Amber, to let her know that he was all right and that he cared about her. She would need to know that, with the baby coming.

Down on the lower bank Harold Wheeler was coming around. He sat up, made it to his hands and knees, and stood, a half-drowned ragged scarecrow steaming in the high sun. Quinn shouted at him and he started for the high bank, walking painfully, favoring his left leg. His pants were torn away there, and Quinn saw the raw, scraped skin where he had been thrown against the rocks. He went down, helped him to ground level and said, "We'd better get moving. You pick a direction and I'll help you walk."

Harold gazed around, then his eyes held eastward and he squinted. "Somebody's comin'. Over there."

At first, Quinn didn't see anyone. Then there was movement in the distance. A man riding a horse, coming toward them. With a sigh, he sat down to wait.

The newcomer was small and wiry, a youngish, nervous-seeming man with a wide hat pulled low over a prominent nose, and stiff whiskers that jutted outward and twitched with each movement of his face. He looked like a mouse, Quinn thought. He also wore a large handgun in a tie-down rig.

"You fellas don't look too good," he said, studying them from his saddle. "Look like men either chasin' somebody or bein' chased, which is it?"

"I don't know if we're bein' chased," Quinn told him. "But we got away from a work camp last night in the flood. People wouldn't let us go. Is there a town hereabouts?"

"A few," the man said. "Here and there. What's the matter with him? He hurt?"

"Banged his leg on the rocks. I could use a bandage for him, if you got anything that would work."

"I got some toweling here someplace." The rider reached into a saddlepocket, never taking his eyes off the two of them. He brought out a wad of cloth and tossed it to Quinn.

Quinn shook it out and began wrapping Harold's leg. "Much obliged," he said. "My name is Quinn. Sterling Quinn. This is Harold Wheeler."

"I'm Bead," the man nodded. "What line of work are you gents in when you're not escapin' from work gangs?"

"Railroads," Quinn said.

"Uh-huh." Bead backed his horse off a few steps, then swung down. "Railroads. You happen to know a gent name of Clive Wilson Jones?"

The two looked at each other blankly, and shook their heads. "Don't think I ever heard the name," Quinn said. "Wonder if you could point us the way to a town? We need to find a telegraph."

"Oh, I believe I can show you a town, all right," Bead approached and looked over Quinn's shoulder. "He doesn't seem to be hurt too bad. Fit to travel, you suppose?"

"I'm just banged up," Harold Wheeler said. "I can make it, if you'll show us the way. My mother's probably wonderin' where I am. I need to let her know."

"And my wife," Quinn said. "She's fixin' to have a baby."

"My," Bead said. "That's quite a story." With an abrupt, flowing movement he stood, drew his gun and thrust its muzzle against Quinn's back. "Stand up and raise your hands," he said. "I got you both dead to . . ."

It was so sudden, so unexpected, that Quinn virtually bolted upright, losing his balance as he did and staggering back against Bead. Bead windmilled, and his gun went sailing off over the bank, glinting in the sunlight. It hit the lower bank, bounced, skidded and hung for a moment right at the edge of the rock shelf. Then it teetered and fell into the water. Bead tripped and fell, landing on his tail.

Quinn regained his balance and stood over Bead, wide-eyed. "What did you do that for?"

"Because you're wanted men," Bead's whiskers twitched furiously. "It's plain as day that you are. Bounty is my business."

"We're not wanted men," Quinn said slowly, trying to understand. "I'm a journeyman tie-setter and Harold's a roustabout."

"Sure you are." Bead got his feet under him and turned full circle, squinting. "Where's my gun?"

"What makes you think we're wanted men?" Quinn demanded.

"Said yourself you're escapees from a work gang. That makes you fugitives from the law."

"It wasn't a *law* work gang. Just some people that didn't want us to leave because they're tryin' to keep a secret."

"Sure." Bead walked past him, searching here and there. "So you say. But you also said you're rail-roaders an' there isn't a railroader alive that doesn't know the name Clive Wilson Jones. I got you dead to rights, an' I aim to collect on you gents. Where the devil is my gun?"

"We're not railroaders and I never said we were," Quinn insisted. "We're railroad *builders*. There's a difference."

"Did you see where my gun went?"

"Well, hell, no, I didn't see where your gun went.

All I know is, you jabbed me with somethin' and told me to stand up. If you can't keep track of your gun, that's your problem."

"I saw where it went," Harold Wheeler said. "It went into the creek."

Bead stared at the torrent, his whiskers twitching. "In there?"

"Bigger'n Dallas," Harold nodded. He finished his own bandaging and stood, easing weight onto his sore leg. There didn't seem to be anything broken. "You said there was towns around here. Where are they?"

Bead didn't seem to hear him for a moment. He was looking at the creek, his whiskers twitching. Then he waved a hand. "There's Rosebud over yonder someplace, and Farley's off that direction, and Six Bit up there somewhere . . . take your pick. What am I gonna do without my gun?"

"Well, you still got your horse," Quinn pointed out. "What you might do is help us get to someplace where there's a telegraph."

Chapter XXVII

Like most everyone in the southwest, Wilbur Short had heard the name of Royal Flanders. He had heard the name spoken in hushed voices and with vague and differing qualifications. "A man-hunter," some said. "Vigilante," some said. "Bounty thing," some said. "Vigilante," some said. "Bounty hunter," said others. But however classified, the name usually was said with respect. Wilbur could not recall ever running across anyone who admitted to having met the man.

Thus, Wilbur Short was stunned and confused to find himself riding westward with Royal Flanders and some — he could never quite be sure how many, because they usually were spread across several miles — of his men. But, more than stunned, Wilbur was saddlesore and shaken. He would never have believed that riders could cover so much distance in so little time. They were like the prairie wind, he felt — pushing on and on, fast, steady and relentless. Each of them had at least two horses, and they swapped saddles from one to another as they went, never stopping for more than a few minutes. Wilbur's choice of travel — for what little he had done before — had been rail or stagecoach. But now, for straight cross-country pace, he decided that there never had been a train or stage that could keep up with these large, heavily-armed men and their running horses.

"The Flanders bunch, that's the bunch that tamed the badlands," Wilbur had heard someone say. He was ready to believe now that they had done it, all of it, and probably on a Sunday afternoon. Even flood-cresting waterways didn't seem to slow them down. They simply altered course to find a wide place where the flow was diminished, crossed and went on, putting seventy or eighty miles a day behind them.

He knew they were taking him back to Perdition, and he knew it was because he was a witness to Jake's robbing the bank there. But there seemed to be a lot more involved. It had to do with Mr. Burton and Mr. Jackson, and unlawful incarceration and forced servitude by somebody involved with some railroad that hadn't been built just yet, and with swindles and counter-swindles and who would pay for the capture of whom, and the more he thought about the few comments he heard, the less he understood them.

"I hope it isn't Jake Creedmore you fellers are after," he had said to one of them at a night stop. "I sort of like ol' Jake."

"It *was* him," the man said, "but times change. Mr. Flanders gets real testy about folks who lie to him and waste his time."

"I hope he doesn't think I did anything like that," Wilbur pled.

"No, not you," the man grinned. "But he knows

288

who did."

Like prairie wind the bunch thundered westward, and Wilbur was swept along with them, the country around him a blur, the brief halts and rests all running together in memory. Then there was a halt that was different. Wilbur was riding behind Royal Flanders himself, and being herded along by one of his deputies, when another one appeared on a hilltop ahead and to the left, and waved his hat. They veered toward him, and when they reached the hilltop the man pointed.

Yonder in the distance was what might once have been a little ranch but now was just a few weathered and scattered timbers. But among them was a speck of garish color, shining in the sun. They rode down to the place and hauled up, and Wilbur's eyes went wide at what was mounted on a post there. "Why, that there is Conrad W. Jackson's painting," he said. "Mr. Jackson put stock in that picture."

"Understand he did," Flanders' cheek twitched in what might have been a grin. He rode to the post, reached up and took down the picture. "Fine likeness of the gentleman," he said. "Looks like he's been eating toads."

"Town yonder a ways," one of the big men said. "Rosebud, I believe."

"Sam's over that way," Flanders said. "He'll check it out. Let's move." And they were off again, Wilbur Short clinging to a flying horse and wondering if he would live long enough to ever tell tales about this wild trip.

Most of the way to Rosebud, Harold Wheeler rode Bead's horse. It was the practical method of getting the three of them there, and though Bead fumed at having to walk, they were going where he wanted to take them. Rosebud had a telegraph, and if it should turn out that these were wanted men — and if he could get his hands on a gun — he would arrest them then and there and claim the reward. Through the remainder of the day, they walked, Harold riding and nursing his sore leg. Once, late in the afternoon, they heard sudden hoofbeats behind them and three riders with extra horses appeared on a rise, coming fast.

Bead's feet were sore and those men had extra horses. As they bore down on them, Bead tipped his hat and waved. "Ho, there! I wonder if . . ."

In a thunder of hooves the six horses and three riders were past them and going away, and Bead wasn't sure they had so much as glanced around. "Folks ought to be more neighborly than that," he muttered.

It was nearly dark when they came to a railroad track, and Bead sat on a rail, motioning for Harold to get down from the horse. "We better rest a while," he said. "Rosebud is yonder, down this track."

"We can rest," Sterling Quinn agreed. "But we don't have time to spend the night here. We have to find a telegraph."

"I have to find a telegraph," Bead said, pulling off his boots to cool his feet. "I have to see if you fellers are wanted anyplace."

"Well, you can wait your turn when we get there.

290

I got to let my wife know I'm all right, and find out if those people have been sending my wages. She needs the money. She's expectin' to have a baby most any time."

"Where is she?"

"Rossville. We'll probably have to route the message through Big Spring."

"Rossville?" Bead tilted his head to look at Quinn from the dark recesses under his hat. "Your wife is one of *those* women?"

"What do you mean, *those* women?"

"Why, all the women pulled out of Rossville. I thought everybody in the country'd heard about that by now. They packed up an' went lookin' for their menfolks 'cause they couldn't find out where they were. Are you them?"

"We're some of 'em, I guess. What do you mean, *went lookin'*? You mean they . . . *went lookin'*? Why?"

"Way I heard it, they was running out of vittles and no money comin' in because all their men had gone off someplace. Then the word got around that Rossville was full of loose women, an' folks started comin' to court, so they just left. Got a notorious outlaw with 'em, last I saw of 'em. The train robber, Clive Wilson Jones."

Quinn and Wheeler looked at each other in the dusk awed. "You actually saw them?" Quinn asked.

"Bigger'n Dallas."

"Which way were they headed?"

"West."

"This is west."

"Well, then, I guess they'll be along eventually."

"Well let's get moving! We have to get to that

291

telegraph!"

"What for? I told you about the women."

"Because if those people buildin' that rail grade find out about them looking for us, there's no telling what they might do. The railroad is a secret and those people are mean."

"A railroad is a secret?" It was Bead's turn to be startled.

"It sure is."

"What railroad?"

"That's a secret."

Harold was already climbing aboard Bead's horse again. As Quinn handed him the reins and Bead pulled his boots back on, Harold scratched his head. "Sterling," he asked, "what's Dallas?"

It was morning when they came to Rosebud, and Bead's feet felt like solid blisters. "Get off my horse," he said. "Telegraph is yonder at the depot. You can use it first, while I . . ."

"While you what?"

Bead didn't answer. He was staring at a horse hitched in front of the little general store. There was a horse and wagon there, too, but what held Bead's attention was the saddlehorse. A fine sorrel racer. He had seen it before. "You all go on," he said. "I got other things to do."

The railroaders headed for the depot. Leading his horse, Bead walked across to the general store and looped its reins at the rail, alongside the sorrel. While he was doing it, he had a look at the sorrel's saddle. There had been insignia hand-tooled in the skirts—or initials—but whatever had been there had been shaved off with a knife. It was all Bead needed to know.

He paused at the door of the place, glanced inside and saw a man with a silver-belly beaver hat pulling bags off a shelf while a man with an apron helped him. Both of them had their backs to him. Bead slipped in, crossed to a display case and selected a pistol similar to the one he had lost. Under the counter were bullets. Quietly he loaded the gun, crept across the room and thrust its muzzle into the back of the man with the white hat. "Hands in the air, Clive . . . no, wait!" Too late, he saw the bag of flour descending upon him.

In early afternoon the wagons, not too badly scattered considering that Maude Wilkinson and Ima Lou Stuckey had been at odds since breakfast over the proper pleating of bodices for morning wear and that Aunt Jessy Wheeler and Lottie Camber weren't speaking to each other again, wound its way through arid hills and down into a narrow valley where a torrent raged and sang through a rock-bound gully. Faced with such an obstacle, they all stopped, forming a front of no more than a quarter mile along the waterway.

"We can't cross that!" Sedonia Mills declared.

"Of course we can cross it," Nora Bennett regarded the floodwaters archly. "We must cross it. It's in the way."

"Can we cross that?" Ophelia Lashlee shouted at Janey McCoy.

"Mercy," came the response, "I don't believe I'd care to try."

293

"How do we cross that?" Henrietta Price asked Annie Coke.

"I don't know, ask Mr. Sneed. He's the man here."

"He'll be less of a man if he touches me again," Holly Bee advised.

"Absolutely shameless," Clara Hayes agreed. "And devious, as well."

"Where is that thespian?" someone shouted.

"Mr. Sneed?" several of them stood on their footboards or benches, shading their eyes to search the surrounding landscape.

"I hope he didn't get lost again," Annie told Holly Bee. "Don't seem right for a wagon party's man to keep gettin' lost like he does."

"Yonder he comes," Holly Bee pointed. "Not lost, just late."

When Sneed arrived at the obstacle, Maude Wilkinson pointed at the creek with her riding crop. She had only lately taken to sporting a riding crop, and some of the ladies felt—more or less privately— that it was a show of ostentation. What, after all, could one do with a riding crop when one was driving a wagon? She pointed. "Mr. Sneed, we have some disagreement about crossing that."

Sneed looked at the little singing river and backed his horse away a few steps. "What is the nature of the disagreement, Ma'am?"

"We don't know whether it's safe to cross," she explained. "Is it?"

"I haven't the foggiest idea," he said. "I myself have not tried to cross it."

"I don't even understand why such a thing is

here," Janey McCoy said. "All this land around here, so very dry, and then there is all this water right here in one place. Does that seem right?"

"It seems factual," Sneed gave her his best fourth-row-back smile.

Maude nudged him with her crop. "Well, do something."

"Do what, Ma'am?"

"Determine whether or not we should cross this stream," Lottie Camber said. "Land, what did you think we wanted you to do? Hamlet's soliloquy?"

"Can you do that?" Coryanne looked up at him with wide-eyed admiration.

In the Lashlee wagon, Amber Quinn's baby began to cry and little Hope Mills in the next wagon took up the chorus.

"I don't really know how to determine whether we should cross," Tyrone admitted. "This is decidedly out of my line."

"What would what's-his-name do if he were here?" Holly Bee asked Annie.

"Charlie? Why, I guess he'd know the answer."

"I believe you must test it," Lottie Camber told Sneed.

"How?" he asked meekly, already knowing the answer.

"You cross it. If you make it, then the rest of us will try."

Sneed pushed his hat down on his head and eyed the stream. He shook his head determinedly. "No, Ma'am, I don't believe I'll do that."

Holly Bee pulled out her rifle. "Cross the crick," she said.

Sneed sighed, stepped down from his horse and handed the reins to Lottie Camber. "If I get in trouble," he said, "I hope someone will have the decency to throw me a line."

"You're not gonna try like that, are you?" Nora Bennett demanded.

"Take off your clothes," Janey McCoy suggested, "If it's deep you'll sog and sink like a rock."

"There are ladies present," Sneed pointed out.

"We'll all turn our backs," Maude said. "Now get on with it."

Clad only in hat, boots and longjohns, Tyrone Sneed approached the torrent. It didn't appear very far across at this point, no more than twenty or thirty feet. But there was a lot of water between the rock banks. He stepped in, disappeared beneath the flood and bobbed up, struggling, several yards downstream.

"Tell us when you're in the water," Maude called over her shoulder. "Then we will turn around and watch."

Sneed didn't hear her. He surfaced again, flailing and gasping, twenty yards farther down, then disappeared once more. Only his hat, floating along beside him, indicated his position.

Annie looked around. "Now where did that jasper go?"

"I don't think we ought to try to cross," Holly Bee said.

"I see his hat," Coryanne pointed. "Maybe he's under it, walking on the bottom."

"Well, if he is, he's lost his way."

"He didn't make it," Lottie decided. "Poor Mr.

Sneed."

"I told you we couldn't get across here," Sedonia Mills pointed out. "But does anybody listen?"

"Then how do we get to the other side?" Nora Bennett wondered.

Some distance downstream, Pleasant and Serenity Higgins tied a castiron trivet to a length of clothesline, cast it out and grappled Sneed with it. In businesslike fashion, they reeled him in. "What were you doing in the water?" Serenity asked him, severely, as he lay coughing water from his lungs. "Did you fall in?"

"I don't think he fell in," Pleasant suggested to her sister. "If he had fell in, he'd be dressed decent."

"Least he might do is button his flap," Serenity pointed out.

"We didn't catch his hat. Do you suppose he'll want his hat?"

"He'll just have to make do without it. Come, Pleasant, we must go and speak to the others. Someone might try to cross this gully, and be damaged. It's better just to wait until the water recedes."

The suggestion was well received by all present, and Lottie Camber declared a rest stop. Jessy Wheeler declared that it was not Lottie Camber's place to declare rest stops, and Maude Wilkinson got into the thick of it on both sides.

By the time Tyrone Sneed, half-drowned and exhausted, managed to get back to where his clothing awaited, the flood had lowered visibly, ebbing from its crest, and Lottie Camber decided that by evening they probably would be able to cross.

A heated discussion followed, based on who had

the authority to make such decisions.

Because of the flood, it was late the following day when the first vehicles to top out on a rise with flats ahead saw the outlines of a small town. Holly Bee rode forward, took one look and galloped her paint back to where Annie was riding. "We come right back to Rosebud!" the girl said. "Annie, I don't want to go to Rosebud. Uncle Roscoe sees me, he'll put me right back to work again."

Annie consulted with several of the others, then comforted Holly Bee. "We ain't goin' into town, child. We don't have money to buy anything, and no time to go shoppin' even if we did. We'll just go on by. That trestle is out yonder somewhere, way on past Rosebud."

They angled to pass the town on the north, and Fredonia Whisenhunt rode ahead to find a smooth grade to cross the railroad tracks that led northward to Six Bit.

Mose Tuttle eyed the little town hungrily from the tailgate of his wagon. "If there's a saloon yonder, I'd stand us all a drink," he suggested.

"Somebody's comin'." Holly Bee told Annie. "Yonder's a wagon comin' this way. Horse tied to the gate . . ." she sucked in her breath, hissing between small white teeth. "Annie, that's him! What's-his-name! Your outlaw."

Within minutes it was obvious to everyone who was approaching. Jake sat disconsolately on the seat of a buckboard wagon, its bed piled high with bags and bundles, while his sorrel trailed behind.

Near the first wagons he reined in, got down and went around to untie his sorrel. When Annie, Holly Bee and several others approached he pulled off his hat. "I'm sorry I let my temper get the better of me," he told them. "Not the first time it's happened, either, but I had no call." He turned a thumb toward the buckboard. "Here's some things you ladies might need, by way of makin' amends before I ride on out."

The wagon was packed with supplies—more and a greater variety than they had started with at Rossville. They gathered around it, looking at first one thing and then another, voicing surprise and pleasure. "White flour! My land. Looky here, this is slabside bacon! Coffee? Coffee, too!" "Canned tomatoes! Land a'mercy!"

"Linen!" someone bubbled. "Just look at all this linen!"

"I think it's cotton muslin," another argued.

"You think I don't know linen when I see it? Oh, an' looky here. Fresh blankets!"

"My land, what is this?" Annie had unwrapped a package and now was holding up a long, pink garment with blue ribbons at the shoulders.

Jake blushed and ducked his head. "It's a dress," he muttered.

First one and then another of them looked at him, then shifted their gazes to Holly Bee. "Well, I declare," Annie said.

Holly Bee's eyes were huge. "A dress," she whispered. Then she turned as Jake set foot to a stirrup. "Jake Creedmore!" she pointed an accusing finger at him. "I ain't shot you yet for runnin' off

299

like you did, but if you try it again you'll be sorry."

"I declare," Annie beamed. "Ain't we doing just fine, though."

"Where'd you get the money for all this?" Holly Bee demanded, suddenly visualizing banks and things of such nature.

"I had a little money left," he shrugged. "And I went over and found Roscoe Sutherland and got him to help out."

"Uncle Roscoe?" Her eyes went wide with disbelief. "What'd you do, shoot him?"

"Naw, I told him a pair of mules identified as his had got loose and turned up over at San Galena and done considerable damage. I reckon he thought maybe I was a hired collector, because he settled up."

Chapter XXVIII

Though Ruby Jessup and Willis Holt may not have been the brightest two stars ever to grace the intellectual constellation of Texas, they did have their skills. Between the cowboy and the mustanger it was no great test to follow the trail of a dozen or so gunmen riding out from Big Spring to stop a convoy of women. They simply picked up the track at Big Spring, put themselves on it and went where the owlhoots went—which was due west. And on the second day out, Willis leaned from his saddle, studied the turf and said, "Well, these ol' boys is hot on them women's tails."

"You can't tell from lookin' at trailsign what kind of mood them boys is in," Ruby pointed out. "An' I don't believe you ought to assume improper intentions."

"What?" Holt raised his head and looked around.

"All we know is, these jaspers is sent to head off those women an' stop 'em. We don't *know* if they got impolite notions about their tails."

Holt shook his head. "Ruby, if you don't beat all. All I meant was, these jaspers have found the trail an' they're on it. I think it's you that's got impolite notions. You ain't been quite the same since you saw that little redhead up at Rossville."

"I don't deny," Ruby said sternly, "that certain notions cross my mind now and again. But I try to be polite in how I talk about 'em."

Crossing a sand flat at evening, Willis studied the sign again. "The ladies have about two days' lead on these jaspers," he said, "but the jaspers is makin' good time an' the ladies is dawdlin'."

"How come they're dawdlin'?"

"Hard to tell. They can't seem to decide how to keep goin' west. They just sort of wander all over God's half acre."

"That feller with the silver-belly beaver hat was supposed to take care of 'em," Ruby snapped. "Where's he?"

"Oh, he's with 'em, all right. See that highline sorrel's cut all over the place. But it looks like ever' time he gets 'em lined up to travel they bust loose all directions like a flock of quail. I never seen the like."

They made cold camp on a rise where they could keep an eye on the pursuer's camp. "What I ain't figured out yet," Willis admitted, "is just what are we gonna do about these jaspers if they do catch up to them ladies."

"What any pair of gentlemen would," Ruby sighed. "We're gonna whip their asses an' chase 'em off, then get acquainted with the ladies."

"Has it crossed your mind," Willis wondered, "that there are a dozen jaspers there and only two of us?"

"We'll think of somethin'. The ladies got that feller with the silver-belly beaver hat. That makes

302

three. Then there's that yellow-haired filly on the paint horse. Land, did you see her shoot the rope off that school bell?"

"Make it three an' a filly, then. There's still a dozen gunmen yonder."

"That's what will make our daring rescue so impressive," Ruby yawned. "You want first watch an' I'll take second?"

"You just want to impress that little redhead."

"Can't hurt. Sweet little thing like that, she needs a man-model."

"A what?"

"She needs a fine, upright example of a man to look to so she can rest easy knowin' she's in good hands in this world."

"Maybe she does. Where's she gonna find one?"

"Right here."

"There ain't anybody here but you and me."

"Well, you let her alone! I seen her first."

Two days later they were still shadowing the hired guns, but Willis Holt was getting nervous. "I keep findin' more and more sign," he told the red-haired cowboy. "Now there's folks out ahead of the ladies, an' folks behind 'em, an' those jaspers ahead of us ain't more'n a few miles from them. Land, it looks like half of Texas is goin' west."

"All the honest folks movin' out," Ruby philosophized. "I knew last election it'd come to this."

Chola and the Hog rode out ahead of the rest when the wending trail of wagons ahead became fresh. They pushed out a mile to look, then came back to report.

"They're just ahead of us, Slick," the Hog said. "We can be on 'em in an hour."

"They ain't even closed up good," Chola said. "Hell, there's wagons an' buggies everyplace."

"Any men with 'em?" Slick asked.

"Two that we could see," Chola grinned. "An' maybe a codger in one of the wagons. Not any more than that."

"I'll take first pick of th' women," the Hog rumbled. "Plenty to go around."

Slick regarded the big man for a moment. "Mr. Burton just said to stop 'em," he said. "He didn't say they're ours."

They gunman called Whisper had moved up on his flank. "As I remember," he said softly, "Mr. Burton told us to do whatever we needed to do."

"They might have money," Chola mused. "We don't know what's in them wagons."

"We know there's women in 'em," the Hog said.

"It's a long way from anyplace out here," Pawnee Bill said. "Seems like whatever we do, that's just up to us."

"All right," Slick decided. "But first things first. Mr. Burton said to stop 'em, so that's the first thing we do. After that, maybe it's a whole 'nother situation."

"I get first pick of the women," Hog reminded him.

"Then if they got money I get first pick of th' money," Chola said. "I can use it."

"You are the brokest jasper I ever saw," Pawnee Bill said. "What do you do with all your money,

Chola?"

"I buy things," Chola shrugged.

"What kind of things?"

"Carnegie Trust, B&O, you know, like that."

"All hard commodities?"

"No, sometimes I buy cotton futures."

"No wonder you never have any money," Whisper said. "I never buy futures on domestic goods. Market's too unstable. I buy coffee, sugar, things like that."

"I could use some breakfast," the Hog said.

"There's folks behind us, Jake!"

Jake looked around, then grinned. Astride her paint pony, with her rifle in her hand, Holly Bee's bright pink dress with blue bows seemed a little inappropriate. But he liked it. It was comforting to him for women to wear clothes a man could see through.

"I saw two riders on that ridge back yonder," she said, "so I went an' had a look. There's must be a dozen of 'em back there. Hardcases if ever I seen any."

Jake was impressed. He had never been quite sure whether Holly Bee Sutherland looked like a girl. Now, come to find out, she certainly did.

"I don't like this, Jake," she said.

"Maybe if you were to comb out your hair instead of rolling it up under your hat . . ."

"Jake Creedmore! You pay attention. There's men back there, comin' up on us. Hardcases. Gunmen. What are we gonna do about it?"

305

"Oh." Jake looked back. "Where are they?"

"Just past that last slope. Mile or so."

"I guess we'd better get these wagons closed up together." He sighed, looking around. The only wagon presently following the path he had indicated was the supply buckboard with Tyrone Sneed driving it. The rest were scattered like ducks on an otter pond. "Get Annie, and see if you can persuade those ladies yonder to come and travel with Mr. Sneed. I'll go talk to those on that side."

"What if they don't want to come?"

"Tell 'em their jelly is burning."

Once again, with the help of his female outriders and some intervention from the Almighty, Jake got the train assembled into a sort of order. But even as Lavinia Tuttle wheeled Mose Tuttle's two-up into line, turning up her nose at Nora Bennett, whom she was disdaining at the moment, the riders came into sight behind them. Jake whistled through his teeth. Holly Bee was right. That was a hard-looking bunch, and there were a lot of them.

Most of the women saw them, too, and suddenly the wagon train closed itself into a line-rank that an experienced overlander would have been proud of. Jake shook his head. "Now how come they haven't done that all along?" he muttered.

Keeping a nervous eye on the off front wheel of Maude Wilkinson's heavy wagon, which had developed an ominous squeal, Jake got them moving as fast as the slower vehicles would accommodate and looked for a place to fort up if it was needed. There was no place he could see that offered any such advantage. The land rolled away in every direction,

306

arid and scrub-mottled, with no cover anywhere.

He spurred ahead, hauling in alongside the supply wagon. "Just keep on, straight ahead, Tyrone," he hollered. "Those gents might be just passing through."

"That's what Genghis Khan was doing in Cathay," Sneed informed him. "Just passing through."

Annie appeared, riding alongside, her shotgun cradled on dimpled arms. "They're veerin' off to go around," she pointed.

"Maybe they *are* just passing through," he noted.

The gang overtook the wagons, came abreast two hundred yards out to the right, and went on, passing them by. But once ahead of them the riders wheeled, pulled into a crescent blocking their route, and stopped, facing them.

"Aw, criminy," Jake said. "Haul up, Tyrone!" He raised his arm to bring the train to a stop.

For a long minute the two parties stared at each other across an interval of a hundred yards—a dozen armed men and an eleven-wagon train carrying women and children. Then Jake thumbed back his hat, loosened his Peacemaker in its holster and rode out ahead. Three of the hardcases came forward.

"Howdy, Gents," Jake said. "Somethin' we can do for you?"

"Yessir," the center one of the three said, "we got orders to stop this bunch of wagons."

"Well, you've done that," Jake pointed out. "Every one of them has stopped."

"Turn around and go back where you came from," the man said.

307

"We don't want to do that. That would be east. We're going west."

"If you don't turn around and go east, we'll start shootin' " the man grinned.

"I get my pick of th' women," a big, beefy man muttered. Jake barely heard the comment on the wind, but it told him what he needed to know. Turn around or not, these men weren't going to let the wagons go.

"Well, hold on a minute," he told them. "I'll have to talk to the ladies."

He rode back and gathered them. "We can't get out of this," he said. "Those men mean to turn us back, but whether we turn back or not, they intend to take whatever they want on this train."

"We don't have anything of value," Nora Bennett snapped, then her eyes widened. "Oh. Oh, yes."

"I say we open fire," Holly Bee opined.

"There isn't a wagon here that could stop a bullet," Jake said. And there isn't a wagon here that isn't full of ladies or babies or both, he thought. "We'll open fire, all right," he told Holly Bee, "But only when these wagons are out of range."

"Well, how are we gonna get them out of range?"

"By turning back."

"You said that wouldn't do any good."

"It'll give a you chance to get a little distance and form a circle. It's better than no chance at all."

"Against a dozen men?" Maude stared at them, waiting just beyond gun range.

Maybe there won't be that many by then, Jake thought. "I'm going to stay and talk to them while all of you ladies pull back," he said. "Maybe I can change their minds or something."

"I'll stay, too," Sneed said.

Jake glanced at the thespian. "Do you have a gun?"

"I have this," Sneed said. From somewhere he drew a stubby, square-looking fistful of murderous intent, a palmful of gun with four short barrels and a hammer-lug. "Sometimes theater crowds get out of hand," he explained.

"You know these boys can shoot back."

"It's better than drowning."

"All right, then. The rest of you . . . what do you mean, *drowning?*"

"Some other time," Sneed said.

"The rest of you, turn around and start back the way we came. Go as far as you can . . . Annie, you be the judge . . . then swing in and make a circle . . . and try to get everybody behind something that will stop bullets." And whoever has guns, get ready to use them, he thought. But he didn't need to say that.

God help you all, he thought . . . unreliable, sharptongued, scatterbrained bunch of damn biddies, y'all take care now, y'hear? "Come on, Tyrone," he said. "Let's go see if we can buy some time."

Sneed started to turn the buckboard, but thought better of that. He handed it over to Annie Coke, climbed down and untied his saddlehorse from the tailgate. "What are we going to talk about?"

"Lord only knows," Jake shrugged. "Whatever'll distract them for a few minutes."

"Then what?"

Jake glanced back. The women were all out of

earshot. "Then I intend to open the ball and see if I can make the odds a little better."

Sneed's grin was pasty, but it was there. "Okay, you call it."

With Sneed following close behind, Jake rode back to face the line of gunmen. "They're turning around," he said. "They're going back."

"Right smart of 'em," the lead man said. He tossed a glance at the one next to him. "I guess that settles what we were sent to do."

"I reckon we're just on our own now," the other agreed.

They lifted their reins, but Jake and Tyrone Sneed were still there, sitting their saddles, facing them.

"Well, what do you want?" the lead man scowled.

"I was wondering," Jake drawled. "We been out of touch lately. Do any of you boys know the latest quotation on Homestake preferred?"

Most of them just stared at him, but one nodded. "Seven an' a quarter last week. That's down a quarter."

"Was that the closing quote?"

"Last week's close," the man said. "I took a bath on that."

"That's why you never have any money, Chola," another said. "Hell, you'll take a flier on anything."

"I'm big in bull markets," Chola snapped.

"Sorta enjoy cattle auctions myself," another mentioned.

The big, beefy one was watching the receding wagons, his eyes glinting with anticipation. Jake glanced at him. You're first, he thought. "Real estate's been my downfall," he told them. "But I solved that problem. I put my money in trust, and let Philo Henderson worry about it."

"What does he do with it?" Chola asked.

"Invests it. Philo keeps up with things a lot better than I have time to."

"I've thought about a middleman," a soft-spoken gunman nodded. " 'Course, I'd want a financial profile on him."

"You're right as rain about that," a mean-looking one to his right said. "Pays to set your own risk-to-gain ratio, too."

"What are them women doin' yonder?" the beefy man's expression had changed to one of heavy suspicion.

"Where would a body find that Henderson feller?" the leader asked.

"Over at Portales."

"You trust him?"

"As the day is long," Jake said. " 'Course, I don't give him carte blanche. I tell him generally what I'm interested in. You know, modest-risk portfolio with blue chips at the base and enough variety to offset short-term setbacks."

"I see two riders comin' " the beefy man squinted.

"Wonder if he's got a line on transportation ventures?" the leader said, thoughtfully. "Railroad issue, maybe?"

"Does he handle commodity futures on the margin?" another asked.

"What's his broker load?" Chola cut in.

"Some of them women are . . ." the beefy man started.

311

"I heard somethin' about coalition pools," a gun-slinger said, "but it sounded a little like group insurance to me."

"Shit, they've crossed us!" the beefy man roared, his hand diving for the gun at his side. Jake's Peacemaker flashed and roared, and the big man pitched backward from his horse.

The leader had his gun in hand, raising it, then he stopped as a hole appeared in his chest, and he sagged forward. The whip-crack ring of a rifle echoed around them.

"Holly Bee, damn it, you're supposed to be with the . . ." Jake levelled and plugged another one. ". . . wagons!"

A shot sang past his ear and was answered by the thumping, stuttering reports of Tyrone Sneed's bullpistol. Abruptly, there was melee. Guns firing, people shouting, they closed in a swirling mass of horses and mayhem. Holly Bee was at Jake's side, her rifle barking, and he saw a gun aimed at her and emptied his Peacemaker at its owner. Two riders flashed past him from behind and cut through the crowd, guns blazing. Holly Bee sighted one of them and Jake knocked her rifle aside. "I think they're on our side!"

"They ain't anybody I know!"

"Well, then, shoot somebody you know!"

She did. The mean-looking jasper with the risk-to-gain ratio was slapped from his horse. Fredonia Whisenhunt and Henrietta Price were there, circling the gunmen, both firing pistols.

"I told them how to do that," Holly Bee said, proudly.

And then there was silence, and men were dropping guns on the ground and raising their hands. Jake gazed around in amazed appreciation. Of the twelve gunmen, five were still upright, and they were ringed by levelled muzzles—his, Holly Bee's, Fredonia's, Henrietta's, Annie's shotgun and an even bigger one held by Lottie Camber, and a pair of Colts in the hands of two cowboys that Jake hadn't had the pleasure of meeting.

Tyrone Sneed was on the ground, bleeding, and a few feet away Pawnee Bill stirred, groaned and tried to raise a pistol. Clara Hayes flattened him with an axe-handle, then crouched beside Sneed. "You're hurt," she said.

"Still better than drowning," he gasped.

Chapter XXIX

"Some of us changed our minds," Jessy Wheeler told Jake as he and Willis Holt loaded Tyrone Sneed into her wagon while Clara supervised. Sneed had a bullet hole in his side, but nothing seemed to be leaking except blood, and they had done something about that.

"We left the ones with children to circle the wagons," Lottie Camber said. "Then some of us came back over here. Annie told us what to do."

"I thought I left you in charge of getting the women to safety," Jake scowled at Annie.

She shrugged. "You ever try to reason with a bunch of women, Charlie?"

"Jake," Holly Bee corrected. "His name's Jake."

Annie turned to watch the distant figures of five defeated gunslingers walking eastward. "You don't think them yahoos will come back to devil us, do you?"

"Not too likely, without horses or guns."

"I'd have shot the varmints if you'd let me," Holly Bee told him. "Still wouldn't mind, come to that."

"I believe they've seen the error of their ways," Lottie Camber said. "Mr. Creedmore told them they ought to lay low and invest wisely. They said they would."

"Obliged to you fellers for steppin' in," Jessy told the mustanger. "Hope it wasn't out of your way."

"No, Ma'am, that's what we came for, was to rescue all you helpless ladies from them varmints. That, an' so ol' Ruby yonder could do what he's doin' now, namely taggin' around after that little redhead."

"That's Coryanne," Annie said. "Mighty sweet little thing. She'll whip him into shape an' make a saint of him if he gives her half a chance."

Willis stared toward where the wagons were grouped. Nearby, Coryanne O'Keefe was strolling toward the supply buckboard, with Ruby trailing behind. He had a grin on his face and about eighty pounds of hardware and supplies in his hands. Coryanne had volunteered to show him where to put it. "Picture that," Willis said softly. "Ruby civilized. Just imagine."

"We're lookin' for a bunch of missin' husbands and fathers," Jake told him.

"And a son," Jessy added.

"And a brother," Fredonia Whisenhunt added.

"We're out to find some missing men," Jake amended. "You and your friend are welcome to come along."

"Thank'ee," Willis nodded. "Yeah, we know about the missin' men. We was at Rossville, remember?"

"That's right! I remember seeing you there. Thought you and your friend looked familiar."

"We went to Big Spring," the mustanger told him. "Got ourselves an education. Did you know about the Burton brothers?"

"Heard they'd got respectable lately."

"I mean what they're doin'? They're fixin' to build a railroad. That's what the Great Central and Pacific Investment Company is all about, it's a financin' cover for the Great Central and Pacific Railroad."

"There isn't any such railroad, is there?"

"There's fixin' to be. They're buildin' it. Abilene through Big Spring and right on out to the Territory to hit both transcontinental routes."

"There's three transcontinental routes."

"Not south of Omaha, there ain't. Just two down here. Anyhow, it was Uno Burton that sent those yahoos out here to stop the women. His brother Dos has got their menfolks out buildin' subgrade, an' they don't want anybody to find out about it."

"Well, that's where we're going," Jake said. "We think we know where they are. You want to trail along?"

Willis grinned, looking off to where Coryanne was helping Ruby load outlaw guns and tack into the buckboard. "I don't believe ol' Ruby would have it any other way." Casually, he turned to Fredonia Whisenhunt. "Believe I heard you say it's a brother you're lookin' for? Not a lost husband?"

When the vehicles were reassembled and Tyrone Sneed was resting easy in Jessy Wheeler's wagon with Clara Hayes to look after him, Jake pulled off his hat and scratched his head, looking west. Far off there, just on the horizon, was a dot that might be a railroad trestle. If they pushed hard, and nothing else came up to stop them, they could be there in a day or so.

He unhitched the sorrel and stepped aboard, raising his arm to get the wagons moving. "Let's go, hoss," he muttered. "Nothing to stop us now, I reckon."

Somewhere behind and to his right, there was a thud. As he looked around a wheel rolled past him, tilted, spun and sprawled against a greasewood snag. Behind, Maude Wilkinson's wagon stood askew on three wheels and a hub.

"It is a sight to see, sure enough," Sam told Royal Flanders, sipping at scalding coffee beside a little fire. "There's stacks of rail out there that a sale barn couldn't hold. And ties . . . looks like half the cedars in Oklahoma was cut to make 'em. Spikes, switches, signal arms, poles . . . shoot, there's everything a railroad needs, just sittin' out there in that hole. There's even a switch-engine with about a hundred barrels of water an' plenty of stoke-wood. And seven flatcars."

"How far north of the grade-line?" Flanders' eyes glowed with deep humor.

"Six miles, no more than that. But a body'd never know all that stuff was there unless he just happened to come up on that valley right where I did. I guess that stuff might have been there fifteen-twenty years. Maybe since the war. Who'd know? It's a twisty little valley," he drew a line in the sand at his feet, where the firelight would show it, "comes downs from the north, kind of does a cutback right there—maybe three-four miles altogether—then heads on south. The thing is, a man

317

could ride across the valley a mile north or a mile south of that hole and never suspect it was there. And that's where all that stuff is. Right there in the cut-back. A mile or so of track on the ground, with the engine and cars sittin' on it, a couple of hand-cars, tools of all kinds, and all that rail and cut ties just stacked along both sides, waitin' to be hauled away."

"Probably was an old spur line," Flanders mused. "Somebody could have hauled all that stuff out there, then took up the rails behind them and plowed over where they'd been. Sounds like Texas politics to me."

"Don't it, though!"

"And that's what the Burtons are basing all this on. Well, I'll give 'em credit. They might just have what it takes to build a railroad."

"And all the secrecy is so they can put together the rights-of-way before anybody knows what they're doing."

"And the whole grade they're buildin' is pointed right out into the Territory, right straight toward that place that Conrad W. Jackson took from Jake Creedmore. The place with the big well." He turned to Wilbur Short, who sat dwarfed and goggle-eyed among them. "What do you think about all this, Wilbur?"

Wilbur swallowed, gulped and shook his head. "I guess if Jake had knowed anything about all that, he sure never would have let his place go back to Mr. Jackson."

"Seems that way to me, too," Flanders said.

"So what do we do about it?" Sam refilled his

coffee mug. "Back to Big Spring? On to the Territory? What?"

Flanders turned to another of his deputies. "What's happenin' over at the worksite, Hank?"

"Same thing. They're layin' down subgrade straight as a string, with one bunch out ahead of the rest layin' in gravel base for maybe a roundhouse or a switch-yard." Hank leaned to extend the valley line that Sam had drawn in the sand. Then he drew an X on top of it. "Right there."

"Staging ground," Flanders said. "They plan to haul the stuff out by rail and start building line back to that trestle."

"There's enough hardware to do that," Sam said. "And maybe a few miles more. There isn't enough to go all the way back to Big Spring or Abilene, though."

"Won't need to," Flanders said. "As soon as Uno has his rights-of-way down pat, he can build from the east to meet them, and he won't need to keep it secret any more. And I guess once they get rail from the north-south mains out to here, it won't be any trick to push right on over into the territory. I'd bet that Conrad W. Jackson already has the right-of-way over there, just waitin' for 'em."

"He does," Wilbur said softly. "I wondered why he was buyin' the land he was buyin'. But that's what it is, all right."

Flanders thought it over for a few minutes, then looked up at Sam. "I reckon we'll just stick around here a little longer," he said. "I'd kind of like to see what happens next."

319

Bead had been gone from Rosebud for only a day, when he returned. The man with him was tall, knife-nosed and nervous. His hands were tied behind him, Bead's new gun was tied to his neck and Bead had his finger firmly on the trigger. Without ceremony, he marched the man into the little marshal's office at Rosebud and said, "I got a wanted man here, an' there's probably a reward on him. I aim to collect."

The marshal's mouth dropped open and for a moment he seemed incapable of closing it.

"Well?" Bead's eyes glinted under his hat. His whiskers twitched. "Can you handle it for me, or do I take my business elsewhere?"

"Well, land, yes, I can handle it," the marshal said. "How'd you catch him?"

"Just walked up and stuck a gun in his back," Bead shrugged. "That's what I generally do. This time it worked out."

"I can't believe it," the marshal said. "You got *him*. An' here he is, right in my office. Ol' buddy, you an' me are both fixin' to be wealthy men."

"You know who he is?"

"Land yes, I know who he is. Don't everybody? That there is the notorious train robber, Clive Wilson Jones."

"No," Bead said. "That's what he's been tryin' to tell me, too, but I know better. Now who is he, really?"

"That's who he is, really. What makes you think he's not?"

"Because I know Clive Wilson Jones. Durn near

320

had him, right down the street yonder at the general store, but he got away again."

"You mean the one that dusted flour all over Luke Haley's floor? That was Jake Creedmore. I've seen a dodger on him."

Bead's whiskers twitched. "Jake Creedmore? Then who's this here?"

"Clive Wilson Jones, damn it! Careful with that trigger, I'd as soon deliver him alive. If you didn't know who he was, how'd you know to catch him?"

"I saw him ridin' along out yonder a ways, saw him stop to make water an' I knew he was an outlaw right off. I know an outlaw when I see one. Bounty is my business."

"You saw him stop to pee an' you knew from that that he was an outlaw? How?"

"He didn't get off his horse. Old outlaw trick. I've seen it before."

The marshal stared at him, speechless, wondering how many lazy but honest cowboys the bounty hunter had brought to justice in learning his trade.

Annie Coke had been meaning to tell Jake about the railroad shares she had registered in his name, but what with one thing and then another, the subject just hadn't come up. Now as she watched him fixing the wheel on Maude Wilkinson's two-up, while Holly Bee stood stubborn guard in her new pink dress and rifle—mostly, Annie knew, standing guard to keep other women away from him—she thought again about the certificate of registration in her saddlebag, and considered telling him about it.

321

It seemed like a man ought to know if he has a fortune in railroad stock just sitting in the bank waiting for him to draw on it—or whatever men did with stocks and things.

Still, it was a beautiful evening. The sun's last slanting rays had left the land and leapt into the sky to throw shafts of brilliance across its vault, and the land lay shadowless and brilliant in cloudlight. Holly Bee looked positively radiant, her long corn-silk hair combed out and hanging from her hat, her new dress hiding the worn tops of her boots, her rifle freshly cleaned and shining, her blue eyes constantly straying toward Jake where he worked.

Riding the devil's trail, that was what the lady sheriff had said about him. Recompense, she had said. Community service and moral restitution, that would straighten him out. Annie had ideas of her own about such things. She knew what it took to straighten out a man. She'd done it herself, many times.

Well on his way to being a saint, she thought now, noticing how Holly Bee watched him. Well on his way to being a saint. And so far, he doesn't even know it.

She thought again about the stock registration and decided it could wait. There he was, crouching and muttering, drenched with sweat and trying to fix an errant wheel on a heavy wagon. And there she was, dressed in her finest and keeping a hawk's eye on him while she cradled her rifle. There was the evening, there was the brilliant afterglow lighting the sky, there was the song of desert birds . . . and there were two young people she had set herself

322

to bring into burgeoning awareness of each other's outstanding qualities.

The whole thing was just so romantic that Annie felt like she might bawl.

In a day or two they would be at the trestle. They could already see it out yonder. Then they would find the menfolks of Rossville and get them back together with their loved ones and maybe take a hand in figuring out where everybody should go from there.

Then would be time enough to spring it on Charlie . . . Jake . . . whatever that he was in the railroad business. No sense upsetting him before it was necessary, she decided.

Chapter XXX

It was, without doubt, a railroad trestle. Poles and timbers that never grew in this arid land supported a grade-level roadbed where it spanned a watercourse, pilings below and high framing above to support the weight of rolling stock. All it needed was ties on its floor and iron rails spiked to them, and trains could cross there.

What crossed on this day was eleven horse-drawn vehicles, seven riders, assorted livestock and a human contingent consisting of twenty-one women, seventeen children and five men.

"See those pilin's!" Callie Tuttle Smith chirped. "That's Pete's work. I know a Pete Smith pilin' when I see one!"

"Looky how that frame brace juts!" Sedonia Mills told her four children. "That's your daddy's work, sure enough!" Billy, Grace, Francis, and even Baby Hope stared wide-eyed at the frame-brace. "Nobody juts like Otis Mills," Sedonia reminded herself.

Mabel Hornby spotted unmistakable evidence of the work of Clyde Hornby in the stubbing of tie-bars and pointed it out gleefully to Bubba, Willie and Aristotle. "Just like old times," she told the children. "Other folks make the parts line up, but it takes your daddy to make them stay there."

Janey McCoy pointed out Roger McCoy's work to Matilda and Roger Junior. Nora Bennett showed Ferdinand and Fastidia the fine way in which Walter Bennett levelled cross-braces. Ophelia Lashlee explained to Sue and Sally how their pa could handle a fresno like nobody else ever could, and Amber Quinn let out a squeal of delight when she saw Sterling Quinn's initials cut into a riser.

Lottie Camber cast a practiced eye over the entire structure and muttered, "Frank, you've done better work."

Jake sweated the entire crossing, dark visions flitting through his mind. "If you ladies break ranks here," he muttered, "you're all going to wind up down yonder in the creek."

Beyond the trestle was gradework—a string-straight line of patches of fresh earth where the low places had been filled and the high places scraped. "Somebody sure as hell is fixin' to build a railroad," Willis Holt nodded. "Don't see how they expect to bring in ties and rails, with no tracks to run out here on, but they sure got *somethin'* in mind."

"There's dust yonder," Holly Bee pointed at the horizon.

Jake started to answer, then turned and swore softly as discord erupted behind him. The sisters Higgins had turned too soon and run their surrey afoul of the trestle's final stub-pile. They were hung up there with one wheel snugged around the upright pole and the last two wagons piled up behind them. "Oh, lordy," Jake sighed. "If it ain't one thing it's six. If I ever get shed of this mess I'll . . . give me a hand, will you, Willis? We'll need Ruby, too, if Coryanne can spare him that long."

"I'll go take a look," Holly Bee said, and spurred her paint.

"Just wait up," Jake swung around. "We'll all go together . . ." But she was already gone, and Jake shook his head, gazing at her backside going away. She was back to wearing pants again, but somehow it was different now. Having seen her in a dress, he had learned to appreciate what was there to see, pants or not.

"Looks like an angel an' rides like the devil," Willis said, admiringly. "What's she like without that rifle, Jake?"

"Can't say. I've never seen her without it."

Annie came from beyond the wagons. "Where's Holly Bee off to, Charlie?"

"She saw dust yonder. Went to see what it is. She was gone before I could stop her."

"You're gonna have to learn to put your foot down, Charlie. That's a high-spirited gal, but she ain't broke to neck-reinin'."

"I've noticed." He dismounted and went to survey the surrey.

Annie followed him. "Well?"

"Well, what?"

"What are you gonna do about Holly Bee?"

"Nothing. She isn't my problem. Willis, we're goin' to need a pry-bar here." He tipped his hat to the Higgins sisters, still sitting prim in their wedged surrey. "Nice going, ladies. I couldn't have snugged up against a post like this better if I'd tried."

"You are supposed to be looking after us," Serenity pointed out. "You should pay more attention."

"What do you mean, not your problem?" Annie snapped. "Didn't you stop off and buy that gal a dress?"

"I was apologizing," he said. "That's all I had in mind. Ruby, can you . . . Ruby! Yes, hello there. Good morning. Can you get those other wagons backed away, please? That rail will do, Willis. Set it right here."

They put their shoulders to it and the surrey budged, budged again, then backed free.

"You can bet your sweet soul that ain't how she sees it," Annie nagged. "You're on your way to winnin' that gal's heart, Charlie. An' if you don't see that, then you don't deserve . . ."

West winds brought the sound of distant gunfire, and Jake stood up so fast he banged his head against the pry-bar that Willis was just pulling loose. More shots sounded, thin with distance and distortion. From the west, where Holly Bee had gone.

While the others were still turning toward the distant sounds, Jake was in the saddle of the sorrel, which bunched its great haunches and took off like a rabbit, throwing gravel and sand in its wake.

He rode as he had never ridden before. He let the sorrel have its head and bent low over the saddlehorn, squinting into the wind. The horse settled to a belly-down run and a quarter mile was behind them, then another. Ahead now, Jake saw riders, coming toward him — one in the lead, trailing a dust plume, others behind in pursuit — and again he heard shots.

327

The gap closed and Jake's breath went ragged. The one leading was Holly Bee. Her hat was gone, and blond hair streamed out behind her. Her rifle was gone, her face was chalk-pale and she rode awkwardly, her right arm dangling at her side, the sleeve bright with blood.

As she neared, he saw clearly those behind her. Three men on fresh horses, barely a hundred yards back and firing as they ran. "Run, Holly Bee!" Jake shouted. "Get to the wagons!" They passed in a rush and Jake heard the whine of a bullet. Like magic, the Peacemaker came to hand and began to roar.

It was over in an instant. The three rail-camp guards might never have known what hit them. Like a scythe through rye, the Peacemaker's thunders licked out at them. Two disappeared from their horses, the third buckled and tried to cling, then slid off and rolled under the hooves of the charging sorrel. With barely a glance at the fallen guards, Jake wheeled and headed back. Ahead of him Holly Bee's little paint was beginning to falter, and Jake shouldered the big sorrel alongside and lifted her from the saddle, holding her close as he headed back to the wagons at the trestle.

"They seen us . . ." her voice in his ear was a whisper. "They was waitin' . . . there's more yonder . . ."

He hauled up among the wagons and handed her down to wanting hands. "Careful, she's hurt," he said. "She's . . . damn, she's bleeding!"

"What happened?" Willis asked.

"People out there shot her. They . . . my God,

what kind of people shoot at women?"

"Jake, listen . . ."

"They shot Holly Bee!"

"Well, simmer down an' . . ."

"They can't do that!" He drummed the spent
sorrel with his heels, trying to turn it, trying to go
back, but hard hands took the reins away and
strong arms were dragging him from the saddle. He
lashed out, wanting to hit someone. Anyone.

"Jake, it's me! Willis! Calm down, now. You're
not goin' anywhere on this horse, not unless you
want to kill him. Jake! Listen!"

Gradually the red haze of fury lifted, and he
shrugged off the hands holding him. They were all
around him, their eyes wide and frightened.

"Jake, she's all right," Annie said. "She'll be just
fine. No more than a little scar, when she heals.
Jake? Do you hear me?"

"She's right, Jake," Ruby stared at him. "Jesus, I
never seen the like, how you put them three on the
ground."

"Jake? Are you listenin' to me? I said she'll be all
right. It's just a little scrape."

"All right?" he felt dizzy . . . disoriented. "Holly
Bee is all right?"

"She will be," Annie said. "Now come on, catch
your breath."

"She'll be all right," he mumbled, suddenly feeling
embarrassed. " 'Course she will. I just . . . well, I
hate to see people shoot at any woman . . . especially . . ."

"Especially Holly Bee," Annie nodded, understanding. "Yeah, I believe you're all right, too."

329

"Annie?"

"What?"

"How come, Jake? What happened to Charlie?"

"I guess you gave 'em something to think about," Ruby said, "but there's a bunch more of 'em out there, waitin' for us."

"When they get tired of waiting, they'll come for us," Tyrone Sneed speculated. "And I don't think that will be very long. They know we know they're here."

"That's Dos Burton out there," Willis reminded.

Jake leaned on his elbows at the tailgate of Jessy Wheeler's wagon. Just inside, Holly Bee slept while Annie and Clara kept watch over her. Sneed, still wearing bandages of his own, leaned against a wheel. Willis squatted on his heels in the wagon's shade, and Ruby paced nervously. "Sons-a-bitches won't stop at anything," the redhead growled.

"Well, they won't have to wait," Jake declared, turning. "They know where we are, but I know where they are, too. I'm going in."

"There's breaks yonder," Willis said. "They'll see you comin' and all they got to do is hide and wait."

"I have to go," Jake said.

"Well, then, I guess I do, too. Any crowd this big deserves more than one damn fool."

"I'll go." Sneed tried to stand up, and had to brace himself against the wheel.

"You're not going anywhere. You stay with the women. And pick out a rifle from that supply wagon. This isn't going to be a bullpistol occasion, however it goes."

"Well, I'm not gonna let that bunch get the chance to come out here," Ruby tugged down his hatbrim. "So count me in."

Jake nodded. "All right, let's get these wagons forted up, right at the end of the trestle. The ladies can cover a lot of ground from here . . . if they have to."

"You just keep your hands off our wagons!" They all turned, startled. Lottie Camber, Jessy Wheeler and Maude Wilkinson stood facing them, most of the other women ranged behind them.

"We had a meetin'," Jessy said.

"Good thing we did, too," Maude snapped. "We figured you boneheads would come up with somethin' chivalrous an' dumb like goin' out after those folks all by yourselves."

"If anybody goes, we all go," Lottie said. "That's what it comes down to, Jake Creedmore. Take it or leave it."

"I don't intend to take women and children out there with those . . ."

"Don't make any difference what you intend. You can't make us stay here. We're goin' with or without your leave."

"They got our menfolks yonder," Flossie Todd said.

Ophelia Lashlee put her fists on her hips. "We aim to get them back. That's what we come all this way for."

"Ladies, those people will shoot. You can't . . ."

"Whether we go to them or they come to us, they'll shoot. So we'll just have to shoot back."

Lottie's eyes dared him to test the logic of that.

"We got a lot more guns now than we started out with," Aunt Jessy Wheeler noted.

Henrietta Price swung aboard her gray horse. "We're goin'," she said.

Fredonia Whisenhunt put her foot in the stirrup of her black and gazed at Willis Holt. "Would you like to meet my brother?"

Annie pushed forward, cradling her shotgun and leading her horse. "It's all settled, Charlie. No sense wastin' time arguin' about it."

"But the children! The babies!"

Clara Hayes took his hand. "Come here, Jake. I want to show you something." She led him to the rear of the Wilkinson wagon, and drew back the flap. Inside the high walls were stacks of bagged flour, beans, salt and every other bulky supply they had. Strung over these were saddles, lapped like shingles, hanging by stirrups from the headrail. And between the barricades were children, crouched and wide-eyed. "We did the same with both of the heavy wagons," Clara said. "And in case you hadn't noticed, we doubled out the harness and hooked on trace chain. These'll be teams of four."

Jake was impressed, despite himself. Then he went thoughtful. "Have you ever driven a four-up? Has anybody here? You can't just take on a four-up team like it was one horse or two. You have to know how."

"I can drive a four-up," Maude said.

"Well, who else?"

For a moment there was silence. Then Tyrone Sneed raised a hand. "I drove a circus wagon for a

332

year. All I need is somebody to help me up and hand me a rifle."

Coryanne O'Keefe led Jake's sorrel to him. Someone had cooled out the animal, flanneled it down and resaddled it. It was as fresh as morning, and Jake realized again what a prize he had taken from Conrad W. Jackson. "Thank you, Coryanne," he said. "I . . ." he stopped, looking at the saddle.

"Oh, I didn't put the saddle on him this time," the girl giggled. "Ruby wouldn't let me. He said that's man's work."

Here where the canyon swung in from the north, opening onto the skirt of plains where subgrade was being put down, the land dropped from canyon on the north to breaks southward, with the right-of-way of the new line bisecting the land between.

When the shooting began, the work guards had turned their attentions eastward to watch the chase — three perimeter guards on horseback running down an intruder. On the banked grade, Frank Camber squinted eastward, then strode to where the surveyor's transit sat on its tripod and swung its telescope around. He sighted, adjusted, sighted again, and muscles bunched in his whiskered jaws. "It's a kid," he said to those around him. "It's just a . . . no! By damn! It's a girl! They're shooting at a girl. Oh, God, I think they hit her."

They crowded around, shading their eyes, trying to see what Frank saw in the distance.

"She's still riding," he said. "There's three after her, right behind it looks like. Can't tell with this

333

thing how far, but they're still shooting. Where's she trying to . . . huh!" He tugged at the adjustments, raising the telescope slightly, changing the focus. "Why, that's . . . oh, my God."

"Damn it, Frank, what is it?"

"Wagons. Buggies. People . . . at the trestle. That's my surrey! Why's my surrey . . . Henry, that highwall carriage of yours, it's there too. And Claude's dray wagon, and . . . and Walter's old cart. What are they doing . . . my God, it's the women!"

"Our women?"

"Our women. There's Lottie, and . . . Lucas, your sister is there, and Maude Wilkinson. Walter, Nora's driving your cart . . ."

"What in God's name are they doin' 'way out here?"

"Which one got shot?"

"I don't know her, but she's . . ." he went silent. His mouth dropped open and he stared through the telescope. "By damn," he whispered. "By damn."

"What?" they pummelled him on the back. "What's goin' on, Frank?"

"Those three guards . . . some jasper on a sorrel horse rode right into 'em. He dropped all three of 'em. I can see 'em, they're dead. All three!"

"That's our women out yonder," men murmured, exchanging glances.

"Where are Burton and his men? And the guards?"

"Scootin' down into that front ravine . . . some of 'em, anyway. I don't see Burton . . . oh, there he is. Him and his thugs, they're on the rise yonder.

334

There they go, down a draw. Looks like they're goin' for the wagons."

Clyde Hornby shrugged the sling off his bad arm and tried to pick up a sledge, then settled for a spade. "Like hell they are," he said.

Roger McCoy picked up the sledge, and Claude Stuckey hoisted a weeding scythe. Richard Todd filled his pockets with rocks and his hands with framing hatchets. Henry Lashlee and Walter Bennett grabbed pry-bars, and Otis Mills found a five-foot length of trace chain. Within a moment there wasn't a man on the grade-site, and the work guards in the breaks, watching eastward, failed to see them coming.

Chapter XXXI

They had fired from cover, Holly Bee said. From the rim of a ravine where the breaks began, they had opened up on her and she had never got off a shot. Then riders had come, pursuing, trying to finish her off. In Jake's mind a still, barely-banked anger smoldered, waiting to burst into flame. What kind of men would point a gun at a woman, much less shoot at her? Murderous scum, he knew where they were and though it worried him to have the wagons at his back he knew it was better to go for them than to wait for them to come.

The wagons rolled now in a tight, grim line, Jake leading, Ruby and Willis riding flank and the mounted ladies bringing up a rear guard. Tyrone Sneed, pale but alert, drove the lead heavy wagon with its saddle armor and four-up team. The second was just behind it, and all of the children were in one or the other. The light vehicles were in midline, where the flankers could protect them if they were rushed.

Where Jake's three dead men lay, he stopped just long enough to pick up their guns and hand them over to Annie at the supply wagon Then he went on, searching the land ahead, waiting. Three hundred yards ahead was the first ravine, and he studied it. Twice he saw movement there, just glimpses of motion veiled beyond the low brush. Once he heard—or thought he heard—a man's voice, high pitched as though in pain. But the sound cut off abruptly and he was not sure he had heard it at all. At two hundred yards from the ravine, holding the sorrel to a slow walk, he drew his Peacemaker and held it ready. Again there was a glimpse of movement beyond—a sudden arc as of a spade swinging over and down. Just ahead of him something on the ground flashed sunlight. Holly Bee's rifle, where she had dropped it. He swung down from the sorrel, not taking his eyes off the nearing ravine, and led it forward, gun in hand. As he approached the fallen rifle there was movement ahead again. He stopped, levelling the Peacemaker.

A man appeared above the ravine's lip, shooting upward as though catapulted from the ground. Jake aligned on him, then hesitated. The man cleared the rim of the ravine and sprawled face-down in front of it, not moving. Immediately a second man flew from the cut, this one feet first, upside down. Then a third, limp and turning in mid-flight to land atop the second one. Jake stared.

Again and again, limp man-forms arced from the ravine to fall in front of it, and they lay where they fell, not moving. From the left, beyond a bend in the ravine, he heard a shout, then several gunshots. A moment later two more limp men flew upward and lit sprawled and unmoving where they fell.

Then there were distinct voices: "Any more that you can see, Clyde?" "Take a look down that way!"

337

"Hey, Frank, one got past me . . . oh, you got him. Good." "Where's Burton an' his thugs? Anybody seen them yet?"

From two wagons back, Jake heard Lottie Camber's delighted voice. "That's Frank! That was my Frank that said that! Don't shoot, anybody! That's our men!"

There was more movement then at the ravine. A head appeared, then several more. "Lottie?" the first one called. "Lottie, is that you?"

Jake put away his pistol and stooped to pick up Holly Bee's rifle. It was full-loaded. She had ridden into ambush and never got off a shot. What kind of people would do that to Holly Bee? Running hoofbeats drummed on the wind and he heard a shout of alarm, then a shot and a bullet ricocheted inches from his boot. Still crouching, he turned and brought up Holly Bee's rifle. Mounted men were angling in on them from somewhere aside, springing from hiding to charge down on the wagons. The one in the lead he knew, from a chance meeting years before. Dos Burton. He aimed, then shifted his sight as the second rider pointed a pistol at Lottie Camber. His shot took the man out of his saddle, and he felt something sting his upper arm. Again he fired, awkwardly this time, and a rider's horse went down, rolling, crushing the man beneath it. He saw Ruby empty his gun into one of them as the man's horse panicked, pivoted and began to buck.

Then he was on the ground, not knowing why, and Dos Burton was above him, pure hatred drawing his lips back from his teeth, his pistol aligning.

338

"You . . ." Burton said. Then his face erupted, as though his left eye had exploded. His gun discharged, kicking sand in Jake's face, and Burton slumped forward and slid off his horse.

Somewhere near but far away a resonant voice, pitched for the back row, complained, "How come nobody takes actors seriously?"

The million stars of desert sky, brilliant above cool night breezes, greeted him when he opened his eyes, and for a while he simply lay there looking up at them. Then he began to sort things out. Somewhere nearby was a campfire, its yellow light dancing on the canvas of a wagon that stood against the night sky. Somewhere people were talking in low, relaxed voices—a lot of people, it seemed, and a lot of separate conversations. He felt pain in his right arm and in his left leg, pain that dwelt there dull and aching, and brought tears to his eyes when he moved those parts.

And someone was holding his hand. He turned his head and there were big, shadow-dark eyes an inch from his own. She gazed at him for a moment, then raised her right arm. It was swathed in bandages, and he knew that his was, too. "Annie's right," she said. "We *are* alike in some respects."

"Who did we lose?" he husked, his throat dry as desert sand.

"Nobody. Everybody's all right . . . well, you and me and Mr. Sneed, of course, we'll be stove up for a time. And that redhaired cowboy has a notch in his ear, but Coryanne'll have him well in no time."

339

"The women . . . and the babies?"

"Nary a scratch. I reckon outlaws are good for somethin' after all. Their saddles made good shieldin' for folks." Still lying beside him, holding his hand, she turned and called softly, "Annie? He's awake, an' could use some water by the sound of him."

She turned back. Her breath was warm and delicious, and Jake had a sudden desire to find out more about it. He shifted, and the pains flooded him. He groaned and settled back. "You behave yourself," she ordered him. "You're in no condition to get frisky."

Others gathered around them, then, silhouettes against the stars with firelight touching a face here and there. There were some among them whom Jake didn't know. Annie squatted beside him, raised his head and gave him water to drink. Somewhere beyond her a man said, "We're all obliged to you, Mister. Lottie an' the rest, they told us how you taken care . . ."

"Hush, Frank," Lottie Camber's voice came from the standing silhouettes. "Tomorrow'll be soon enough. Let the poor man rest."

Someone else crouched beside him and removed his hat. "Howdy, Jake," he said. "It's me, Wilbur. Wilbur Short, from Perdition."

"Wilbur . . . ?"

"And this here is Mr. Royal Flanders. I bet you've heard of him."

"Creedmore," Flanders rumbled. "How do you feel?"

"Little stove up at the moment, but I guess I'll

340

mend. Flanders?" The name soaked in. *"Royal Flan-ders?* What are you doing here?"

"Gettin' a little business wrapped up," the big man said. "Most of what's left is business between you and me, but we can talk about it later."

"You and me?" Jake pushed himself up to his good elbow, ignoring the pain. "What kind of business have you got with me?"

Flanders nodded. "Don't want to wait, huh? Neither would I. Well, sir, I set out at the request of Mr. Conrad W. Jackson to bring in the man who robbed the Perdition bank, and collect a substantial reward on him." He raised a hand. "Hear me out, now! The thing is, Mr. Creedmore, I never have in my whole life not done a thing I set out to do, an' it wouldn't be good business to start now, if you follow."

"I follow," Jake sighed, wishing Holly Bee's hand in his weren't such a distraction at a crucial moment. "I guess I always figured somebody like you would turn up. I sure must have aggravated Conrad W. Jackson, for him to have brought you into it, though."

"Offhand I'd say you aggravated him some, yes. Well, sir, I said I'd bring Jake Creedmore back, so naturally I have to take you back. And I said I'd bring back the painting of Mr. Jackson—which I have in my possession now—so naturally I'll take that back too. And I said I'd collect a substantial reward, which is where the problem comes in."

"What problem?"

"How much reward are you prepared to offer for the man who robbed the Perdition bank, Mr.

Creedmore?"

"How much . . . but that was me. I robbed it. Wilbur was there, he'll tell you."

"As I see it, you made a cash-and-kind withdrawal. Wilbur told me all about it. But shortly afterward, that bank was robbed of nearly twenty thousand dollars, and I believe you should post a reward for the man who did it, otherwise how can I justify my time and trouble?"

"Well, who did it?"

"Conrad W. Jackson."

Jake lay back, staring at the sky, and a few things began to make sense that hadn't made sense before. He shook his head. "Wouldn't you just know he'd do a thing like that!" He paused, then sighed. "I don't know how I'd pay any reward, Mr. Flanders. I don't have any money that I can get my hands on. I left it with Philo Henderson, to invest."

"Henderson, yes," Flanders said. "What kind of investments does he handle?"

"Diversified. He kind of favors the short-range rollover markets, but I told him to leave me out of that. I like real estate, myself."

"Know what you mean. Each man to his own notion. Lately I've got real interested in railroad shares, especially single-issue prime capital stock. You interested in that kind of thing?"

"I guess not. I wouldn't know what to do with that kind of stuff if I had it."

"Well, then, I guess we can both solve our problems. I've got an agreement already drawn up, and all you need to do is sign it in front of witnesses. We seem to have plenty of those."

"What kind of agreement?"

"It sets up a capital trust, for the management of any and all railroad stock registered in your name . . ."

"But I don't have any . . ."

"Yes, you do. Don't worry, you won't lose it, you'll just sign over the rights to manage it, to a trust."

"I told you, I don't have any . . ."

"Yes, you do," Annie said. "Tell you about it later, but right now just hush. The gentlemen is tryin' to make a right nice deal with you."

"I don't . . ."

The soft fingers in his hand became strong, pressing soft fingers. "Annie said hush. So hush," Holly Bee said.

"I b'lieve he's hushed now," Annie told Flanders.

"All right, then I'll continue. As I said, your railroad stock . . . any stock that you might happen to have of that nature . . . becomes a managed trust, and you appoint me as manager and agent of record. You do that, and I'll accept it as my reward for apprehending the man who robbed the Perdition Bank."

"That is ridiculous," Jake said. "Even if I had railroad stock, and set up a trust with you as its agent, how do you stand to gain from that? There's no money just in being an agent, especially if there's nothing to pay commissions on."

"Oh, I have a plan," Flanders grinned. "As your trust's agent, I intend to go back to Big Spring and have myself a chat with Uno Burton. He's been in the railroad business long enough. I'm going to

343

execute a leveraged buyout."

Another large man, standing beside him, also grinned. "When we get things tended to at Perdition, Mr. Flanders wants to handle that buyout business personally. He figures he'll stop over at Limestone and have a glass of lemonade."

"That's enough about that, Sam," Flanders rumbled. "Well, is it a deal, Creedmore?"

"Far as I'm concerned, I guess. Shoot, I don't even know what the deal is, but it won't be the first time I've acted through a middleman."

By lanternlight he signed the document Flanders had drawn up, and handed it back to him. "Railroad stock," he muttered. "That's the craziest idea I ever heard. I never in my life had any . . ."

"I told you Conrad W. Jackson put stock in that paintin' of hisself," Wilbur Short said. "I just didn't know at the time how many ways he done that."

Chapter XXXII

Sim Hoover had gone to Mission to look at a turkey farm, then stopped over at Las Palomas to visit Flossie. It hadn't taken long to visit the turkey farm, but the visit with Flossie had run into weeks, so Sim had been somewhat out of touch of late. Now, nearing Perdition, he reined in and shaded his eyes. "What's goin' on yonder?" he muttered.

The closer he got to town, the more mystified he became. There were people there. Smoke arose from chimneys, and there were people in the streets. At the edge of town he stopped to gawk at a brightly-painted sign on upright posts. "Clearwater City," it said. "Metropolis on the Make."

"Metropolis on the make?" Sim muttered, squinting. "What in hell does that mean? An' what happened to Perdition?" Mystified, he went on. Ahead, a lumber wagon was making the turn from the north road, and beyond that he saw people laying fresh shingles on a roof. Two men on horseback — strangers to him — passed and thumbed their hats. "Howdy," one said. Women in sunbonnets came and went around a canvas-topped arcade that seemed to be a produce market. A buckboard loaded with cans of milk angled into the street from an alley and the driver glanced at Sim. "Howdy," he said.

"Isn't this Perdition?" Sim asked.

"Used to be," the man nodded. "But it got over it."

Sim felt he had ridden off the edge of the world and found himself in another one. Grimly, he set his hat and headed for the livery stable, half expecting not to find it. But it was there, right where he had left it, and it was busy. A farrier was at work in the front lot, someone was breaking horses out back and the stalls were full of animals. Sim rode up, reined in and a redhaired cowboy peered from the toolshed door. "You need a stall or just a bait of feed?"

"Who are you?" Sim asked.

"I'm Ruby an' I'm kind of busy. What do you need?"

"What are you doin' here?"

"What does it look like? I'm tendin' this place until the owner gets back, an' I wish he'd show up because he owes me wages."

Sim lapped his mount's reins over a rail and walked down the street, wide-eyed. He didn't see any linoleum signs, or any boarded-up buildings, and for a time he saw no familiar faces. Then a shop door opened and Opal Hayes came out, carrying a covered basket. "Mornin', Sim," she said. "Are you back?"

"I don't rightly know," he pulled off his hat. "Where did all these people come from?"

"Here an' there," she said brightly. "You know how people are. What do you think of the water?"

"What water?"

"Why, from the new well yonder. Where have you been, Sim?"

He looked where she pointed. Down the street, a

new waist-high wall of fresh adobe stood in front of the hotel, encircling a stubby frame of peeled timbers with a rope pulley mounted on it. "That well? They found water, then?"

"Oh, my, yes. Sweetest water you ever tasted, an' all a body could want. They drilled for it."

"Water . . ." Sim muttered. "I declare." He turned to Opal, but she had gone on her way. Sim walked on, then saw Homer Boles sitting on the bench in front of the marshal's office. A gray-haired, pleasant-faced woman sat beside him, holding a shotgun on her lap. Sim turned toward them.

The woman was talking, and Homer seemed sort of glazed-over. ". . . saint most ways," she was saying. "I told him, though, many's the time, I'd say, 'Woodrow,' that was his name, was Woodrow, 'Woodrow,' I said, 'Woodrow, that's gonna be th' death of you, actin' like that, you wait an' see. But he just couldn't never seem to change, bless his heart. So sure enough . . ."

Homer saw him and came unglazed. "Sim! When'd you get in?"

"Just now. Homer, what in thunder is goin' on here?"

"A Lord's plenty, Sim. You didn't know about it? I reckon you been out to see Flossie. Sim Hoover, this here is Annie Coke. She come with Jake an' them."

"Howdy," the woman said.

Sim pulled off his hat. "Howdy, Ma'am." He squinted at Homer. "Jake an' them? Who?"

"Jake Creedmore. How many Jakes do you know?"

"Jake's back?"

"As ever was. He brought in a bunch of women that had lost their menfolks, an' Royal Flanders an'

347

his bunch, an' Wilbur Short's back, too, an' we just got folks comin' from all over since they heard about the railroad."

"What railroad?"

"The one them women's menfolk is buildin'. Out yonder, headin' for Clearwater. 'Cept Clearwater's here now, not up yonder. Conrad W. Jackson had all these fine signs, y'see, an' it was a shame to waste 'em, so we changed the name to Clearwater. Sim, you look like you're tryin' to catch flies, your mouth hangin' open that way. I guess you been to see Flossie, all right."

"Did you say . . . Royal Flanders? He's here?"

"Was. He brought in a prisoner, then he went back to Texas to buy out that railroad that Uno Burton's been fixin' to build. Since we got all this water now, it's gonna come right through here."

It was all a little much for Sim. He sat down on the porch and tried to make sense of it. Then he stood up again, gawking. Down the way, Jake Creedmore had emerged from the hotel, escorting a pretty blond woman in a pink dress. Each of them had one arm in a sling, and Jake walked with a limp, but there was no mistaking who he was.

"Yonder's Charlie an' Holly Bee," the woman with Homer pointed. "Land, don't they make a handsome couple?"

"That's Jake Creedmore," Sim said.

"Sure is," the woman said.

"Sit down, Sim," Homer said. "I can see we got a lot to talk about."

"What are those men doin' yonder?" Sim pointed.

"Diggin' a trench. They're goin' to pipe water out to where the railyards will be, then we're thinkin' about maybe layin' pipe all over town."

Sim scratched his head. "That Henderson feller that was here . . . did he start all this, Homer?"

"He got the drillin' started, then he had to get on back to Portales. Seems like he's got an investment company up there that he can't hardly keep up with any more. But Jake's lookin' after things here. Did you know the bank's open again? Wilbur Short's clerkin' it, but it belongs to a citizens' trust. Town can't hardly get by without a bank, you know. Did I tell you who my prisoner is? Conrad W. Jackson, that's who. I got him in the lockup, waitin' for a circuit judge."

"Conrad W. . . . ?"

"It was him that robbed the bank, turns out."

Sim sat down again, wondering.

"We got a feller tendin' your stables," Homer said. "But you got to pay him wages. Name's Ruby."

"Homer, can I ask you somethin'?"

"Ask away."

"All this . . ." Sim waved an arm vaguely. "Water pipes, drillin', new roofs . . . Homer, who's goin' to pay for all this?"

"Oh, we got that figured out," Boles said. "We're gonna issue municipal bonds."

"Bonds." Sim ran a hand across his grizzled cheek. He tried to grasp the enormity of it all.

"Probably revenue bonds," Homer shrugged. "But we might need to do us a general obligation bond issue, too. With all the folks here now, we'll need a school, and schools don't produce revenue . . . just peace of mind."

"Civilizin' influence," Annie Coke said. "Like jails an' town socials."

Sim glanced around at her, confused.

"Put th' big varmints in jail," she explained, "an' the little ones in school, it gives folks time to plan town socials."

Now Homer was confused, too. "Are we gonna have a town social?"

"Some of th' ladies have been talkin' about it," Annie said. "Nothin' definite just yet, because some of 'em wants to lay on a spread of fried chicken an' some of the others is opposed to that. They claim folks get greasy when they eat fried chicken, an' a greasy town social lacks class. 'Bout half of 'em ain't talkin' to the other half right now, but they'll work it out. Brings to mind my husband Henry. He couldn't get within ten feet of a drumstick without gettin' grease all over him. I used to tell him, 'Henry,' I'd say . . . that was his name — Henry . . . I'd say, 'Henry, you gettin' slicked down like you do, it's gonna be th' death of you, sure enough.' But he just never could seem to change. Bless his heart, he was a saint most ways in spite of his bad habits. Well sir, sure enough, one mornin' he . . ."

Sim stood, tipped his hat, shook his head and started walking, back the way he had come. One thing at a time, he told himself. Just take it one thing at a time and eventually it's all going to make sense. It's bound to. Just one thing at a time.

The thing to do now, he decided, was to head on back to the livery stable and introduce himself to his employee.

350

POWELL'S ARMY
BY TERENCE DUNCAN

#1: UNCHAINED LIGHTNING   (1994, $2.50)

Thundering out of the past, a trio of deadly enforcers dispenses its own brand of frontier justice throughout the untamed American West! Two men and one woman, they are the U.S. Army's most lethal secret weapon—they are POWELL'S ARMY!

#2: APACHE RAIDERS   (2073, $2.50)

The disappearance of seventeen Apache maidens brings tribal unrest to the violent breaking point. To prevent an explosion of bloodshed, Powell's Army races through a nightmare world south of the border—and into the deadly clutches of a vicious band of Mexican flesh merchants!

#3: MUSTANG WARRIORS   (2171, $2.50)

Someone is selling cavalry guns and horses to the Comanche—and that spells trouble for the bluecoats' campaign against Chief Quanah Parker's bloodthirsty Kwahadi warriors. But Powell's Army are no strangers to trouble. When the showdown comes, they'll be ready—and someone is going to die!

#4: ROBBERS ROOST   (2285, $2.50)

After hijacking an army payroll wagon and killing the troopers riding guard, Three-Fingered Jack and his gang high-tail it into Virginia City to spend their ill-gotten gains. But Powell's Army plans to apprehend the murderous hardcases before the local vigilantes do—to make sure that Jack and his slimy band stretch hemp the legal way!